# BEYOND THE PARMALEE BOTTOM

A Novel By
Jake Keeling

ISBN: 978-1-936497-38-6

Photo credits:
Mary Curry

First Edition: September 24, 2022

Published By
**Jumbo Exchange and Communications**
8515 State Hwy. 315
Long Branch, TX 75669
903.658.0128
jumboexchangeandcommunications@gmail.com
or visit our Facebook page

# Dedication

With love and appreciation, once again, to Jennifer Davis Green
and Sandy Simmons Gatlin.

Ms. Sandy, your Christian love, loyalty, and resilience in the face of adversity never cease to amaze me. You are always counted among my greatest blessings. Jenny, you are dearer to me than you will ever know. Our friendship is a priceless gift.

# Contents

# Chapter One

(East Texas: late May, 2015)

"Let her by," the graceful, darkhaired rider called automatically, peeling another tiger-striped heifer away from the main bunch of cattle.

Serena Durham Hollister, still called Miss Sis by those who knew her best, glanced approvingly toward her nephew as he followed her rapid-fire instructions. The young horseman reined his little bay aside for the heifer. Working together seamlessly, horse and rider sprang back into the gate just in time to turn a cow.

Ches Durham's compact frame never added much height, but he showed the passage of time in other ways. At thirty, he looked somewhat broader across the shoulders. Thicker through the waist, too, with a little softness over his belt buckle. Cerebral palsy and days spent in a wheelchair limited other forms of exercise, but Ches sat his horse with practiced ease. The animal's power and athleticism brought an exhilarated grin, and at the same time, made him reach down to tighten the safety rigging. Not given to overmuch praise, Sis refused to acknowledge her nephew's disability by cheering him on like a kid playing t-ball. She simply eased her dun-colored mare around the cattle until she came up next to him.

"There's one left in there, honey," she said with a smile. "Go cut her out; I'll work the gate for you."

"Yes'm."

Ches sat a little straighter in the saddle, having just received the biggest compliment his aunt knew how to give. Sis glowed with loving pride as she applied a touch of leg pressure and sidled old Pumpkin into place.

"That'll do," she said with a wink, leaning from the saddle to chain the gate good and tight once he'd put the last heifer out. "Short Stuff has come a mighty long way since you gathered him out of the Parmalee Bottom."

"Yeah," Ches agreed, reaching down to stroke his horse's neck. "I still miss Twister, but he never really got over his lameness. I couldn't ask for a better replacement than this little fella. Besides, he's the last one you ever broke and trained."

"Don't be too sure about that, honey. He might be the last if your Uncle Andrew gets his way, but I'm not ready for the rocking chair just yet."

"Well, now, Uncle Andrew's just trying to look out for you. Nobody expects you to quit riding or anything that drastic. He only asked you to stick to the gentle ones."

"I know it," she replied, wrinkling her nose in mild irritation, "but one hip replacement and a few more candles on the birthday cake don't exactly turn me into a china doll! Speaking of Andrew, though, we'd better get back. Steak supper with your folks tonight."

Terry and Jenna Durham had watched their son pine for his aunt, the horse-sale crowd, and "home" for as long as they could stand it. Both eventually located jobs nearby, and their day-to-day lives were not all that different from the ones they'd left behind in Dallas.

"Don't be too hard on Cassidy," Ches suggested gently as the pair rode along side by side, "not after all the fun we've had this evening."

"That girl," his aunt responded on a sigh. "I declare, Ches, some days it's a good thing you're around to remind me how long I waited and prayed for the chance to be a mother. Do you know what the colonel would have done to me for mixing stock like that after we'd separated them?"

"You wouldn't have left a gate open in the first place," he pointed out dryly, "but we can't expect Cassidy to be another Miss Sis Durham."

Back at the sale barn, Sis used a mounting ramp and special overhead hoist to transfer Ches safely into his latest motorized wheelchair. They tended their horses and then headed up to join the rest of the family at the big house.

Home to Sis, Andrew, and their daughter Cassidy, the old white frame structure served as a sort of headquarters for family and friends. Preferring not to spend too much time in the wheelchair, Ches stepped carefully out of it and into a ladder-backed chair at the supper table.

Even though vital tasks had kept them out late, Sis felt slightly neglectful of her hostess duties and chose to make light of her own unease.

"Well, y'all," she said, flashing her lovely smile around the table as Andrew pulled out a chair to seat her, "I did make the sweet tea before we headed out this morning. Ches, honey, why don't you bless the food."

"Steaks cut from our own grass-fed beef," Andrew announced minutes later as he helped everybody's plate, and the pride in his voice was easy enough to forgive.

Andrew earned his living elsewhere but took a special interest in their cow-calf operation. While his wife loved horseback work and knew her way around cattle almost instinctively, he studied carcass quality, birth weights, and mothering ability.

"Cut it with a butter knife," Terry Durham observed, praising his brother-in-law's efforts.

"Guess what popped up on Facebook today," Jenna offered brightly by way of table conversation.

"I saw it."

Ches didn't mean to be short with his mom but hoped intensely that he could head off this particular subject.

Sis considered Facebook the silliest invention since canned biscuits. In this case, though, curiosity overcame her distain for social media.

"Well, Jenna, what was it?"

"Serena Kate got married today! Just a little courthouse affair, but she made a lovely bride. She's lost weight, too."

"Wasted away, more like," Ches muttered.

News about the little crossroads community of McKendrick and its residents, past or present, generally reached Miss Sis without benefit of a username or password. She spoke in a soothing East Texas drawl which, to the untrained ear, might have concealed all the protective instincts roused by this troublesome topic.

"I helped raise that girl. Then she went and cut us off without a backward glance. Surely to goodness we've got better things to discuss over a nice sit-down supper."

Ches chewed and swallowed automatically but his uncle's prized steak had lost all flavor. Even so, he tried to focus on the goodness of God and the many blessings he enjoyed.

The old Durham horse sale operated on a monthly instead of a weekly basis these days, but the corresponding reduction in costs ensured a decent profit. Though his parents never showed much interest in the homeplace, they applauded his every accomplishment and seemed to have settled into the close-knit rural community around McKendrick. Aunt Sis, for her part, stood in as business partner, saddle pal, and steadfast anchor.

There was just one sore spot in his life, a kind of aching loneliness where Serena Kate was concerned. Jim Rex McKendrick's redheaded daughter, now somewhere in her early thirties, had never been anything more than a friend during their growing up years. Her little brother, Scooter, was his main running buddy. Somewhere along the line, though, his feelings for Serena Kate had deepened considerably.

At the end of a strangely silent meal, Sis turned her full attention on Ches, practically willing him to look up and meet her gaze.

"Come on, honey. Let's go smoke."

She hadn't lit a cigarette in years and certainly never passed the habit along to him. This was just her mischievous sense of humor coming out, a lighthearted reference to all those not-so-very-long-ago talks in her porch swing.

"Oh, Mother…"

Cassidy rolled her eyes in a typical teenage response to the little joke, but Miss Sis cut her off mildly.

"Y'all leave the dishes 'til I get back. Why don't you recite some of your lines for Uncle Terry and Aunt Jenna?"

"They're not my lines until I get the part, Mother."

"She'll get that part alright," Sis asserted, holding the old swing steady from force of habit as Ches made the transfer. "Do you know another junior high girl who can sing like a little bird and mock me to-a-T while she's doin' it?"

"You noticed, huh?" Ches responded, mustering up a genuine chuckle. "Laurey from *Oklahoma* sounds like she'd be right at home running the horse sale."

Sis breathed in the earthy, reassuring smell of fresh-cut hay drifting up from the bottomland and finally cleared her throat to speak.

"Scooter tells me Serena Kate and that new husband of hers are coming back here to live. Having them right underfoot is apt to make it rough on you, honey."

"Yes'm," he admitted dryly, "but there ain't a thing we can do about it."

"Well… I always had a soft spot where that girl was concerned, but they can starve plumb to death before either one of them works on this place."

*Beyond the Parmalee Bottom* 9

"Aw, Aunt Sis...That don't sound much like you, not with those sweet twins to consider. Corrie and Torrie ain't done nothing. I wouldn't bother you with this a'tall, except..."

"I understand, honey, and I'm here."

This statement reminded Ches how much he valued the gift of his aunt's presence. Miss Sis offered her loved ones a singular combination of gentleness, strength, and unshakeable loyalty. Words failed him, so he gave her hand a squeeze.

The swing creaked steadily along and crickets hummed on the warm night air, but these familiar surroundings brought more frustration than comfort. If he couldn't find happiness here, with all these blessings so near at hand, it must be his own fault.

His aunt's flock of half-wild guineas roosted in the treetops on the far edges of the yard. A saddled horse often passed the night tied to the large oak at one end of the porch, but none stood there this evening. Only the stock dogs remained close by. Ches's particular favorite climbed the steps with toenails clicking against heart-pine lumber and padded over to stand before them.

A little over a year old, Roxy was a throwback- a smaller, feminine version of the old Rhett dog that headed his aunt's pack for so many years. Ches reached out to stroke her head, and she laid it in his lap. Her long, shuddering sigh somehow jump started his own voice, and he continued the conversation with Aunt Sis.

"Serena Kate's got a right to her own choices, and we all know I'm not the greatest catch. Still, to go and waste herself on some no-account stranger... I loved her an awful lot, Aunt Sis. Maybe I still do."

"Serena Kate's plenty smart until it comes to looking out for herself."

"Yes'm... Corrie and Torrie's daddy showed us that, I reckon."

"Me and old Nash tied a can to his tail," Sis recalled, years softening the unpleasant business into a rather satisfying memory. "From what Scooter tells me, this Ethan Fisher ain't apt to drown in his own sweat. Be that as it may... My worry's closer to home."

"Please don't fret over me, Aunt Sis. I feel just like a fool. Folks everywhere dealing with real trouble, and here I'm pining over a girl who probably never cared anything about me in the first place."

"Serena Kate loves you after her fashion, but that don't take the hurt away. It ain't easy lookin' ahead to that next mountaintop when you're a-way down in the valley. Still, the Lord expects His children to lean on Him and keep pluggin' along. Feelings oughtn't change what you believe, what you know is true, but that don't mean you've got to be grinnin' all the time."

"No, ma'am..."

"I'm praying, Ches, just like you are. You'll find the right young lady one of these days, and there may come a time when you can look at Serena Kate as an old friend. Right now, though... Did I hear your mom say something about a chance to take a little trip and do some speaking?"

"Remember that leadership forum a-way out in the Hill Country?" he asked, answering her question with one of his own. "A summer camp for young people with disabilities... It don't amount to much, really."

"Not to you," she chided gently, taking in the Durham homeplace around them with an all-encompassing wave of her hand, "but the chance to get outside and romp a little is probably a rare thing for most of those kids. Besides, a change of scene might do you some good. Does it pay anything?"

"Just expenses."

"What about your magazine articles?" she wondered. "I know you generally keep some stuff filed away..."

"Yes'm," he admitted almost reluctantly, "I've got enough material put back to keep the Mayfield bunch satisfied for a little while. Still, I'd hate to leave you shorthanded around here."

"I'll miss you like my right arm, honey, but I can manage for a couple of weeks. You go on; maybe it'll take your mind off of things."

"I spent my time as a camper missing you and the homeplace. Why would I up and volunteer to do it all over again?"

*Beyond the Parmalee Bottom* 11

"Of course, you got homesick! I was your whole world back then." A little toss of her dark curls and a fleeting smile said she hadn't minded one bit. Still, her next words came in a serious tone. "You never used to be unhappy here on the homeplace, but I can't fix what's ailing you now."

"Aunt Sis was right as usual," Ches reflected a week later as he watched his mom and Cassidy pull away from the campground.

They were bound for two weeks of shopping and spa treatments while he passed the time out here amongst rocks and sticker bushes that wouldn't run a cow and calf to every twenty acres. He wasn't stuck in McKendrick just waiting to welcome the new Mrs. Fisher home, though, and somehow the thought gave him a kind of a friendly feeling toward those sticker bushes.

"Hi, Chester!" the latest camp director greeted him overenthusiastically. "It's always a thrill to welcome one of our former campers back as a speaker and counselor."

"Thank you, ma'am. I'm glad to be here, and I generally answer to Ches."

"Great! Great! We'll make sure your name tag is filled out correctly. You're an author, right?"

"Well, you might say that. I write for Tom Mayfield's *Ranch Horse Gazette* and furnish content for several agribusiness websites. I also buy and sell livestock in partnership with my aunt."

In spite of his pride in the long-running family business, Ches purposely skimmed over the details. People outside the horse-sale culture sometimes looked as shocked as if you'd just admitted to auctioning off small children for a living.

"I suppose your involvement in the livestock industry provides a lot of subject matter for the articles."

"Yes, ma'am. Then too, whenever the opportunity presents itself, I try and educate folks to the therapeutic benefits of horseback riding."

"Great! Great! We have a couple of horses that were donated to the camp menagerie. I'd love to get your input on a full-scale program."

Her rapid-fire conversation didn't leave much time for deliberation, but he glanced around briefly as if visualizing a barn and set of corrals right there in the courtyard.

"Maintaining a string of reliable horses to use for a few months out of the year can get mighty expensive," he finally said. "Have you ever thought about farming it out?"

"Farming... We just want to let the campers ride around on them."

"Yes, ma'am, poor choice of words. Have you ever considered a contract with someone to supply the horses and a certain number of wranglers every summer?"

"People actually do that? All those brainstorming sessions and nobody ever... Great! Great! I think you just created yourself an extra assignment! Write me up some kind of proposal and I'll take it before the board."

"Ma'am, I can't rent you a string of horses. It's three hundred miles from here back to McKendrick."

"No, no," she answered with a laugh. "I just want you to write down what you've told me. Only... Sell the idea. Put your creative skills to work, but don't lose too much sleep over it. Incoming campers tomorrow!"

Sizing up his burnt toast and dried-out scrambled eggs the next morning, Ches decided orange juice would have to do until noontime and joined somewhat reluctantly in the organized chaos of arrival day.

"Watch out... Hey, catch that dog!"

Most people surged toward the cry, but Ches didn't think much of their chances. Wheeling around, he motored away from the crowd and waited. Sure enough, a smallish lab mix emerged from the forest of legs. A couple of people grabbed for the wildly flopping leash, but Blackie was headed for parts unknown.

Sliding forward in his wheelchair, Ches dropped one boot off the footrest and stepped solidly on the leash as it slithered past.

"Easy, buster... Where you goin' anyhow?"

"His name's not Buster; it's Onyx!"

The voice was pitched high with excitement but not quite reproachful. Ches frowned slightly at the unfamiliar name, but his expression soon relaxed into an easy grin.

"Try Buster, or Jet, or Blackie. Maybe he won't be in such an all-fired hurry to leave."

"There's nothing wrong with Onyx! It's a very sophisticated name," the pale, fragile-looking teen retorted from her own motorized wheelchair.

"That may be, but this here is a dog."

"Onyx is a highly trained service animal."

"Still a dog..."

When the pup quieted under a firm but gentle hand, his owner decided not to take offense.

"Anyway, thanks for catching him. My name is Erica; I've been coming here forever. You must be one of the new counselors this year."

After a short visit, Erica and Onyx headed off to one of the girls' cabins, a nice young lady and a sweet-natured pup. Badly mismatched, though, both of them full of nervous energy.

Ches gave large-group talks and made one-on-one connections with several campers. Onyx, the highly trained service animal, escaped several more times, but good Samaritans usually pounced on him before things got too far out of hand. Erica seemed well-spoken and popular. Toward the end of the first week, though, Ches was surprised to find her waiting outside the main office with tear marks plainly visible on her cheeks.

"Hey, there," he ventured, reaching down automatically to pet the dog. "How's Buster Bill this evening?"

"Onyx is terrible," she sniffled, trying her best to smile. "He's an absolute Tasmanian Devil! They're taking a group to the fair tomorrow, but because of him, I can't go."

"Turn him loose with old Molly," he suggested, mentioning the three-legged camp mascot. "I expect he'll stick around pretty close."

"Turn him loose?" she echoed in horror. "I was on a waiting list for six months, and you can't begin to imagine the red tape I went through to qualify for a service dog. Besides, the horrid creature is my best friend!"

"He's not a horrid creature," Ches corrected her gently. "He's just a dog, half-grown pup at that. Say, I've got an idea. Y'all wait right here."

"I'm not going anywhere," Erica answered, voice still a little shaky, "but who knows about Onyx."

Early the next morning, Ches found himself aboard a large charter bus with Onyx, better known as Buster Bill, a bundle of nerves on the seat beside him.

Self-imposed dog duty notwithstanding, Ches stayed fairly close to the main group of campers. He enjoyed watching them take in the fair while exposing the puppy to new sights, sounds, and smells. Buster Bill's nose was a lot keener than his own. Nevertheless, Ches identified the faintest suggestion of a favorite scent.

"Popcorn, turkey legs, and cotton candy are alright," he told the dog conversationally. "But there's horses workin' somewhere, and that smells like home."

As the motorized wheelchair bounced him along toward the outer edge of the fairgrounds, Ches noticed a lady's voice lifted in song. Carried to him on the breeze, the drawling lyrics sounded quite tender and sentimental.

"Flow gently, sweet Afton, among thy green braes. Flow gently, I'll sing thee a song in thy praise; my darling's asleep by the murmuring stream. Flow gently, sweet Afton, disturb not his dream."

Ches figured the soloist must be drumming up trade for one booth or another. In reality, her song was intended to sooth an anxious child. Most kids like the idea of ponies, but parents don't buy tickets for timid children who refuse to ride.

*Hot Apple Fritters and the Prescott Ponies: Phineas Absalom Prescott,*
*Proprietor*

"Phineas Absalom Prescott," Ches read softly from the colorful but somewhat faded banner overhead. "Now there's a medicine show huckster for you."

Shifting his gaze from the sign, he watched a lovely young lady walk her slow circle alongside a Shetland pony. This girl was built close to the ground, scarcely five feet tall, but faded denim outlined very definite curves. Sandy-blond hair hung in a single carefully plaited braid while runover western boots and a pink T-shirt completed the picture. The ponies knew their job and were secured by a carousel apparatus, but she continued the old ballad as they ambled along, one hand resting lightly on the back of a fretful rider.

The blond-headed wrangler looked to be somewhere around his own age, and yet, Ches noted just a hint of stiffness in her right knee. This tiny defect somehow accentuated the feminine motion of her hips. Never particularly girl-crazy, Ches had only ever confronted the fine line between natural, God-given attraction and unwholesome thoughts where Serena Kate was concerned. Still, those blue jeans- just a tad snug from too many washings- and that honey coated singing voice...

"My biggest old pony might tote you, son, but you'll have to tie the dog first. Otherwise, how 'bout a fritter?"

Ches flinched, startled by this interruption of his private musings, but a glance at the speaker made him smile. The very picture of a southern gentleman gone to seed, this character sat reared back in the shade of a portable pavilion. Rumpled white linen strained slightly across his ample midsection, and a felt hat belied the hot weather. With a bit more shaping, the little Stetson might have been a cowboy hat, but he wore it like a fedora.

Without the slightest intention of taking a pony ride, Ches noted a buckskin-and-white gelding, just about Welsh sized and easily big enough to carry him.

"Reckon I'd get a private concert with my ride?" he drawled by way of an answer.

"Throw your money in," the old man shot back, jerking a thumb toward his cash box. "If she don't sing to you, I will."

"How much for the fritter?" Ches decided wryly.

"Dollar an' six bits... Every one made by hand, and they're worth twice that."

"I wouldn't doubt it," Ches answered, fumbling for the correct change as he rolled closer to the booth. "Stayin' busy?"

"Pony ride angle's clip-cloppin' right along. Weather's kinda hot for fritters, though."

This man spoke his language, the fritter tasted good, and homesickness hit him like a wave.

"By the way, sir, my name's Ches Durham."

"Phineas Absalom Prescott, at your service," the old showman responded, and since the sugary glaze coated Ches's left hand instead of his right, they shook.

"Ches Durham... Ches... Now, that's not your average ordinary kind of handle. Durham... Ches Durham... Did you ever hear tell of a little place way over in the piney woods called McKinley or some such thing?"

"We call it McKendrick," Ches supplied with a grin.

"That's right," Prescott cried, slapping his makeshift counter hard enough to rattle the cash box, "just as sure as we're sittin' here! And there was a fella named Durham used to run a good many horses through this little country auction."

The sting of tears caught Ches totally off guard.

"Dadgum blowin' dust," he said, and casually flipped a business card up onto the counter. "I'm the grandson."

Old Prescott started to chuckle and then laughed until his own eyes watered.

"And here I'm trying to sell a pony ride... Old Colonel Durham's a regular pistol, if you'll forgive my sayin' so. Why, I can just see him stomp and snort at the very notion!"

*Beyond the Parmalee Bottom* 17

"You've got the advantage on me there," Ches admitted. "I never knew him."

"I figured that old ramrod might just live forever, but I guess none of us do. Say, Ruthanne," he called suddenly in the general direction of his pretty helper. "Wrap that deal up and get over here!"

"Be right with you, Pap," she answered cheerfully, and Ches got the distinct impression that working all day in the summer heat- running back and forth on his beck and call- was nothing out of the ordinary.

"What kin are you to Miss Sis, anyhow? I reckon she's runnin' things with the colonel gone."

"She's my aunt, Daddy's older sister."

"I remember, now. The colonel did have a boy. Kind of a bookish little fella, and not near as handy-like as Miss Sis. She was a wonder, every inch the little lady, and ride like a wild Comanche!"

The comparison was hardly new to Ches, and he met it with a grin.

"You sure pegged Aunt Sis. She's still a wonder! Daddy figures not being a top hand will keep him from ending his days poor and stove up."

"Is that how you figure it, too?" Prescott inquired, one eyebrow shooting up quizzically.

"Well, sir, I was born stove up, so I just strap myself down good and tight and ride hard tryin' to keep up with Aunt Sis."

"Strap yourself..." Here, the old man paused for a low whistle. "Now, that's grittier than used flypaper. If you can ride up with Miss Sis, you'll sure enough do."

"Time for a fresh batch of fritters?" the young lady inquired brightly.

"Ask him; he just ate one. But that ain't what I called you over for, Ruthie girl. You recollect those tales I used to spin about a little, country sale barn in East Texas and a teenage belle who could stick on a horse like part of his natural hide?"

"Why, sure, Pap... Miss Sis was as big a deal to me as Lucille Mulhall or Annie Oakley!"

"Well, hold on to your hat, missy... This young fella is her nephew, Ches Durham." Then, completing the introduction, "My granddaughter, Miss Ruthanne Prescott."

"You don't mean it," Ruthanne practically gushed.

"Yep, I tried to sell him a pony ride, but he settled for one of your fritters."

"Well, for pity's sake... He ought to get plenty of chances to ride." She offered her hand across the counter and then noticed the remnants of homemade glaze on Ches's free hand and britches leg. "Let me get you a damp cloth," she said, immediately moving to do so. "Pap's a fine storyteller but kinda lax when it comes to customer service."

"Thank you, Miss Prescott. I'm awfully pleased to meet you," Ches ventured, instantly second guessing his own formality.

"Oh, Ches," she responded, accepting the gentle courtesy without a bobble, "you just don't know how glad I am to meet you. I've wondered over the years if Pap made the Durham horse sale up out of his head to entertain a bothersome little girl."

"I can't say much about your granddaddy's customer service or the workings of his imagination, but Aunt Sis is as real as they come. She'd dearly love to meet you." Ruthanne's delighted smile only increased her beauty, but Ches managed to shift his attention briefly to the old showman. "Say, Mr. Prescott, how'd you come to know so much about us?"

"Call me Pap, son, everybody else does."

"Yes," the young lady put in, "and I'm Ruthanne. You worked for the Durhams once upon a time, didn't you Pap?"

"I drifted through McKendrick back in the mid-70s and hung around the barn for a while. There was always plenty of work to go around on sale night, and I drew a check or two. Finally circled on home, though. Your Gram took me back again, and that ended my wandering days until..."

"It really is a small world," Ches observed. "I tend to get pretty lonesome when I'm away from home, and running into y'all is just what I needed today."

"I'm glad," Ruthanne answered simply, applying glaze to a half-dozen hot fritters as she spoke.

"What are you doing a-way out here, anyhow?" Pap wanted to know.

"I'm volunteering at a camp just outside of town. Aunt Sis wanted me to get away for a couple of weeks and maybe encourage some young people facing similar physical challenges."

"Do you always travel with a dog at your side? The way I remember it, little Miss Sis had six or eight following her all the time."

"We like a stock dog… I'm afraid Aunt Sis wouldn't have this one. Onyx here belongs to one of the campers, but he's kind of a handful."

"Is that a fact? What ever happened to dogs named Blackie and Spot?"

Ches made way for a high-spirited family group with a taste for apple fritters and then returned to the counter just as Ruthanne spied some pony ride prospects.

"I've got to run," she told him regretfully. Then to her grandfather, "Why don't you let me take your picture with Ches, Pap? It's not every day you run into the grandson of an old friend."

"To tell you the truth, Ruthanne," Ches broke in before the old man could answer, "I'd enjoy a good, long visit with y'all. You're busy right now, but the food out at the camp ain't none too shiny. If y'all would consider picking me up this evening, I'd be tickled to buy supper for us."

"Oh, Ches, of course we'll go! Just set things up with Pap, and I'll see you later."

Her usual sense of decorum overruled by the joy of this chance meeting and a pressing rush to get back to work, she favored Ches with a quick hug before dashing off toward the ponies.

"Ruthanne's right, son," Pap said as they watched her go. "I drag her from pillar to post like an old-time road trader. We don't make too many connections aside from other vendors and such. I think it'll do her a world of good to have supper with you, and we ought to be able to roll your wheelchair right up into the back of the van."

"I've got my forearm crutches back at camp," Ches assured him. "It won't hurt me to walk."

"Make it easy on yourself."

"Whatever you say. For the time being, though, I better ease on. I'd hate to turn away trade by sittin' here visiting."

A thought seemed to strike Pap Prescott, and he put out a hand to stop the younger man.

"Whoa up a minute… You talk to Miss Sis much while you're travelin'?"

"At least once a day," Ches assured him. The old rascal nodded, his expectations confirmed, and reached reluctantly into the cashbox. "What's this?"

"Twenty-seven dollars and a half; you can tell 'er I'm paid up."

Returning the roguish grin, Ches slipped the money into a shirt pocket. He gave Pap the camp's address and then motored off to find his group.

"Oh, won't you please take him along?" Erica begged that afternoon when he tried to return her dog. "Onyx can go anywhere with his vest on, and he needs more experience in restaurants."

"I'm hoping for a nice visit with this young lady and her grandfather, and I don't want your cotton-pickin' pup underfoot."

"He can keep the grandfather company if this special date of yours really has one," she retorted.

"Everybody's got a grandfather," Ches grumbled, "two of 'em. Never said she was my date… I'll hang onto the dog if it means that much to you."

"Pap begged off," Ruthanne explained a little while later, her tone cheerful and yet somewhat apologetic. "He said I was to pick you up here. I wonder, now and again, just what he gets up to."

"You look very nice this evening, Ruthanne. I'm sorry about the dog."

His sincere compliment made her eyes sparkle even as the apology brought a dismissive shake of her head.

"Don't you worry about it, Ches. Won't be the first meal I've eaten with some old pup layin' under the table."

"It may take both of us to keep this one off the table," he quipped and was rewarded by her musical laughter.

"I don't get to wear my dresses very much," she confessed offhandedly. "Pap calls this the appaloosa getup."

Ruthanne wore a white 1950s style dress with small black dots scattered over it like dapples on a horse. Soft, lustrous hair- flowing loose past her shoulders- retained just the right amount of wave from that morning's braiding. A dainty patent leather belt and matching shoes provided the finishing touches. The dress was sleeveless, but otherwise, this ladylike outfit reminded him of something from his aunt's closet.

Finally, Ches gave his head a slight shake to clear it. What was old Pap Prescott thinking to send this angelic girl off alone with a virtual stranger, and for that matter, what was wrong with him? He had loved Serena Kate enough to make himself nearly sick with grief. Now, to have his head turned by this other girl...

Poor Serena Kate... Sweet, precious Serena Kate who gave and gave and gave with never a moment to spare for herself. The single mom, overwhelmed and exhausted, who never thought to rest unless he reminded her. Guilt pulled at his heartstrings. That didn't make much sense, though, not after Serena Kate ignored his phone calls for over a year and then married somebody else.

"Ches? Say, Ches... Is everything okay?"

The sound of Ruthanne's voice pulled him back to the moment.

"Sure," he answered with a genuine smile. "Let's go."

Their transportation was a large maroon van with the Prescott logo emblazoned across the side, but the two young people, lost in each other's company, never gave it a second thought.

"It may sound strange," Ruthanne said, making conversation easily as she drove, "but your Aunt Sis is forever a young girl in my mind because of Pap's tales. You have to understand, I soaked up stories like a sponge, and his recollections of a horse-crazy East Texas belle naturally piqued my interest."

"I wonder why?" Ches answered, teasing her a little. "Aunt Sis is married, now, with a teenage daughter of her own. But she wouldn't mind the notion of being forever young in your imagination, not one little bit."

"I'd love to meet your aunt, Ches, and see McKendrick for myself. We travel all over the country, but there's not much call for a pony ride service in rural areas. Although, if we fall any further down the totem pole..."

"What do you mean?" he wondered. "The apple fritter I had this afternoon tasted delicious and your ponies are in good shape..."

"Well, there's kind of a hierarchy when it comes to traveling concessions. We got to be a big-time outfit back when I was performing. Pap kept a hired hand to help with the ponies and cooked fritters himself. Depending on the venue, I'd either do ticketed shows or run through my routines for free to drum up pony ride business. But when a nasty fall ended my performing days, things sorta went downhill for us."

They settled on a barbeque restaurant, and before the meal was over, Ches felt like he'd known Ruthanne for years. She told him of leaving her South Carolina home at age twelve for the nomadic lifestyle of a professional trick rider and about performing, three or four times a day, right up into the recent past. He shared some of his childhood struggles with cerebral palsy. The emphasis, though, was on how Aunt Sis taught him to live beyond his handicap.

"Thank you so much for the meal, Ches, and for the company. Everything's been lovely. Why, even the pup behaved fairly well."

"I've owned some mighty good dogs over the years, but none I'd trust inside a barbeque joint. Have a piece of pie with me?"

"Mercy, no. Livin' off day-old fritters will just about ruin a girl for sweets."

Looking back on it later, Ches hated to think this adorable little lady might not have whatever she wanted to eat whenever she wanted it. The humor sparkling in her eyes proved contagious, though, and at the time her statements struck him as funny.

"I hate to take up too much of your time, Ruthanne. Still, visiting with you is almost like coming home, and I'm not quite ready to go back to that camp dormitory."

"You're not keepin' me," she assured him. "I may be havin' more fun than you are! Tell you what, Pap's a pretty good hand with that old guitar of his. Let's circle back to the fairgrounds for a sing along before we call it an evening."

"I heard you singing earlier today," he admitted, "and that's an invitation I can't turn down."

The shoestring carnival lost any pretense of sparkle after sundown, and Ches followed Ruthanne carefully across the dark, semi-deserted grounds.

"Pap? Say, Pap," she called, checking inside the fritter stand and all around the livestock trailer. "Everything's quiet on the picket line," she said, gesturing toward the horses, "but there's not a sign of Pap."

"Not a sign is right," a man's voice jeered disgustedly out of the darkness. "That country fried conman has flown the coop again!"

Ruthanne stiffened in anger, and maybe just a touch of fear, as a huge form emerged from the night around them.

"Phineas Absalom Prescott's no con artist, Tiny. If you can't trade with Pap without losin' your shirt, then you ought to quit trying."

"Don't you take that Sunday School tone with me, Miss High and Mighty. It's easy for a man to come out the winner when he makes all his own rules."

"I don't have the faintest idea what you're—"

Suddenly, this Tiny character hemmed her in next to the horse trailer. He wasn't pressed up against her, not yet, but enormous arms and the sheer mass of his body prevented escape.

"Climb down off your high horse, girlie, and start digging around for that cash box. Unless you can think of a more interesting way to square Pap's account ..."

# Chapter Two

Ches sat off to one side a little in his wheelchair, shocked temporarily into silence as the situation spiraled out of control, but Tiny's menacing stance and thinly veiled threat demanded action.

"Mister, you need to leave."

The words rang with genuine authority. He might be crippled and alone, but Ches spoke as if Aunt Sis and two or three of their toughest sale-barn hands were ready and waiting to back his play. Tiny knew the boy and dog were there before he ever revealed himself, but matching wits with Ruthanne taxed him considerably. As a result, their presence had slipped his mind. The big man whirled, poised for flight, but the concern on his face quickly faded into a sardonic sneer.

"Be real still and quiet, runt. Maybe I won't feel the need to hoist you out of that chair and paddle your behind."

"I don't figure you've got that much nerve. If I was the least bit worried, I'd just set this dog loose and get it over with." Beady eyes flicked momentarily down to Onyx, and Ches knew he'd won. "Now, do like I tell you and carry your big self on down the road."

Anger flashed briefly across the man's face, but old Pap Prescott chose that moment to amble onto the scene.

"Aw, Tiny, you needn't be too concerned about that dog. Still, I know this boy's family. There ain't no way in the world Miss Sis sent him out of the county without a pistol on him somewhere. Besides, if you so much as bloody his nose, that bunch'll hunt you for the next thirty years."

Tiny's gaze bounced rapidly from Pap to Ches to Ruthanne and back again.

"You hayseeds are too crazy to be running loose," he decided, "but there's always another day."

"Make it another dark night," Pap taunted. "Might even the odds some."

"Mercy sakes," Ruthanne breathed, sinking onto a handy folding chair.

"Thank you much, son," Pap offered sincerely.

Seeing the vulnerability behind Ruthanne's brave front made Ches feel a little wobbly inside, but he grasped her grandfather's outstretched hand.

"Tiny was right about one thing, Pap. You're crazier than a road lizard. I can't have a gun around that special-needs camp."

"I hear you, but Blackie don't exactly look like no attack dog. Just satisfy an old man's curiosity… Did Miss Sis ask you to tote a sidearm?"

"Well, yeah, but her being right might not've helped us much."

"You and the dog started Tiny backin' up," Pap admitted. "When I put in with that talk about a pistol, he just had to cut and run."

Still a little shaky, Ruthanne got to her feet and went into the fritter stand to fix glasses of ice water for the three of them.

"I'm sorry to pull you into our troubles, Ches," she said quietly, handing over a Styrofoam cup, "but I'm glad you were here with me."

"Me, too," Ches replied wholeheartedly but not before a sip or two of water to make sure his voice wouldn't break. "Who is that Tiny fella, anyway?"

"He likes to throw his weight around," Pap answered dismissively. "Runs a rickety old Ferris wheel and lords it over this particular bunch of carnival folk. Keeps three or four toughs around and him big as an ox besides. I 'spect he gets protection money off a lot of these vendors."

"Y'all best load up and pull out of here tonight. There's plenty of room over at the teens camp."

"Son, this is our living," Pap answered with a dry chuckle, "and I don't figure to run."

"How long did you watch Tiny's little show before you finally took a hand?" Ches asked bluntly. "I'll never forget the sight of your granddaughter up against that trailer. Fact of business, there are two voices in my head. One's quoting Scripture, 'Vengeance is mine sayeth the Lord.' The other tells me, 'That rats' nest needs a good burnin' out!' Both voices sound suspiciously like Aunt Sis, but if you don't get Ruthanne out of here right quick, the Scripture quoting side ain't got much chance."

"It's not as bad as all that, Ches," Ruthanne put in soothingly. "I wear a sharp little sheath knife on my belt when I'm working so as to cut a lead rope right quick if we get in a bind. But I could just as easily trim Tiny's nose hairs with it. He caught me all dressed up and playing at normal life, that's all."

The words "playing at normal life" seemed to affect Pap more than Ches's little speech.

"Start loadin' horses, Ruthie girl. We're pulling out."

"I'd like that, Pap, if you're sure."

"All this junk ain't likely to pack itself. Scat, girl..."

"Yes, sir!" Ruthanne answered with a radiant smile.

The Prescotts used their biggest pony for impromptu rides the next morning. Ruthanne even pulled her trick horse off the picket line to accommodate larger riders. Campers enjoyed a new experience, and several remarked that Thimble, the buckskin-and-white pony, looked like a scaled down model of her horse.

The disabled teens laughed and hugged and showed their gratitude until even Pap temporarily forgot the loss of a day's income. Once everyone with the desire and physical ability to sit a horse had ridden as long as they wanted, he cleared a big circle and looked from Ruthanne to the trick horse with an expectant grin.

"Now, Pap," she said, her tone more amused than scolding. "Me and Buttons haven't made so much as a practice run since the accident, and this knee still lets me know when it's comin' on to rain."

"Just like riding a bicycle," he quipped, looking beyond the day's entertainment to a more profitable comeback.

The campers couldn't exactly hear this exchange, but their anxious faces proved too much for Ruthanne.

"Alright, maybe just a couple of basic tricks. Come on, Buttons," she murmured, swinging expertly into the saddle. "Let's go to work." She spun the horse around a time or two, just to warm him up, but even this brought oohing and aahing from the uninitiated audience. After a dust-raising gallop earned enthusiastic applause, she leaned down and spoke to Buttons. "We wouldn't even have to try any tricks, but I can see Pap running up your feed bill in his head. Here goes!"

Without slackening the pace, Ruthanne dropped off the horse's left side. Her million-dollar smile was part muscle memory and part exhilaration, but waving to the crowd with her free hand seemed to take more nerve than it once had. She made one whole circuit, attempted another, and then noticed her strength fading halfway around.

Ruthanne pulled back up into the saddle but felt almost clumsy getting it done. She wondered in passing whether the heat in her face came from exertion or embarrassment. The smile never wavered, though, and Buttons executed his bow to perfection. Sliding off to stand near his head, the lovely rider tried not to gulp for air as she took a bow of her own.

Ruthanne, pleased with the kids' obvious enjoyment if not with her performance, was signing autographs for amazed campers and staff when Ches finally handed her a Gatorade.

"Thank you, darling," was her heartfelt response as she raised the ice-cold bottle to her forehead.

Sudden realization of what she had said brought fresh heat to her cheeks, and the next autograph wavered a little.

"My pleasure," he assured her, passing over the unplanned endearment without comment. "The memories you gave these young people here today will last a lifetime."

"Oh, Ches," she sighed, "at least I managed not to fall off. I'd like to gripe about how out of shape I've gotten since my little mishap. Truth is, I could've caught myself that day if I'd been in top form."

"Accidents happen…"

"That's a comforting thought," she quipped, continuing the conversation once the last autograph had been signed. "I never was any great hand to exercise, not unless I could do it from horseback. When birthdays began to interfere with my girlish metabolism… Well, gravity makes precious few allowances for a trick rider."

Stung by her casual self-criticism, Ches took her hand ever so gently, drew back uncertainly, and finally cleared his throat to speak.

"Ruthanne, people aren't… Men don't… I'm not concerned about the teenage athlete you used to be. You're a beautiful woman. A piece of God's most gorgeous handiwork… Why, if you just stood beside your horse and smiled, you'd be a heartstopper. Don't you know that?" Afraid he had overstepped polite boundaries, Ches looked around rather desperately for a change of subject. Finally, he spotted Erica and realized she'd watched all the excitement from afar. "Yonder's the girl who owns Onyx," he murmured discreetly. "Might do a world of good if you'd spend a few minutes with her."

Hoping a quick sip of Gatorade would settle the butterflies in her stomach, Ruthanne twisted the bottlecap back on and gave him a gentle sort of smile.

"Well, then, I'll just carry my beautiful little self on over there and have a talk with Miss Erica."

Ruthanne picketed Buttons once again, being sure to loosen the girth and slip him a piece of stale apple fritter in the process. Acting on a hunch, she untied Tinker, a good-natured little Shetland mare, and led her over to use as a conversation starter when she approached Erica.

While the regular camp activities resumed around them, Pap and Ches parked themselves under a lone shade tree within sight- but not hearing distance- of Ruthanne's impromptu counseling session. Tilting his chair back against the live oak, Pap stretched booted feet out before him, laced weathered fingers atop his stomach, and opened the conversation.

"Ruthanne did fine out there today, but she's favoring that knee. I can see it from here. Your name is Durham, son, so I know you for a trader. What's the goin' rate on highly trained trick horses?"

"Why, you old scoundrel," Ches drawled, his bemused chuckle taking any sting from the words. "You'd sell that horse right out from under her and leave me lookin' like the coldhearted opportunist out for a quick buck!"

The old showman's mouth quirked upward, acknowledging the truth of the statement.

"Take you a breath, sonny, and settle down. Can't blame a fella for trying. In round figures, just conversationally, what do you figure old Buttons might be worth? A twelve-year-old paint gelding with more extras on him than a new Oldsmobile..."

"More than I'll give for him," Ches shot back.

"Naturally, naturally... Even so, you're the only live buyer ready to hand. What do you say?"

"I've known some horses to stay twelve forever," Ches said almost automatically while gathering his thoughts.

"Aw, I don't know his age right down to the minute. We'll ask Ruthanne. You wouldn't doubt her word, I guess."

"You guess right, but I'll do the asking. If Ruthanne puts him closer to twelve than twenty, I'll give fifteen hundred right where he stands. You'll have to take a check, but that leaves me huntin' a way to get him home."

"Me and Ruthanne are kind of at loose ends after last night. What'll you give for him standin' in the barn at McKendrick?"

"Oh, eighteen hundred, I guess. That's something over a dollar a mile, and I'll do away with the check, too."

"Say what?"

"Aunt Sis'll meet you at the gate with hundred-dollar bills."

Pap studied the toes of his dust-covered boots for a long minute before allowing himself a wide grin.

"If you never knew the old colonel, Miss Sis taught you right well. Tighter than bark on a tree... But you just went into the trick horse business."

"No, I ain't, neither. Not 'til Ruthanne makes up her mind. I don't know which one really owns the horse, and I don't care. If he's bought with my money, Aunt Sis will count it right into your granddaughter's pretty little hand. Y'all can sort it out from there."

"Not quite two days, and you're already henpecked," Pap lamented, feigning severe disappointment before his grin returned in full force. "Just so long as we get a little folding money and lighten up on the expenses."

"This morning was phenomenal, Ches!" the camp director enthused a little while later. "When I asked you about a horse program, I wasn't expecting such immediate results. Our campers will talk about this for months on end!"

"No need for thanks, ma'am. Horses bring a lot of joy to my life, and it's always a privilege to share that with others. Besides, I appreciate you letting my friends camp here last night. Mind if I give you a little advice?"

"No, of course not."

"Those two horses that were gifted to the camp will never suit your purpose. Both are untrained, their feet need trimming badly, and that gray is a stud."

"He is quite the handsome boy! But I suppose most horses are beautiful."

"No, I don't think you understand. This one's all boy. He's a stallion, ma'am, and if he ever figures it out, he'll go to bitin' and squealin' and actin' a fool."

"Oh, no... We can't have that! The riding, as much as it thrilled our campers, was a liability nightmare. A rampaging stallion sounds even worse! I'll have to call animal control right away."

"Hold up a minute. I know pony rides weren't exactly figured into your budget, but the Prescotts do this for a living. If you'd consider passing those two horses along to Pap, it might kill two birds with one stone."

As she headed for her office to consult the board members by telephone, Pap scowled at his newfound friend.

"Just who you trying to help, son? I got a little room on the trailer, but the kind of horses you're talking about ain't fixin' to take no prizes."

"I'll buy them off you," Ches explained. "Run 'em through the next sale and at least get my money back... I've got enough cash to pay you here and now. That'll make traveling money until you collect for Buttons. Besides, Aunt Sis wouldn't give as much for these nags as I will."

"Well, ain't you just broke out with generosity all of a sudden."

"It's either buy these horses from you a little high or slip Ruthanne a hundred for the road."

"She's eatin' regular," the old man harrumphed.

"Her pride won't stand for a handout, anyhow, but this'll sure help my feelings."

Their eyes locked for several seconds before Pap closed the subject with a solemn nod. His sharp old gaze then drifted over to where Ruthanne and Erica were finishing their conversation with a hug.

"The girl's got a way with kids. Then again, it's just her way in general. Works about the same with grown folks or bronc horses."

"Ruthanne knows just who she is, and that gives her a very soothing presence,"

Ches agreed.

"She can work a crowd, like in the old performing days, but one-on-one is where my granddaughter really shines. If she ever gets one, horse or human, hemmed up in a corner of the corral and starts that sweet talk, they'll eat out of her hand directly."

"You're in business to buy and sell," Ruthanne said minutes later, reluctantly agreeing to part with her special favorite. "I can't ask you to keep Buttons forever. If you think kindly of me, though, please take a little extra care as to who gets him."

"Oh, Ruthanne..." Looking into those tear-bright hazel eyes, Ches could have sworn on oath to hold an entire band of brood mares until judgement day, but some promises get hard to keep. "If I sell your horse, it'll take a mighty special buyer to get him."

As soon as Pap's ownership of the two camp horses was confirmed, Ches paid him a couple of hundred dollars apiece. Ruthanne used Buttons and a lariat rope to catch and load them, rigging up a partition to protect her ponies in the trailer.

"I'll be so tickled to finally meet Miss Sis," the young lady said as she and her grandfather got ready to leave. She sounded almost giddy, but her tone switched to an anxious sort of hopefulness when she spoke again. "How long until you come home, Ches?"

"I'm committed here for another week," he answered regretfully.

"I'll hold Pap there as long as I can, but a week is a mighty long time. If I don't see you in McKendrick..."

Choking up, she squeezed a colorful but somewhat faded business card into his palm and turned quickly away.

As the Prescotts bounced off down the rocky access road, Pap driving the van and Ruthanne following with their aging pickup and horse trailer, Ches felt strangely isolated. There were plenty of people around him but no homefolks and certainly nobody like Ruthanne. After spending so much of the last year missing Serena Kate, loneliness seemed almost natural. Still, he considered the feeling a little foolish.

*Beyond the Parmalee Bottom* 35

For a long time, staying close to Aunt Sis and living the life they loved had been enough. She was a tangible connection to family roots, his tie to the community, and the one who had taught him the most about his faith. He loved and cherished his parents, but Aunt Sis lived on a little pedestal all her own. How could he yearn for something more when this special lady was happy, healthy, and working by his side. Foolish or not, though, the feeling persisted. Was there something wrong with him, some defect that would keep him forever pining after someone or something?

Ches gave his head an exasperated shake.

"I'm so mixed up 'til I don't know if I'm missing Ruthanne or just sad because Serena Kate ain't hardly got sense enough to come in out of the rain." Abruptly, he shifted from irritable muttering to prayer. "Help me, Lord. Help me to live each day with a thankful heart and trust in your provision for my future."

The popularity of Ruthanne's performance made Ches a minor hero around the camp. Before returning to his regular duties, though, he found a quiet spot and dialed the number he had learned so well as a lonely kid in Dallas. His aunt owned a cell phone, had for years, but the line he called rang a rotary dial phone on the colonel's old desk and two or three wall mounts throughout the sale barn. The phone rang several times before a familiar but slightly breathless drawl ended his wait.

"Durham Auction Company; this is Sis."

"I thought I might catch you at the desk, but I should've known better."

"Hey, honey! I'm just riding Cassidy's mare up and down the alley a little. My daughter begged for this high-headed, glass-eyed creature and then let her stand around idle 'til she's nearly as dangerous as a teased snake."

Visualizing the long, tall red-and-white mare, Ches realized he had just bought the perfect replacement. Ruthanne's trusted mount offered all the flashy paint-horse color without the many drawbacks of riding an idiot.

"I'm sorry I didn't call you last night, something kind of—"

"Oh, I did a little stall walking, but your Uncle Andrew made me promise not to pester you. He said you'd call in your own good time."

*Beyond the Parmalee Bottom* 36

"I sure missed our visit, but things got kind of busy."

"What about your supper with old Pap Prescott and his granddaughter? Any man who'd take nearly forty years to pay back twenty-some-odd dollars…"

"Aw, now… I knew Pap for a slick one the minute I laid eyes on him. He don't mean no harm, though. Ruthanne is sweet as she can be, and she's sure got the touch with a horse. That's one reason I called, Aunt Sis. They just left me headed your way."

"Pap's an awful good pitchman, honey, but even he'd starve to death trying to sell pony rides a-way out here in the woods."

"Yes, ma'am," he answered with a grin she could hear in his voice. "I bought a topnotch little gelding from Ruthanne, still owe her eighteen hundred in cash. I'd appreciate it if you'd take care of that first thing. She's also hauling a couple of rough-edged nags I bought from Pap, but I've already paid him."

"Good; if he tries to collect again, I'll set the dogs on him."

"I don't think he'd embarrass Ruthanne that-a-way. When it comes to the thought of meeting you, she's just like a kid at Christmastime."

"I declare, Ches, you've got to stop singing my praises to anybody that'll listen."

"I just tell the truth," he protested, "but it wasn't me this time. Pap did it. Remembered his time in McKendrick and spun a bunch of tales to little Ruthanne while they were traveling up and down the road."

"Well, heavens to Betsy…"

"There's something special about Ruthanne, Aunt Sis. She's got a hard life, traipsing after old Pap. Do me a favor; spoil that girl. Make her a batch of your biscuits, too. Another thing, just hold the little buckskin-and-white for me. He ain't exactly trade stock."

"You bet, Ches. I'll take care of things."

"Know something, Aunt Sis?"

"Tell me…"

"I sure do love you."

"I love you, too, honey, a bushel and a peck!"

As he ended the call, Ches felt his smile spill over into a chuckle. Thoughts of home now focused on Aunt Sis and Ruthanne enjoying their time together. Serena Kate, her redheaded twins, and their brand-new stepdaddy faded into the background.

Putting his own troubles aside, Ches worked to make a difference at every opportunity. The second week brought a fresh crop of campers and a type of homesickness he knew well. Not the sad, rootless feeling from a few days ago but an eager anticipation of his return to McKendrick.

Ches appreciated his experience volunteering at camp and made a point to thank the director. But when that minivan rolled up with his mom at the wheel and Cassidy waving from a window, Ches sat waiting with a duffel bag atop his knees. He didn't fuss much about a stop at Cracker Barrel but only because it was his first decent meal since the barbecue plate he'd enjoyed with Ruthanne. They talked all through lunch, but once back on the road, conversation began to wind down.

"Poor Dad," Cassidy finally observed with a slight giggle.

"What's wrong with Uncle Andrew?" Ches wanted to know.

"Well," she explained, "you've been gone two whole weeks. I bet Mother's fit to be tied."

"What do you mean, you bet?" he asked a little sharply. "Haven't you talked to her?"

"Yeah, once or twice."

"Once or twice? You're her daughter, Cassidy. If my being gone has upset her, don't you reckon she's missing you?"

"Doubt it…"

*Beyond the Parmalee Bottom* 38

"She rode your horse," he challenged.

"She did what? If I've heard it once, I've heard it a thousand times, 'You picked this high-headed, glass-eyed Indian pony. Now, you ride her.' Of course, she rides your horse once or twice a week just to make sure the oh-so-perfect Short Stuff stays fine- tuned for her oh-so-perfect nephew."

"Cassidy," Jenna put in from the driver's seat, "you have to admit that Ches's situation is a little different. Being strapped to his saddle and all, he can't afford even the slightest mishap. Your mother expects a lot when it comes to your riding, maybe too much. That's not exactly new in the Durham family, but it has nothing to do with her love for you."

"All I meant to say," Ches qualified, "was that maybe you ought to've considered your mother's feelings while you were off having fun. Give her a big hug when we get home, though, and that'll go a long way to make up for it."

"I knew you'd call her, so what's the big deal?" Cassidy retorted before changing her tune. "Okay... Okay... The hug's probably not a bad idea. I can't believe she rode Fancy for me!"

"She did, and that says I miss my Cassidy in big capital letters."

They traveled in silence for a mile or two, and Cassidy took on a rather thoughtful expression.

"Hey, Aunt Jenna," she finally ventured. "Let's stop off at the sale barn first thing."

When the travelers arrived at home, Ches hung back and gave Cassidy time for a little reunion with her mother. The dogs milled around as usual, and Roxy trotted up to place her head on his knee. She blew out a heavy breath that spoke of every long day without him. Two weeks probably seemed the next thing to eternity in a dog's mind. Finally, though, Aunt Sis nudged the little red gyp aside to claim her hug.

"Short Stuff and Pumpkin are saddled and ready, been standin' that way since this morning. I figured we'd take a little welcome home tour."

"Can I go, too, Mother?"

"Sure, darling. Run catch Fancy. Don't expect a permanent reform, but I think you'll find her easier to handle today."

"How 'bout the little buckskin-and-white?" Ches asked a few minutes later as Aunt Sis fussed around getting him situated in the saddle.

"Buttons settled in just fine, honey. I was a little skeptical as to the price, but if we can show him half as well as Ruthanne, he'll bring your money back and then some."

"I'd like to keep the horse around a while," he admitted a little sheepishly.

"That's a good bit of money to tie up," his aunt suggested gently, "and Ruthanne, as sweet as she is, may never drift back this way again."

"I figured they'd moved on. You were pretty quiet on that subject when we talked yesterday. I don't know, Aunt Sis... She didn't want to sell the horse, and I just don't feel like shipping him right on down the line. If she does make her way back in the next month or two, Buttons ought to be here."

"You're awfully tenderhearted for a horse trader, honey child."

"Well, for better or worse... I learned the business from you, not old Colonel Durham. Figured Buttons might help build Cassidy's confidence as a rider... I don't expect you to buy him or anything. I'll just hold what I've got and let her ride him whenever she feels like it."

"You just might have something there, Ches. Here she comes now with that high-headed, glass-eyed... Why don't y'all ride a circle or two. I'll turn old Pumpkin out and catch Buttons for myself so she can get a look at him."

The three enjoyed their ride, and Cassidy got by with only a minor fit or two on Fancy's part.

"Mother," she complained at one point, "I wish you'd warn me before you slap her across the hindquarters like that!"

"Well, darling," Sis answered almost apologetically, "when she balks on you, I don't plan my reaction. I just ride in and swat her a time or two."

They rode for an hour and a half, but by the time everyone gathered at the big house, Sis had thrown together a quick supper of homemade biscuits with sausage gravy, scrambled eggs, and vine-ripe tomatoes. She liked the idea of a garden but- with Nash gone, livestock to see about, and the horse sale to run- seldom put the time into it. Neighbors Bowie and Lillian Tate doted on Miss Sis and kept her well supplied all summer long.

"What did you think of the little horse I rode today?" she asked her daughter halfway through the meal.

"I told you... His coloring is beyond cool. He seemed well-behaved, too, but you can make the average rodeo bronc look gentle."

"Oh, he's easy to ride. Lots easier than that high-headed—"

"Mother!"

"Anyhow, darling, Ches is set on keepin' Buttons around. We thought you might want to sell your horse and ride this one for a little while."

"Sell Fancy? I just don't know what you have against her, Mother."

Ches opened his mouth to run through a laundry list of the mare's shortcomings, but his own mom cut him off with a look. Though she never quite understood the conventional family wisdom against high heads and glass eyes, Jenna didn't like the unpredictable animal any better than they did. Using a little wisdom of her own, she took a different approach.

"Fancy's very pretty, but you don't always get along with her. If Ches wants to keep this other horse and let you use him, why not sell her and put the money in your college fund. Someone else might really enjoy Fancy. Besides, your mother is the horse expert with Ches running a close second."

"You didn't have to say it out loud," Cassidy answered, suddenly teasing. "They already think they know everything."

"They don't know everything," Terry Durham put in with a sympathetic chuckle. "Plunk these two down in the middle of New York City, and you'd soon find out. Still, what they know, they know. I wish now I'd paid a little more attention to things the colonel tried to teach me."

"Guess you're right," Cassidy responded. "I'll try Buttons out and then decide about putting Fancy in the next auction."

The table went silent then until Miss Sis flashed a saucy smile at her brother.

"We'd end up in Central Park driving a carriage apiece."

"What?" he asked blankly.

"Me and Ches in New York City," she explained smugly.

"I wouldn't doubt it, not one little bit," he admitted with a snort. "Now, let's cut Bowie's watermelon for dessert."

Ches, having felt at ease in the big house since that very first summer, decided to stay the night. The cousins swapped homes fairly often, but this time Cassidy opted to stay put. Promising to see everyone at church the next morning, Terry and Jenna headed out for the moonlight stroll back to their house.

"I never saw anybody so keen on traipsin' across pastures at night," Miss Sis muttered. "If some old mama cow runs 'em up a tree, you know it'll be all my fault."

Used to the gap between his aunt's worldview and that of his parents, Ches just smiled at her and shrugged.

"Goodnight, Aunt Sis."

"Night, honey. I'm awful glad to have you home."

Andrew fried bacon and eggs the next morning to go with his wife's leftover biscuits. Having slept like a baby amid the familiar creaks and sighs of the old house, Ches was surprised to find his appetite missing.

"I didn't burn that bacon, Ches," Andrew chided good-naturedly. "Now, quit shovin' it around the plate, and eat it."

"Yes, sir," Ches answered with a grin but directed his fretful question to Aunt Sis. "Have Serena Kate and her family been to church?"

"Now and again, but not too regular," she answered matter-of-factly.

Cassidy, not normally a morning person, sounded almost chipper when she joined the conversation.

"I hope they come. It'll be great seeing Corrie and Torrie again!"

"Yeah," Ches agreed without much enthusiasm, "it's been a while." Alone on the porch a few minutes later, he felt a hand drop onto his shoulder.

"Just about ready?"

"Believe I'll lay out today, Aunt Sis."

"I don't think that's a good idea, honey. You can't avoid her forever, and you needn't let it run your life."

"I don't care about avoiding her. She'll always be Serena Kate, no matter the choices she makes, but if I can steer clear of that Ethan Fisher... You're right," he admitted, catching hold of her hand to squeeze it. "It's not a good idea, but it's what I'm fixin' to do."

"Alright then; I'll change clothes and catch our horses."

"Oh, Aunt Sis, I never meant for you—" he started, but Cassidy interrupted from her listening post in the doorway.

"Good grief; the world's coming to an end!"

"Not today, darling, and that means you've got to play the piano."

"Mother... You know I hate playing in front of people. Besides, if you two aren't coming, we might as well scrap the whole thing and try again next Sunday."

"Hush that silly talk, and go pick out some songs," Sis advised in a tone that brooked no further argument. "You're just lucky your dad leads the singing these days. I played for Uncle Elmer and learned whatever songs he happened to pick out, please and thank you."

"Yes... That is how you got so good." Cassidy spoke each phrase slowly and distinctly as if explaining something to a toddler. "And... That is why you and Ches can't just ride off into the sunrise whenever things don't suit you."

# Chapter Three

Miss Sis never considered herself a very strict parent. Still, old-fashioned sensibilities recoiled from the notion of allowing a sassy teenager to dictate what she could or couldn't do. The white lace gloves held casually in one hand were a far cry from her leather quirt, but the flash of temper in her eyes left Cassidy very little time to ponder this minor detail as she scurried back into the relative safety of the house.

"Know something," Ches observed grudgingly, "she's right."

"You'll go?"

"Yes, ma'am. Just promise me one thing. You've got to be cool, calm, and sweeter than sugar. I know you can't hardly stand to see me hurting... But what's done is done, and there's no use gettin' mad."

"If sweet's what you need me to be, Ches, butter won't melt in my mouth," she promised solemnly, and they headed off to church.

Visiting quietly with Ms. Edna Crawford- widow of their longtime pastor- before Sunday School, Ches felt a slap on the shoulder and turned his wheelchair to face the newcomer.

"Say, bud, I'd begun to think you wouldn't make it back in time for the horse sale on Friday," redheaded Scooter McKendrick said with a grin.

"Aw, you and Aunt Sis could handle it," Ches answered, reaching up to shake his friend's hand.

"Maybe so, but she gets awfully edgy and hard to work for if you ain't around. Worse than an old woman…"

"I am an old woman, knot head," Miss Sis commented as she sailed by. As promised, though, her tone was honey-sweet.

The summer before Ches entered college, he and Scooter had gone through auctioneer school together. Ches all but dragged his less-than-studious friend through the bookwork, but Scooter made a jimdandy auctioneer with plenty of style and a keen eye for livestock pricing.

Voice slightly affected by cerebral palsy, all Ches wanted was the certification. He auctioned off a horse or two on occasion just to keep his license active under Texas law. Scooter, on the other hand, worked several cattle markets each week and came home to the Durham horse sale once a month.

"Good old foot-in-mouth disease," Scooter commented wryly.

"She don't ever pay you much attention," Ches assured him, gesturing after Aunt Sis who was already seated at the piano.

"That's probably for the best," his pal admitted with a shrug.

Ches truly enjoyed the worship service, and his mood picked up steadily as the morning progressed without any sign of the new-made Fisher family. Soon, though, he began to question even that sense of relief. "Now, what kind of attitude is that?" he chided himself inwardly. "Do you really want Corrie and Torrie raised outside of church just so you can feel more comfortable?"

Scooter showed up with a different girl on his arm every month or so, and some folks assumed that only the wheelchair stood between Ches and a similar revolving string of girlfriends. Chalking the real difference up to his friend's tender heart and keen sense of loyalty, Scooter carefully avoided any mention of his sister.

Ms. Edna, now well into her nineties but still quite active, stopped Sis after church with a hand on her arm.

"Who all's going to the nursing home this afternoon, darling?"

"Looks like just me and Ches, Ms. Edna. You'd be more than welcome to come with us."

"Well, now, Sis... Are you sure it won't be any trouble?"

"Trouble? When has your company ever troubled me?"

"Please come, Ms. Edna," Ches added. "The folks out there'll be tickled to see you."

Sunday afternoon visits to the county seat rest home were pretty much routine for Miss Sis. Andrew often accompanied her as did the new pastor and his wife. Terry and Jenna went sometimes, and Cassidy joined the group only when she was forced into it.

"Old people just adore Mother, but that piano needs tuning bad."

Ches recalled a time when his aunt had refused to even darken the door of a nursing home and made it his business to stay at her side. Her fears of growing old alone were long past, now, but he still felt more than a little protective.

"Play us *The Great Homecoming*."

Giles Parmalee leased his pastureland to Ches, rented his house out to Scooter, and terrorized the hallways of Pinevale in a newly-acquired mobility chair.

"That old Jimmie Davis tune?" Miss Sis inquired. "You know good and well I can't get halfway through it without bawling."

"Well, if you want to let a few little tears stop you... *Waltz Across Texas!*"

Ms. Edna's breath caught audibly, somewhere between a gasp and a chuckle, but this reaction was overshadowed by more strident objections from Aunt Hattie.

"This is Sunday, you worthless old rogue!"

Miss Sis's only surviving aunt ran Giles a close race as Pinevale's most opinionated resident. Both fiercely independent individuals spent their lives around the rural crossroads of McKendrick until age and infirmity forced them into the nursing home.

Having already enjoyed several hymns, the many residents who didn't feel personally entitled to order Sis around were content to sit back and watch the developing squabble. Figuring Mr. Giles would pick at her mercilessly until she sang the Jimmie Davis tearjerker or played him something country, Sis caught a flash of inspiration.

"It 'is' Sunday," she conceded. "Here's *The Waltz of the Angels*."

Ches loved to watch his aunt's fingers as they floated effortlessly over the keys, but the gentle waltz-time melody made his eyelids heavy.

"Nobody plays quite like Miss Sis."

As the soft whisper sounded in his ear, a hand trailed briefly across his shoulders.

"Mmm," he agreed, enjoying a sweet familiarity in the momentary contact.

"Don't sit there and play possum on me, Ches Durham. You've never taken a nap in your entire adult life." The voice, teasing and gentle as it was, shattered his composure. Eyes now wide-open, Ches stared up at the girl he had once considered his dearest treasure. Thinner, yes... Maybe even a little haggard... But her expressive gaze still seemed deep enough to fall into, and that McKendrick hair had to be some of the reddest God ever made. Serena Kate stood there, brimming with affection and genuinely oblivious to all the heartache she had caused. "You're not still mad because I didn't return your calls?" she asked, giving him a pained look.

Knowing something must have shown in his face, Ches instantly regretted upsetting her. When she knelt down, dropping to his eye level, he accepted a hug and even returned it.

"No, baby girl," he breathed, "I'm not mad at you."

In that moment, the words were true. Of course, Ches felt a sudden rush of embarrassment. This was Mrs. Ethan Fisher, not his "baby girl".

Ches represented most of the good things in Serena Kate's past, the one friend who stuck it out with a smile when the twins hit their terrible twos and she found herself quite literally sick and tired. A clean break had seemed the least stressful way to leave all those months earlier. Now, she let out a long, quivering sigh against his shoulder. He was still her friend, so that much in life was okay.

Getting to her feet as Miss Sis finished the song, Serena Kate stepped over and plopped down on the edge of the piano bench.

"Hey, lady…"

Years of horse trading served Sis well when it came to maintaining outward composure, but her heartbeat skittered into a gallop as she fought contrasting impulses to either grab this girl by the throat or kiss her on the cheek.

"Hey yourself…"

"I meant to tell you Serena Kate had come to work out here," Hattie put in conversationally. "It's nice to see a familiar face now and then. I'd started to think they had some kind of a policy against hiring anybody raised in this county."

"Speaking of work," Serena Kate quipped, "I best get back to it." Then, well under her breath, "Hattie ain't changed much, but don't you worry, Miss Sis… I take extra good care of the old dragon just 'cause she's your aunt."

Ches settled down at the computer on Monday morning and struggled to ignore the lingering pain of Serena Kate's absence. In addition to running the office on sale nights, she had typed for him all through college and the early stages of his working life. The whole process, writing with the aid of a typist, held too many memories. Still, it provided a necessary part of his living.

After Serena Kate, he'd made the mistake of hiring one of Scooter's girlfriends. An epic bust up propelled her back to long, tiring days at the local grocery store. Now, Cassidy was filling in for the summer. They turned out three articles, gave each one a little polish job, and sent them off to Tom Mayfield's daughter-in-law. She, in turn, would upload two articles to the *Gazette*'s website and save one for the printed edition. The cousins stopped for a quick break before moving on to some Facebook ads for a saddle maker out of Crockett, Texas.

"How long 'til you find out who gets to play Laurey?" Ches asked, as she handed him a glass of tea.

"They'll tell us the day school starts," she informed him. "That way, we can start rehearsing."

"Did you put down a second choice?"

"Nope, how often is the female lead going to be a doe-eyed farm girl? If I'm doomed to live the life, I might as well get some limelight out of it. Besides," she added with a little pirouette, "I was born to be a star!"

"Well, I'm rooting for you, cuz. Much competition for the part?"

"Not so's you'd notice," she drawled in her best Laurey or Miss Sis voice. Then, speaking normally, "One of the girls actually sings the phrase 'my honey lamb and I' as if it involved three distinct individuals."

"And you didn't think your country raisin' would ever pay off..." he teased, reaching up to tousle her hair.

She smiled sweetly but couldn't resist rolling her eyes.

"What a quote for my yearbook, 'Class Hick'."

Just then, his cellphone rang.

"Durham Auction Company; this is Ches."

"You need more hobbies," Scooter McKendrick quipped.

"Say what?"

"I'm not callin' to buy a horse, Ches."

"Good; I'll hang up now."

"How about coming to the Willards' sale with me tomorrow?"

"I reckon not. There's always another article to write, and horses are starting to come in for Friday."

"Come on... You sore because I didn't tip y'all off about Serena Kate working at the old folks' home? If I try to sneeze my head off again, you may have to sell for a while."

"See if Aunt Sis'll go; she's a topnotch auctioneer. If those cattle buyers listen to me fumble around for long, it's apt to get you fired."'

"You could always sell a few goats, just for the practice. I'll pick you up 'bout eleven o'clock in the morning. We need to talk."

"I'll just bet we do; you let me wander in there like a settin' duck."

"I kept my mouth shut... Same as I've done for most of a year, nothing more and nothing less..."

"Come on by in the morning," Ches finally relented. "We'll take my van."

"If you're going with Scooter tomorrow," Cassidy observed, watching as he returned the phone to a shirt pocket, "I might just try out that new little horse. You really think he's a good one?"

"I know he is," Ches assured her. "You won't know how to act, riding one that's not high-strung and scared to death all the time. Ask your mother to go with you. She'd like that."

"But she'll have her regular appointment with Ms. Lillian that afternoon."

"You're right; she ain't gonna miss that weekly shampoo and set. I'll probably run into Bowie at the cow sale," he reflected, mentioning the beauty operator's good-natured husband. "Anyhow, maybe y'all can take a little evening jaunt after she gets back."

"Do you stay awake nights thinking up ways to make Miss Sis smile? All I ever hear is 'You ought to do this for your mother' or 'No, don't do that. It might upset her.'"

"I reckon it all seems sappy and a little overboard to you, Cassidy, but she's done so much for me over the years. Still goes out of her way to make time for our little visits and include me in everything…Thinking about what makes her happy just comes natural."

"Oh, I know Mother is practically perfect," the girl admitted with a sigh. "I just can't decide whether to gag or feel guilty for not measuring up to her."

"You don't have to measure up to anybody. Why, Aunt Sis has been thinking and praying about you for as long as I've known her. You're nothin' less than a miracle in her book."

"Whatever…"

"Here's a dose of honesty, cuz. The way you idle away your time with computer games and play practice, ignoring all these good horses and the beauty of the homeplace, sometimes strikes me as a waste of an able body. Aunt Sis sees the same thing and smiles, content to know her baby girl is having fun."

"Guess it's kinda tough being stuck in that chair, huh? I feel pretty dumb for not realizing sooner."

"You're not dumb, Cassidy, just growing up."

"And Mother has always…"

"That's right. We're enough alike that she can imagine herself with my limitations, and it just about kills her. Aunt Sis would never pity me, but she understands. Her sympathy comes out as time, wisdom, and friendship poured into my life."

"I've never been crazy enough to try and come between you two. After this little chat, though, maybe I won't feel so jealous. Now, let's get back to work before things get any mushier around here."

"Just for the record, Cassidy, I don't think you're a waste of space. I only meant to say that my love is not as unconditional as your mother's."

"Join the club," she quipped. "Nobody measures up to Miss Sis."

Ches looked forward to watching Scooter work. As an auctioneer, the redheaded rascal came in second only to Miss Sis. Their conversation on the drive didn't amount to much, but Ches's irritation faded quickly. As his friend and Serena Kate's little brother, Scooter was caught uncomfortably in the middle. Staying quiet actually made a good deal of sense. By the time Scooter practically carried Ches up to the auctioneer's box, the two were swapping jokes like always.

"Looks like there's a couple of horses here today," Scooter observed. "Let me do the work on them while you decide if they might be worth buying. When we get past that little dab, you can sell the goats and bottle calves. I'll knock out the cows and then tackle the yearlings. Barring another sneezing fit or a case of the hiccups, you can sit back and watch me roll through 'em."

"Suits me," Ches agreed with a grin.

Raymond Willard made a short opening speech, and turned things over to his auctioneer at exactly half past twelve. Taking the microphone, Scooter went right to work.

"Swing the gate!"

It was six o'clock that evening when they finally left the auction barn.

"I ought to get some kind of prize," Ches joked. "Bet you nobody else ever took five and a half hours to sell two billy goats and seven nannies."

"Yeah, but having you there takes a load off my mind. Big Ray gets kinda hostile if the sale stalls out. Not as bad as Miss Sis, but he can't step in there and do it for me."

"He got a good auctioneer when he hired you, smoother than a Cadillac."

"Pop had plenty of style," Scooter reflected, mentioning his father. "Just never could seem to get it all together without Miss Sis nursemaiding him every step of the way. But you know something, Ches? I would've put my mind to it and really tried before I gave it up to freeze my tail off workin' some North Dakota drilling rig."

"Serena Kate went up there for a while, didn't she?" Ches asked against his better judgement.

*Beyond the Parmalee Bottom* 53

"Yeah... Pop paints a glowing picture, but a lot of the time he's just talking and don't mean anything by it. 'You oughta see this big country at the edge of the Badlands,' and 'Nobody ever got anywhere knockin' around after Miss Sis,' and 'I'd sure like to see you, sugar bear.' Plenty of working hands up there making all kinds of money, and he let her take up with the fry cook. You're not gonna like Ethan Fisher, Ches, and that's just the way it is. I don't like him much, either, but she picked him all by herself."

"Serena Kate's so stinkin' sweet... It's awful hard to turn loose."

"Maybe so, but you've got to. Me and Seth have just about washed our hands of the whole mess. Same goes for Miss Sis, only she never would have until you got hurt. It'll be good to see Corrie and Torrie once in a while, but my sister can just paddle her own canoe. Of course, that may get hard to do with Ethan weighing the boat down."

Seth, the oldest of Jim Rex McKendrick's kids, made his living as a timber buyer up around Quitman, Texas. He had married his high school sweetheart and, according to Scooter's brotherly ribbing, sold his saddle. He ignored the jokes and visited around the sale barn occasionally but steadfastly refused to buy a pony for his three children.

"You can't just turn your back on her. I won't. Things may not ever be like they were, but she'll need her friends."

"Sounds like an uphill battle to me. Quit pickin' at that sore place and move along. What about old Pap Prescott's granddaughter? She gave us all an earful as to just how wonderful you are."

"Ruthanne's a very special young lady, but she's not here. That girl could have just about any fella that struck her fancy. Why tie herself to a cripple? Serena Kate is—"

"Married. To an idiot, I'll grant you, but still married."

Voice worn out from the auction, Scooter opened himself a Dr Pepper and let the subject drop.

Ches bounced over the threshold and into his parents' kitchen just as they sat down to supper. Doc Parmalee, a neighbor and distant relative, owned one of the earliest ranch-style brick homes in the area. Andrew Hollister bought it and lived there for a time before he married Miss Sis. A single story and built on a concrete slab, the house was- quite accidentally- handicap accessible. Terry and Jenna purchased the old doctor's home and pastureland when they finally moved back to McKendrick.

"Hey, son," Jenna greeted him. "I pulled this lasagna out of the freezer. We weren't sure how late you might be."

"Not much tellin' about a cow sale," Terry answered for him. "Want me to move a chair, Ches?"

"No, sir. I'm good and tired of this wheelchair," Ches responded before dropping lightly to the floor and knee walking over to the table.

"Did you get to do some auctioneering?"

"Sold a handful of goats... Scooter didn't really need my help. But I got a little aggravated with him the other day, and he wanted enough time to kid me out of it. Anyhow, we enjoyed the day. That knot-headed buddy of mine can sure enough roll through a sale."

"I think he's every bit as good as the colonel," Terry agreed. "Of course, your Aunt Sis would consider that opinion disloyal, ungrateful, and who knows what all else."

"Well, I never heard the colonel, but Scooter ain't quite as good as Aunt Sis."

"Maybe, but you're more than a little partial. She was really good in her teens and twenties, even better than the colonel, but nobody ever admitted it."

Completely uninterested in who might have been the best auctioneer to ever work the Durham horse sale, Jenna tried to redirect the conversation.

"What happened to make you mad at Scooter?"

"Nothing much..."

"You don't generally raise a fuss over nothing," Terry observed.

"Scooter's the closest thing I've got to a brother. The redheaded booger is bound to get on my nerves every once in a while. Ain't no call to worry."

"Cassidy and Sis rode by just as I was getting home from work," Jenna told her son. "The horse you bought from that carnival girl is very pretty."

"Cassidy's smile was a mile wide," Terry added, "and Sis looked like a cat that got into the cream. That's a nice little gelding, son. He'll probably do Cassidy a world of good."

"I hope so." Then, to his mom, "Miss Ruthanne Prescott's no carnival girl, and if you ask me, she's prettier than the horse."

"I didn't mean anything by it," she assured him with a smile, and Ches realized he had just stepped into her carefully laid trap. "It's about time you showed interest in other girls instead of just moping around over Serena Kate McKendrick."

"Fisher," Ches corrected in the most disinterested tone he could manage.

"You should give 'Miss Ruthanne' a call sometime. She seemed very sweet."

Thursday afternoon found Ches, Aunt Sis, and Cassidy spending time together on horseback. Playing around in the outdoor arena behind the sale barn kept them close enough to lend a hand with incoming horses. Time spent in the arena or just riding around the sale barn was nothing new for Ches and his aunt, but to have Cassidy join in willingly... Miss Sis glowed with loving pride, and Ches liked seeing her happy.

"Mom thinks I ought to call Ruthanne," he murmured, pulling his horse in close beside Pumpkin as they watched Cassidy fool around with the barrel pattern.

"Do you even know how to get a-hold of them?"

"Oh, yes ma'am, it's not that. But I... It don't hardly seem right to call her just because I'm lonesome for Serena Kate."

"I love Serena Kate, too, honey. Helped raise her. Even so, she was never the kind of girl I would've picked for my Ches. You're inclined to hard work and generally try to do right. Serena Kate knows how to work; no doubt about that.

But she'll take the path of least resistance nearly every time."

"You never said anything," he recalled in genuine surprise.

"Maybe I'm not quite as meddlesome as everybody seems to think," she answered with a half-smile. "Besides, I love you both and wanted everything to work out."

"I know it," he said tightly and reached down to stroke his horse's neck.

"Reckon you might be just plain lonesome? Your mom's not suggesting that you snatch little Ruthanne up and plug her into the empty spot Serena Kate left; just call and visit with her. I think you'd both enjoy it."

"I don't know why," Cassidy said, sounding almost giddy as she stopped Buttons near them, "but I don't mind letting this one go a little faster. In fact, I think it's kinda cool!"

"He's got a shorter stride," Sis explained, "so you're not covering quite as much ground. 'Course, he ain't insane, either."

"Mother…" Cassidy objected predictably, but this time it came out with a short burst of laughter. "Should I go get Fancy and practice with her in the sale ring?"

"I wouldn't, darling, not unless you just want to. That ring ain't big enough for her to make a mistake. She'll bounce from one corner to the other on her own. All you need to do is look confident, like the whole thing's your idea."

"Good; I'll just keep riding Buttons. He's really neat, Ches! When are you going to try him out yourself?"

"I generally stick to Short Stuff," he answered, stating the obvious.

"Buttons is good enough for you to ride if you wanted to, honey," Sis observed.

"I may try him," he drawled with a grin, "but I'll just wait 'til Cassidy goes back to her computer screen."

"Now that you mention it," and she matched his teasing tone without missing a beat. "It is kinda hot out here."

*Beyond the Parmalee Bottom* 57

"Not kinda," Miss Sis chimed in, "it's awful hot. Still, there's nowhere else I'd rather be."

"Spin old Pumpkin around them trash cans a time or two. Let's show your daughter what a sure-enough cowgirl looks like," Ches suggested, and that was all the encouragement she needed.

Sis's barrel run was hardly greased lightening by professional standards, but she did it with ease and fast enough to raise an impressive dust cloud. Just as her mother slid Pumpkin to a perfect stop, Cassidy noticed a classmate hanging on the fence. She considered kicking into a barrel run of her own, but rather than set herself up for comparison with Mother, trotted over to speak to him.

"Hi, Cassidy," the boy called before she reached him.

"Hey; I've never seen you around the horse sale before."

"This is my first time," he explained. "Is that your mom out there?"

"Yes, that's Mother."

"Wow, she just about made that horse fly! Can you do that?"

"More or less," she answered, hoping her momentary hesitation would pass for modesty.

"Well, anyway, you've got the coolest mom ever!"

Cassidy's mind flitted back to a time, not so very long ago, when Miss Sis showed up to the PTA meeting in a Sunday dress and pearls. "You're overdoing it, Mother," she'd complained, mortified, "way overdoing it!" When the next meeting rolled around, a gooseneck trailer crowded with low-end horses stuck out among the minivans. Manure-splattered boots and a pair of spurs put quite a damper on Cassidy's fifth-grade social life, but Colonel Durham's daughter simply would not be molded into a stereotypical soccer mom.

"Kid didn't get here by himself," Ches stated, gesturing toward Cassidy's school friend. "I'll go check for incoming horses. She'll get through visiting directly, and you two can keep riding."

"That'll work. For once in her life, my daughter's actually having fun in the saddle."

Leaving the arena, Ches rode around to the offloading chute. He couldn't quite place the battered pickup and rusted out stock trailer, but when a well-made sorrel gelding with a good bit of age on him stepped from the trailer, he drew in a breath and called out to the check-in hand.

"Hold up a minute. Don't tag that horse."

A young woman- not yet forty but showing the effects of a good many hard miles- stepped into sight, already on the defensive.

"Is this a horse sale or not?" she demanded. "Here's a horse or what's left of one, and I brought him to sell."

"Yes, ma'am... I'd just like to clear it with my aunt before we tag him."

"Oh, I've heard all about your aunt. The high-and-mighty, holier-than-thou—"

"Look, lady, I don't know anything about you or what you've heard, but I know for a fact that if Lonnie Ray Leggett comes rip roarin' in here and finds a sale tag glued in his horse's tail, he'll threaten to kill at least three or four of our hands before Aunt Sis can get him gentled down again."

As he turned his head to holler, Sis rode up beside him.

"That's a fairly accurate prediction, honey. Y'all put old Topper in a pen to himself. Give him a flake of good alfalfa hay and plenty of clean water."

"What about the tag?" the young woman challenged.

"No tag, ever, and he don't run through the sale until I hear it from Mr. Leggett."

"Mr. Leggett," the girl retorted, "that's rich... Lonnie Ray don't know this old horse is in the world. Besides... I'm his daughter-in-law, or soon will be."

"Where is Sonny Boy these days?"

"Gone to work, but he's the one who decided to sell the horse."

Sis gave the girl a hard-edged smile.

"Gone is a pretty good place to be when you take a notion to sell Lonnie Ray Leggett's horse out from under him."

"What does it matter? The old man's dyin'."

"Well, now, sugar… You wouldn't be the first to miss that bet."

Back in the arena Cassidy and her classmate discussed school friends and next year's musical.

"Must be some kind of problem over there," she finally confided, gesturing toward the offloading chute.

"What…"

"Did you see the way Mother eased out of here? She's got a sixth sense when it comes to trouble, especially where Ches is involved. I guess she'd be the same way with me, but I don't ever get into that kind of situation. Ches is so much like her that excitement seems to follow him around."

"I better go," he finally decided. "That's my sister over there."

"Your sister?"

"Yeah, the oldest one. She's dating Sonny Boy Leggett, and we brought his daddy's cow horse to the sale. I'll think over what you said about trying out for the musical, Cassidy."

"Good to see you," she called after him. "Tell your sister to be polite, and they'll treat her the same way. I feel kinda sorry for anybody who gets crossways with those two."

The excitement of preparing for these monthly horse sales topped even the anticipation Ches recalled from the old weekly operation. Now, waiting to see what Lonnie Ray Leggett might do added a touch of suspense.

Rapidly declining health aside, the old cowboy was known as a tough customer. He'd ended a short but explosive telephone rant the evening before with, "Don't you worry, Sis. I'll be there tomorrow." He would be, too, but that didn't tell them if he wanted to sell his horse, load it up and take it home, whip somebody with a wet rope, or some combination of the three.

"When you get a minute, Ches," Aunt Sis drawled almost cheerfully amid the pre-sale rush, "run up to the rest home and get Mr. Giles. If Lonnie Ray puts on a show tonight, he'd sure hate to miss it."

Leaving his wheelchair at the sale barn, Ches made his way to the county seat with an empty van to accommodate Giles Parmalee's mobility scooter. As Aunt Sis had predicted, he found their longtime neighbor dressed and raring to go.

"'Preciate you coming after me, boy. Going to the horse sale once in a while sure makes me feel alive. Besides, Serena Kate's off this evening. Hattie'll be squawking about one thing or another all night. Can't nobody else do to suit her."

"You notice I didn't stick my head in Aunt Hattie's room?" Ches replied, mustering up what passed for a grin.

"Didn't have your wheels; that's as good an excuse as any. Say, Ches, what about you and Serena Kate? I kinda thought you might marry that girl."

Swallowing a sudden lump in his throat, Ches decided to keep his answer short but honest.

"I did, too… She run off before I ever got around to asking. Had marrying on her mind, I guess, just not to me."

"Reckon she was scared of Sis?" the old man wondered aloud.

"Aunt Sis always handled her with kid gloves, especially after we started going together. I don't know why Serena Kate left unless she just inherited the travelin' itch from old Jim Rex. Anyhow, so far as I'm concerned, her coming back is just as rough as the leaving."

"Sorry to've dug up a sore subject, boy, but you'd best get ready. Serena Kate said something about bringing them twins and her new husband out to see the horse sale."

Ches drove home on auto pilot, his usual sale-day enthusiasm flattened right along with any curiosity as to Lonnie Ray Leggett's intentions.

"My name is Serena Durham Hollister," she said into the microphone that afternoon, "but most of you know me as Sis. I'd like to welcome each one out to McKendrick, Texas and the Durham horse sale."

"Tell 'em somethin' else," Scooter quipped. "I want to finish this milkshake."

"Sale day is a very special time for us each month, and I hope y'all enjoy it as much as we do. Ches is set up across the way, running our online bidding today. My daughter's in the back with a horse of her own to sell, and Andrew's floating around here somewhere. I've got the Mouth of McKendrick up here in the auctioneer's box beside me... You 'bout through suckin' on that malt, Scooter?"

"I reckon so... Let's have us a horse sale."

"Remember, now," Miss Sis told the crowd, "first horse is generally the cheapest. Bring one!"

The gate clanged open and young Zeke Claymore, the newest barn rider, entered the ring on a black quarter horse mare. Breathing in the familiar scents of the sale barn, Ches shut his eyes for just a second. Broken heart or not, this was his world, and he loved it. Online service had replaced telephone bidding, but the technology was such that he could speak to his computer through a headset rather than trying to type.

Lonnie Ray Leggett showed up, looking gaunt and pale. But his fiery gaze, pearl-snap khaki shirt, and matching saddle-marked britches remained stubbornly indifferent to the illness that wracked his body. The notorious rounder seemed a little unsteady, but nonetheless determined, as he sailed up to the auctioneer's box for a quick talk with Miss Sis.

Ches hardly had time to wish for a seat beside his aunt before he caught a familiar flash of red hair. Serena Kate's blue-jean shorts and tank top showed her recent weight loss much plainer than the loose-fitting scrubs she wore at work. To Ches, she looked almost as skinny and frail as poor old Lonnie Ray.

The twins, barely a year younger than Cassidy, ran ahead to the top of the bleachers, but Serena Kate lagged behind them. Ches resisted the familiar pull on his heartstrings. There was no way he could see dark circles under her eyes at this distance. Still, the big, clumsy arm draped possessively over her shoulders nearly turned his stomach.

# Chapter Four

Ches focused intently on taking online bids rather than watch the little family settle in atop the bleachers. Soon, though, one of the twins scurried down again and headed off toward the café. Probably to bring back a Mountain Dew, he reflected. Serena Kate downed gallons of the stuff to keep herself going, and had done so long before she started working twelve and fourteen hours a day.

Without taking time to analyze the thought, he hoped Torrie knew that she could still cut through the kitchen rather than wait in line. In the next moment, though, Ches shook his head in aggravation. It wasn't his worry whether Serena Kate got another soda before her headache kicked in and never would be again.

Finally, his attention shifted back to the auctioneer's box where Lonnie Ray Leggett, despite his unsteady gait, gave the rather courtly impression of assisting Aunt Sis down the ramp. Ches watched the two of them disappear into the back of the barn and wondered almost absentmindedly what might come next.

Scooter sold eight or ten horses before Miss Sis returned and motioned for him to hand over the microphone.

"Look out folks," he drawled. "The boss lady's fixin' to sell one, and it ain't just to give me a break. This here's bound to be something special."

"Scooter's right, y'all. This next horse is pretty special. I've ridden alongside

Lonnie Ray Leggett, and anybody here that can say the same will have a story to tell you about old Topper."

"You bet," somebody hollered in ready agreement.

Riding confidently into the ring, Lonnie Ray put the sorrel gelding through his paces. They spun, rolled back, and even hit a lope within the constraints of the small pen. The old man showed a sliding stop and then highlighted the horse's transition from full-throttle athleticism to levelheaded tranquility.

"Look there, boys," Sis directed, eager excitement ringing in her already musical voice. "Turn him on and off like a water faucet... Topper's seventeen this year, but don't let that scare you. He can put in a hard day's work or teach your child to make a hand on horseback."

"You'd better quit talkin', Miss Sis, before I decide not to sell him," Lonnie Ray called up to her with a touch of humor in his weathered voice.

"Mr. Leggett is a friend, and if Topper's got to go, I'm proud to see him come through the Durham sale."

"Does that old high-backed saddle go with him?" some unsentimental soul inquired from the crowd.

Lonnie Ray's temper flared, a rather common occurrence, but he looked up in time to catch a steadying glance from the auctioneer's box.

"Miss Sis gets my saddle, and the rest of you can go plumb to... Kalamazoo."

The old horseman's meaningful pause brought a wry smile even to Ches's face, but the sight of Serena Kate's head settling onto her husband's shoulder made him swallow it.

Not knowing what else to say, Sis fell into a familiar rhythm.

"Welllll, alright now... Nine hundred on the money, and we ain't backin' up... Who'll give ten?"

The bids rolled upward, and Lonnie Ray put Topper back into action. With all the balance and grace of a natural-born rider, he reached forward with one bony hand and dropped the bit out of his horse's mouth. Now answering only to the pressure of a bridle rein on his neck, the stocky sorrel gelding performed flawlessly.

"I ain't been on a horse in thirty years," Giles Parmalee muttered to his unsuspecting neighbor. "Lonnie Ray's near 'bout dead, but there's not more than two or three people here tonight could outride him."

On his horse, Lonnie Ray Leggett wasn't sick, frail, or afraid to die. He was simply one of the best.

"Twenty-one hundred, once," Miss Sis singsonged. "Twenty-one hundred, twice... Annnd... I have... sold'im! Twenty-one hundred to buyer number 1683; you got a good one, ma'am. Thank y'all... Stick around, Mr. Leggett. You might wanna buy a colt."

"Oh, I want to, puddin'. You can bet on that."

Sis left her place in the auctioneer's box once again to make sure Lonnie Ray got safely off his horse and found a comfortable seat in the crowd. Meanwhile, Ches found himself blinking back tears. Never particularly proud of his tender heart, he had long ago accepted it as a fact of life, and his own deep-seated loneliness made the old cowboy's failing health all the more poignant.

Topper sold inhouse, but the show he and Lonnie Ray put on prompted a wave of online activity. Ches bid almost constantly, and internet buyers won several horses. One of these virtual bidders purchased Fancy, the high-headed, glass-eyed calico mare for twelve hundred dollars. Ches caught his aunt's eye across the expanse of the room, and they shared a long-awaited sigh of relief.

"How come Cassidy sold her horse?"

Ches turned his head at the familiar, inquisitive voice and realized with a start that Corrie and Torrie McKendrick had climbed up and settled on either side of him. The girls carried their mother's maiden name and the red hair that went with it.

"I found a better one for her to ride," he answered, reaching over to ruffle Torrie's hair.

"Bet it ain't as pretty," Corrie challenged.

"I wouldn't be too hasty with that bet, young lady," he teased right back. "Besides, remember what Miss Sis always says—"

"Pretty is as pretty does," the girls recited in unison.

"That's the truth… For horses, or for little redheaded beauties. Did you get what you needed from the café?" he asked Torrie.

"Yep; I grabbed Mama's caffeine fix and some other stuff. Want something?"

"No, but you might check on Miss Sis and your Uncle Scooter."

"You trying to get rid of us?"

"Now, what gave you that idea? I missed y'all."

"We finally got to spend a little time with Grandpop," Corrie volunteered and then, as if imparting a secret, "but it's cold up there!"

"I've known your grandpop most of my life. Jim Rex is a sure-enough character, but I ain't goin' a-way yonder to see him."

"Corrie can run to the café for Uncle Scooter and them," Torrie decided. "I'll stay here with you."

Both twins happened to be with him later that night, not paying much attention to the sale but too happy to complain of boredom, when Scooter knocked off a little Appaloosa mule for six hundred and seventy-five dollars.

"Well, girls," Ches teased gently, "that's the one we been huntin'."

"Do what?" Corrie inquired with a start. "I missed it."

"Why would we be hunting a little spotted mule?" Torrie wanted to know.

"Last one for the night," he explained with a grin. "Go find your mama. She's probably dead on her feet and ready to get out of here."

"Mama's always tired," Torrie observed without much sympathy as they trooped down the ramp to ground level. "That don't stop her from going along with pretty much anything Ethan wants to do."

"She says you're okay with…everything," Corrie sputtered in sudden agitation. "Makes me think about what old Nash used to tell us."

"What's that?" he inquired against his better judgement.

"Well, me and Torrie were 'born in the night but not last night.'"

"He did say that, didn't he? I've always wanted the best for Serena Kate. Don't much matter whether or not I like the way things turned out."

Corrie snorted her dissatisfaction with the answer, and Torrie stopped in her tracks, turning to face him as he sat in the wheelchair.

"Matters to us, Ches."

He wanted to thank her and assure them he'd always be around if they needed him, but Lonnie Ray Leggett emerged from the crowd. The old man leaned against the wheelchair for nearly a full minute, fighting to regain some strength before he spoke.

"Say, Ches… Good horses are finally bringin' some pretty decent money."

"Yes, sir. If we could call back Topper's youth and put him in front of the right crowd, he'd fetch six or eight thousand at least."

"Some people's got more money than sense. They'll never pay for one like that by ranchin' off him."

"I couldn't hardly believe you sold Topper."

"Well… The old hayburner looks fixed to outlive me, and Sonny Boy's apt to starve him to death. If that woman that bought him likes him to the tune of twenty-one hundred dollars… Topper may end his days sleepin' at the foot of her bed."

"Wish I could ride the way you did tonight," Ches admitted by way of a compliment.

"Always was kinda handy on a horse. Never managed to keep a wife very long or rake together much money at one time, but I could ride and stand my ground in most any kind of a scrap. You notice I say 'could', Ches. Miss Sis... She had to help me get on and off this evening. I ain't never backed up from nothing, boy," he confided, "but this deal's got me scared."

"What deal? Being without a horse to ride? Come out here any time and—"

"A horse? I'd as soon never look at one again as to have somebody put me up in the saddle."

Suddenly remembering the younger man's physical limitations, Lonnie Ray regretted the words. He'd spoken the truth, though, and it wasn't in him to fumble around over an apology.

"I can see how that'd be hard on your pride. What's worrying you?"

"I want to face up to it like Colonel Durham. That rascal lived with the heart failure for four or five years. Doc Parmalee was a brother-in-law or something..."

"His uncle," Ches clarified, and Lonnie Ray acknowledged it with a brief nod.

"Why, I was standing right next to him in that set of pens up at the big house when old Doc told him the next heart attack would kill him. Kind of took the wind outta me, but the colonel never turned a hair. We just went back to workin' stock. How does a man look death right in the face, take a couple of swipes across the whet rock with his Case knife, and call for the next set of calves?"

Finally realizing what the old horseman was driving at, Ches felt his mouth go dry. He had been raised to respect Lonnie Ray's skill and his age, if not the choices he'd made in life. "Oh, Lord," he prayed inwardly, "give me the right words... Words You'd have me to say."

"I'm here to tell you; it never fazed him. 'If you're not gonna help,' he told Doc, 'go on up to the house and cut yourself a piece of buttermilk pie. Sis made it fresh this morning.'"

"Sounds about right," Ches drawled appreciatively before turning to more serious matters. "So... The thought of dying, that's what's working on you?"

"Yeah. Nobody figured I'd live long enough to die in bed, least of all me. I'd like to go on livin' right up to the last minute the way your granddaddy done, but..."

"The colonel knew the Lord, Mr. Leggett. That makes all the difference."

"It's a little late to start preachin' at me, ain't it, boy?"

It took everything Ches had to meet that steely gaze without flinching. But he did it, and that carried some weight with Lonnie Ray.

"I ain't preaching. You asked me. You keep talkin' about the colonel; let's go get Aunt Sis to tell you what he said on his death bed."

"Passin' the buck, are you?"

"No, sir, but she was there."

"I got nothin' better to do. Need to see Miss Sis, anyhow. I'm gonna give her some cash to put with the money I got comin' from Topper and have her pay for my funeral. I wouldn't trust Sonny Boy or any of my ex-wives to square up a parkin' ticket for me. Sis got old Nash Holloway buried, so I reckon she'll do as much for me."

"Nash traded old man Bird a gaited paint stallion for his funeral the summer Aunt Sis turned seventeen, but that's another story."

"A paint stud, huh? Good old Nash; he never missed a trick."

Lonnie Ray shook his head, grinned, and headed off to find Miss Sis. Taking in his surroundings for the first time since the conversation started, Ches was surprised to find Serena Kate and her new husband standing with the twins just a little ways behind him.

"You did good, Ches," she declared, blinking back tears as she dropped a hand naturally onto his shoulder. "I'm never sure what to say in that kind of situation, and old Lonnie Ray can be scary on a good day."

"I feel bad for the old rascal. Maybe it helped."

"Hope so... Hey, I want you to meet my husband. Ethan, this is Ches Durham."

"How do?" Ches managed, reaching up to shake hands.

The oversized paw felt soft and clammy in his grasp. Grain-fed... That was the first adjective he settled on for this transplanted Yankee, and it contrasted jarringly with Serena Kate's now waiflike appearance.

"Ches is one of my oldest and dearest friends, babe. We even dated once upon a time, didn't we?"

She gazed up at the big klutz adoringly, switching her glance only momentarily to ask the rhetorical question.

"We sure did," Ches answered shortly, trying to come across like Lonnie Ray and every other weather-beaten, hard-eyed cowhand he'd ever been around.

"You really believe what you told the old geezer about God and dying, don't you?" Ethan inquired almost tentatively.

"Well, yeah..."

Ches's heartbeat quickened and his insides flopped around in a sort of panic that Lonnie Ray's half-soured attitude could never arouse. His resentment for this outsider bordered on hatred. Lord help; he even coveted the man's wife. He hoped to surrender both sinful attitudes sooner rather than later but wasn't anywhere near ready to witness to the lazy bum tonight. Trouble was, he knew he should be. Thankfully, though, Lonnie Ray stopped a quarter of the way across the room and hollered at him.

"You comin' along or ain't you?"

"Yes, sir."

Serena Kate and her family tagged behind at a safe distance, but Ches put them out of his mind as he caught up to the old man.

"There's generally more than one filly runnin' in the herd," Lonnie Ray growled just under his labored breathing, expressing what was for him tender concern. "I always favored the wild ones. Had it to do over again, I'd hunt one with enough grit to stand hitched. Likely, though, you'll be a lot easier to live with than what I was in my time."

Miss Sis was personally supervising the out gate, but a word from Ches cleared her schedule.

"Got a minute?"

Pointing him to her office with a nod, she addressed Serena Kate in a tone that left little room for questions.

"Work this gate. Anybody tries to load a horse that don't match the paperwork," she added, gaze traveling up Ethan Fisher and back down for the very first time, "sic Paul Bunyan on 'em."

When they reached the inner office, Lonnie Ray handed her a wad of bills, explained what he wanted in just a few words, and then moved on to more pressing concerns.

"Ches tells me you were with the colonel when he died. I've been wild and wooly all my life, and now right up at the jumping off place... How did Chester take it, there at the last?"

"I wasn't with him at the very end, Mr. Leggett, but I know the story Ches is thinking of."

"Yeah?"

"I wanted to stay with Daddy. Part of me still wishes I had, but I'd been minding him all my life."

"Him and nobody else," Lonnie Ray snorted.

"Anyhow, I stayed by his bedside for most of three days and nights, but he sent me away on that last morning. 'I told Nash to saddle your horse. Go check the water in the Bateman pasture. That little pond ain't much good this time of year.'"

"And you went?"

"I said, Daddy, I don't want to leave you. Nash can go see about, but he cut me off. 'I told you to do it. Run along, now, and enjoy your little ride.' I got to the doorway before he called out and stopped me. 'Don't take it too hard, Miss Sis. We've done this at least a thousand times. I'll lope on ahead and set the gates. You drop back and keep the bunch pushed up nice and neat.'"

"Well, I'll be..."

"Brother Crawford and Uncle Doc both said he passed peacefully. I didn't know until years later that he sent Nash to follow me at a distance. 'She'll make a cornered wildcat look gentle when the grief hits her, but it'll pass. Just try to see that she don't hurt herself or cripple a horse ridin' off from all this.'"

"Sounds like he was more worried about you than anything else. Tell you the truth, Miss Sis, now that old Topper's squared away, I ain't frettin' over nobody but myself. I've ducked out of many a tight, but the end's comin' fast."

Sis reached over, took one bony hand in both of hers, and sat there with moisture welling in her eyes.

"That business about loping ahead to set the gates was just Daddy's way of teasing me out of my tears. He was going on before me, trusting that I could handle myself in this life without him. See, Mr. Leggett, Daddy knew he was bound for Heaven. He knew I'd see him again one day, and I believe that with all my heart."

"I believe in Heaven, puddin'. I just don't think much of this old cowboy's chances. I've lied, cheated, even relocated some livestock by moonlight. Not so much as a dogie calf off the Durham place, you understand," he added quickly. "The colonel... I won't say I was ever afraid of him, but I respected him enough to walk around him. Now, if somebody could be pushed, I didn't exactly mind tryin' my luck. I've got plenty to answer for, girl, and Judgement Day's a-coming. I'd find it mighty comforting if I could just be dead, plain and simple, like an old cow dog that finally got himself stomped."

"Oh, Lonnie Ray, you don't—"

"I know. I know, puddin'. Granny Leggett taught all us kids better than that, and

I reckon I've got to pay for this reckless life of mine."

"It's already paid for, Mr. Leggett," Ches assured him with Aunt Sis nodding along. "Jesus Christ shed His blood on the cross to pay for your sins and mine."

"Yeah, but what would He want with me, more 'specially right here at the end?"

"You're no different than me, Lonnie Ray Leggett," Sis said passionately. "We come from the same way of livin' and thinkin'. Why, you just heard me say it. I was so high-strung 'til the colonel worried I'd break a horse's leg or my own neck trying to ride clear of the pain."

"You might have, too. I never saw a girl any crazier about her daddy."

"I might have," she agreed, "but the Lord kept me from it. I couldn't have lived those years between Daddy's death and Ches finding his way to McKendrick without faith. The world wasn't offering me much hope back then, but the Lord carried me through. You've done a lot of things wrong in this life; I won't argue with that. But our Heavenly Father's given you one more chance to make it right."

"Thank you, Miss Sis. And many thanks to you, Ches. I think it's time for me to go check the water in that old Bateman pasture..."

"Sure," Sis agreed gently. "You go on and think things over. We'll be around if you need us."

"You and Ches are about the only ones left around... I worked for the colonel on and off. Treated him fair, and he did me the same. I watched you grow up, from a distance you might say. Now, you're the last human being I trust enough to get me buried. Kinda sad, ain't it?"

"Whatever your faults," Sis told him, swallowing a lump in her throat as she rose to her feet, "you kept good horses, rode them right, and looked after them. I count it an honor that you'd pick me to handle your affairs. I warn you, now, though..." she managed with a little smile, "If Sonny Boy crosses me, I'll take a quirt to him."

"I'm countin' on it," he replied with a grin on his way out the door.

"We'd best relieve Serena Kate and them," Sis told her nephew. "It's been a good while since she worked for us, but old habits die hard."

They continued loading horses Saturday morning but had the barn cleared out before noon. Ches slid from his wheelchair into the driver's seat of his minivan and then called to Aunt Sis through the open window.

"Anything you need me to do this afternoon? You'll want to spend a little time with Uncle Andrew before he leaves."

"Nothing I can think of, honey, but you just as well come on up to the house. I'll fix us up a bite of something to eat if Andrew hasn't already done it."

"Oh, I'll just ease on over to Mom and Daddy's. Tell Uncle Andrew that we'll miss him at church tomorrow."

"I'll do it," she answered with a nod. "I'm thankful he's working so much from home these days instead of making that weekly drive to Dallas and back, but when he does go out in the field, it makes for a long, roundabout trip."

"I know you don't mind having me underfoot all the time, but I figure he might appreciate a few hours with just his wife and daughter. Besides, Mom and Daddy kinda like for me to show up once in a while."

"Horsefeathers," she said with a loving smile. "Andrew knew you were part of the package when he signed on. As for his daughter… Well, I expect you'll find her with your parents. Jenna scheduled pedicures or some such foolishness for the two of them. Ches, you know I'm as particular about my appearance as the next woman and a sight more careful than some, but who looks at toes?"

"Beats me, but if it keeps those two happy, we oughtn't complain."

"I do love you, honey child."

"A bushel and a peck?" he questioned, cocking an eyebrow.

"And a hug around the neck," she finished with a very definite nod.

A real good hug would have been difficult to manage with him in the car, so she rose on tiptoe and leaned through the window to brush his cheek with a kiss.

*Beyond the Parmalee Bottom* 76

Sure enough, Cassidy opened the front door for him.

"Hey, you. Off to the toe parlor?"

"Yes, and you and Mother can snicker all you want. I'm just thankful for my Aunt Jenna."

"Say, you done a good job showing Fancy. Everybody on the place gave out with a sigh of relief when old Scooter dropped the hammer on her."

"Me, too," she confided in a mock whisper. "Don't tell Mother, but riding Buttons is lots more fun."

"I've told you not to 'don't tell Mother' me and expect it to mean anything, but I think we can make an exception this time."

"At least you're honest," Terry Durham observed, clapping his son on the shoulder as he entered the room. Then, to Cassidy, "Don't even expect him to keep quiet long enough to spring some kind of a celebration on your mother. He'll get to thinking about how she don't care much for surprises, and the beans are as good as spilt."

Jenna entered the living room in time to catch their shared laughter.

"You three are certainly in a good mood," she said with a smile. "Hello, son. Sorry to run off just as you're getting here, but…"

"Don't worry about it, Mom," he said and rolled across the room for a quick hug.

"There's chicken salad in the refrigerator. Cassidy and I'll be back later on."

"You know, the refrigerator," his younger cousin teased in an overly helpful tone. "That'd be like the icebox up at Mother's."

Jenna dialed down her own amusement to another quick smile, and with a hand on Cassidy's back, ushered her out the front door.

"Little bit thinks she's pretty funny," Ches observed good-naturedly as he and his daddy drifted into the kitchen.

"She is funny," Terry shot back. "She and I didn't fall headlong into the horse business, but we inherited a few family traits. When Cassidy starts runnin' her mouth, that's the Durham wit coming back at you."

Ches fixed himself a glass of ice water and opted for peanut butter spread over saltine crackers.

"Take a little ride with me when it starts to cool off this evening?"

"Boy, don't you ever get enough?"

"Enough time in the saddle... Not yet, anyhow. Aunt Sis has got a pretty good head start on me, and she ain't never slacked up."

"Sure; I'll go. Just point me out a gentle nag. I don't hardly take the trouble to notice one from the other anymore."

"Yes, sir. I'll put you on Buttons. Haven't ridden him myself, but by all accounts, he's good as gold."

As it turned out, Miss Sis joined them on the evening ride. She and Terry truly enjoyed one another these days, making up for lost time. Ches rode along in contented silence feeling Short Stuff's measured stride and listening to their brother-sister antics. Riding out across the homeplace with Daddy and Aunt Sis never failed to make him count his blessings.

Running into Ethan Fisher at the sale barn had been a bitter pill to swallow, but with that initial meeting over and done, he no longer dreaded the sight of Serena Kate's little family. When they didn't show up at church the next morning, Ches figured she needed the overtime.

People around Ches tended to hold him up as some kind of super Christian. Knowing better, he counted cerebral palsy as a blessing in disguise and considered himself just crippled enough to avoid some of the temptations common to the wilder side of cowboy life. On this particular morning, though, Brother W. C. Waller preached from Psalm 115:4-11.

Their idols are silver and gold, the work of men's hands. They have mouths, but they speak not: eyes have they, but they see not: They have ears, but they hear not: noses have they, but they smell not: They have hands, but they handle not:

feet have they, but they walk not: neither speak they through their throat. They that make them are like unto them; so is every one that trusteth in them. O Israel, trust thou in the LORD: he is their help and their shield. O house of Aaron, trust in the LORD: he is their help and their shield. Ye that fear the LORD, trust in the LORD: he is their help and their shield.

Through life experience and absolute trust in the Word of God, Ches understood his sinful nature and the need for daily repentance. Still, of all the wrong a body could do, idolatry had never even crossed his mind. The notion of worshipping a statue or a mountain or a cow critter seemed so farfetched as to be almost laughable. However, when God's Word is preached, the Holy Spirit can always lay a finger right on the tender spot.

Ches swallowed hard and even lost track of Brother Waller's voice for a time as he contemplated Serena Kate's place in his life. Maybe she needed his friendship. But he had gone beyond friendship to adoration and beyond adoration to...

Studying the toes of his boots, faint scuff marks showing through the glossy black polish, he fought an urge to reach for his aunt's hand. Her nearness steadied him some. But this uncomfortable revelation was between him and the Lord, and he decided to keep it that way.

Miss Sis noticed her nephew's comparative silence during their Sunday afternoon nursing home visit and the week that followed, but didn't press him for an explanation. Knowing he would tell her all about it when and if he got ready, she opted for prayers and an extra hug or two in place of their usual back-porch chat. Ches took care of day-to-day business and did some praying of his own. Long-delayed repentance brought deep sorrow and an awareness of having grieved God by his sin.

Reflecting on time spent with Serena Kate as well as the pain of her sudden departure and year-long silence, he slowly put aside the feelings of abandonment and betrayal. In fact, Ches began to wonder if he had wronged his friend. Serena Kate was a few years older than him, but poor choices and hard realities had given her a tough outer shell and a surprisingly fragile heart.

Maybe running away was the least painful way she knew to deal with his infatuation. Their friendship started with Ches showing her God's unconditional love. Instead of building on that solid foundation, though, he made her happiness the number one priority in his life. Having known so little happiness, she seemed to thrive on the attention he gave, but this misplaced focus encouraged selfishness in her and hampered his own Christian walk.

God's gentleness, patience, and mercy never ceased to amaze him. If his horse, Short Stuff, ever acted half as bullheaded as he had for the past year, Aunt Sis might watch for as long as five minutes before offering succinct instructions. "Slap that sucker and make him get right."

As Ches once again experienced the joys of life without the deadening overlay of sin and heartache, he debated whether or not to call Pap Prescott's lovely wide-eyed granddaughter. Realizing his single-minded adoration of Serena Kate had interfered with the most important things in life, he cautioned himself against rushing into anything else. Still, he hated to give up on the idea of companionship altogether.

From long habit, Ches almost asked his aunt's advice, but he bit back the question. This wasn't a decision Aunt Sis could make for him. A week later, after another Sunday afternoon at the nursing home, he drifted down to the sale barn, found a quiet spot that offered some shade from the hot July sun, and took out his cell phone.

Ches prepared himself to leave a message, or the way things had been running for him, wake Pap Prescott out of a good Sunday afternoon nap, but he didn't get recorded instructions or a sleepy headed old grouch. The gentle lilt of a feminine voice floated effortlessly across the miles.

"Prescott Ponies; how may I help—"

"Yes, ma'am… I'd like to book some pony rides for a big celebration in McKendrick, Texas."

Laughter bubbled up immediately, but she managed to play along.

"Alrighty, when does this celebration start?"

"Just as soon as the pony-ride lady shows up!"

"How about some hot apple fritters to sweeten the festivities?"

"Weather's kinda hot for fritters," he quipped. "Matter of fact... I don't even care whether or not you bring the ponies."

"Hello, Ches! It's good to hear your voice. I've been wondering if you'd call."

Ruthanne spoke the truth without hesitation but quickly second-guessed herself. No need to hint at how many times she'd checked this cell phone in the last couple of weeks. Was the battery charged? Had she missed a call? Had Pap neglected to mention...

"I should've already checked on you," he apologized. "Thought about it a dozen times... If you want to know the truth, I figured you'd be too busy to talk and too polite to say so."

"Ches Durham, when would I be too busy to talk to you? I've even thought about calling Miss Sis, but..."

"She really enjoyed her time with you, Ruthanne."

"Your aunt is a jewel! I was her shadow for several days and loved every minute of it. A'horseback... At church... In the kitchen... I loved it all but especially my visits to McKendrick Missionary Baptist Church. I read the Bible and pray, Ches, but church attendance gets pretty spotty."

"Yeah, that crossed my mind," he sympathized. "I imagine all the traveling makes it pretty tough."

"Life on the road has its ups and downs, just like anything else, but you didn't call to listen to me complain."

"Sharing everyday troubles and trials with a friend don't hardly count as complaining. I'd like to be your friend, Ruthanne, or at least start out that-a-way. Listening kind of goes with the territory."

"Aww, Ches... I've already been counting you as a friend. Right at first you were the missing piece from Pap's tales of McKendrick, filling in the gaps of Miss Sis's life story for me, but ever since I talked your ear off in that Hill Country barbecue joint... Not to mention that little run-in with Tiny back at the fairgrounds."

"Yeah, our friendship like to have kicked off with a real scrap."

"I don't believe there's much fight in Tiny. Still, if you hadn't been there with me..."

"Don't even let your mind go that way," he advised quickly. "The Good Lord watched over us. In the end, that's all that matters."

"He always does," she answered cheerfully. "Me and Pap are all set up on some little hometown rodeo grounds not too far outside of Alexandria, Louisiana. The fair starts tomorrow and wraps up with a rodeo on Thursday, Friday, and Saturday nights."

"Big doin's, huh?"

"It's hard to find that kind of good, long run these days, but a few towns are still hanging on to the notion of rodeo week. I wish you were here this evening, Ches. We could drop in somewhere for church services, and I might even let you buy my supper again."

"I'd like that very much, Ruthanne. I've got friends outside of Leesville, Louisiana," he added thoughtfully, "and we like that A & A Western Store in Alexandria."

"Leesv— You know, I think that's where we are."

"Really!" Then, with humor and a note of excitement in his voice, "Sit tight, honey child. I may get you a good supper yet!"

# Chapter Five

Ruthanne felt a warm glow as the phone call ended. She had a friend. Little cowboys and cowgirls all across the country adored her, at least until the excitement of their pony ride faded. Most of Pap's generation admired her level head and good manners. But to have someone her own age, someone who seemed to enjoy their conversations as much as she did... "Now, what in the world could Ches be up to?" she wondered with a fond chuckle.

Her question was answered when Judd and Shirley Matthews, a super-friendly couple in their late forties, drove up to the campsite and introduced themselves.

"Ches calls us his Louisiana kinfolk," Judd explained with a contagious smile. "I bought some mules and a wagon from him several years ago, and I don't know, we just..."

"There's something pretty special about Ches," Shirley volunteered warmly. "We hit it off first thing!"

"I went out of the mule business in a hurry," her husband added. "Cross-grained freaks of nature if you ask me. But meeting Ches made the whole experience worthwhile! Any friend of his is a friend of ours."

"I appreciate that, and I couldn't agree with you more. The whole Durham family is pretty special. Miss Sis opened her heart and home to me like nobody else I've ever run across."

"Yes," Shirley agreed, "Miss Sis is quite a lady. I know Ches enjoys his visits with us, but he'll just about get the nervous twitches if you keep him away from her too long. Missing Serena Kate only made it worse."

Wondering if she'd said too much, Shirley cast around for another topic of conversation, but the subject of Serena Kate fizzled out conveniently enough when Ruthanne heard the chime of an incoming text message.

"Mr. Judd and Ms. Shirley are the cream of the crop," Ches had typed. "They opened their hearts and home to me like you wouldn't believe!"

The nearly identical wording struck Ruthanne as funny, and she wiped tears of laughter from her eyes as she handed the phone to Shirley for a look. With her quick wit and natural exuberance, it didn't take Shirley long to get in on the fun, and shared laughter provided as good a reason as any to pull Ruthanne into a hug.

The racket outside roused Pap Prescott, and he stepped gingerly from the back of the van.

"What did you do, girl? Drag up some long-lost relatives ..."

"No, sir, not exactly. Ches called and told his friends that we were in town for the rodeo. Mr. and Mrs. Matthews... This is my grandfather, Pap Prescott."

"Y'all care for an apple fritter? You caught 'em right in the sweet spot today, free but not too stale to eat."

"For pity's sake, Pap..." Ruthanne exclaimed with heat rushing into her cheeks.

Shirley placed a comforting hand on the embarrassed girl's arm, even as she doubled over with renewed laughter. Judd grinned broadly, shook his head, and drew in a breath to speak.

"I've got to say, Mr. Prescott, Ches described you to a T! If it's all the same to you, we'll come back later in the week and pay for one that's hot and fresh."

"Matter of fact," Shirley said, still chuckling as she tried to catch her breath, "we were thinking of inviting y'all to supper."

Pap quit kidding around and doffed his hat in a courtly gesture.

"The kind offer's much appreciated, ma'am, but my lot in life involves riding herd on ten small equines. My granddaughter, on the other hand, is young and carefree. Light as her workload is, I'm still inclined to think that getting away from this makeshift camp and sitting up to a real, civilized supper table might do her some good."

"Ruthanne's more than welcome," Judd said by way of seconding his wife's invitation. "You both are."

"What do you think, Ruthie?" the old man inquired of his granddaughter with a wink. "Don't see many kidnappers circulating 'round in a late-model Chevrolet one-ton..."

"For pity's sake, Pap," Ruthanne chided and then laughed at her repetition of the familiar phrase.

"Go easy on your grandfather," Judd advised. "I wouldn't feel real comfortable sending a daughter or granddaughter of mine off with folks I'd just met." Then, swinging his gaze from Ruthanne to Shirley, "If y'all aren't too hungry yet, let's kick around the rodeo grounds for a while and get to know each other."

"Sounds good to me," his wife agreed. "I'll need a little time to get supper, but there's no real hurry about it. We can go right on visiting while I cook."

"The Prescotts aren't the only vendors already on site," Judd observed. "The grounds are so choked with people during the fair and rodeo until you can't hardly turn around without steppin' on somebody. Today might be just the time for a little stroll."

"There's not much to look at," Ruthanne cautioned, "but then I've seen many a rodeo or fairgrounds on the afternoon before opening day. Can I at least offer y'all a cold drink or maybe some ice water? Remember, you just invited me home to supper, so there's no need to be shy."

"I'll take a Sprite if it's not any trouble," Shirley decided.

*Beyond the Parmalee Bottom* 85

"And a glass of ice water sounds pretty good to me," Judd said with a smile.

"Water for you, too, Pap?" she asked but went into hostess mode without waiting for his answer.

"The day we met Ches," Prescott explained as his granddaughter stepped into the fritter stand which doubled as their kitchen, "Ruthanne and I left the little carnival we'd been traveling with."

"Oh, really?"

"Yes, ma'am. I knew old Colonel Durham and Miss Sis from a-way back. Ches and I made the connection, and he bought a horse from Ruthanne. We pulled out of the Texas Hill Country, delivered the horse to McKendrick, and spent a week or so around the sale barn."

"A visit to the Durham homeplace feels like stepping back in time. Four or five stock dogs running loose on the yard and guinea birds roosting in the trees to keep clear of them... I cook a lot when we're at home. Judd can be a picky eater, but I've never seen him turn down anything Miss Sis fixed. Did you know she keeps a horse saddled all the time? One for her, at least, and sometimes another for Ches."

"You don't see many like Miss Sis anymore," he acknowledged. "We left there and kept goin' east until we hooked up with this little bunch. I'm not real well acquainted with most of these folks, but I'll mosey 'round with y'all. If you find something you want to buy or ride or so forth, I bet we can roust out somebody who'll be glad for a little early trade."

"We don't want to put you to any trouble," Judd assured the old man.

"No trouble a'tall, I'll just grab my walkin' stick."

The light cane saw more use bumping tires, rattling along the bottom rail of fences, or making sweeping gestures than it did in actual walking, but Pap brought it into play occasionally to correct a miscalculation in his shuffling gait.

"Before we wander off too far," Judd said, "I'd like to look at your ponies."

"That's easily arranged, my friend, and it don't cost nothin' to look."

*Beyond the Parmalee Bottom* 86

Ruthanne shook her head in fond exasperation. Smiling, she caught Shirley's eye and gestured to a couple of lawn chairs set up in the shade.

"I'm so glad y'all dropped by," Ruthanne said, and her tone bespoke real joy. "We don't generally stay in one spot long enough to develop any lasting ties. Running into Ches was an unexpected blessing, and now to meet good friends of his... Well, it's a nice extension of that special connection."

"Ches thinks an awful lot of you, sweetheart. He was so excited for us to meet you. I probably shouldn't say... He wouldn't want to embarrass you, but Ches asked me to give you a homecooked meal and a little break from the road as a special favor to him."

"He's very thoughtful, but I wouldn't want to impose on your hospitality."

"No, no, no... I didn't say it to make you feel that-a-way, just wanted to give you a glimpse of our friend's kind heart. Besides, I'm a pretty good judge of people. If Judd and I had bumped into you somewhere, I think we'd of all hit it off, even without the connection to Ches."

"You mentioned Serena Kate earlier," Ruthanne ventured somewhat reluctantly. "Did you know she and her girls turned up back in McKendrick?"

"No..."

"Yes, ma'am, with a brand-new husband in tow."

"She got married?" The question conveyed shock that bordered on disbelief but definitely not disappointment. "Oh... Poor Ches. Did she at least pick out a decent man?"

"Well, I was only there for a week. Anything I could say might come across as judgmental, so I think I'll just hush before I get started."

"Me and Judd just came home off an extended pipeline job. I knew things had been awfully quiet on Ches's end, but we had no idea. I can't say I'm surprised about Serena Kate, but the sorrier her husband is, the worse it's gonna tear Ches up."

"If they were close, Ches must have seen something in her, but anybody who would just turn her back and..."

Unexpected emotion choked Ruthanne's voice and tears shimmered in her eyes, but Shirley brightened in a moment of speculative calculation.

"As long as she's married and off the market... That kinda works in your favor, huh?"

Stunned, Ruthanne felt her unshed tears evaporate. A rush of embarrassment followed, but Shirley's contagious chuckle brought a shy and somewhat hopeful smile.

"Well, ma'am, I never exactly thought of it like that."

"Say, what was Ches doing in the Hill Country anyway? He generally doesn't travel unless it's with us or Miss Sis, and she don't exactly keep her suitcase packed."

Soon enough, the ladies joined Pap and Judd for a late afternoon tour of the grounds. All four were talkers, but with the possible exception of Pap, they were the kind of talkers who also enjoyed listening to one another. The time passed quickly, and Judd finally turned to his wife with an impish grin.

"Woman, if you're gonna cook supper, we best be moving along. I'd hate for you to have to wash the dishes, turn right around, and start breakfast."

"That ain't happenin', buster, so you can just quit worrying about it."

This couple genuinely enjoyed one another, Ruthanne reflected as she and Pap joined in their laughter. A few minutes later, she kissed her grandfather on the cheek and stepped up on the running board of the Chevrolet truck. But Shirley stopped her with a hand on the arm before she could duck into the back seat.

"You're welcome to bring some laundry, sweetheart, and take care of it while we're at the house."

"It won't take me a minute to gather up some things that need washing," the girl replied, smiling her appreciation.

"I'd like to show you my horses," Judd commented as the trio finally headed off down the road. "I've got a couple of two-year-olds and one coming four, all registered quarter horses."

"Yes, sir. I'd love to see them."

"All three go back to Poco Bueno," he volunteered. "They're Louisiana bred but carry a lot of that old foundation blood, the King Ranch, Waggoner's, and…"

"Ches can't quite understand the money we put into young horses," Shirley said conversationally. "Miss Sis taught him to value a horse for what it can do. The bloodlines give us an idea of what we're getting, though, and there's just something about watching a good one develop."

"Ches don't hardly get around well enough to fool with untrained colts," Ruthanne offered in an attempt to reconcile opposing viewpoints. "It's only natural he'd lean toward broke horses."

"I'm not exactly a rough-stock rider myself," Judd admitted with a chuckle.

"With our crazy work schedule," Shirley lamented, "we end up paying for training and then turning the horse back out."

"Ches knows what those bloodlines can mean," Judd declared. "In fact… His little horse, Short Stuff, carries a lot of the same breeding."

"Yeah," Shirley agreed, stifling a chuckle, "but our Louisiana breeder is a lot more reputable than old man Parmalee."

"Mr. Parmalee's a character, alright," Judd admitted with a grin. "I don't think they even got the papers on Short Stuff, but that's the horse they brought up out of the Parmalee bottom the day Miss Sis had her accident."

"Judd likes a horse sixteen hands high. All of ours are somewhere around that mark, but a lot of those Poco Bueno horses are a little on the small side. Then, too, Mr. Parmalee's mare was older than water. I doubt if she gave much milk, and the lack may have stunted Short Stuff. But when Miss Sis put him on good grass… The little joker's nearly as wide as he is tall."

"He's a good-looking horse," Ruthanne said, "and just right for Ches."

"He is that," Judd agreed. "Miss Sis saw something that might suit Ches, and she didn't give two hoots about the papers. She's a top hand and keeps people around her who can ride. If they would really concentrate on the registered horse business…"

They drove along in silence for a minute or two before Shirley hit on an explanation.

"Their customers have always been working people: ranchers, farmers, and weekend trail riders. Ches just can't fathom a high-bred gelding bringing tens of thousands of dollars."

"Oh, well," Judd said, dismissing the subject, "you just about have to hobnob with the rich folks to get that kind of money for one. The Durham sale has chugged along for years and years. Ches and Miss Sis ain't exactly jumpin' up and down to change their operation."

"I kinda lean toward the tried and true myself," Ruthanne admitted. "Tell you the truth, I'm sick to death of traveling, but it's all I've ever known."

"This is Anacoco," Shirley explained as they negotiated a four-way stop, "where Judd and I went through school. Not far to the house now."

The Matthews home sat on a well-timbered piece of high ground. Judd weaved his truck between pine and hardwood trees as he passed the red brick house and headed directly for the barn.

"What a pretty place," Ruthanne sighed in genuine appreciation. "There's something peaceful about it."

"When you get inside," Shirley cautioned, "try not to look at the clutter. We're hardly ever here, and on top of that, we've got too much junk."

Ruthanne allowed the comment to pass and stepped out of the truck as it rolled to a stop. The horses, two bays and a buckskin with black points, had completely captured her attention.

"You've got three sure-enough beauties here, Mr. Judd," she said over her shoulder, already climbing up to perch atop the weather-beaten plank fence.

"Thanks," he said, pleased by her enthusiasm, "and call me Judd. All they need is riding."

"How about Mr. Judd and Ms. Shirley?" she ventured and then returned to the subject of his colts with a whimsical little smile. "Wet saddle blankets and lots of 'em, that's what Miss Sis would prescribe. They've all been started?"

"The buckskin's had way over ninety days of professional training, but not all at once," Shirley answered as she joined them at the fence. "The other two are just babies; they've had thirty days apiece."

"Not one of them ever bucked," Judd offered proudly. "That's what the right bloodlines and good handling can give you."

"Well, shucks," Ruthanne exclaimed as realization dawned, "all they need is some miles put on them! I'd ride them for you in a heartbeat, but I'm not going to dump my washin' off onto Miss Shirley."

"She's used to it," Judd teased. "Just point out the one you want caught and saddled."

"Hold it... Wait just a minute. Believe me, Ruthanne, I'd gladly do your laundry in exchange for riding these colts. But Ches intended for you to get a homecooked meal and some rest. Besides, I'm sure you'd rather ride in your own saddle. If you're interested in doing some riding for us, we'll try to make that happen. In the meantime, though, you're company. I don't aim to see you ride for your supper."

"Wouldn't be the first time," Ruthanne quipped, eyes alight with laughter as she observed Judd's obvious disappointment.

She helped with the evening feeding, making quick work of it, before the three of them piled back into the truck for the short drive up to the house. They entered through a crowded carport, and Judd smiled as he unlocked the door.

"Now, Ruthanne, just make yourself right at home. If you need something and can't find it, be sure to holler at one of us."

The door led directly into the laundry room, but four or five high-quality saddles scattered about on racks nearly obscured the washer and dryer.

"How do you like Judd's tack shed?" Shirley inquired in a voice full of good-natured sarcasm.

Ruthanne smiled as she spoke, making every effort to stay neutral.

"That's one way to keep leather goods out of the weather."

"You might as well come on through and see the rest of it," Shirley invited. "Judd will bring your things in from the truck."

"Yes, ma'am."

Western décor mixed haphazardly throughout the home with souvenirs from their many trips.

"Like I told you, sweetheart, just try to ignore the clutter."

"Your home is lovely," Ruthanne gushed, laying a gentle hand on her arm. "What you call junk, I see as the natural outcome of staying in one spot long enough to accumulate some nice things."

Recognizing a thinly veiled longing behind the words, Shirley gave her a tender smile.

"Our home is a blessing," she admitted, "but stuff is just stuff."

They shared a laugh, and the girl finally nodded in agreement.

"I'll just run start my laundry and then I can help you get supper."

Shirley's methods in the kitchen came so naturally that they appeared almost haphazard. In between loads of laundry, Ruthanne made every effort to lend a hand without getting in the way.

"I'd planned on a meatloaf; that's one of Judd's favorites. I hope you'll like it, too."

"Yes'm, I'm sure anything you fixed would be delicious."

"We'll have new potatoes, snap beans, sliced tomatoes, and cornbread."

"Mercy," Ruthanne breathed, slightly overwhelmed by Shirley's idea of a simple supper.

Judd took up a stool at the island and visited with the ladies, only leaving the room occasionally to see about some household chore or glance through internet ads for horses, trailers, and other interesting items.

"Ches tells us you're a trick rider," he ventured at one point.

"No, sir. I'm a pony wrangler who used to do some trick riding," was her lighthearted answer. "I won't teach your colts any circus stunts if that's what you're worried about."

"Aw, durn," he teased right back, "I was hoping you could train them to square dance or at least jump fences backwards."

"Do you miss trick riding?" Shirley inquired when the laughter finally died down.

"I don't know," Ruthanne answered slowly. "I liked having those skills. I liked making people happy, too, and then there's the thrill of it. But a good trick rider puts in an awful lot of work, and when you do that day after day after day... I was pretty well burnt out and just hated to admit it."

"Ches bought your last trick horse?"

"Yes... Pap operates on the theory that it's better to ask forgiveness than permission. But Ches refused to buy Buttons until I okayed it, and even though Pap made the deal, Ches insisted on paying me directly. He was just so sweet about all of it."

"How did you start out trick riding?" Judd wanted to know.

"Well, sir... My earliest memories go back to Fairview, my grandmother's family home near McColl, South Carolina. It never was what you'd call a large plantation, and the years had whittled it down some. But Gram... Well, you know how Miss Sis feels about the Durham place."

"Ches, too," Shirley interjected.

"Uh-huh… Fairview was the center of her world. She introduced me to sidesaddle riding because it was elegant and ladylike. When I showed some balance and nerve, Pap took to calling me his little monkey and figured out some basic tricks for me to learn. Before too long, he got hold of a video tape somewhere and the rest is history."

"No professional training at all?"

"I never even thought about lessons, not until internet access brought a world of information to our fingertips."

"Amazing; you pretty much taught yourself."

"Gram got more and more frail as the years passed. She had a stroke, or some sort of episode, when I was twelve. There was an accident on the way to the hospital, and she was killed along with my parents. Pap's always been sort of a drifter at heart. When bill collectors got to sniffin' around Fairview… Well, I could ride pretty good by then, so off down the road we went. I've still got some kinfolks back there in Marlboro County, but they never cared too much for Pap. Didn't exactly help matters when he cut the old place loose and let it go to the bank."

"Oh, Ruthanne," Shirley murmured sympathetically.

"Well," the girl drawled in a considering tone, "young'uns seem to take their licks easier somehow. If I had to face up to all that, now, as a young lady and then leave Fairview with its lifetime of memories behind… Back then, I just figured I still had Pap and that I belonged with him."

Judd rose suddenly and left the kitchen. Shirley, as deeply moved as her husband, blinked back tears and busied herself over the stovetop.

"I'm just cooking these blueberries down for pie filling," she explained. "It's my mama's recipe, and we all like it. Judd calls it a million-dollar pie."

"Ms. Shirley, I never meant to upset—"

"Hush, Ruthanne… I'm just glad you felt comfortable enough to share your story with us."

*Beyond the Parmalee Bottom* 94

Judd reentered the room with his trademark grin back in place, cleared a space on the crowded island, and deposited a large stack of magazines.

"Ever read any of the articles Ches writes?" he inquired brightly. "He publishes stuff in other places, too, but we've got every issue of the *Ranch Horse Gazette* going back to 2008 when they picked up his East Texas column."

"How wonderful," she exclaimed. "I knew Ches was a writer, but I've never seen any of his work."

"Well," Judd invited, "knock yourself out. It's some mighty good reading!"

"Yes, sir, and I'll enjoy every word. Right now, though, I'm trying to watch Ms. Shirley cook. Man cannot live by apple fritter alone!"

"Pap been complaining?" Shirley asked, and one eyebrow arched heavenward as her voice vibrated with barely suppressed humor.

Somehow missing these signs, Ruthanne opened her mouth and sent Mr. and Mrs. Matthews into waves of laughter.

"Well'm, I wasn't exactly thinking of Pap."

Heat rushed to the girl's face, but soon she found herself laughing with them.

"Why apple fritters instead of funnel cakes or corny dogs?" Judd finally panted as their amusement subsided.

Ruthanne latched on to his question eagerly, still avoiding eye contact with Ms. Shirley to keep from having her giggle box tumped all over again.

"We lived in upstate South Carolina, right on the state line," she explained, spirits still high from the shared laughter. "They raised cotton on Fairview until it wouldn't hardly pay for the ginning. By the time I came along, the livestock consisted of our riding horses, some laying hens, and a few gentle old Jersey-cross cows. Gram did a lot of gardening and canning just to get by, and we had a little apple orchard not far from the house."

"Well, how 'bout that."

*Beyond the Parmalee Bottom* 95

"They weren't Red Delicious or whatever else you might see in a grocery store, but I've never found anything to beat them for cookin' apples. We put up apple butter, made cider, and always sliced up a bunch to bake with. Hot apple fritters were a favorite childhood treat for Gram, and she passed that down to the rest of us."

"So, you carried a little piece of home with you on the road," Shirley ventured.

"When we started traveling, making the fairs and such, you couldn't turn around good without bumping into a funnel cake stand. Pap caught one of the proprietors on a bad day and... Well, to be perfectly honest, I think he won it gamblin'. With that old boy hard up enough to risk it all on a throw of the dice, we didn't exactly want to follow his business plan. Pap never could boil water, but he came up with a box of apples and told me to get after it."

"Didn't all that cooking kinda interfere with your trick riding?" Judd wanted to know.

"Not really, you'd be surprised how fast a twelve- or thirteen-year-old girl can scamper back and forth. But Pap needed me out front as the main attraction, so he finally broke down and learned to make fritters himself."

"What made him see the light?" Shirley wondered.

"For one thing, it was easier to hire somebody to work with the ponies than it was to find reliable kitchen help. For another, I set back like a borrowed dog when it came to giving out Gram's recipe to some fly-by-night fry cook."

Once everything was in place, Shirley snapped a picture of the heavily laden dining room table so she could send it to Ches and aggravate him a little. Judd blessed the food and conversation waned for a time as they enjoyed the homecooked supper.

"Here, Ruthanne, won't you take just another sliver of meatloaf."

"No, ma'am. It's delicious, but I just couldn't hold another bite." Shirley frowned in momentary disappointment, but a sudden thought occurred to Ruthanne. "What about your pies?"

"Good gravy... I forgot all about the pies!"

"I'll get 'em," Ruthanne offered quickly, jumping to her feet, "if you think it's time."

"Should be; if they look done to you, just set them somewhere to cool a little."

A minute or two later Ruthanne returned to the dining room. Too full and sleepy to risk sitting right back down, she paused for a moment with one hand resting on the back of her vacated chair.

"That was some supper, Ms. Shirley! I can't tell you how much I appreciate the hospitality. You, too, Mr. Judd."

"Don't be thanking us just yet," Judd protested. "You've still got to eat a piece of pie."

"Give me a few minutes," she answered with a somewhat doubtful smile, "and I might manage a little piece. Don't tell Ches, though. I turned down pie when we ate supper together. 'Course, I didn't have to smell that one cooking or take it out of the oven."

"So, Ches took you out to supper," Shirley mused in an interested tone. "Was this a date?"

"Well, I sure hope so!" Judd shot back before Ruthanne could speak.

"Me and Ches are quite a pair when it comes to dating," Ruthanne chuckled, surprised at how comfortable she felt talking to these goodhearted strangers. "His only sure-enough date was to the prom in high school. Being homeschooled over the road, I never even did that."

"Nobody ever took your eye?" Shirley inquired softly and without the least trace of humor.

"Not like Ches," Ruthanne admitted as she finally sank into her chair. "I've had my share of hopes and dreams, but they've never centered around anyone in particular."

"Never?"

"The pony ride business doesn't exactly draw unattached men, except for the occasional uncle or big brother. Besides, we hardly ever stay in one place more than two or three days at a time. The experience of loving Serena Kate puts Ches just a little ahead of me. Then again, having his heart tossed aside that-a-way..."

"I wasn't sure how much you knew about all of that."

"Ches hinted around it during our short time together, but I spent a week on the Durham place with Miss Sis."

"She must really like you," Judd decided.

"Don't worry, sweetheart," Shirley guffawed at her husband's expense. "We like you, too."

"Y-yeah," he stuttered, "sure we do, but Miss Sis generally plays her cards pretty close to the vest. She's awful protective of Ches, too."

Gifted with a charming wit of her own, one nearly as automatic as Shirley's, Ruthanne decided to lighten the mood a little.

"I know what you mean about Miss Sis," she told Judd innocently enough, "but I don't think she'd appreciate the card playin' metaphor."

"Can't argue with that," Judd agreed with a ready smile. "She's a lady through and through."

"Kinda like somebody else we're gettin' to know," Shirley observed.

The compliment made Ruthanne blush. In fact, she changed the subject rather than try to come up with an answer.

"I'd dearly love to ride those colts for y'all, but I don't know how we can work it out. Maybe early mornings before the fair opens... A week-long stand is rare these days, and Pap depends on me to keep everything rolling."

"Here," Shirley suggested as she slid matching dessert plates in front of Judd and their guest, "y'all think about it over a piece of pie."

"Oh, Ms. Shirley," Ruthanne said after the first forkful, "that's just about the best thing I ever tasted! I'm not particularly crazy about sweets, but your blueberry pie…"

"Just wait 'til you taste Mama's. She's over in Mississippi right now visiting one of my sisters. The whole family's crazy about Ches, and I figure you'll meet them before too long. Bet lots of cute kiddos show up for a pony ride…"

"Every day, and you should see those little faces light up when they touch a pony's soft muzzle or feel him move under them for the first time."

"Mmm," Shirley murmured in a considering tone. "Judd and I just love the little ones. What if we took turns helping Mr. Prescott this week, or if he needed both of us to fill your shoes…"

"That just might work," Ruthanne said enthusiastically. "I'll gladly swap out the riding for your time workin' the fair."

"Wait a minute, Ruthanne," Judd cautioned. "The kind of riding you're offerin' don't come cheap. Believe me; I know. And we wouldn't want to take advantage of you."

"I appreciate that, Mr. Judd, but I've walked a million miles after them cotton-pickin' Shetlands. 'Round and 'round and around we go… A week of riding your good horses out across open country sounds like some kind of dream vacation!"

"Open country… Where would she ride?"

"Camp Baker, but she'd need to take the measure of each colt before leavin' here. Crossing the highway would be the only tricky part." Judd's excitement and enthusiasm grew as he answered Shirley's question, but he still had a few reservations about her plan. "Working the pony rides with Mr. Prescott sounds like fun, but there's a lot I need to get done around here while we're home."

"Really?" Shirley answered in mock surprise. "I can't think of a single thing I need to do in this house." Then, dropping the teasing tone, "Come on, Judd… You're always griping about how bad the colts need riding, and an opportunity like this don't come along every day. Just think about all those darling babies, some of them on their very first ride."

"Yeah," he said slowly, almost convinced, "but do we really want to send

Ruthanne out alone with only a general idea of where she'll be riding? Our horses are gentle... But they're young, too, and that makes them unpredictable."

"I'll look after myself alright," the girl tried to assure them, but Judd's cautionary words left his wife slightly deflated.

They sat there in silence for a minute, and he scraped the last traces of blueberry pie off his plate.

"Got it," Shirley burst out, startling both of them with the exclamation and a sudden snap of her fingers. "No riding tomorrow... Ruthanne, you'll help your Pap like always. Judd, you better work like a dog around here. Me, I'm gonna make a flyin' trip over to McKendrick!"

# Chapter Six

"Do you really think he'd come?" Ruthanne breathed, sounding almost starry-eyed.

"These horses ain't nowhere near ready for Ches," Judd chided. "They're green. That's the whole point of gettin' Ruthanne to put some miles on them."

"You better believe it, sweetheart. He'll come. And of course, I don't expect Ches to ride one of our horses. We'll bring Short Stuff back with us. He'll be a good, steady influence on the colts, and that'll put Ches on hand with his cell phone if Ruthanne gets into any kind of a jackpot."

"You can't pull a trailer all the way over to McKendrick and back," Judd objected halfheartedly as he tried to hide his rising enthusiasm.

"Done it before, but I'm not taking our trailer. Don't you remember? Miss Sis had one of theirs rigged up with a pulley system to hoist Ches up into the saddle."

"I guess that would make it easier on Ruthanne," Judd quipped, jokingly excluding himself from any heavy lifting, "but I still don't want you making that drive by yourself. There's nothing I've got to do around here that won't keep just about as well as your housework. We'll both go."

"Hard head," she accused and then smiled at him. "It's nearly eleven o'clock, Ruthanne. Won't you just stay the night?"

"Well'm, I hadn't planned on it. Left the cell phone with Pap so I could get ahold of him, but he's long since asleep."

"You run Ruthanne back out to the fairgrounds," Judd suggested. "I'll clean up around here."

"Would you be just as comfortable riding back with Judd, sweetheart? If he starts messing around in the kitchen, some of these dishes may never be seen again."

"Yes, ma'am, but I ought to stay and help you."

"No, you run along. Take the rest of this pie with you, and I'll put the other one in the icebox until Ches gets here. Grab a couple of those magazines, too, but I want them back."

"You'll get 'em and the pie plate, too."

"We'll bring you a riding partner sometime tomorrow afternoon. Sound like a fair swap?"

"More than fair," the girl beamed and then pulled Shirley into a spontaneous hug.

"Sleep tight, sweetheart," Shirley advised softly. "Tomorrow just might be a big day!"

Ruthanne slept soundly, and in spite of the late night, she rose early the next morning to brush and saddle ponies. Their current string included eight Shetlands, plus Thimble. Every time she looked at the larger Welsh-type pony, she thought automatically of her boy, Buttons. The two animals carried virtually the same buckskin-and-white color pattern. Despite obvious differences in size and breeding, crowds all over the southeast got a big kick out of the exceptional paint gelding and his little lookalike.

Slowly, almost reluctantly, she allowed the memories of her last- and probably her favorite- trick horse to give way to thoughts of his new owner. Kind and attentive, Ches seemed genuinely fond of her. But with Miss Sis, loving parents, and the old Durham homeplace anchoring his life, she and Pap must seem like a couple of rootless gypsies.

Ruthanne wished fervently that she could somehow turn back time and show him Fairview as it was in her childhood. Show him that she had a family history, too. Nobody cared much about that sort of thing in this day and time, but Ches did because. . . Well, because he was her kind of people. She sighed deeply then and pressed a hand firmly against her stomach to quiet the butterflies. Finally, though, she gave her head a rather impatient shake and threw herself back into the grooming process.

Ruthanne knew each and every pony. She understood their strengths, weaknesses, and individual quirks. The small equines, for their part, appreciated her well-established routine, kind voice, and gentle hand. The youngest Shetland, a little pinto called Scout, generally needed time to settle in before starting his workday, so he got saddled first and tied on the carousel to walk off his nervous jitters.

Moving right along, Ruthanne worked through the string until she came to old Tinker. The diminutive, white mare was the oldest and least excitable Prescott pony. She nuzzled Ruthanne's pockets, got a piece of stale apple fritter for her trouble, and sighed philosophically as the girl tightened her cinch.

"Hang in there, old lady," Ruthanne said, amusement bubbling just under the soft-spoken phrase. "It's not the end of the world, just another day on the job. We've made lots of memories for lots of little boys and girls, you and me…"

Being a well-broke little horse and capable of a lot more than walking circles all day, Thimble could fall first, last, or anywhere in the morning routine. Instead of what they called "the big-kid saddle", Ruthanne fit him out with her own rigging and swung lightly onto his back for a quick jog around the fairgrounds before returning to fix her grandfather's breakfast.

"What's this ridin' job pay?" Pap Prescott asked bluntly when she mentioned her new plans for the week.

"Now, Pap, you let me worry about that. It'll be a nice change of pace, anyhow."

"Nice for you," he retorted, "while I'm left with a couple of greenhorns to educate."

"Yes, nice for me," she agreed in a soothing tone of voice. "Is there anything wrong with that? Besides, Pap, it ain't like they don't know which end of a pony to put the bridle on."

The old man hated to give in, but a big piece of blueberry pie with his scrambled eggs quieted any further objections. Business was good all day, and that didn't exactly hurt his mood, either.

As usual, Shirley insisted on putting Ches in the front seat next to Judd. All three laughed and chatted happily as they started back toward Leesville.

"Say, Judd, is it just me or what? I don't think he's been this excited about coming to see us in a long time."

"Banana pudding and a good visit are one thing," Judd declared, joining in the fun, "but a pretty girl is something else."

"That's okay, Ches. We like her, too. Ruthanne's a real sweetheart. Kinda reminded me of when we first met you. We just fell in love with her right off."

"Yeah," Judd's agreement sounded sincere, but that little twinkle still shone in his eyes. "She's well-mannered and pretty, and if she's still around when I get through using her for a crash dummy on them colts, you'll know she's got the stayin' power."

"Judd Matthews!" Shirley cried, reaching up from the backseat to swat him playfully, "you know those colts aren't going to hurt her. And if one of them did, you'd never forgive yourself."

"You're right," he admitted, still chuckling at his little joke.

"I say it's about time, Ches. The deal with Serena Kate always looked one-sided to me. You're a kind, affectionate young man with a fairly small circle of close family and friends. You had all that love to give, and with life demanding so much from her, she gladly sat back and soaked it up like rain after a drought."

"Maybe," he admitted reluctantly, "but I was tickled to death to find somebody who wanted my time and attention."

*Beyond the Parmalee Bottom* 104

"I know it, but that kind of thing ought to be a two-way street."

"Ruthanne could never be second best or some kind of a replacement for..."

"Surely you don't think about her that way?"

"No, of course not."

"Well, just make sure she knows that. I'm telling you, Ches, I don't intend to let this one get away. Beat around the bush too long, and I'll do your talking for you."

"Boy howdy," he answered with a rueful shake of his head, "it pays to have friends."

"I'll say," Shirley teased. "Who else could you just call up and get them to cook supper for your girlfriend?"

"Girlfriend?" Ches snorted. After a long pause, though, he took a deep breath and started over. "Ruthanne's caught my interest alright. I'd be lying if I told you any different, but why would a young lady like her pay any attention to me? Why would any girl? If Serena Kate didn't need what I had to give..."

"Ches Durham," Shirley snapped almost impatiently, "the only thing you're not qualified for is long walks on the beach."

This dose of humor interjected into a very serious discussion was trademark Shirley Matthews. Rather than list his many good qualities, which she figured Ruthanne could do much more convincingly, she and Judd set out to make him forget his doubts.

Most people's suppertime had come and gone before they finally pulled onto the fairgrounds that evening. Ches slid hurriedly from the truck, wobbling a little as he got his crutches situated, and old Pap Prescott reached out a hand to steady him.

"Hey, there, sonny... You write some pretty good stuff. Trouble is, I ain't got a lick of work out of my granddaughter all day. Every time I look up, she's got her nose stuck in a magazine. What's worse, I think she's been into my blueberry pie!"

"Now, Mr. Prescott," Shirley objected, "I gave that pie to Ruthanne."

"Look here, lady, if you and me are fixin' to work together…"

At that point, they both dissolved in laughter, and Ruthanne approached Ches almost shyly. He smiled and spoke her name, so she laid a hand gently on his arm.

"There's a chair over yonder; come and sit."

"How have you been?" he wanted to know almost immediately.

"Wonderful, thanks to you. Mr. Judd and Ms. Shirley are just the sweetest people!"

"I know it; a fella couldn't ask for better friends. Let's go out to eat and save Ms. Shirley the trouble of cooking."

"I'm tickled to death as long as we get a chance to visit. But, Ches, she's got enough leftovers to feed a starvin' army!"

"Yeah… She'll never be satisfied putting out leftovers, though, not if we go to the house. Besides, if we get us a bite somewhere in town, you can probably talk Pap into leaving the ponies unattended long enough to come and eat."

"He might just do that," she agreed with a nod.

Accustomed to Shirley's good meals, Judd could be hard to please in a restaurant, but the little group got so caught up visiting that they paid very little attention to food.

"Say, Pap," Ches ventured as their evening drew to a close, "how 'bout letting me camp with you?"

"With me and Ruthanne?" the old man questioned, and his bushy brows knit together as he spoke.

"No, sir. I kinda figured she could take my room at Mr. Judd and Ms. Shirley's. We call it my room, anyhow. A few nights in a real bed wouldn't hurt her none."

"Just get her spoiled," Pap mumbled in a dismissive tone but flashed a grin as the younger man's jaw muscle clinched. "I reckon she could do with a little spoilin' at that. Fine by me, if it's alright with your friends."

Pap's snoring reminded Ches of a dying goat, and the summer night kept the back end of the Ford van uncomfortably warm for sleeping. But he never once wished for that soft, queen-size bed at Judd and Shirley's. Instead, his thoughts focused on Ruthanne's daily existence and the basic comforts it lacked.

"Me and Ms. Shirley fixed y'all a hot breakfast," Ruthanne called happily the next morning as she moved steaming dishes from Shirley's SUV to the fritter stand. "Mr. Judd wanted to feed and groom his colts, so he'll be along directly."

"A good night's rest looks awful pretty on you," Ches murmured softly.

"Beg pardon?"

"Oh, you look very nice this morning."

"Why, thank you."

She continued laying out the food with graceful efficiency, missing only half a beat to glance down at herself with a pleased but slightly puzzled expression. Dressed for riding, she had on the same faded t-shirt, snug blue jeans, and dilapidated boots she'd worn the day he first met her.

"You and Ches can take the car," Shirley said after the hurried but delicious meal. "Just put these dishes in the sink and hit the saddle before it gets too awfully hot."

"Don't you worry about me," Ruthanne answered with a smile. "Hot weather makes those wet saddle blankets easier to come by."

"Maybe so, but y'all better drink plenty of water!"

"Thanks for coming, Ches," Ruthanne said tentatively as she drove back toward Anacoco. "I didn't exactly need anybody to go along on these rides, but... Well, I'm awful glad you're here!"

"Me, too. It'll make Judd and Shirley feel better, and I'm glad for the chance to spend a little time with you."

Ruthanne stopped at the house to unload their breakfast dishes, but they didn't see Judd until they rolled to a stop in front of the weathered barn.

"Ms. Shirley said you wouldn't take time to eat," Ruthanne admitted, smiling as she handed over sausage and biscuit wrapped in a paper towel.

Grinning his thanks, he bit into it immediately, strode over to his truck for a bottle of water, and came back to them.

"I'll stay long enough to get Ches on his horse, make sure y'all don't have any problems right off, and then get on over to the fairgrounds to help Shirley and Pap."

"Yes, sir," Ruthanne answered brightly. "You just show me how to work the hoist. I bet we can manage after today."

"I'd start with the buckskin. He's had the most riding. But now, you do it however you like."

"Well, sir... I know they're all pretty honest colts, but I'd as soon not start with the gentlest one."

"In that case," he answered thoughtfully, rubbing the back of his neck, "you might try the lighter colored bay. I've been callin' him George after a friend of mine. He's got a little more mischief about him, just playful really."

All three colts stood caught and tied, so Ruthanne saddled George and then helped Ches settle into his rigging.

"Slick as a whistle," she said with an admiring glance toward the long, hinged pole and pulley system attached to the side of his stock trailer.

"Daddy and Aunt Sis worked it out."

"I think Georgie boy will do just fine," Ruthanne said, giving Ches a long look as she fastened the safety belt at his waist, "but if he decides to blow the cork, you stay out of his way. Likely as not, I'll hang in there 'til the dust settles. If I don't, you can help gather my hat and spare change."

"I've sat by and watched Aunt Sis in many a ticklish situation," he answered gently, brushing her hand momentarily with his own. "Like 'em or not, Ruthanne, I know my limitations. I'll help you all I can without taking any wild chances."

Ches rode into the pen as she swung up on George, near enough to let Short Stuff be an anchor and a comfort to the colt but not so close that they couldn't get out of the way in a hurry. They made several circuits in the round pen with the young horse walking on eggshells, but Ruthanne's patient handling and Short Stuff's calm, almost lazy, presence settled him down without a fuss.

Judd stayed around to see them safely across the two-lane highway, and Ches waved to him as they hit the sandy, unpaved roads around old Camp Baker. The young couple rode along comfortably for fifteen or twenty minutes. Only a word or two passed between them, and even the steady rhythm of hoofbeats fell like whispers against the loose white sand.

"It's mighty peaceful back here," Ruthanne finally observed, "but I kind of pictured our first ride together happenin' on the Durham place. Maybe with Miss Sis along for a nice picnic beside the swimming hole."

"Thought I was the only one to daydream about stuff like that," Ches admitted quietly as their horses moved along side by side.

"No," she replied lightly, "you're just the only one with sense enough to keep it under your hat. I'm riding along nice and easy, watching the colt pretty close but letting my mind wander, and somehow my mouth slips into gear."

"Well'm, I sure do like the way your mind wanders."

"I had the ride with Miss Sis several times over, and even a picnic. You might say my dreams all but came true. We missed you that week, Ches, both of us."

"I know what it's like... missin' somebody," he said almost tenderly, "but I'm here now."

"Tell me about Serena Kate," she ventured, second guessing the request almost before she spoke.

"I've just wasted a year of my life pining over her. But it was all my fault, not hers. I reckon that's the short version."

"I don't want to sound nosy or too forward, but that hurt is a part of you. I'm not here for the short version."

"I don't mind telling you more, just as soon as I figure out where to start."

"Take your time, Ches. These colts need all the miles we can give them."

"Serena Kate was sixteen years old when I first met her," he started hesitantly after a long silence, "trying hard to look after her daddy and brothers. Being a little younger, I saw her as a close family friend but not my friend in particular."

"Did those feelings change quickly?"

"Not really," he answered thoughtfully. "The next two or three years were some of the happiest I've ever known. See, I kind of found my niche working alongside Aunt Sis, but those same years were pretty rough for Serena Kate."

"I thought her twins must've come along awfully early," Ruthanne ventured tentatively.

"That's right. By the time I started college and needed some help with my typing, Serena Kate was a stressed-out single mother chasing after two toddlers."

"Was she still working for your Aunt Sis?"

"Uh-huh, but we'd backed the horse sale off from a weekly deal to once a month. Serena Kate needed extra work and seemed like the natural choice. She'd been through a lot, and working together almost every day... I don't know, we just sort of clicked."

"Having a friend around to talk to can be a great blessing," Ruthanne ventured softly.

"As Serena Kate began to tell me her troubles," he continued, "I naturally started taking care of her. She's got to have a Mountain Dew most all the time, so I kept plenty of that along with her favorite candy. We got my schoolwork and other writing done, but we visited a lot, too."

The thought of Ches spending that much time and effort on another girl bothered Ruthanne more than she cared to admit. Scolding herself inwardly for what she saw as a petty reaction, she nudged the colt into a trot to mask her feelings. Ches followed suit, but with the July morning warming up fast, they couldn't afford to push their mounts too hard.

"You and Serena Kate never actually dated?" Ruthanne inquired as they slackened their pace once more.

"We never called it that, but I enjoyed spoiling her. A surprise gift here and there, or we might go out to eat… I treated her like my girlfriend, and she gave me a warm, gentle kind of appreciation that felt an awful lot like love."

They rode along a narrow ribbon of sand that meandered its way through dense pine and hardwood timber. Not sure how to respond, Ruthanne allowed the steady creak of saddle leather to fill the silence.

The plodding rhythm of her horse's walk, the smell of deep woods baking in summer heat, and even the considerable humidity proved strangely comforting, but she just couldn't seem to organize her thoughts and feelings into words. Finally, the road widened a little, and Ruthanne reined to a stop. She swung down, stretched the stiffness gingerly from her right knee, and smiled up at Ches who sat watching her from horseback.

"It don't hardly seem fair that you can't step down for a break," she said, reaching up automatically to stroke his horse's neck.

"Getting on and off always seems like more trouble than it's worth," he replied, accepting a bottle of water she handed him. "Listen, I didn't mean to upset you by rattling on about Serena Kate."

The smile flickered ever so slightly, but her lovely eyes remained soft with understanding.

"You haven't upset me, Ches. Besides, I asked you to tell me. I may not always know how to answer right off, but I'd like to hear the rest of it."

They eventually rode on, and Ches searched for the right words to continue his narrative.

"More often than not, Serena Kate showed up dead tired. She knew how to push through it and get things done. But after she'd typed for me a couple of years it got to where I'd rub her shoulders, play with her hair, just anything to help her relax. She might even stretch out in the other room for a nap while I organized my thoughts on the next project."

"Y'all must've been awfully…" Ruthanne trailed off, uncertain.

"I never exactly knew how to talk to her about dating. Kinda seemed like we fell into it naturally. After college, when I found a steady market for my writing, I wanted to marry her."

"Oh, Ches…" Ruthanne murmured, heart aching over all he'd been through. "I don't know Serena Kate or understand what could make a girl just up and walk away from someone who treats her like a precious jewel."

"Ruthanne, I haven't told anybody this, not even Aunt Sis, but the way I'd treated her… That's where the trouble started."

Rather than leaping automatically to his defense or trying to convince him that she could keep his secrets, Ruthanne simply waited. Eyes full of unwavering compassion, she gazed steadily at Ches for several strides and then finally glanced away, murmuring softly to her horse to break the tension.

"Steady, George. There's a good fella."

"I set Serena Kate up so high that, being human, she was bound to take a fall. Worse than that, I let my fascination with her come between me and God."

"That's very personal, Ches. Thank you for trusting me."

"The Lord's been awfully patient, and it's all straightened out now."

"Even when you know God deserves first place in the hearts and lives of His children," Ruthanne pointed out, "this old world promotes the notion that romantic love ought to surpass everything else."

"Love and marriage are wonderful gifts from God, but without Him at the top…"

"That kind of absolute adoration," she confessed after a few minutes of quiet, "would be awful hard to pass up, precarious elevation and all. Sounds like life misused her heart pretty badly before you ever tried to make a claim."

"There's three of those McKendrick kids: an older brother, a younger brother, and Serena Kate in the middle. Miss Sis was the only consistent maternal figure in their lives. She and Serena Kate butted heads occasionally, but they loved one another."

"And their daddy?"

"Jim Rex was consistently Jim Rex... He wanted his kids around; I'll say that for him."

"Loving but not very dependable," Ruthanne guessed perceptively.

"When it comes to men, Serena Kate's got this weakness for the underdog. Fellas like Jim Rex, come to think of it. That rascal is a perpetual hard-luck story, and the women just eat it up. Even my sweet aunt felt the pull of his charms. In fact, things kind of fell into a pattern. Aunt Sis helped raise those kids and dated Jim Rex, respectably of course, in between his wild women. About the time I got there, though, it all started to change. She married Uncle Andrew, and I guess Jim Rex felt crowded out."

"Well, I certainly hope so," Ruthanne answered lightly.

"He managed to get some money together, took Scooter with him, and bought part interest in a livestock auction. A cow deal mostly, down south of us. Being a senior in high school, Serena Kate wanted to stay put. We asked her to move out to the homeplace, but Aunt Sis and Uncle Andrew had just set up housekeeping together. Besides, I guess she had a kind of sentimental attachment to the McKendrick house."

"That fine old home just off the square?"

"What's left of the square," he confirmed. "Aunt Sis ended up buying the house when Jim Rex ran short of money, but so far as I know, she never charged Serena Kate any rent. Living by herself, I reckon that's where the trouble started."

"Mmm," Ruthanne murmured, "and she'd always had a houseful of family to look after."

"Yep... It wasn't long before she had a houseful again, only they weren't kinfolk or very nice people, either. For some reason, she started to see my aunt as this sort of unrealistic embodiment of the proper Christian lady. 'I kept telling myself Miss Sis was probably human just like the rest of us, and then y'all took away her cigarettes! Now, she really is perfect!'"

"People come up with some mighty strange notions," Ruthanne commented, "it's not as if smoking made Miss Sis any less a lady or any less a Christian."

"No, she would've compared it to a diabetic who can't stay out of the candy dish, 'May not be the best thing for me, but I sure do like it.'"

"With or without her cigarettes, Miss Sis is one of the finest ladies I ever hope to meet."

"She's very precious to me," Ches said with a ready nod. "Still, nobody's perfect, and she never claimed to be."

"Of course not, but from the perspective of a confused teenage girl, she could sure look that-a-way. What about the father of Serena Kate's twins?"

"Not hardly worth mentioning. It's enough to say he had the biggest puppy dog eyes and the sorriest low-down nature I've ever run across. Serena Kate was barely eighteen when the girls came along, with no wedding ring in sight. She helped at the sale barn whenever she could, and I think Aunt Sis paid her whether she showed up or not. Still, their life choices drove them further and further apart."

"I imagine so," Ruthanne said quietly and then in a more conversational tone, "Reckon this road will circle us back to the highway? Time to see about switching colts."

"Ought to," Ches speculated as he turned Short Stuff up the road in question. "The old timers around McKendrick had never run up against a drug problem, but there got to be some pretty wild parties in Serena Kate's family home. Bums and delinquents laid up all over the place."

"I only saw Serena Kate once or twice while I was in McKendrick," Ruthanne ventured almost reluctantly. But I've heard y'all talk about her, and she doesn't seem like the type to..."

"Well, Serena Kate pretty much stayed on the edges of all that mess. But Aunt Sis wasn't about to sit still and let... After all, they were right there off the old town square in a house that she owned."

"What about the authorities?" Ruthanne wondered.

"Never could catch 'em or even gather up enough evidence for a raid. I remember one phone call in particular that my aunt made to Sheriff Wainwright over at the county seat. 'Serena Kate and her girls are out of the house today, Marvin. If you can't find enough sand left in your craw to scatter that little bunch of riffraff, we'll tend to it ourselves. Ain't nothin' wrong up there that I couldn't fix with a jug of coal oil and a kitchen match.'"

"Mercy," Ruthanne breathed.

"Aunt Sis is one of the sweetest ladies who ever drew breath, but she loves our little crossroads town and the community around it something fierce. That's the world she planned to share with her daughter."

"I see your point."

"Sheriff Wainwright gave her a long-winded explanation about squatter's rights and the fact that his hands were tied. Said he'd probably end up having to arrest her. She told him exactly what she thought about that, paced back and forth across the colonel's old office several hundred times, and then called him back to apologize and regroup."

Ches fell silent for a time, suddenly tired of reminiscing and ready to just enjoy the ride.

"I declare, you ought to write suspense novels instead of magazine articles," Ruthanne chided after a while. "Are you gonna tell me what happened, or not?"

Laughing a little at her impatience, he shrugged and recited both sides of that memorable phone call as if it had taken place only a day or two ago.

*Beyond the Parmalee Bottom* 115

"Say, Marvin… Me and Nash are headed up there for a neighborly little discussion about overdue rent. No guns, no ill will, no nothing. If we're not back in an hour, Ches is gonna call your office. What I want you to do is bring a handpicked bunch of deputies, men raised around here to think like we do, kick the ant pile, and stomp everything that runs."

"Let me get this straight, Miss Sis. You're going in there with a bull whip and Nash with a good stout walkin' cane. And if things go south, I'm meant to finish the job before any kind of outside law can make a move."

"That's one way to put it. Can I count on you?"

"Well, if anything happened to you or Nash, that'd give me plenty of justification, but it seems like a mighty high price to pay."

"And?" Ruthanne inquired almost breathlessly, bringing him back to the present.

"You know how petite and ladylike Aunt Sis is, and Nash was old as the hills. But with the two of them good and stirred up… Well, that little bunch of thugs scattered like a covey of quail. Uncle Andrew was working in Dallas then. We picked little Cassidy up from Mrs. Crawford's that evening, and nobody ever knew the difference."

"Mother's Day Out," Ruthanne quipped, shaking her head in mild amazement.

"I guess you could call it that," Ches answered with a grin.

"How did Serena Kate react?"

"She was better off without her so-called boyfriend and his crew. I think she knew it, too. Things had been kind of tense between her and Aunt Sis for a long time, but that all cleared up pretty quick."

"And she started helping you not long afterwards?"

"Yeah… When she took off, Ruthanne, I didn't just lose my typist or my sweetheart. I lost my dearest friend."

"I'm sure her leaving is hard to forgive, Ches. Still, you needn't give up that friendship forever." These words came somewhat hesitantly at first as

Ruthanne's tender heart fought to rise above jealousy, but she finished in a single breathless rush. "And then, well, there's always me."

# Chapter Seven

It took several seconds for her words to register. When they finally did, Ches could only compare it with the pleasant shock of diving into cold water on a hot summer day. Short Stuff leapt ahead, reacting to the sudden tightening of his rider's muscles, but a quick tug on the bridle checked this forward rush.

"Steady, boy," Ches drawled, stroking his horse's neck in automatic apology.

As an experienced rider, Ruthanne understood this transmission of energy but chose to make light of the situation.

"Hey, don't run off," she called laughingly, coming up alongside him once more.

"You're not gettin' rid of me that easy, Miss Ruthanne Prescott."

"Good," she answered, still teasing. "I like a challenge."

"Ruthanne, what you said just now, it really means a lot. With everything I've told you, would you even consider getting to know me better? Dating, I mean, or whatever we're supposed to call it nowadays…"

"Absolutely, Ches…" Then with a little laugh, "let's just call it goin' steady. I'm not sure how many actual dates we'll get with me a-following Pap up and down the road."

They smiled into each other's eyes for a long, thrilling moment. Nobody drew rein, but the horses slowed gradually to a stop. Giving the colt a little pressure with her outside leg, Ruthanne sidled him closer to Short Stuff and leaned over to hug Ches.

"I'm not apt to forget this day," he murmured softly against her neck.

Back at Judd's barn, Ruthanne swapped her saddle to the darker bay colt and glanced affectionately up at her riding partner.

"Sure you don't want down for a minute? How about something to eat or drink?"

"No, I'm doing alright. Did you want something?"

"I don't generally stop to eat as long as I'm busy. Ought to slim down without half trying. Only… Apple fritters just don't play fair."

"I reckon you're near-bout perfect, Ruthanne, just the way you are."

"I'm certainly glad you think so," she answered with a laugh.

After a few minutes rest in the shade around the barn, she swung carefully into the saddle and untracked her new mount. This colt moved out freely, and Ruthanne soon labeled him as quite a bit steadier than the one she'd ridden that morning. Ches fell in alongside as she headed off down the drive. Recrossing the highway without incident, they picked another dirt road for the next leg of their ride.

"Now that I've talked your ear off," Ches finally ventured, "why don't you share some of your own memories?"

More of a listener than a talker, Ruthanne proved reluctant, but after asking him outright to tell her about Serena Kate, she felt obliged to share something of herself. She told of childhood days at Fairview, the loss of her parents, and a kind of minor-league stardom on the fair and rodeo circuit.

"Maybe you don't think you've had much experience with this kind of thing,

Ches. Dating, I mean... Well, I've had even less. A handful of fellas showed interest over the years, but some of their intentions were less than honorable. Me and Pap culled that kind out right quick. The good ones, or those that might have been, just stood there waving and lookin' kinda sad while we drifted off down the road."

"Things must've gotten pretty lonesome for you," he guessed, voice filled with tender concern.

They rode along in easy silence for a good while as she sought a label for her feelings.

"More wistful, really, a longing for something I'd never known. Now, you... Getting accustomed to that special kind of companionship with Serena Kate and having it suddenly taken away, that's what I'd call lonesome."

Ches figured Ruthanne's gentle compassion would always give her more sympathy for others' hardships than for her own. Before he could open his mouth, though, something rounded a curve in the dirt road and came barreling straight at them.

Ches's brain registered a small Palomino horse dragging what remained of a cart in the split second before Ruthanne's previously calm mount snorted and shied, crashing into the woods on the opposite edge of the road with one sideways jump. Short Stuff pricked his ears and cleared his nostrils in surprise, but he never completely lost it. Ches found the remarkable gelding right up in the bridle, primed to answer the slightest pressure whenever his rider decided to make a move.

Ruthanne probably didn't need help, and if she did, there was little enough he could provide. Stopping the runaway seemed like a good idea, but if he jumped Short Stuff right into the Palomino's path, the little horse would try to dart by them. With the two-wheeled wreck still hitched on behind, darting around might prove a complicated proposition.

Ches wheeled Short Stuff and, acting on a split-second decision, galloped back up the road. Finally judging that they had gained enough ground, he stopped his mount and turned him broadside in the center of the road. One hand reached up for his straw hat and brought it down in a sweeping arc. He wanted the runaway horse to see the obstacle in its path in time to make a reasonable decision.

*Beyond the Parmalee Bottom* 121

"Hey, booger. Hey, hey…" he called, striving to keep his voice gentle and make it carry at the same time. "Whoa. Whoa, now, I say."

Slowing his flight, the Palomino started to double back the way he'd come, but found himself hampered a little by what remained of the cart. He eventually figured things out and swapped ends, but Ruthanne trotted up, her mount back under control, and stepped down to grab a trailing line.

"Come get this colt," and she managed to convey urgency without betraying any nerves or excitement. "I doubt if I can hold him and little Secretariat at the same time."

Her own straw hat was gone, one shoulder of her t-shirt was partially ripped, and blood oozed from a scratch just above her left eyebrow. Acting almost instantly on her request, Ches rode over at a deliberate walk, took charge of her mount, and led him quietly out of the way.

"You okay?"

"Uh-huh…"

The little Palomino never even tried to pull away from Ruthanne as she worked up the line toward him. In fact, he showed so much sense that she took a firm grip on his headstall and, talking softly all the time, encouraged him to drag the ruined cart out of the roadway. That done, she stripped the tangled harness off him, dropped the bit out of his mouth, and secured one of the driving lines to his halter.

"Bet I looked like a real knight in shining armor," Ches finally ventured with a chuckle, "cuttin' a trail for the way off yonder."

"Oh, I knew exactly what you were doing," Ruthanne assured him. "Things were happening awful fast along about then… Still, I'm pretty sure I thanked God you had the presence of mind not to jump Short Stuff right out in front of that train wreck. Take a couple of wraps around your saddle horn with this line," she advised, walking over to exchange the Palomino for her riding horse.

"Come on, booger," Ches murmured softly. "Let's go see if your driver is laying in the ditch or a-walkin' back up the road."

"I know Mr. Judd is your good friend," Ruthanne said with a muffled grunt as she heaved herself back into the saddle. "I think the world of him, too, but I've got to question his love for tall horses."

"Amen to that," Ches answered with a grin.

"Rats, I ought to've walked up yonder for my hat. Don't know if I like it well enough to get off and back on again."

"Maybe we could break off a handy-sized limb and fish for it," Ches speculated as their two mounts and the extra pony started off in a contented little bunch.

"Worth a try," Ruthanne decided whimsically.

She picked out a long limb and snagged her hat off the ground without much trouble, but bringing it back to her hand on the end of that stick put rollers in the colt's nose. Opting out of another fuss, Ruthanne passed the hat to Ches who then handed it back to her.

They kept an eye out as they rode and eventually spotted a bare-headed man in overalls limping purposefully toward them. At sight of the riders this unwilling hiker stopped, conserving his energy, and allowed them to trot up to him.

"Whatcha know, roadside assistance," he quipped with a shamefaced grin.

"You hurt, friend?" Ches inquired of the white-headed stranger.

"Nothing but my pride," he grimaced, reaching up to claim the pony's lead line. Ches and Ruthanne exchanged worried glances as he casually tied the free end back into the halter for a rein and scrambled up bareback. "Rides good," he explained, catching the look. "Maybe I was a little hasty about hittin' the open road with my cart, but I ain't about to walk all the way home!"

"My name's Ches Durham," the younger man volunteered as they rode off together, "and this is Miss Ruthanne Prescott."

"Earl... Earl Littlejohn. 'Preciate y'all catching my pony. Reckon where he lost the cart?"

"Ruthanne drug it out of the road a good ways back yonder and unhitched your horse from what was left."

"Least the little booger didn't cripple himself," he observed philosophically.

"Funny," Ches responded, "Booger's what I've been calling him."

"How's the little horse bred?" Ruthanne wanted to know.

"He's just a Choctaw pony. I reckon he was headed back to Peason Ridge and the rest of them wild broomtails."

"Looks settled enough now," she responded noncommittally.

"Yeah, my grandkids rode him all over the place before their daddy moved 'em to Houston so he could make a living."

"What'll you take for him?" Ches inquired.

"Nothin' like a fella that knows when to buy cheap! How much money you got?"

"I could let you have two hundred for him."

"Anybody ridin' them kind of horses," he said, nodding to indicate Short Stuff and Judd's colt, "ought to could dig a little deeper than that."

"Stole 'em off the side of the highway up yonder. We just loped off down here to see which one might be worth keeping."

"Yeah, I bet. Three and a quarter to you… Two seventy-five to the pretty girl."

"Loan me the money, Ches?"

"You know it."

"Well, Mr. Littlejohn, you just parted ways with a pony."

"Call me Earl, missy, but I ain't sold out yet. That's two seventy-five when I get off at my front stoop."

"Fair enough," she agreed with a smile.

They accompanied Earl back to his secluded farmstead, completed the transaction, and took his advice on a shortcut back to the Matthews place so that Ruthanne could ride the third and final colt before dark.

"You can have the pony if you want, Ches. I never meant to run in under you. We bought him with your money, anyhow."

"He's worth more than two seventy-five," Ches assured her. "Let's see what Pap thinks of your investment before you back out of it."

"Oh, Pap'll take him at that price. I just thought you ought to have first chance."

"You bought him, Ruthanne. All I'm due is my money back. I'd give you the pony if I thought you fancied him for your own use, but I don't feel no overwhelmin' urge to give him to Pap."

"I can understand that," she answered with a playful smile.

"Wish you'd run in the house and put some peroxide or something on that cut," he said back at Judd and Shirley's.

"It's more of a scrape than a cut. Besides, I'd hate to go in the house without changing out of this torn shirt, and then I'd hate to put on a clean shirt without a bath. A good long soak in the tub, and I'd be out like a light. Shirley and them might find you sitting out here on your horse when they got home from the fairgrounds."

"Alright, alright... I know a thing or two about hardheaded cowgirls. One of 'em helped raise me, so we'll finish the job before we quit. Let's ease out the back way. We can cut across a fire lane to Shirley's uncle's place and the Dixon Loop. It's a shorter ride, but Judd won't care. Besides, hardheadedness can only carry a body so far."

"Lead out," she agreed, "and say a little prayer that this buckskin is as gentle as Judd has him figured. My tailfeathers are draggin' some."

"Nobody could tell it by looking. You just get more and more beautiful as the day goes along."

"Aww, that's real sweet… I wouldn't dare question your honesty. So, naturally, I'm left to wonder about your eyesight."

In reality, though, Ches spoke the truth. He had always admired Serena Kate's pretty, pale skin with its smattering of freckles, but Ruthanne's healthy outdoor complexion seemed practically flawless under the added sheen of perspiration.

The passing thought of Serena Kate raised a question as to whether he had shared too much earlier in the day. As he looked at Ruthanne sitting there a'horseback, smile still bright at the end of a grueling day, he let go of his doubts. This girl deserved the whole truth.

Later that evening, he caught a minute with Judd and Shirley in their kitchen. Tired but a long way from worn out, the couple recounted their day and told of all the cute little buckaroos who showed up for a ride on the Prescott Ponies. Being local people, they saw several families they knew and even got some pictures with a great nephew during his ride.

"How did it go with my colts?" Judd finally inquired. "George looked a little uncertain when y'all rode out this morning."

"Ruthanne nursed him along real easy, and he settled in just fine. Sarge is probably steadier overall, but he shied from a runaway cart. Dark like to have caught us before we could fool with Willy. But you hired a rider that won't quit. She carried him around the Dixon Loop without any trouble."

Before Judd could respond, Shirley cut in with a chuckle.

"Say, hold up a minute. What did you say scared Sarge?"

"You heard right. The only traffic we saw down around Camp Baker was Earl Littlejohn's Palomino pony dragging what was left of a two-wheel cart. Pony's down there at your barn, now. Ruthanne bought him."

"Bought him?" Shirley exclaimed. "That wouldn't have been my first reaction."

"Oh, I'm the one started it," he confided with a grin, "but Mr. Littlejohn wanted to sell his horse to the pretty girl. He offered Ruthanne a better price."

"I think Ches has done found him a wife," Judd quipped, "any girl that would buy a runaway pony off the side of the road was born to marry a Durham."

Ches flushed bright red but smiled in spite of himself.

"Hush that talk," he pleaded with a worried glance in the direction of the hallway. "Let's not scare her off on the first day."

"What do you mean the first day?" Shirley inquired, eyes suddenly bright with interest.

"Well'm," he answered, overjoyed but reticent at the same time, "Ruthanne said she'd go steady with me."

Shirley opened her mouth to whoop, swallowed it, and snatched the cap off Judd's head so she could at least fling something into the air.

"Are we the first you've told?" she asked in an excited whisper as Judd grabbed Ches for a quick bear hug.

"Sent Aunt Sis a text message," he admitted a little sheepishly. "I don't know what that precious girl sees in me, but I'm prayin' she don't snap out of it."

"Ruthanne or Miss Sis?" Shirley questioned, voice full of teasing sarcasm.

"I ain't worried none about Aunt Sis," he shot back. "Look up loyalty in the dictionary, and you'll find her picture!"

"Don't waste too much worry on Ruthanne, either," Shirley advised with a laugh. "I believe she's cut from the same cloth."

"Say, y'all have already done so much... I hate to ask another favor."

"I don't mind tellin' you no," Shirley joked, stepping over to squeeze his shoulder fondly, "but how can we make up our minds if you don't even ask?"

"Pap ought to look at this horse Ruthanne bought. And I feel like I need to, you know, ask his permission or something."

"Ruthanne is a grownup young lady, Ches. Y'all don't exactly need Pap's blessing to date. Come to think of it, though, I know what you mean."

"I'll camp with him again tonight, but I'd like for him to come over here and… Trouble is, he won't leave those ponies in camp that long."

"I'll go over there and watch his camp," Judd volunteered.

"No need for you to go over there and sit by yourself," Shirley said quickly. "I'll come, too. There's plenty of leftovers here, and Ruthanne won't mind laying them out."

"If she can hold her eyes open that long," Ches worried.

"That girl's tougher than you give her credit for. The food's already here, and y'all can just sort of enjoy one another." Then, turning to Judd, "Make us a couple of meatloaf sandwiches. I'll holler at Ruthanne so she don't jump straight into her pajamas. We'd best hurry if we're gonna catch Pap before he goes to roost for the night."

Ches never drove for the fun of it, especially not at night over unfamiliar roads, but he didn't require hand controls or other special adaptations on a vehicle, either. Figuring Pap knew even less about the area, he decided to tag along and bring the old showman back for a nice little sit-down supper.

Ruthanne dried and brushed out her hair, rifled through a stack of jeans and T-shirts, and finally remembered her last-minute decision to bring along one nice dress. Light blue in color with touches of white lace trimming the neck and short sleeves, the dress made her think of picnics, ice cream suppers, and other summertime fun, but she'd only ever worn it once, to some kind of rodeo banquet. She remembered feeling very pretty at first, but once lost in a room full of strangers, it seemed that a trick-riding costume might have served her just as well.

Making her way to the kitchen, Ruthanne located a pair of aprons and borrowed one to protect her dress. She loved Judd and Shirley, even after such a short acquaintance, but their absence allowed her to play out a cherished dream. Tonight, she could act as hostess in a real, honest-to-goodness house.

Her imagination toyed with the idea of having prepared this delicious, homecooked meal especially for Ches and Pap instead of just heating up Shirley's leftovers. Her practical nature wanted to dismiss the notion, but her normally unlined brow furrowed as she considered the ordeal of receiving even an occasional guest in a fritter stand that offered little more than shade from the noonday sun. Giving her sandy blond locks an unconscious little toss, Ruthanne decided to allow herself a bit of harmless fantasy.

When Pap rapped on the door a few minutes later, she hung up the apron, smoothed the front of her dress, and greeted them with a smile.

"Y'all come on in here; supper's on the table."

"Now, that's what I like to hear," the old man quipped, brushing past her, but Ches was practically stunned by this vision in blue.

"Ruthanne, I... The dress is... Do you have any idea how beautiful you are?"

Pap turned back briefly, pinched his granddaughter's cheek, and sized her up from head to toe in a single glance.

"Missed you today, Ruthie girl. You do clean up pretty good."

Ches wanted to pull out one of the dining room chairs for Ruthanne but didn't quite know how to get it done on his crutches. In the end, all three seated themselves. Pap reached immediately for a serving fork, but Ruthanne cleared her throat gently. "Ches, would you return thanks?"

"Dear Heavenly Father, we come humbly before You thanking You for the blessings of this day and for Your watch care over us. I thank You particularly for Ruthanne and her grandfather and this time You've allowed us to spend together. I ask, Lord, that You'd continue to bless and keep them both. Bless this food, now, to the nourishment of our bodies and our bodies to Thy service. Forgive my sins for in Jesus' precious name I pray. Amen."

"Regular little homemaker, ain't she," Pap observed around a mouthful of meatloaf, and Ches nodded without taking his eyes off Ruthanne.

"I hope you don't mind, but I went ahead and told Pap what we talked about today."

"About goin' steady?" she asked, smiling softly.

"Uh-huh... It seemed like the respectful thing to do, but you might have wanted to tell him yourself.

"No, Ches, I'm glad y'all had that conversation."

"I figured you'd latch onto somebody one day, Ruthie," Pap said bluntly, "but remember what I taught you about buying a pony. Given my druthers, I'd have you pick one sound in his legs."

Color rushed to Ruthanne's cheeks and then drained away as she shot to her feet, leaving her almost pale in the grip of a cold fury.

"Phineas Absalom Prescott, Ches is perfectly capable of... Well, just about anything! If you can't see that, then I don't know—"

"Take it easy, Ruthie," the old man said as he patted the air in a placating gesture. "Just settle yourself down. Young Mr. Durham is a lucky man. If you felt sorry for him, you would've launched into a long-winded explanation of all the reasons why he's good enough. If you were embarrassed by his limitations, you'd have stuttered and fussed around making excuses. But when that backbone snapped straight and those pretty eyes flashed at me... Well, I reckon he's won a place in your heart."

"For pity's sake, Pap," she sighed heavily and then sank back into her chair, replacing the cloth napkin just so in her lap before she spoke again. "I was so very happy to have the three of us sitting down together at a real supper table, but there's nothing like a sudden spike in blood pressure to clear the stars from a girl's eyes."

"I don't deserve her, Pap," Ches interjected in a quiet but firm tone of voice. "Still, I guarantee you she'll be treated like a princess for as long... As long as she'll let me."

"This boy's a hardheaded Durham, Ruthie. Crippled or not, if he's made up his mind to be good to you, I reckon that's all there is to it."

"I think Ches is just wonderful," she sighed, starry-eyed once again.

"You're the wonder, pretty lady! That tongue lashing you gave Pap even scared me a little."

The words brought genuine laughter from Ruthanne, and she reached almost unconsciously across the table to clasp his hand for the very first time. Pap noted the warmth of this brief contact before turning the conversation to more practical matters.

"Ches told me about the little Palomino you bought, Ruthie, but he offered me a chance to make up my own mind before we pay off. Bring the pony to the fairgrounds in the morning when you come with Judd and Shirley. We'll try him out and see about some kind of trade."

"I borrowed the money and bought the horse in good faith," Ruthanne protested. "We ought to go ahead and pay Ches."

"You got a good deal on the pony," the younger man assured her quickly. "We're just trying to decide if you bought him for me or Pap. Like I told you before, I'm happy either way."

They recounted their day, bragged on Judd's colts, and told how they had come to find the pony. Pap's eyes widened a little when he heard about the smashed-up cart, but his business didn't exactly call for a driving pony.

"There's blueberry pie," Ruthanne offered and rose to get it from the kitchen.

"Thought you didn't like sweets," Pap commented as she cut a generous slice for each of them.

"Well," Ruthanne admitted somewhat sheepishly, "I get kinda tired of leftover fritters, but after a day or two without them, I reckon I'm due for a little sugar rush."

"Nothin' wrong with that," Ches assured her. "Miss Shirley's blueberry pie is hard to beat."

"We'd better get on back to camp, son," Pap finally observed. "Can't leave those good folks sitting over there all night."

Ruthanne hummed softly as she cleaned up the kitchen. She felt the slight ache of long hours in the saddle and a definite need for sleep, but those things couldn't dim her contented smile. She waited around to say good night to Judd and Shirley before heading off to bed. Something between a groan and a sigh

*Beyond the Parmalee Bottom* 131

escaped as she lowered herself onto the soft mattress, and she fell asleep almost before her head hit the pillow.

Breakfast the next morning was a hurried affair, but Shirley insisted on bringing leftover biscuits to camp and heating two at a time in Pap's small toaster oven. Meanwhile, Ruthanne introduced the little Palomino gelding to the pony ride carousel. He tossed his head nervously at first, but the next five minutes saw him walking sedate circles with Ruthanne on his back and a Shetland in front and behind.

"This little fella's okay, Pap," she called, stroking the pony's neck. "Flashy colored and plenty cheap..."

"Don't crowd me," her grandfather quipped, rubbing the back of his neck in thought. "I'm studying on it. Say, Ches, how 'bout letting me use him. He makes the day alright, and I'll see if I can't trade with you."

"Good enough, Pap, and if you skip town with my pony, I'm keepin' this pretty granddaughter of yours."

Ruthanne and Ches enjoyed their saddle time together immensely. They talked a lot but also rode along in periods of easy silence. The network of dirt roads turned out a little busier than on the previous day. They met a pickup, a go-cart, and a battered Lincoln Continental. Not having a runaway pony to contend with, Ruthanne made sure to divide her time equally between Judd's three horses.

"You holding up alright?" she finally questioned, handing Ches a bottle of water.

"If I could ride all day every day, I would," he assured her with a smile, "and that's without the lure of a gorgeous young lady. So, you needn't waste time looking around for me and Short Stuff. We're right in your back pocket."

Their new status as a couple eased Ches's shyness, and he seemed to possess an endless string of compliments. She was gorgeous, her eyes were pretty, he liked the sound of her voice. Ruthanne knew good and well she wasn't ugly. But she wasn't the stick-thin Hollywood ideal, either. However she looked, it was more the good Lord's doing than her own, and while his little kindnesses thrilled her, she never knew exactly how to respond.

"Riding colts in this July heat can sure take the sap out of a girl. But with just a few hours in that nice, soft bed at Ms. Shirley's, I'm rarin' to go again."

"I thought you looked tired last night," he observed, voice full of concern. "Well, I don't mean that, not exactly. You looked just as beautiful as always but awful sleepy at the same time."

"I've been worried about you," she shot back, dismissing any weariness of her own. "Bunking in the back of our old van don't exactly make for restful nights. That little oscillating fan ain't good for much except to make a racket and stir the warm night air; I ought to know."

"Being hot ain't so bad, but Pap ought to look into one of them sleep machines or something. I figure he snored some of them dents into the van! I can take most anything for a week, but it really bothers me to think about you camping that-a-way. Hot in the summer, cold in the winter, cooking in that fritter stand the year 'round, and trying to do up your clothes in some public washhouse…"

"Washateria," she murmured, stroking her horse's neck as she considered this new perspective. "Life on the road is pretty much all I've ever known. Can't scarcely call it a hardship."

"Maybe you can't," Ches qualified, "but I sure can! Don't get me wrong. Most folks today are a-way too comfortable for their own good. A lovely young lady like you, though, you ought to be a little spoiled and soft. Camp life is alright for an old rounder like Pap, but you deserve so much better!"

Ruthanne's breath caught in her throat as she blinked away tears. There wasn't an ounce of self-pity in her, but his loving concern grabbed at her heartstrings.

"I remember an upstairs, corner bedroom at Fairview with double windows to draw the breeze," she confided in a reflective tone, "but that seems a mighty long time ago now."

Most horses required definite pressure from the outside leg to side pass, but with a little help from a bridle rein, Short Stuff could almost read his rider's mind. As the savvy little bay edged closer to Ruthanne's mount, Ches reached up gently to brush a sandy blonde ringlet off her cheek.

"Oh, sweet girl…"

"I've never had a real good shoulder to cry into, Ches, but this day's too pretty to ruin it with messy tears. Let's just ride on."

"Sweet as sugar and tough as nails," Ches marveled. "My shoulder's here whenever you get ready."

All three colts got a good workout that day, and Ches sent Shirley a text message asking her and Judd to wait around at the fairgrounds until he and Ruthanne could get there.

"I started to feed for you, Mr. Judd," Ruthanne explained as the long summer day faded into dusk, "but we figured you might want to let the buckskin cool out first. I turned him loose in the round pen to roll and get the sweat off his back."

"Aunt Sis always says that a horse or mule is worth a hundred every time he turns over," Ches recalled with a chuckle, "and I think the colonel said it before her."

"Make it a thousand or fifteen hundred," Judd quipped, "and he won't have to roll over so many times to get me out of the hole."

Pap Prescott often complained of bad eyesight. But he possessed a rare knack for counting money, even in dwindling light. Thumbing the day's take like some riverboat gambler might handle a deck of cards, he arranged the bills by value, totaled up the loose coins, and dropped the lid snugly onto his cashbox.

"Best two days we've had in a long time, Ruthie," he declared conversationally. "If the rest of the week holds up like this, I just might take Judd and Shirley on the road."

"Fame sure is fleeting," his granddaughter sighed in mock dismay. "Star trick rider one summer and chopped liver by the next."

"Teach you to go 'round falling off your horse," Judd quipped.

He froze for a brief moment, wondering if he had gone too far, but his quick addition to the constant Prescott banter made Ruthanne laugh until she gave out a darling little snort and then ducked her head in embarrassment.

"Ches, my boy," Pap observed as the laughter died down, "that little Palomino spent all day on the carousel, and he ain't rolled over a time this evening. I reckon you ought to just give him to me."

"Uh-huh," Ches drawled in response, "but I ain't."

"Tell you what I'll do... Old Thimble, my buckskin-and-white pony, matches up pretty good with the horse you bought from us. Count me out five hundred-dollar bills and take him home with you. We'll put that yellow runaway in his place."

"Well, now, Pap... I can't see five hundred dollars' worth of difference between Thimble and the Palomino."

"Thimble knows more than just walkin' circles with the carousel string," Ruthanne advised quietly. "I think you'd like him for riding outside, but the yellow pony's younger."

"We've still got Buttons at home; matching up to him is worth something. How 'bout three of them hundred-dollar bills?"

"Believe I could get four out of you... But you're a Durham, and we'd be here 'til daylight. Pay me and go eat your supper."

"Fair enough; I might even bring you a plate."

"Why don't you ride Thimble tomorrow, Ches?" Ruthanne suggested. "When I come after you in the morning, we'll haul him back over to the house with Pap's truck and trailer. High time we quit running Ms. Shirley's car back and forth, anyhow."

The little paint pony showed all the steadiness of an oilfield pumpjack. He kept up doggedly with the larger, longer-legged colts but never betrayed the least sign of nerves or excitement.

Days passed by in a happy blur. Judd and Shirley adored working with children, and they even learned to enjoy Pap, natural-born scoundrel that he was. Ches and Ruthanne soaked up one another's company and tried hard to ignore the fast-approaching end of this special week.

Despite the rising knot of dread in her stomach, Ruthanne arrived in camp early

Saturday morning. She planned to feed, brush, saddle, and generally make things ready before heading out on one last ride with Ches.

"Leave that," Pap ordered almost gruffly. "No use doing Gilderoy's chores for him."

"Gilderoy?" she questioned with a sudden edge in her voice.

"Don't fret, now. Tiny and his boy's ain't nowhere around. You always kinda liked Gilderoy and his old lady, anyhow."

"Mrs. Gilderoy is kindhearted," Ruthanne admitted, "even if she does claim to tell fortunes."

"I expect they'll go back to Tiny's bunch sooner or later. Gilderoy don't scare easy, and that old Ferris wheel kinda draws a crowd. In the meantime, they swung up this-a-way on their own."

"I understand," she answered, in a more settled tone, "but what's Gilderoy got to do with our ponies?"

"His ponies," the old man corrected nonchalantly. "I sold out."

"S-sold out," Ruthanne stammered, mind reeling from his unexpected revelation. "This is as good a string of ponies as we've ever owned. How do you figure we'll make a living without 'em?"

"Gilderoy called himself a magician right up 'til the worldwide web made folks hard to impress. Lately, he's been workin' on boots and other leather goods. Offered me a mobile leather shop for the ponies and everything that pertains to 'em."

"And you took him up?"

"I did... Pony rides are apt to starve a man to death staying in one spot, 'specially in a little bitty country town."

"Stayin' in one little bitty country town?" Ruthanne murmured in disbelief.

"Yep," he drawled with a grin. "The little bitty country town of McKendrick for instance."

"You'd do that for me?" she practically gushed. "I can help you in the leather trade and work for Miss Sis and maybe clean a few houses. We'll make it; I promise!"

"Always have," he said without even a trace of concern. "We'll keep the fritter stand to run on horse-sale days. I don't expect to last forever, Ruthie girl, but the old Durham crowd are good folks. Whether or not this little romance works out between you and Ches, they'll treat you right."

"Oh, Pap," she whispered, stepping over to lay a hand on his arm. "Maybe my childhood wasn't what most folks think of as normal, but you provided everything I ever needed. Everything except... And now you're giving me the chance to put down roots, to be part of a community and maybe even a family."

Phineas Absalom Prescott swallowed a lump in his throat but waved a hand dismissively.

"Hush that sappy talk. I've just got too old for all this drifting and picked us a spot to light."

"One thing worries me, Pap. Will Gilderoy take good care of the ponies? Does he even know how?"

"That rascal's older than he looks. Spent his youth trailing after a genuine horse-drawn gypsy wagon. Now, he may not be above barbecuing one if times get hard, but he'll look after his investment."

A sickly expression washed over Ruthanne's features, and she pressed a hand unconsciously to her stomach.

"Lordy, I wish I'd never asked. Yet and still, I'm mighty glad Ches got hold of Thimble."

"Give an old fox a little credit," Pap replied, tapping a finger against his temple.

Having motioned Judd and Shirley around behind the Prescott van to allow Pap this conversation with his granddaughter, Ches finally moved back into sight on his crutches.

*Beyond the Parmalee Bottom* 137

"Ches Durham," Ruthanne called, her joy spilling over into laughter as she ran the few steps to meet him. "How long have you known about this?"

When he knelt down and discarded the crutches, Ruthanne dropped to his level for a long hug.

"Not too long, sugar pie, but I did call Aunt Sis. She's already lined up a house for y'all to rent."

"A house?" she choked out in genuine shock.

Remembering his promise of a shoulder if she ever got ready to cry, Ches stayed contentedly on his knees in front of the old fritter stand and held Ruthanne while she sobbed.

# Chapter Eight

(East Texas: late September, 2015)

Corrie and Torrie lived with their mother and step-father in the county seat, just sixteen miles from the rural crossroads that bore their family name, and a trip down the farm-to-market road passed quickly in comparison to the long drive home from North Dakota. They loved spending time in Mac Town. Uncle Scooter occasionally kept half an eye on them, and at other times Miss Sis took charge. Cute, spunky redheads named McKendrick generally had the run of the place.

The twins showed little interest in drama club or virtual reality but enjoyed riding the side-by-side with Cassidy. All three looked forward to the rare occasions when they escaped Miss Sis's notice long enough to go zooming up the blacktop road and around the deserted square at Mac Town. On this particular Saturday joyride, a mid-morning shower caught them out in the open.

"Let's make a run for Ruthanne's," Cassidy called over the engine noise and sudden downpour. "It's the closest."

"Do we have to go there?" Corrie hollered directly into her friend's ear. "Mama might not like it."

"What Mama don't know won't hurt her," Torrie shouted, trying to shield her face from the blowing rain. "I'm fixin' to drown here!"

Cassidy drove them directly into the sheltering carport and grew bored before the engine cooled.

"Let's go inside. Ruthanne won't care; she's real sweet."

Corrie shot her sister a worried look but got only a shrug in return, and they trooped after Cassidy. Observing their waterlogged arrival from a window, Ruthanne smiled to herself and threw some clean towels into the dryer. When the three girls finally sloshed their way up to the doorstep, she met them with an armload of readymade warmth.

"Kinda hurts my feelings to know y'all went swimmin' without me," she teased.

Not knowing the McKendrick twins nearly as well, Ruthanne simply handed them a couple of towels. But Cassidy's dark curls got a vigorous rubdown.

"Swimming?" The towel muffled Cassidy's voice, but her girlish excitement came through loud and clear. "I was just driving across the pasture and this wall of water hit us out of nowhere. Torrie almost drowned!"

"Well, we can't have that," Ruthanne answered lightly. "Y'all come on into the kitchen while I hunt up some dry clothes. A little water won't hurt that floor."

"These clothes will dry out okay," Cassidy assured her, "and the warm towels feel nice. You got any coffee?"

"I thought Miss Sis told you to stick to just one cup in the morning time."

"You're getting as bad as Ches," the younger girl accused playfully. "Mother may be the queen of the realm, but she can't watch everybody all the time."

"Maybe that's what she's got me and Ches for," Ruthanne teased right back.

"But you're a free spirit fresh from the open road, remember? Lots of cream and sugar, pretty please!"

"Okay, just this once. And we'll cut the air conditioner off for a minute."

"Kitchen's a lot cleaner than it was when Uncle Scooter lived here," Torrie observed, gazing all around with bright-eyed curiosity.

"Mmm, your uncle did live here for a while, didn't he?"

"Yes, ma'am. He rented this place from the time Giles Parmalee went into the nursing home until y'all came along."

"I love this house. Pap and Mr. Parmalee enjoy one another, too. They carry on like a couple of long-lost brothers. But how come Scooter to move?"

"Miss Sis put him back in the McKendrick house right off the old square."

"Put him back..." Ruthanne let the question trail off in favor of a simpler one as she busied herself with an old-fashioned stovetop percolator. "You girls drink coffee, too?"

"Put him back, asked him to move... It's all the same coming from Mother," Cassidy quipped. "Most folks around here act like she hung the moon or something."

"No coffee for us," Corrie said, wrinkling her nose in distaste. "Got any Coke?"

"Sure, there's all kinds of soda water left in the fritter stand."

"Miss Sis owns the old McKendrick house," Torrie explained, "but she didn't like the idea of charging rent. Not with you being Ches's new lady friend and all. Uncle Scooter grew up in that house, so she just stuck him back in it and fixed things up where y'all could lease from Mr. Parmalee. This is closer to the sale barn, anyhow."

"Plus, it keeps us from moving out of our little apartment and back into the McKendrick house," Corrie realized with a thoughtful frown. "Miss Sis is always sweet to me and Torrie, but I don't think Mama's real high on her list right now."

Tactful enough to keep silent, Ruthanne flashed the girls a reassuring smile and stepped from the room to locate their soft drinks.

"Two Coca Colas on ice and one sugar-milk with a dash of hot coffee." A born hostess, even when her company consisted of three rain-wet young girls, Ruthanne took a seat at the kitchen table and gave them her full attention.

"Good stuff," Cassidy sighed after the first sip.

"You'd already talked me into breaking the rules," Ruthanne confessed with a laugh, "so I put in some extra sugar."

Cassidy smiled her thanks but then asked a question.

"What are you doing at home, anyway?"

"Well, Ches is busy writing today and—"

"Did he get somebody else to type for him, Cassidy? Now that summer's over and you're back at school," Corrie interrupted.

"Yep," Cassidy answered, "some lady who used to work with Aunt Jenna at the dentist's office is helping him. She's semi-retired, and it looks like she might actually stay for a while."

"Longer than any of Uncle Scooter's girlfriends, huh?" Torrie joked, but her grin soon faltered. "I was kinda hoping he still needed help. Thought Mama might take her old job back instead of working 'round the clock at that stupid nursin' home, but I guess it's too late for that."

"Why don't you type for him, Ruthanne?" Cassidy wondered.

"Y'all were practically born in front of a keyboard or touchscreen," the older girl answered with a laugh. "Most people my age can say the same, but a traveling trick rider doesn't develop many computer skills."

"It's not like you have to type fast. He's sitting there making the stuff up as he goes along."

"Oh, I could probably get by, but I don't want your mama's old job. Ches partners with Miss Sis, but I can help out around the sale barn without working directly for him. We're both more comfortable that way."

"I bet," Cassidy muttered under her breath. "He fell in love with one typist, and she took off for the Canadian border."

"Pap's fixing up a few bridles to put in the next horse sale," Ruthanne told them, hurriedly moving the conversation forward. "Me and Miss Sis figured on rain this morning, so I decided to spend a quiet Saturday around the house. I'm awful glad y'all stopped by."

"Mother never said anything to me about this storm," Cassidy complained.

"Even a chicken's got sense enough to get outta the rain, honey child," Ruthanne teased.

"Ches is honey child; I'm darling! If you're going to mimic Mother in front of the expert," she chided, indicating herself, "you'd better get it right."

"Want to know something?" Ruthanne drawled, her hazel eyes alight with fun. "I never meant to imitate her. South Carolina yardbirds know how to get outta the rain, too!"

"Oh, no," Cassidy groaned, lowering her head dramatically to the tabletop. "What did I do? What did I ever do to deserve this? I'm surrounded by hicks!"

"Your mother is not a hick," Ruthanne corrected gently, all playfulness gone from her tone. "She's a genuine southern lady, and this old world could use some more like her."

Cassidy reflected on the words for a moment and even considered a serious reply, but her sense of humor would not be denied.

"Oh, I don't want y'all to go extinct or anything," she said in an overly sincere tone of voice, "but us normal people are starting to feel outnumbered."

"Well," Ruthanne sniffed, a smile playing around the corners of her mouth, "carry your normal self on over to the telephone and let Miss Sis know y'all are here with me. No use worrying her."

Ruthanne asked the twins about school, but when that subject dried up rather quickly, she clapped her hands together in sudden inspiration.

"Hey, do y'all want to help me try out a new recipe? Well, not new exactly...

It's a recipe for teacakes that came down from Grandmother Durham. Miss Sis gave it to me the other day but said she'd never tried to make them."

"I'm pretty sure Mother could turn out a batch of biscuits in her sleep," Cassidy observed, returning to the conversation. "Everybody brags on her homemade biscuits, and she's more than a little partial to them herself. Other than that, I think she'd rather avoid the kitchen altogether."

"Miss Sis has a real gift with horses, and she's probably the ablest manager I've ever known. She cooks to eat and to feed her loved ones, but it's gettin' to be a hobby with me."

"I've heard of chocolate cake, pound cake, and even angel food cake, but what are teacakes?" Torrie wanted to know.

"They're kind of like cookies, I guess," Ruthanne offered for lack of a better description. "Let's make us a batch and then you'll know what they are."

"Did my grandmother write this?" Cassidy asked minutes later as she studied the recipe card.

"No, silly, I copied it down."

"Don't silly me; you've got old lady handwriting. It's kinda pretty, though."

Judging by the quantity of each ingredient, Ruthanne saw right away that the old recipe would probably turn out several dozen teacakes, but she decided to forge ahead and bake them in shifts. As rain poured down outside, giggles and the pleasant scent of baking filled the house. Cassidy already regarded Ruthanne as a sort of big sister, and the twins soon placed her in a similar role.

"There's nothing to it, really. We'll dig up my old pictures later, and y'all can look at those," Ruthanne told her wide-eyed listeners as she neared the end of a rather offhand explanation of trick riding. "It doesn't take much to learn the basics, and I guarantee you Buttons ain't forgot nothing. I'm the one got old and stove-up..."

"You're not old," the girls chorused, making her laugh.

"Old-fashioned, maybe," Cassidy qualified, "but not old. That's why Ches is so silly over you. He finally found somebody young and pretty who thinks like him and Mother. I didn't think that girl existed."

"Y'all make me feel young," Ruthanne told them warmly. "I'm not so very old in years, but when I think about all the miles behind me..."

"I like Buttons a lot," Cassidy admitted, turning their conversation back to the trick horse, "but I'll stick to trotting through the pasture with Mother close by in case anything happens. Her gift with horses skipped me completely. Uncle Terry rides better than I do, and he don't even like it much."

"Everybody's different," Ruthanne conceded. "Ches doesn't consider himself a natural-born rider like your mother. Says he just loves it enough to make up the difference, but I'm not so sure."

"Everybody knows he's horse crazy."

"Yes, but I believe he's got some natural ability, too. Riding without good balance and control of his limbs is bound to be a fearful thing. Still, Ches doesn't telegraph anxiety to his horse. His skill's not as plain to be seen as your mother's, or even mine, but it's there."

"That's sweet and all, but a wooden Indian could ride Short Stuff."

"Can I have another teacake, please?" Corrie wondered, eyeing the first and second batches cooling on the counter.

"You better believe it," Ruthanne quipped, still smiling, "but be careful not to spoil your dinner."

Feeling slightly more at home than her sister, Torrie reached for another of the treats without asking.

"Let's just have these for lunch," she suggested around a mouthful.

"Mercy sakes!" Ruthanne answered with a sudden glance at the wall clock. "Pap'll be eating teacakes, too, unless I get busy and do something about dinner."

Even as she spoke the words, Ruthanne swooped down and grabbed a big saucepan from under the cabinet. The girls looked on with a touch of curiosity as she dumped in three large cans of beef vegetable stew and another of carrots, added water and placed the pan over a burner.

"Your microwave quit working?" Cassidy wanted to know, glancing dubiously at an appliance that looked to be left over from Mr. Parmalee's time at home.

"No, it works. The grocery stores just nearly give this stuff away, and if you'd ever tried to eat it straight out of the can, you'd know why. Add good, clean water to cut the salt, flour or something to thicken it up again, and black pepper to help the flavor. Few minutes over a decent flame, and it's pretty well fit to eat."

"Hey, Ruthanne," and the older girl met Torrie's searching gaze, prepared to answer some kind of a cooking question. "You love Ches as much as we do, don't you?"

Ruthanne took a breath and then another, lowered the heat under her stew, and allowed the wooden spoon to rest on the edge of the pan.

"I love Ches very much," she confided softly, wiping her hands with a dry cloth more as a distraction than from actual need. "Y'all have known him longer, I guess, but a young lady's love for her fella is... Well, it's different."

"Mama's worried you're just some fly-by-night gold digger who'll use Ches and then break his heart," Corrie almost whispered, "but I don't think so."

"Th-thank you, sweetheart," Ruthanne managed before turning quickly away to bury her face in the dishcloth.

"Are you for real?" Cassidy asked her friend in open-mouthed disbelief.

"Y'all don't fuss," Ruthanne chided gently, drawing in a long, shuddering breath as she regained her composure. "Ches and I are still learning one another's ways, courting as the old folks used to call it, but he's already very special to me."

"We didn't mean to hurt your feelings, Ruthanne."

Torrie placed a hand lightly on the older girl's arm as she spoke, hoping to restore the easy friendship they had shared moments earlier, and Corrie overcame her embarrassment in time to add an apology of her own.

"I'm really sorry, too, Ruthanne. After overhearing what Mama said to Ms. Hattie the other day, I just couldn't quit thinking about it. But you're not like that at all."

"You girls didn't do anything wrong," she answered reassuringly, "just gave me a kind of a shock. Only our Heavenly Father knows the paths Ches and I will take in the future, but I'd never intentionally break that kind, gentle heart of his."

"We love Mama," Torrie confided, "but nobody's right all the time."

Corrie nodded, acknowledging the truth of her sister's statement, while Ruthanne prayed inwardly for the right words. She genuinely liked the twins and wanted them to feel comfortable in her presence. However, she couldn't knowingly encourage them to disregard their mother's opinions.

"Your Mama and I barely know each other," she began carefully, "but maybe that'll change in time. I'm sure Serena Kate is a lovely person. Otherwise, Ches would never have invested so much of himself in their friendship. I know she works awfully hard to provide the things y'all need and take care of you girls. Tell you what, let's just enjoy one another. Y'all listen to your Mama and mind what she tells you, but let me worry about Ches's heart. I promise to take real good care of it!"

"Sounds good to me," Corrie agreed readily.

"Yep, that'll work," Torrie put in, snagging herself another teacake.

Ches showed up with Pap, his typist having gone home for the day, and the six of them enjoyed a quick lunch of stew and grilled cheese sandwiches.

"Put more water in the soup," Pap joked, sweeping a glance over the sizeable crowd at his kitchen table. "There's better times a-coming."

Later, he strummed an old Gibson guitar and hummed under his breath while their visitors poured over Ruthanne's old photo album. She told them all about the horses pictured, downplaying her own skill as a trick rider. Her pretty face, alight with fond memories, held more fascination for Ches than any number of old photographs, but the girls gawked openmouthed at some of the more difficult poses.

Cassidy often told herself that she preferred the quiet normalcy of Uncle Terry's home over time spent at the big house with her parents, but she considered the McKendrick twins- all of fifteen months younger- a little hyper and not nearly sophisticated enough for her Aunt Jenna. Thankfully, Mother's brand of country hospitality extended even to these rowdy childhood friends.

"We got nearly two inches," Andrew informed his wife as she joined him in the porch swing. "Looked like a morning shower at first, but it set in and rained for a while."

Fitting naturally into the crook of his arm, Sis leaned against him and allowed herself a contented little sigh.

"Maybe we'll have a wet fall. Keep the pastures going 'til frost."

Andrew's fingers rubbed the back of her neck ever so gently, and "the boss lady" purred like a kitten. Cassidy sat a few feet away on the top step, relying on the uncertain evening light to hide a spontaneous smile. Some teens might have gagged at the sight of their parents snuggling up to each other, but Cassidy liked glimpsing this tender, still-smitten side of Miss Sis. Besides, Corrie and Torrie hardly counted as company, not like the town kids in her circle at school.

"Grass looks good right now," he observed, "the cattle, too."

"You do a good job of managing them," she answered sweetly. "Me and Ches put in a little cowboy work whenever it's needed, but that's our idea of fun."

"I like fat cows and pretty calves, but achieving something for you to see and be proud of, that's the best part. A spreadsheet or bank balance just don't mean much in your world, baby doll."

"You'd make a go of anything you turned your hand to, Andrew. You're a great provider for this family."

"Hasn't stopped you from trading horses like your life depends on it and squeezing every deal for all it's worth," he answered, chuckling even as he scolded her.

"Old habits die hard."

"Or not at all... Some men complain that their wives won't get off the couch while I try and convince mine to take life a little easier. You just don't know how, do you?"

"Mmm," she responded, the tone almost as soft as her smile, "I'm feeling pretty lazy right this minute."

"Maybe so, but it never lasts long."

"I know you'll take care of us, Andrew, and provide for Cassidy's future. I'm trading for the fun of it and putting almost everything back into the family business. Because of you, I'll leave Ches a going concern one of these days without feeling that I've wronged our daughter."

It almost seemed a shame to disrupt the sappy, Hallmark sweetness of the moment, but Cassidy couldn't resist a teasing little jab at Mother.

"I never wanted your dumb old horse sale, anyhow."

Miss Sis whipped herself upright, transitioning instantly from lazy contentment to vibrating intensity.

"That 'dumb old horse sale' fed and clothed us for most of two generations after the East Texas cotton market fell in on itself. Kept this place together, too, if that means anything to you."

"Shh, shh," Andrew comforted, hugging his wife close once again. "She knows; she knows."

Their daughter laughed, having achieved the desired reaction, and Miss Sis managed a rueful smile.

"Pushing my buttons that-a-way used to be a dangerous thing, Cassidy Hollister, but your dad's made me soft in my old age."

"You're not old, Mother," Cassidy answered placatingly.

"That's better," Miss Sis quipped, playing up the moment with a highly satisfied nod.

"Where's Ches this evening?" Andrew asked a little while later.

"I reckon he's still visiting with Ruthanne and her grandfather."

"Aren't you just the least little bit jealous?" he teased.

"Who, me? Well... No girl will ever be quite good enough for my Ches, but Miss Ruthanne Prescott comes awfully close."

"She's not as much like you as the girl I figured he'd choose," Andrew admitted.

"No, Ruthanne's more of what I always figured I ought to be. Gentle and kind, always the sweet-natured homemaker. She's a worker, but without the hard-driving edge me and Ches inherited from the colonel."

"She can cook, too," Torrie McKendrick chimed in as she came out of the house munching on another homemade teacake.

This prompted Cassidy to brag on the doctored-up stew they had eaten at noontime.

"Stock Ruthanne's kitchen with a few decent supplies," Andrew observed casually, "and she might be about half dangerous."

"That girl's no charity case," Sis said as if to herself, frowning slightly in concentration. "I can't just show up over there with a bushel of peas and a stack of porkchops for her deepfreeze."

"You'll figure it out, Miss Sis."

"She always does," Cassidy agreed.

"Know something, baby doll?" Andrew asked a minute or two later, pretending deep concentration of his own. "I might just pick you all over again, hard-driving edge and all."

That said, he kissed her in gentle adoration. Miss Sis gazed up at her husband with love and unshakeable loyalty in her expressive brown eyes. Those eyes, still soft with the tenderness of the moment, clouded briefly as she registered squeals of delighted laughter from the three girls.

"I didn't raise y'all to hoop and holler like a bunch of heathens. If you can't sit up here on the porch and conduct yourselves as young ladies, then go play in the yard!" Far too contented to stay mad, she soon changed her tune. "That rain pulled some cooler air in behind it. We might just take us a little ride after church tomorrow."

The twins squealed all the louder in their excitement, and even Cassidy wasn't exactly put off by the prospect of another ride on a clever, eye-catching trick horse.

"Sounds like a winner to me," Andrew agreed. "I'll fix us up a picnic lunch."

"Might as well take the wagon and team," his wife decided. "I can get Pap to drive. That'll accommodate the dinner basket, Ethan, and any other excess baggage."

Andrew shot a meaningful glance toward the girls, but Corrie and Torrie only snickered at this apt description of their newly acquired stepfather.

After making coffee and mixing up a batch of her biscuits, Sis turned Sunday morning breakfast over to Andrew and stepped out to feed the current generation of stock dogs. The familiar racket of black mouth cur pups playfighting under the back porch assured her that cherished bloodlines would go on for a while longer. Peg and Rip grabbed a bite or two of Ol' Roy, charged down the hill toward the sale barn, and then doubled back to fall in step with her.

From ages three to thirty-five Doc Parmalee, a great-uncle, had never failed to greet her with a genuine compliment. "Well, Miss Sis, you're looking mighty pretty today..." Beyond that, he treated whatever might be ailing and sent her on her way with a handful of butterscotch or cinnamon discs.

Newfangled doctors dispensed meddlesome advice in place of hard candy, but morning strolls to the sale barn struck her as a reasonable alternative to the latest fitness craze. She thanked God for her health, took the occasional respiratory ailment in stride, and politely deflected lectures on the cardiovascular benefits of more strenuous exercise.

*Beyond the Parmalee Bottom* 151

A night horse waited just under the overhang of the barn. Saddling him seemed like an unnecessary chore this morning, but Andrew would pitch a running fit if he caught her riding bareback again. Instead, she rattled around a little longer than usual, setting the necessary gates, and waited for her dogs to figure out the business at hand. Rip and Peg gathered two little bunches of horses while the boss lady whooped her approval.

"Ain't no such thing as too many gates." The colonel's words came back to her as she cut a team of mules and a couple of sale-barn horses out of one bunch before sending the rest back to pasture. The second bunch consisted of the family's personal riding horses. She bragged on her dogs as they panted and wriggled joyfully around her feet. Suitably rewarded, Peg and Rip took to a nearby patch of shade and watched her work.

Singing hymns under her breath as she moved around the horses, Sis glanced up in mild surprise as a familiar minivan rolled onto the scene. Ruthanne Prescott stepped from behind the wheel, and a wheelchair ramp deployed on the other side.

"Ches told me you'd be down here by yourself this morning getting everything ready. So, I asked him to pick me up, and we came on over to help. I brought along some church clothes that I can change into when the work's all done."

"Morning, sugar. Y'all didn't have to go to all that trouble."

"Well'm… You don't exactly have to furnish me a horse to ride and go out of your way to include me, either."

"I do if I want to keep our boy happy," Sis quipped laughingly, "but you're a pleasure, anyhow."

"I'm glad," Ruthanne answered shyly.

"Ches, honey…" Aunt Sis bent down for a hug as he reached up to her from the motorized wheelchair. "I've saddled Short Stuff and the nag I picked for myself. We'll get Ruthanne fitted out with a mount and then see about hitching the mules."

"You're not riding Pumpkin?" he wanted to know.

"Nope, I left her for Corrie or Torrie. The other can take Thimble, and you know Cassidy's just about claimed Buttons. That puts me and Ruthanne on sale-barn horses, but they need the riding."

"Show me which saddle goes where, and I'll get to work," Ruthanne offered.

"Put your own riggin' on that sorrel mare, and let it go at that. Ches gets special privileges, but those girls will saddle their own horses if they ride with me."

"Pap's awful excited about driving your mules," Ruthanne offered later as they worked over the team. "I reckon you've noticed... His church attendance is kinda spotty, but he's all dressed up and ready this morning."

"I'm glad he's willing to drive for me. It gave me the idea to invite Brother and Mrs. Waller. They're not horse people but always open to a new opportunity for fellowship."

"I've never been around wagons too much, but it looks like a lot of fun."

"Let Ches teach you to drive sometime. Of course, Pap could do it, too. He's welcome to take this team out any time. I've just about talked myself out of the notion of selling them."

Ches ate breakfast with Uncle Andrew and the girls while the two ladies changed clothes, and they all headed off to church.

Pap spent most of the service tugging at the collar of his white suit but fell naturally into the role of showman when he finally climbed aboard the rubber-tired wagon and took up the driving lines.

"Hold on tight, folks," he advised the wagon bunch, wheeling his team expertly out in front of the horseback riders. "This wagon train's westward bound!"

"You're headin' southeast, Pap," Miss Sis quipped and then trilled out a rather unnecessary call for her little pack of stock dogs to fall in with the ride. Roxy whined and romped around with the other dogs, anxious to come along, but Ches worried some about her stamina and the length of time away from her pups. A word or two, gentle but firm, sent her reluctantly back up to the house.

"Just keep 'em lined out down the road, and don't fret over the little nitpicking details," Andrew advised jokingly.

"Not on your life," Pap hollered back. "We best get them details nailed down good and proper, 'specially since y'all got me hauling the preacher."

Brother and Mrs. Waller laughed good-naturedly from the back of the wagon, and even Ethan Fisher- who didn't particularly want to be there- snickered at his first exposure to Phineas Absalom Prescott.

"I hope we didn't take Mrs. Crawford's place in the wagon…"

Mrs. Waller's sweet voice held a note of uncertainty, but Serena Kate tossed the graceful brunette a rather indifferent shrug.

"I haven't been on one of these little jaunts lately. I'll tell you this, though… Nobody's gonna bump Ms. Edna out of anything, not with Miss Sis running the show."

The moment lapsed into a semi-awkward silence until Sis rode over on a big gray gelding. A running-bred quarter horse, he crawfished alongside the unfamiliar wagon faster than the average horse could have managed in a good flat walk.

"I'm so glad y'all came along with us," she told the Wallers with real joy in her voice.

"And we're glad you thought of us," the pastor answered.

"Yes, thanks for having us," his wife added. "I was just asking about Mrs. Crawford."

"Oh?" Sis responded, working to hold her mount to the casual pace but doing it so skillfully that Mrs. Waller never noticed. "Ms. Edna's had a plenty of this in her day. She never was exactly horse crazy, and now… She's glad we can enjoy a little saddle time, but that's about the extent of it. Terry and Jenna invited her out to eat, but I think she carried them home with her instead."

"Bless her heart," Andrew commented, riding up beside his wife, "Ms. Edna still likes to fix for company. Now, Brother Crawford, he always kept a horse or two."

"He sure did," Sis recalled. "Managed to give Ms. Edna some pretty good scares over the years, too."

"I know how she felt," Andrew quipped with a dubious glance at the nervous gray.

"Brother Crawford didn't necessarily thrive on the challenge like I do. He just didn't have any nerves at all. I don't think you could have excited the man by chasing him with a chop axe."

"You ought to have married Brother Crawford or somebody like him," Andrew joked. "You and that catfooted racehorse are setting every nerve I've got on edge."

"Aw," Miss Sis answered dismissively, "he don't mean no harm. We can travel sidewise all day, but I won't have him running off like some kind of idiot while I'm trying to carry on a conversation."

"Sounds like Colonel Durham's daughter, don't she?" Pap Prescott drawled almost to himself.

"Along in the late 60s," Miss Sis remembered with a fond chuckle, "Brother Crawford traded for a big, black Hancock-bred colt. A day or two later, this colt made his way back to the house toting Brother Crawford's empty saddle."

"Oh, dear," Mrs. Waller breathed.

"Poor Ms. Edna was fit to be tied. Not knowing what else to do, she jumped in their Pontiac and came flying over to our place. Mama almost never left home during the week, and the colonel didn't go too many places either, unless he was scouting around for some horses to buy. For whatever reason, though, Ms. Edna found me and Terry there alone."

"What about Nash?" Serena Kate questioned, interested in spite of herself.

"Seems like he was off helpin' Uncle Doc that day or maybe gone fishing. Well, I told her right quick that I'd find Brother Crawford. Ms. Edna was more than willing to watch Terry for me, but she couldn't drive a truck and trailer to haul my horse over there. She figured it would take me too long to ride over, so I loaded a couple of dogs in the turtle hull and—"

*Beyond the Parmalee Bottom* 155

"Wait a minute; wait a minute," Andrew interrupted his wife through a fit of laughter. "These people don't know what a turtle hull is. She put them dogs in the trunk of that big old Pontiac! Ches, get over here. Y'all need to hear this."

"Well, Ms. Edna wouldn't have them up front, not even in an emergency. They had some biscuit hounds over there, but I hated to trust to them when my own good dogs were right handy and wanting to go."

"And just how old were you at the time, little miss search-and-rescue?"

# Chapter Nine

"Oh, I couldn't have been much over eight or nine," Sis decided, continuing her story as they rode along.

"Just a child," Mrs. Waller observed with a sharp little intake of breath.

"Maybe so… But Ms. Edna was a-way out of her element, and I considered myself near enough grown when it came to handling horses."

Keeping the fractious gray in check with light but positive hands on the bridle reins, Sis smiled lovingly at Ches and listened with approval as he provided a little context for her story.

"The colonel liked having a pretty little daughter," he put in, "but wasn't about to pay an extra hand if he could get around it. He treated Aunt Sis like an adult and expected a full day's work. He got it, plus a sweet smile. And a batch of biscuits, too, if her Mama was otherwise occupied."

"Ms. Edna's eyes got big as saucers," Sis remembered, "but I eased up to that black colt, caught him, and retightened the saddle."

The natural cadence of East Texas storytelling seemed tailored to the rocking motion from the team as the wagon rolled along. For Brother and Mrs. Waller, recent transplants in their early forties, the lighthearted tale offered a glimpse into the long-gone way of life that had shaped and polished this rare jewel of a lady.

"Surely she didn't expect you to hunt Brother Crawford a'foot?" Ches asked.

The Wallers shot him startled glances, so Ruthanne tried to explain.

"Miss Sis couldn't keep up with the dogs or see the country around her on foot. If somebody's out there- maybe needing help bad- and there's a horse handy, you check the saddle, stick your foot in the stirrup, and see what he'll do."

"I suppose so," Brother Waller answered, polite but still unconvinced.

"I can still see that colt," Miss Sis told them, her voice taking on a far-off quality. "Big and stout with a white star in his forehead and a shine on that black coat like patent leather. He rolled his nose and snorted like I was some kind of horse-eating monster. I talked to him for a minute, trying to soothe him, but I wanted to get to Brother Crawford. I kept hearing the colonel in the back of my mind. 'Quit tiptoeing around that big rascal and show him who's boss.'"

"You didn't miss it much," Pap observed with a chuckle. "I can hear him now."

"I'd left home without my spurs, and there was no sign of a quirt on Brother Crawford's saddle. So, I turned to my kid brother. 'Give me your belt.' Terry hadn't grown up on the Durham place without learning a thing or two. He snatched that little belt out through the loops on his britches, passed it to me, then reached up and caught Ms. Edna by the hand. 'Come on; time to get outta the way.'"

"Smart kid," Ethan mumbled from his place inside the wagon.

"Brother Crawford's stirrups hung a-way too long for me but I caught one, bounced off it, and landed in the saddle. I gathered my reins and took a good, solid mane hold with the same hand. Blackie never knew I was there until that belt came down across his rump. He bellowed like a fighting bull and bucked right through the yard fence. White pickets went flying every which way. The colt lost his footing somehow and landed flat out on that hard-packed ground."

Mrs. Waller looked physically ill, and Serena Kate made an involuntary noise in the back of her throat as she envisioned one of her daughters in such a predicament, but Miss Sis seemed exhilarated by the telling of it.

"So much for showing the horse who's boss," Brother Waller quipped in an attempt to break the suspense with a little humor.

"Oh," Sis answered lightly, "I felt bad about the yard fence. They'd just whitewashed it, and anybody ought've had sense enough to lead a bronc outside the gate before getting on him. Still, the whole business added considerably to that colt's education. Only the Good Lord above kept him from landing on me, but that fall knocked some of the wind and a lot of the fight out of him. When I cut him one more good lick with the belt, he scrambled to his feet and lined out in a ground-eating trot."

"Felt bad about the yard fence?" her pastor echoed in disbelief.

"Well, I did... The colonel offered to fix their fence, but Ms. Edna said the sight of it would only call up a moment that took ten years off her life."

"I don't doubt it," Mrs. Waller breathed, still shaken by the mental image of a small child being tossed around like a rag doll on the back of a wildly pitching horse.

"The dogs didn't know exactly what I was after, but they knew their business and ranged out ahead. Ike was a tough old yella dog born the same day I was, and Priss was a young brindle-colored gyp. Sure enough, they found Brother Crawford before I did. He had a big yard dog with him. Ike rolled the mutt on general principle, but I called him off before the fight really commenced."

Having heard quite a bit about the well-loved former pastor, Brother Waller found himself invested in the story.

"How badly was he injured?"

"The dog? Why, they never even had time to bloody each other."

"No, ma'am... I was wondering about Brother Crawford."

Miss Sis smiled fondly, but tears welled in her eyes as her tender heart lost itself in the past.

"Tough as an old boot... I rode up on him picking wild plums down along the creek. He grinned at the sight of me sitting way up there on that black horse and shook his head. 'How do you like that; bucked off by a kid's pony! Edna's been needin' a mess of plums to make jelly, but I've been too busy fooling with that colt. When he unloaded me right here next to this plum thicket, I just started in to pick.'"

"He wasn't hurt at all?" Ethan asked incredulously.

"Just said the Lord had many ways of humbling a man, and big stout high-bred colts were as good as any. He showed me a half gallon or so of ripe plums gathered up inside a white cotton undershirt and picked three or four more, handing them up for me to eat. I thanked him and kinda worked up an apology for riding the bronc over and through his picket fence."

"That's about right," Serena Kate muttered in mild irritation. "The two of y'all passing the time of day while poor Ms. Edna was still worried out of her mind."

"Brother Crawford sized up the colt with a glance and then grinned at me again. 'Tore up the yard fence, huh? Reckon he'll pack both of us back to the house?'"

"P-pack you both?" Mrs. Waller stuttered. "What did you say to that?"

"Ain't but one way to find out," Ches and Ruthanne guessed in near-perfect unison.

"True back then," Miss Sis observed laughingly, "and it's true today. Sliding over the cantle, I reached down and took the makeshift bundle. Brother Crawford stepped into the saddle with nary a sign of trouble from the colt, so I locked an arm around his waist. We jogged off to the house neat as you please, wild plums and all."

"Just when I think I've heard all the stories, every funny or exciting or poignant memory," Ches said fondly to his aunt, "you come up with something else. This one ought to make a magazine article: 'The Preacher, The Plums, and the Big Hancock Colt.'"

"You've always soaked up my old tales like a sponge, honey, but it never once occurred to me that you'd reproduce them in print."

"I changed her name in the very first article I published," he explained to Ruthanne, "but the 'Aunt Sadie' stories have always been a big hit with readers."

The young couple managed a few quiet minutes together before Cassidy and the twins crowded around them once more.

"Show us some of your tricks," Torrie pleaded.

"Just the easy ones," Cassidy added in a persuasive tone.

Pleased by their interest but not about to give in, Ruthanne shook her head and glided a reassuring hand down the sorrel's neck.

"This little mare seems pretty steady," she admitted, "but I'd hate to blow her mind. Why don't you tell me how things are going with the school musical?"

"I still can't believe you've never seen *Oklahoma*... Not even the old Rodgers and Hammerstein movie?"

"No, but I enjoy reading lines with you. We'll do it again any time you need somebody."

"You and Ches and Mother are better than the actual cast." Cassidy giggled with a mischievous little sparkle in her eyes. "If I could bottle all that country and sprinkle it out on the theater class, we'd bring the house down!"

"Nothin' like the real thing," Ruthanne drawled brightly.

Always keenly observant of speech patterns, mannerisms, and other little things that could be folded into her bag of tricks, Cassidy warmed to the subject.

"We all know the cerebral palsy affects your voice," she said matter-of-factly to her cousin, "but it's not too distracting. Something I can't quite put my finger on, though... You can sit around in your wheelchair, reading lines, and come off more like a cowboy than my classmates do strutting back and forth across the stage."

"Give your mother a big part of the credit for that, cuz. By the time I came down to spend that first summer with her, the old colonel was long gone and the

Durham line had just about run out of horsemen. Miss Sis took what the Good Lord sent her way and made one."

"Yes," Ruthanne added quietly, "and I'd say she done a fine job of it."

Recognizing this shy compliment for what it was, Torrie McKendrick opened her mouth to tease the young couple, but just then, realization hit Cassidy.

"Hey, Ruthanne," she moaned, drawing out the words for effect, "you changed the subject. Quit talking, and show us the Roman ride or hang off one side of your saddle and then flip to the other. I know you can do it!"

"I tried to tell y'all before," Ruthanne chided with a longsuffering shake of her head, "trick riding takes a bright smile, quick reflexes, strength, and flexibility."

"Your smile would melt anybody's heart," Ches told her sincerely, "one-on-one or by the grandstand full."

"Aww… Thank you, darling," she sighed, laughing a little as she remembered the embarrassment of speaking those words to him accidentally. "I hold up fine for ordinary horseback work and day-to-day chores, but performing is quite another matter."

"Well, thanks for letting me ride Buttons, anyhow," Cassidy said, finally managing to give up gracefully.

"The horse belongs to Ches," Ruthanne reminded her. "So does Thimble, for that matter. If you're going to thank somebody, thank your cousin."

"Thimble and Buttons wouldn't still be here if they hadn't belonged to you," the younger girl observed with a knowing smile. "You so much as hint at wanting to ride your trick horse, and I'll find myself in the wagon."

"Don't be so sure about that, Cassidy Diane. I may trump you… But watching you ride makes your mother happy, and I wouldn't touch that with a ten-foot pole."

Having ridden ahead, Miss Sis circled back to join the group as if on cue.

"Y'all better not be pestering Ruthanne," she warned the girls. "If she felt like doing all those stunts, she'd still be traveling up and down the road."

Ruthanne smiled reassuringly at the younger girls and then listened as Ches and his aunt discussed the upcoming auction.

"They eat, sleep, and breathe horse sale," Cassidy muttered by way of a warning. "Come and find us whenever you get tired of it."

"The girls aren't any bother," Ruthanne said as they drifted off. "Cassidy and the twins treat me like a favorite aunt or an older sister. I'm kinda flattered by all the attention, but the new'll wear off directly."

"I don't know about that," Ches objected with a chuckle. "Letting them make teacakes with you was a big hit."

"You're naturally sweet and kind," Miss Sis added. "More accepting than the high school girls they think are so cool but still young enough to hold some interest."

"Cassidy accuses me of acting just like you," Ruthanne confided with a chuckle, "but it hasn't stopped her from hanging around."

"All three girls will probably accept little hints and pointers more readily from you than they would from me."

"Why do you say that?"

"I was past forty by the time Cassidy was born, and at that, I was the youngest in my circle of friends. Ches is a boy, so what could he possibly know... My daughter's never had too many young ladies she could look to as role models. You may be a little old fashioned for her taste, but she'll gladly overlook that minor detail."

A bright child, naturally gifted with horses and eager to please, little Miss Sis had readily adopted the lifestyle of her parents and grandparents. Somewhat naively, she had expected the same from her daughter. Love of the land, the presence of mind to shut a gate after you came through it, and even good manners were supposed to come as naturally as breathing.

"How 'bout that little patch of shade just inside the gate on the old Bateman place?" Andrew asked, breaking her reverie as he rode up alongside.

"That ought to do for a picnic ground. I'll lope ahead and get the gate."

"Let me do that, baby doll. It'll give me a chance to stretch Galahad out and let him really walk," he said in reference to his tall, slender-made gaited horse.

Everyone enjoyed the quiet, restful spot along with a good dinner and some more conversation. The distant sound of a pickup's horn reached them as they left the Bateman pasture behind and headed back toward the sale barn, three long blasts, a pause, and the same signal repeated.

Miss Sis gazed intently in the direction of the sound, not because she expected to see anything but out of the same highly focused attention that animates a bird dog on point.

"Ches, honey?" she asked softly, almost absentmindedly.

"No, ma'am," he said clearly, apologizing even as he answered her unspoken question.

"Mr. Prescott?"

Her voice rose ever so slightly, carrying this polite inquiry to the white-suited rascal she generally addressed as Pap.

"Yo," the old man affirmed quietly.

"One time," she instructed, and a .22 pistol cracked sharply into the afternoon stillness.

"Holy Toledo!" Ethan Fisher yelped. "Don't you people ever use cell phones?"

The startled mules lunged into their collars, snatching the wagon forward, but Pap stowed his gun away in time to apply steadying pressure through the driving lines and brake pedal.

One gunshot failed to incite much commotion among the riding horses, and nobody took time to answer Ethan's complaint. Instead, the little group looked instinctively to Miss Sis.

*Beyond the Parmalee Bottom* 164

"Bring the wagon in slow, Pap," she said calmly. "You girls can just ease along with him."

Ready and willing to go, the big gray reacted to an almost imperceptible shifting of her weight in the saddle. By the time Cassidy and the McKendrick twins realized they had been left out of a bracing gallop, any chance to complain was long gone.

Scarcely over thirteen hands and blocky, Short Stuff moved differently than the running-bred gray, but an urgent hiss or two from Ches had the little cowpony digging for all he was worth. Ruthanne entered the race half a jump later, and Andrew put his lanky Tennessee Walker into a road-eating gait behind the quarter horses.

"Figured I could call y'all in," Lonnie Ray Leggett observed, never turning a hair as Miss Sis slid to a halt beside his pickup with her dogs a little in the lead and a string of riders coming up from behind.

The battered Chevrolet had once been cream-colored or maybe yellow, but forty-odd years of grime and rust obscured the original paint job. Lonnie Ray stepped carefully from the vehicle, resting most of his negligible weight against the passenger door. Telltale signs of pain lurked around his eyes and in the rasping old voice, but a smile twitched at the corners of his mouth. Colonel Durham's daughter made quite the picture on horseback, and years fell away as he gazed up through the gentle fall sunlight. Miss Sis, a beauty at any age, looked about seventeen perched up there atop the dancing gray gelding.

"You might've waited," she scolded laughingly. "We were headed back, anyhow."

"I quit buyin' green bananas a couple months ago, Sis. Waitin' around ain't much of an option these days."

Concern flickered behind her teasing expression as she stepped lightly to the ground and handed a lead line to Ches. Her gaze took in Sonny Boy Leggett, waiting patiently behind the wheel, and then settled once again on the old horseman.

"In that case, I'll get right down to business. What brings you out this-a-way?"

Instead of answering, Lonnie Ray sized up the fractious gray and then allowed his practiced eye to skim the other riders.

"Big old rascal's got more energy than he knows what to do with, and you're likewise afflicted. Why don't you switch horses with the blond-headed girl? I expect blondie'll calm that scamp down a right smart, and you'll stir up the sleepy-eyed sorrel mare to where she'll do some good."

"Makes for interesting speculation," Sis admitted. "Both horses belong to the barn, and I wanted Ruthanne to enjoy her ride, not spend it in fear of her life."

The flinty old eyes gave Ruthanne a few moments of deeper scrutiny before Lonnie Ray spoke again.

"This girl will never equal you for style and flash, Miss Sis, but the horse that overmatches her will be a sure-enough bad son of a gun."

"I don't doubt Ruthanne would be hard to overmatch," Sis drawled, arching an eyebrow as she considered the young lady's success as a showstopping carnival rider, "but she's pretty special to Ches. I figure to keep her off the bad ones."

"That do put a different light on it… But the boy's crazy about his Aunt Sis, and that never kept you off the rough string. Anyhow, I didn't come out here to meddle in your business."

"Sure enough?" Sis asked, fighting to keep the chuckle out of her voice.

"How do, Ches?" he inquired briefly, redirecting the conversation.

"Just fine, Mr. Leggett. It's good to see you."

"You and Miss Sis steered me right that night at the horse sale, and I thought y'all might like to know that the Good Lord finally got ahold of me."

Sis reached quickly to hug the old man's neck, and Ches leaned from the saddle to shake his hand.

"I don't know nothin' about religion," Sonny Boy admitted, emerging from the pickup to lean across the hood, "but the old buzzard's changed a plenty. I'll vouch for that."

*Beyond the Parmalee Bottom* 166

"Sonny's good to read the Bible to me of an evening. We've been talking, too. Hope he comes around quicker than I did, but y'all may have to keep workin' on him after I'm gone."

While Ches listened intently to Lonnie Ray, Sonny Boy caught Sis's eye and spoke in a lowered tone.

"He ain't had the strength to stand in three days, Miss Sis. Not until he seen y'all ride up... Hurting all the time, and still, never a cross word. I figured we'd drag him into Pinevale kickin' and cussin' one day if he didn't get horned, stomped, or killed in a bar fight first. But, now, he claims it's all part of God's plan."

A brief frown of concern failed to erase the joy that shone in her eyes, and before she could assist the old-time cowhand back into his truck, his gaze drifted off up the road.

"Who's a-driving them mules?" he demanded, eyes narrowing in an attempt at recognition.

"Pap Prescott," Ches answered obligingly.

"Why, that old windbag," Lonnie Ray chuckled in friendly recollection. "When did he drift back into this country?"

Ches shot a quick glance at his sweetheart, but Ruthanne looked more bemused than offended by the offhand characterization of her grandfather. They waited then, in companionable silence, until Pap arrived with trace chains and harness jangling. When his passengers alighted to stretch their legs, Cassidy and the McKendrick twins followed suit, dropping easily down from their saddles.

Miss Sis introduced the pastor and his wife, including Ethan Fisher almost as an afterthought.

"I reckon you know everybody else, Lonnie Ray."

Pap delivered a lighthearted insult or two, tactfully concealing his shock at the old rounder's physical decline. Serena Kate's perpetual weariness lifted at the sight of someone so obviously in need. She spoke the truth kindly and without a hint of embarrassment or apology.

"You look bad, Mr. Leggett."

Childhood fears of the old man's rough tongue and rougher reputation fell away as she laid a hand on his arm, gave a nurturing pat, and tried to guide him back into the truck. Instead of shaking her hand off, Lonnie Ray covered it gently with one of his own, but he remained standing.

"I feel worse than I look, child, and that's one reason I'm here. Want you to have my saddle, Miss Sis. I'm goin' into Pinevale of my own accord."

"You reckon it's come to that?"

"I had a pistol layin' ready, and reason enough to handle things my way, but God's been a-working on my heart. The next few days or weeks ain't likely to be too pleasant, but knowing all He's done for me and a little of the good a-waitin' on the other side, I'll just string along with Him."

A lengthy pause followed this statement, but Miss Sis finally spoke with only the slightest tremor behind her words. Fighting the lump in his own throat, Ches wondered how she managed to find her voice at all.

"Well, sir, me and Serena Kate will go into town with you. She's been working at Pinevale and knows the place like the back of her hand."

At this, Ethan bulldozed his way up into the conversation.

"Wait a minute," he snapped. "You can't just volunteer my wife as a free nurse for every old, worn-out bum who comes asking. She spends most of her time working as it is!"

Despite her boots and their underslung riding heel, the big deadbeat towered over Miss Sis. With straight spine and flashing eyes, though, she gave the impression of looking down at him.

"Serena Kate may be your wife, but she's also a McKendrick. I can remember her great-grandparents, and I've known every one of the redheaded firecrackers since. Whatever their faults, the McKendricks never needed anybody to think for them."

"I've wasted my whole afternoon out here bouncing around in a covered wagon, and I don't intend to spend the rest of the day babysitting. Don't even try that queen-bee glare on me!"

Chafing under the stigma of a loudmouthed outsider, Ethan grabbed her arm roughly as he spat the last words. Andrew Hollister swung a leg over to dismount, and Ches snatched at the bullwhip on his aunt's saddle. But Lonnie Ray's right hand struck like a snake, bony fingers clamping down on the overgrown youngster's throat.

Ethan felt his back slam against the cold metal fender as the old man reversed their positions. With no other way to prop himself up, Lonnie Ray hung from his chokehold like a cow dog swinging from a bovine's ear. Dropping his leg back into place, Andrew settled in his saddle to watch the show. Ches allowed the whip to hang loose and ready in his hand while Ruthanne, for her part, moved up to take charge of the startled gray.

"Never lay a hand on the boss lady," Lonnie Ray rasped. "For that matter, don't raise your voice to her. We don't call her Miss Sis on account of a bank balance and not just out of respect for her old daddy, either. She stayed on the land, wheelin' and dealin' to scratch up enough work for the rest of us, when she could've lived soft and easy somewhere else."

As a more-or-less detached observer, Pap began to worry about the length of this speech and the sickly green pallor of Ethan Fisher's face.

"Steady, now, Lonnie Ray..." he muttered as if to himself. "Better let the boy take a breath."

"I can't make you get right with the Lord, junior, but I'd sure advise it. In the meantime, let me tell you this. Old Amos McKendrick's only granddaughter left here pert, sassy, and maybe just a mite overfed. She came home bone tired and poor as a snake. We don't aim to set by and watch her support your lazy self."

"Ugg, ahh..." Ethan gagged, somewhere between a moan and a squeak.

"One week... Get you a job, or clear out of this county." Then with a glance toward Miss Sis, "You got enough old-time hands to make that stick?"

Nodding, she gave him a tight little smile.

"I don't need a tough crew for that; me and Ches'll see to it."

Satisfied, Lonnie Ray relaxed his hold and took one long step back. Ethan coughed and sputtered, rubbing his throat, but remained fairly steady on his feet. The tall old horseman swayed dangerously, and only swift intervention from Miss Sis kept him upright.

"Let's get him in the pickup," Serena Kate suggested, moving in quickly on Lonnie Ray's other side with little more than a passing glance toward her discomfited husband.

"Want me to trail along?"

Ches didn't raise his voice or put any form of address on the question, but everyone knew it was meant for Miss Sis.

"Thanks, honey, but I'll let you hear something. Finish out the ride and go on to church, just keep the twins close."

"Y'all stay with Ches and mind whatever Miss Ruthanne tells you," Serena Kate tossed automatically over her shoulder.

Corrie and Torrie knew how to fend for themselves, but their mother's sudden and almost unconscious elevation of Ruthanne brought out matching grins.

"Ww-what should I do?" Ethan inquired meekly after several ragged, gulping breaths.

"Keys are in the car," she advised curtly. "Look for me when you see me coming."

"I didn't always show up at school with the nicest clothes or the newest toy," Sonny Boy Leggett mused as if to himself. "I had one thing for sure, though, and still do today. I had the toughest old man who ever drew breath."

Serena Kate possessed a caring spirit and months of practical nursing experience, but in time of emergency she looked instinctively to the one person who had always been there.

"Miss Sis... His pulse... It's awful ragged."

Lonnie Ray sat contentedly on the worn bench seat, eyes roving past his caregivers to the little group of spectators. Gesturing feebly, he beckoned Brother Waller to his side.

"Give me your knife..."

"I haven't got one on me, sir."

"Well," Lonnie Ray observed reaching into his own pocket, "a country preacher sure ought to tote one. Take mine. I'd count it a favor if you wouldn't mention this little ruckus at my funeral. Tell 'em I lived hard, and given another chance, I'd do different. Tell 'em the way to be saved, and make 'em see how important it is..."

"That's my privilege, Mr. Leggett. My privilege and my calling..."

Lonnie Ray shook the preacher's hand and then looked from Sis to Serena Kate.

"Can you girls scooch in here amongst us, or do we put Sonny Boy out in the road?"

As the pickup pulled away toward town, Ruthanne dismounted and tied her sorrel to the back of the wagon.

"The safest place around this gray horse is on him," she explained, retightened the cinch and stepped casually aboard.

Brother and Mrs. Waller climbed back into the wagon, but when Ethan placed a foot on the bottom step, Ches flicked his aunt's whip out menacingly.

"Back up, knot head. I'll have somebody pull that car out to the road ditch. You don't step foot on Durham land until Miss Sis says different. Nor in a Durham wagon, either... Let 'em roll, Pap."

They rode nearly out of sight of the trudging figure behind them before Andrew worked his way up alongside Ches.

"It's got to be almost two miles back to the sale barn..."

"Shame it ain't further," his nephew responded, and the tight little smile looked almost eerily familiar.

"We don't charge no extra for the show," Pap joked to the preacher and his wife.

"Old Lonnie Ray was right," Ches said quietly to Ruthanne as they rode. "That gray settled right down for you."

"Where Miss Sis stays keyed up and ready," she replied with a smile and a shrug, "I stay about half sleepy. Most horses have got sense enough to know the difference."

Ruthanne never seemed to hurry, but she proved highly efficient when it came to helping Ches down from the saddle and back into his wheelchair. So, Andrew brushed the sweat from his own horse's back and turned him loose in the pasture.

Ches felt compelled to apologize to Brother and Mrs. Waller but wondered how to go about it in the absence of any great remorse. He and Aunt Sis had stood side by side for years, meeting every threat with hard-edged resolve. They practiced Christian charity and forbearance, but it wasn't always the warm and cuddly variety. For the first time, he found himself wondering how such tactics looked to the outside observer.

"I'm right sorry y'all got caught up in the middle of that little deal. Hope it won't stop you from riding with us again."

Drawing in a long breath, the pastor considered his response.

"I don't think young Ethan would have acted the way he did if he hadn't been allowed to walk over people in the past. Be that as it may... Our actions as Christians should reflect a higher standard, not mirror the way we are treated. All in all, I was thankful to see you reach for a bullwhip instead of calling on Mr. Prescott and his pistol."

"Me and Aunt Sis don't like to use a heavier hand than what's called for, but I won't see her pushed around. Not ever..."

# Chapter Ten

Brother and Mrs. Waller took their departure, and with everything else turned out to graze, the rest of the little group gathered around the wagon and team.

"Why not leave the mules hitched?" Ruthanne inquired brightly. "They're not tired, and Miss Sis mentioned something about you teaching me how to drive."

"Nothing to it," Ches assured her, "not for a topnotch rider like you. Time's running a little short, but I guess we could take 'em to church."

"Oh, I couldn't go looking like this," she answered regretfully. "I reckon the driving lesson'll have to wait."

"You look very pretty, like always."

"Just keep on telling me that, Ches. I like to hear it. But these are barn clothes, not church clothes."

"Cassidy, take Ruthanne up to the house and show her those dresses your mother laid out early this morning. I don't imagine Sis figured you'd need one today," Andrew continued. "She wanted you to have the dresses, though, and digging them out gave her something to do besides fidget and wait for daylight."

"Take them," Cassidy pleaded. "Ms. Edna's arthritis is the only reason they

*Beyond the Parmalee Bottom* 173

haven't already been cut down for me. They're pretty and all but went out of style about a hundred years ago."

"Just the ticket for me," Ruthanne observed, laughing at herself as well as the younger girl's exaggeration.

"Oh, I didn't mean..." Cassidy started in a moment of seriousness but then found herself caught up in the laughter.

"I'll untie the mules for Ches," Andrew told them. "We'll make us a little circle before he picks you girls up at the house."

"Y'all unload your stuff," Ches called to the twins, "so somebody can move that car outside the gate."

"I'll move it," Torrie volunteered, jumping at a chance to get behind the wheel. "It won't take all of us to powder Ruthanne's nose and help her pick out a dress."

Pulling up alongside the familiar white pickets that marked the edge of the yard, Ches rested one foot on the brake pedal and let the lines hang slack. He and Torrie settled down to wait, but Pap caught a ride with Uncle Andrew.

"Wonder what's keeping them," the redheaded girl scoffed impatiently. "There can't be much to choose from. Miss Sis never gets rid of anything."

"The boss lady wouldn't even look like herself if she changed with every passing trend."

"Huh, I never really thought of it like that."

Minutes later, Ruthanne stepped out onto the porch. A pale pink dress with white tatting at the collar made her honey-colored locks glisten in the afternoon sunlight. The dress complemented her feminine shape, too, without sacrificing the demure beauty she always projected. When Ches finally managed to speak, practicality sidelined half a dozen heartfelt compliments.

"Grab a towel so Ruthanne doesn't mess up her dress," he called to the younger girls. Cassidy rolled her eyes as he knocked dirt and horsehair from the upholstery to prove his point. "Stand at their heads a minute while I help her into the wagon."

"Zip the dress, fetch the towel, hold the mules," Cassidy enumerated in a voice full of high drama. "What am I, Cinderella?"

But Corrie McKendrick stepped forward obligingly to pet the team and talk to them while Ches crawled to the back of the wagon and offered his hand.

"Cassidy's right," Ruthanne chided, but the hushed warmth of her tone bespoke intimacy rather than complaint. "You're spoiling me rotten, Ches, and we mustn't run the girls off their feet."

"That's what kids are for," he assured her with a grin, "to fetch and carry and open the gate. Besides, if anybody ever needed spoiling, it's you."

"Fetch and carry and open the gate… Straight from your Aunt Sis, I expect."

"She's generally right, too."

"Well," Ruthanne decided with a loving smile as she arranged her towel on the bucket seat from a '97 Buick sedan, "I hope Cassidy and the twins are watching close enough to learn how they ought to be treated someday."

"Wish I had a pair of gloves for you," Ches observed, hesitating as he handed over the driving lines.

"A Sunday-go-to-meeting dress doesn't change who I am, Ches. I ride barehanded, and if you can manage a team that way, I can, too."

"I guess trick riding and stunt routines ain't the lightest work in the world," he said with a chuckle.

The younger girls piled noisily onto the rear seats, but Ches only had eyes for Ruthanne. After a few basic pointers from him, she eased off the brake pedal and spoke to the mules.

"Haw around there," she called with quiet confidence in her voice.

The team swung obediently into a wide turn, heading downhill toward the blacktop.

"Sure you've never driven before?" Ches questioned as they lined out down the road.

"Somehow the opportunity never came up," she reflected lightly. "We've been around commercial carriage rides, rodeo grand entries, and draft horse hitches, but I never actually handled the lines."

"You must've watched pretty close," he decided with a smile in his voice. "They're working just right for you."

Eight hooves beat a musical rhythm against the road's hard surface, and jangling harness made for a pleasant counterpoint. Even the girls' chattering voices blended into a lively buzzing sound. The young couple up front enjoyed a comfortable silence, soaking up each other's presence as naturally as they breathed the crisp afternoon air.

"I like the smell of wood smoke," Ruthanne said quietly.

"Mmm," he agreed. "Daddy must've touched off his brush pile after they got home from Ms. Edna's."

"Reckon he'll leave it long enough to come to church?"

"I'm not sure exactly when he set it afire, but it's just a little one on the edge of his yard. Maybe it's burnt down enough to leave."

"Gee over, Mack," Ruthanne directed coolly, pulling the mules and wagon aside for a passing car.

The familiar cadence of hoofbeats continued as Ches lapsed into observation of his beautiful companion. After a while, though, his quiet admiration spilled over into words.

"I don't think you've got the least notion what a gorgeous sight I'm seeing, Ruthanne. I'm afraid telling you all the time will start to sound silly or take away from the meaning, but I just can't seem to help it. You're not only the prettiest girl I've ever laid eyes on but also a real lady whose beauty starts on the inside."

"Ches Durham," she murmured plaintively, "I don't know how you expect me to

*Beyond the Parmalee Bottom* 176

drive these mules and cry at the same time."

He reached over to take the driving lines, but she shook her head with a teary-eyed smile. When an unexpected thought crowded in on the joy of the moment, she glanced quickly over her shoulder to check the twins' level of distraction.

"Am I as pretty as Serena Kate?" she asked with obvious reluctance.

Ches drew in a long breath and prayed for the right words.

"I was altogether infatuated with Serena Kate," he finally admitted, "and I loved the idea that somebody actually needed me."

"Oh, Ches, plenty of us count on you. Miss Sis and your parents, Cassidy and Uncle Andrew…"

"I'm blessed, alright," he conceded readily, "but they've all given me more than I could ever give in return. I wanted somebody my own age to love, and spoil, and see after."

"Mmm…"

"Serena Kate functions on caffeine, fast food, and maybe three hours of sleep a night. She's lived under constant stress and still kept her looks. That's amazing in itself. But believe me, Ruthanne, your kind of beauty is in a class all its own."

"Well, then, how come…"

"Aunt Sis set a pretty high mark in my mind, but I finally decided that kind of young lady must be an awfully rare jewel in today's world. If one did exist, what would she want with me? Serena Kate deserved a soft place to land, and I thought I could give her that."

"Serena Kate McKendrick is a fool," she whispered with a vehemence that snapped his head around. "Oh, Ches, I don't mean to sound ugly," came the instant apology. "I'm just so grateful God put you in my path."

Ches snatched the Stetson off his head automatically but still had the presence of mind not to crush Colonel Durham's good hat. Resting his free hand on Ruthanne's arm, he leaned in to place a gentle kiss on her cheek.

"I'm grateful, too," he breathed directly into her ear.

Ruthanne's long, blissful sigh echoed the pleasant tingle that rushed up the back of his neck.

"Mercy me," Cassidy sang out in an exaggerated drawl. "What *would* Miss Sis say?"

Ches stiffened in shock. Concern for Ruthanne and her potential embarrassment dispelled his own heady excitement. Calm and collected as always, his sweetheart met the situation with a radiant smile.

"She'd say children ought to be seen and not heard."

The humor sparkling in Ruthanne's hazel eyes proved hard to resist, and Cassidy laughed until she cried.

"You two are about as slow as Christmas," she accused good-naturedly, "but things may heat up sooner than I ever guessed!"

Caught up in their friends' amusement, the McKendrick girls hooped and hollered until the mules upped their steady stride to a shambling trot.

"Walk, now, Mack... Easy, General." Her voice and a little pressure on the driving lines brought them right back down to the desired pace. That done, Ruthanne decided to use Cassidy's joking observation as a teachable moment. "Ches and I respect the Lord and each other. Even so, our feelings run plenty hot. It doesn't take mussed clothes or hay in your hair to let a gentleman know you care for him."

Whether or not Cassidy and the twins fully understood this bit of homespun wisdom, they settled right down.

"What a girl," Ches marveled in silent admiration of Ruthanne's wholesome, unselfconscious outlook. Then, his thoughts turned to prayer, "Call that little speech to mind, Lord, when they're old enough to need it."

The wagon and team wasn't a particularly uncommon sight at McKendrick Missionary Baptist, but it drew a certain amount of attention. Though careful of her lovely dress, Ruthanne passed the lines to Ches and hopped nimbly down to tie the mules.

Despite the frailty of advanced years, Edna Crawford reached up in an automatic attempt to steady Ches as he stepped carefully down.

"I reckon Miss Sis took everything in stride?" the elderly lady inquired, having already learned of Lonnie Ray Leggett's near collapse. "If she was upset or flustered, you'd still be with her."

"Yes'm… Aunt Sis is alright, but Mr. Leggett looks to be in a bad way."

Ms. Edna walked alongside Ches as they crossed the churchyard while Ruthanne trailed slightly behind.

"I do feel for the man, but only God's abundant mercies could've kept him alive long enough to repent of his wicked ways. Of course," she reflected, "the same could be said for us all."

Cassidy dodged the task of filling in for Miss Sis at the piano but only because Pap enjoyed picking his guitar. Ches missed his aunt's playing, but the old hymns still touched his heart. Meeting with the church family allowed him to feel the presence of God in a very special way, and Ruthanne's nearness in the pew beside him proved an unaccustomed blessing.

Ches appreciated Brother Waller and the amount of study he put in but still missed Brother Crawford's old-time sermons, delivered in an East Texas drawl almost as comforting as the familiar King James phrasing.

"Y'all load up quick if you're ridin' home with us," he told Cassidy and the twins when the service ended. "We'd best scat before dark catches us."

"Be careful on the road," Ms. Edna cautioned, "and tell Sis we missed her tonight."

"Yes, ma'am, we sure will," Ches answered, glancing back just long enough to see Ruthanne lean in for a quick hug.

"Every road-worn ex-trick rider needs a wagon, Ches," she quipped, nestling back into the comfort of her bucket seat, "especially those of us who've gone soft and lazy."

*Beyond the Parmalee Bottom* 179

"There's not a lazy bone in your body," he snorted, rejecting the self-criticism.

"Well," she answered almost playfully, "let's don't argue." Then in a more serious tone, "My heart goes out to Mr. Leggett, but I've certainly enjoyed our day."

"Any day with you is a good one, Ruthanne. Lonnie Ray lived tough and about half mean. Still, he's been good to the Durham clan or as good as he knew how to be. It's hard to see him backed into a corner."

"I know, but you can be thankful for his salvation. It's an added blessing that the Lord used you and Miss Sis to reach him. We'll go and visit him, Ches, if you'd like. Meantime, the notion of courting as we jog to and from church behind a team is awfully sweet."

"Not nearly as sweet as you are," he countered. "Besides, a light driving horse and fancy buggy would serve better than this pair of mules."

"Mack and General suit me just fine," she answered, laughing softly, "and so do you."

"Would you two quit sweet-talking each other and let those mules trot," Cassidy interrupted. "We'll never get home at this rate."

Ruthanne smiled sheepishly and then raised an eyebrow at Ches in unspoken inquiry.

"I don't generally trot 'em back toward the barn, bad habits and all that, but I doubt it'll hurt much of anything this evening. We can trot a ways and then slow down for the last quarter mile or so."

"Alrighty," she agreed. "Hang onto your hat."

By the time Ruthanne brought the mules back down to a walk, Torrie could see the sale barn ahead.

"Our car's gone," she observed.

"Yep," her sister agreed as they turned into the driveway, "but everybody else is parked up at the big house."

"She's right," Ches observed, taking in the extra vehicles up on the hill. "Looks like the whole bunch has gathered to wait for Aunt Sis to come home. I'll get Scooter or Daddy or somebody to help me see about the mules."

"I don't mind helping, Ches."

"In that dress? No, ma'am, you won't."

"Mother left me to unhitch them once while she went and did something else," Cassidy volunteered. "I tangled the harness so badly that she was probably tempted to disown me, but I never had to do it again."

Sure enough, they found Scooter up at the house. He tousled his nieces' hair as they unloaded, helped Ruthanne down, and then settled himself in the wagon beside Ches.

"Would've made the ride today," he joked, stripping off harness in the lighted hallway of the sale barn, "if I'd known Lonnie Ray was gonna give my new brother-in-law a good choking."

"I expect that was the old renegade's last scrap, but he sure got his point across. I'm just glad things turned out as well as they did."

"Thanks for taking care of the twins after things went haywire. If it wasn't for you and Miss Sis... Well, I ain't nothin' but a good-time bachelor uncle. Still, anybody can see them girls have got a tough row. I sometimes think they'd be better off with Seth and his wife, but Serena Kate won't never stand still for that."

Infatuation with Serena Kate seemed a distant memory, now, but the idea of her parting from the twins triggered a much deeper pang of sympathy than Ches expected.

"She's got to have something to hold on to," he insisted. "We'll get 'em raised if it takes the whole community. Aunt Sis rode herd on all of us, didn't she?"

"She did that," Scooter agreed, and his trademark grin crept slowly back into place. "You had two good parents, but they wouldn't put you a'horseback so you just packed up and left. Beat anything I ever saw!"

"Mom and Daddy finally came around," Ches countered. "It just took them a little while to figure out what the homeplace meant to me."

"I swear, you're every bit as hardheaded as the boss lady. It runs in the Durham line like red hair on us McKendricks."

"Red hair and a few other traits I could name…"

"My sister kinda stood your world on end, didn't she? And still, I've never heard you say an unkind word about her."

"Unkind word? Why would I? You know how silly I was over her. I held her up as some kind of angelic creature that could do no wrong when she'd already shown us just how wrong she could go. Whatever trouble and heartache followed, I brought it all on myself. Serena Kate can be as sweet and cuddly as a speckled pup, but it won't do to hang any hopes on her."

"My sister had you starry-eyed, alright," Scooter admitted with a smile that seemed at least half grimace. "But ain't you jumped from the frying pan into the fire with your little Carolina belle?"

Ches drew in a long breath and gave careful examination to the faint scratches his odd gait had already produced in the black leather of his Sunday boots. When he finally lifted his gaze, though, he looked his old friend squarely in the eye.

"I've been praying about that, Scooter, and I don't think so. I'm awfully crazy about Ruthanne, but she holds on tight to her faith. We share that and would never place our love for each other above our love of the Lord."

"I'm thankful to say I know the Lord, but I may not ever be as grounded as you. Guess I'll just have to keep changing them girls out so I don't set one up too high."

"Well, now, Scooter…" Ches drawled with a grin, "I'm not exactly sure that's what God intended either. Jim Rex sure showed you how to do it, though. Anyhow, you tend to your business, and I'll tend to mine."

Days passed, and Lonnie Ray lay on his back, too sick to get better and too tough to die. Giles Parmalee and Aunt Hattie seldom agreed on anything, but a common tie to Miss Sis and to the McKendrick community prompted frequent trips up the hall to the old cowhand's bedside. The boss lady visited every chance she got while Pap Prescott, not given to overmuch work, showed up with his guitar almost daily. Ches and Ruthanne dropped by fairly often, too.

Serena Kate's heartfelt compassion made her a favorite throughout the nursing home. But with so many family friends gathered in the Leggett room, she naturally gravitated there, tending to Lonnie Ray's every need while also letting herself be petted and fussed over by folks she had known since childhood.

Despite his unwavering loyalty to Ruthanne, Ches watched with satisfaction as the dark circles under Serena Kate's eyes began to fade. The can of Mountain Dew remained a more or less permanent fixture, and she gradually lost her thin, haggard look as Ethan settled into his new job with a local painter.

"My husband would like to talk to you, Mr. Leggett," the redhead confided one day as she brushed the silver locks from his forehead in an almost motherly gesture. "Would it be alright if he came by?"

"You may not like it, pretty girl, but I reckon that's up to Ches and the boss lady. If that old boy's welcome on the Durham place, I'll see him. Otherwise…"

"Miss Sis doesn't own this nursing home," she shot back, sounding more playful than argumentative. "Were y'all really gonna run Ethan out of the county if he didn't take that job painting houses with Billy John Stanley?"

"Now, what do you think?" he asked, a grim smile struggling against the pain on his face.

"What about me and my girls…" she protested as his meaning became clear.

Not particularly fond of Colonel Chester Durham, either before or after he married her late sister, Hattie seldom applauded his unyielding ethics in her niece. But Serena Kate's total misreading of the situation compelled her to explain.

"That's the only reason they care, child. He could've bummed around here the rest of his life, but nobody marries a McKendrick girl and then saddles her with the task of supporting him."

"He's your husband," Lonnie Ray added, tiring of the whole unnecessary discussion. "You could've gone with him or not. Now, whether Miss Sis would've let him carry off the twins…"

"You people are nuts," Serena Kate decided, but even this accusation came in a friendly tone.

"They've always been a little crazy," Hattie observed, getting in her last word on the subject, "but they're your people. Just like a safety net… You know it's there, learn to appreciate it, and then put it out of your mind and get on about the business of life."

"You see Miss Sis, girlie," Lonnie Ray murmured just under the faint rattle of his breathing. "If she's agreeable to a little visit, I am, too."

Serena Kate reentered the room later and found her patient asleep. She smiled a greeting to Pap Prescott and his granddaughter, smoothed the covers expertly, and then dropped wearily into a chair.

"He resting easy?" she inquired of Ruthanne.

Feeling somewhat awkward with the new girl in Ches's life, Serena Kate nevertheless felt sure this little Suzy Homemaker type could offer more sickroom insight than an old guitar-picking drifter.

"I reckon," Ruthanne whispered, backing up her answer with a decisive nod. "He hasn't stirred, and we came in nearly an hour ago."

Serena Kate arched her aching back in a lazy, feline kind of stretch before settling deeper into the padded armchair. That done, she kicked off white orthopedic shoes and wriggled her toes luxuriantly.

"It's good of y'all to come. I mean, it's not like you really…"

"Oh, you know how it is around the horse sale. Miss Sis took us into that circle, and we're glad to do what we can for Lonnie Ray. It puts her mind at ease, too, knowing somebody's here. By the way, she sent you a case of soda water."

Ruthanne kept her voice low, and the murmured conversation held a soothing note in deference to Lonnie Ray's delicate condition. Finally, she gestured toward the bedside refrigerator and its fresh supply of Mountain Dew.

"Oh, good," Serena Kate breathed on a sigh of relief and then left her chair just long enough to grab a cold drink. "The boss lady can be difficult with a capital D, but she'll come through when it counts."

"Say, missy," Pap ventured when Serena Kate had settled comfortably into her unofficial but much-needed evening break, "What about asking your girls to help me come sale night? Running my little leather shop and the fritter stand too is a tall order for just one old man."

"I'm surprised Miss Sis hasn't put 'em to work already," she replied with a chuckle.

"Well, they were kind of young when y'all left here," Ruthanne observed. "Torrie's a good little rider, though, and we could probably use her some."

"Yeah, but Corrie's more like me. I know she'd rather sit around with your grandpa drinking Coke and eatin' candy."

"The girl sounds qualified," Pap quipped, "and she's a-way too little to eat up all my profit. Can she make change?"

"Yep."

"I can't pay much but..."

"Miss Sis started my brothers off at a dollar a ride. Now, they might ride fifty or sixty horses in one night, but nobody ever accused her of overpaying."

"Now, there's a lady after my own heart," Pap said expansively. "No sense throwing good money away." Placing a finger to her lips, Ruthanne gave her head a quick shake. "Settle down, miss priss. Old Lonnie Ray never stopped to worry over nobody's rest before he cut loose on a midnight romp. I can tell you that much for sure."

In spite of the grumbling, the old man lowered his voice appropriately. His granddaughter's smile was warm and loving but also the tiniest bit smug.

"Peanut butter cookie?"

She directed the polite inquiry to Serena Kate, but Pap intercepted it handily.

"Thought you'd never ask…"

Laughing softly, Serena Kate stuck her hand into the container alongside his.

She found herself warming up to Ruthanne, but couldn't pass up a chance to have some fun with this near-perfect little Southern belle.

"You do know these things come in a precut roll down at the Walmart?" she inquired, eyes dancing with mischief. "Yours are better, but not so much better that I'll write down some long recipe and pretend I might use it."

"Mercy me!" Ruthanne shot back wide-eyed, giving her best imitation of a scandalized gasp.

Drawn together by shared laughter, the two young women settled in to chat like old friends. They lost all track of time until Giles Parmalee returned from the dining hall. When Hattie arrived pushing her walker, Serena Kate kissed the old lady's cheek, slipped back into her shoes, and darted off for one last round of the hallways.

Lonnie Ray roused shortly after her departure and was fully alert, nibbling at a peanut butter cookie, when the facility's top administrator stuck her head through the door.

"What's going on here?" she asked in a less than pleasant tone.

"I'm dying, they're watching, and you're butting in," Lonnie Ray answered curtly.

"We don't allow our residents to congregate at the bedside like this, and you shouldn't speak flippantly of death. Have you seen our psychologist?"

"No'm, but unless he can figure a way to set my odometer back, I ain't lookin' for him. I'll cash in just the same whether we talk about it or not, and what's more, it don't bother me none."

"What did you say?" the efficient bureaucrat inquired, moving into the room.

"Was a time, not so long ago, when the odds looked pretty well stacked against me. Now that I'm right with the good Lord, I ain't backing off from nothing."

"I will definitely put you down for a visit from the psychologist, and your friends cannot congregate in here. Visitors are one thing, but other residents… It might prove harmful to their own emotional stability."

"Look around you, lady. Aside from Ruthanne, this bunch is older than dirt. They've seen everything at least twice."

"Nevertheless, we cannot allow it. This kind of thing is most definitely against our policy."

Serena Kate watched undetected from the doorway until muffled giggling revealed her presence. Pulling herself together, she tried to offer a serious piece of advice.

"Take it easy, Evelyn. All these folks are from McKendrick. Mess with them and you'll bring Miss Sis down on us like a duck on a June bug."

"Duck on a… I never heard of any place called McKendrick, and whoever this Miss Sis is, she has no authority to override our corporate guidelines."

"Maybe not," Serena Kate conceded, doubt thick in her voice, "but she'll sure yank this bunch out of here and move them all up to the big house. That wouldn't do much for the corporate balance sheet, would it?"

"I am not easily intimidated by idle threats!"

"Maybe not," Lonnie Ray echoed. "But time them brown eyes snap and that pretty-talkin' drawl comes real slow, you'll run off to the corner and hide your face."

"Look, Evelyn… I've been good help, right? I work the extra shifts. I don't complain. I care about the residents. You're not from around here, so just trust me. Go back to your office and leave this alone. Please?"

"Stay, then," she decided abruptly. "You should all be on hand when the psychologist comes!"

Those left in the room eyed one another with barely contained humor until Serena Kate finally spoke into the silence.

"Her big-bad psychologist is a Methodist from up around Hallsville... Y'all won't have no trouble out of him."

Laughter broke forth in waves then, doing Lonnie Ray more good than all the medicine his doctors could prescribe.

As they prepared for the October horse sale, Ches couldn't help marveling at Ruthanne. Settled into her role at the barn, she worked like an old hand. Presale hustle and bustle never left her agitated or breathless. The girl remained calm and unhurried even as she matched his aunt's breakneck pace.

Her natural self-possession left some to wonder if Ruthanne might be immune to the electric energy of sale day, but Ches saw an added spark in her expressive hazel eyes.

"Looks like a good run tonight, m'darlin!"

The drawling statement came softly, but it also vibrated with contained excitement. She had eased into the "m'darlin" business over the last couple of weeks, but the words gave him a warm tingle each time she spoke them.

"I'd like to have you sit out here with me all night," he confided, "but you're worth your weight in gold running that alley and showing horses."

"It's no trouble... I just keep 'em moving. That, and ride a few."

"You can make it out as simple as you want to, but the sales are running smoother than they have since Nash got too stove-up to manage things back there. Whoever's out back needs to read the boss lady's mind and use plenty of their own good judgement besides."

"A tail goin' out and a head comin' in... It don't get much simpler than that. How about a fritter?" Ruthanne inquired, changing the subject. "I made the first batch."

"When did you have time to do that? Never mind; I'll roll out front and grab us a couple."

"That's awful sweet, but I'll go. Need to check on Pap, anyhow."

Ches intended to wait right there, but he and Aunt Sis shared a kind of sixth sense that drew them together in time of trouble or uncertainty. Without thinking much about it, he drifted over toward the narrow hallway and then down to her office.

Sure enough, she stood just outside the door, eyeing Serena Kate with a hesitant frown.

"Well, now, you and the girls are welcome here anytime, but I just don't—"

"I told you he's sorry, Miss Sis. Ethan never even guessed at the chance he took in laying a hand on you. Out in the real world, people talk noise to each other all the time. Maybe Colonel Durham and those old-time hands of his stayed soft-spoken and mannerly right up to the point of a killin', but things are different today."

"Different don't necessarily mean better," Sis murmured distractedly before catching sight of her nephew. "Oh, there you are. The twins are helping Pap Prescott tonight, and Serena Kate wants to know if she can bring her husband in to watch the sale. Billy John tells me he's made pretty fair help, but I just... This deal's half yours, honey child. What about it?"

"Well, Corrie's helpin' Pap. Torrie's gonna ride some horses for us."

"Mmm, third generation. We've had lots of little redheaded barn help."

"I don't particularly care if Ethan Fisher comes in or not," Ches drawled but reached out gently to touch his aunt's hand. "Does it worry you any, having him around?"

"Not one little bit," she quipped and met his concerned gaze with that reckless Durham grin.

"That settles it," he decided with a nod and then turned to Serena Kate. "Tell your man to come ahead. I'm warning you, though, he's on notice like a biting dog. Trouble comes, every hand on the place knows to take the first lick and make it count."

"Won't be any trouble, Ches. Now, I wish you'd come talk to that crazy little brother of mine. He's leaning on the hood of my car sharpening that long-bladed pocketknife he got when Nash died."

Ches smiled wryly, picturing Scooter's display of loyalty, but a wordless nod let Serena Kate know that he would call for a truce.

"Good evening, folks," Miss Sis said brightly, taking her usual place in the auctioneer's box. "I'd like to welcome y'all to the Durham Auction Company's monthly horse sale and to McKendrick, Texas."

"Now, Miss Sis..." Scooter interrupted, leaning in to reach the microphone, "folks who don't know where they're at ain't apt to buy too many horses!"

The boss lady cut her eyes and took a swat at him but couldn't hold back a longsuffering grin.

"We've got some fine-looking animals here tonight, and you've had ample opportunity to check them for yourselves. I'll call any faults I see in the ring, but all sales are final. I'm a licensed auctioneer and so is my nephew, Chester J. Durham. Believe it or not, the State of Texas even gave Scooter a license. Ches, honey, would you start us off with a word of prayer."

Ches prayed for harmony between buyers and sellers, asking the Lord's watch care over everyone involved, and then turned to the business of taking online bids.

"Welllll, alright boys..." Scooter sang out, falling into a familiar cadence. "Here's a good little buckskin mare. Give me twelve hundred, and let's roll!"

Ches knew that his writing career brought in more money with considerably less physical effort, but the supercharged atmosphere of the horse sale stirred something in his blood. He communicated remote bids to the auctioneer's box with a nod or a shout while the inhouse crowd did their own bidding.

Equines of every description glistened under the electric lights. Gates rattled and hooves pounded while the customers laughed or squabbled or talked business. Scooter McKendrick's voice rang out clear and strong above it all. That chant practically enticed bids with its fever-pitch intensity.

Ruthanne rode into the ring on just about every third or fourth horse, and still managed to keep things moving in the back. If a horse was iron jawed, panicked, or just plain ignorant, she made a pretty passenger. Rather than fight with an animal and highlight its faults, she understood when to just sit up there and smile. If a horse knew a little something, though, she could spin, roll back, and do whatever it took to show his good points.

Smiles from his sweetheart marked the high points of Ches's night, but he also looked forward to the brief intervals when Aunt Sis took over the auctioneering.

"Can't nobody sell 'em like the boss lady," a longtime customer called enthusiastically.

Wholehearted in his agreement and blissfully unaware of any trouble in the back, Ches answered with a wide grin. Just out of sight, though, a young sorrel stallion balked at the in-gate. The animal quivered with pent-up energy as an ominous groaning sound telegraphed rage and fear. When the stud squatted as if to pitch, Zeke Claymore stepped nimbly to the ground.

"They don't pay me enough to take this kinda gamble," he told Ruthanne shortly. "I'll just lead him through."

"Easy there, big fella..." Ruthanne stroked the stallion's neck almost lovingly and then turned her attention briefly to Zeke. "The ticket says saddle and ride, don't it?" she asked rhetorically, hopping up into place.

Aware of his new rider, the stud went through his whole little routine again, but instead of stepping off, Ruthanne took a deeper seat.

"Y'all gone to sleep back there?" Miss Sis inquired good-naturedly over the P.A. system.

"Let's go, you red booger," Ruthanne coaxed gently, adding kissing noises in hopes of achieving some forward movement.

"Somebody better come a-riding," the boss lady called with less humor in her tone.

Against her better judgement, Ruthanne applied a little touch of spur. The stallion bawled like a fighting bull and leaped headlong into the ring. Ruthanne managed to duck the crossbar over the gate but the maneuver kept her from catching the horse's rhythm. She started the ride half a jump behind, and Zeke's stirrups hung too long to give her much support.

Thinking of the eardrums in the crowd as well as his own, Scooter snatched the microphone away from Miss Sis right before she cut loose with a Texas yell. Ruthanne couldn't hear the collective intake of breath from the crowd, but the boss lady's high-spirited encouragement gained her a couple of extra jumps. Even so, the stud finally sling-shotted his determined little rider out of the saddle.

# Chapter Eleven

Though Ruthanne landed in a seated position, something hit her in the back with a resounding thud. The solid partition at the bottom of the sale ring kept animals from sticking a foot through, but it hardly made for an easy landing. It seemed as though Ches maneuvered the wheelchair down from his little corner platform while she was still in the air. Ringside, he dropped to his knees, reached over the partition, and groped for her hand.

Ruthanne took his hand and squeezed it, gazing up wide-eyed as she fought for breath. Feeling sure in her own mind that she would come out of the incident with nothing more than some nasty bruising across her back, she longed to share this knowledge. Ruthanne tried to tell him with her eyes, but her lungs burned for want of air.

"Oh, Ruthanne… You're gonna be alright, sweet baby. Tell me where it hurts."

The terror she saw written on his face caused a tear to slip down her cheek, and that provided little of the reassurance she was fighting so hard to convey. Ches almost quit breathing himself, but the familiar scent of White Shoulders perfume cut through the usual sale-barn smells, and a reassuring arm dropped lightly across his shoulders.

"She's alright, honey, just had the wind knocked out of her is all. It ain't a pleasant feeling, but it never killed nobody yet."

Hearing Miss Sis give voice to her thoughts, Ruthanne nodded vigorously and even mustered up a little smile.

"Thank God," Ches breathed reverently.

Ruthanne's wordless gaze held his eyes like a magnet. When he finally looked around, though, he spotted the stud trembling in a far corner.

"Big rascal's scared to death," Sis observed, catching his quick glance, "but I'll get ahold of him."

She stood, let herself in the gate, and caught the horse handily. While Miss Sis talked the bronc down, Ruthanne caught hold of the fence and pulled shakily up to her feet.

"Sorry I scared you so bad, m'darlin. The look on your face pretty well broke my heart, but there's nothing else busted."

Suddenly, Ches felt another familiar presence beside him. Serena Kate reached through the fence with a couple of pills in one hand and a can of Mountain Dew in the other.

"Extra strength Tylenol," she explained shortly to Ruthanne. "You'll thank me in the morning."

"Thanks," Ches said gratefully. "That was a pretty solid lick she took."

Ruthanne tossed the capsules back, followed them with a long swig from the can, and shuddered at the unfamiliar taste. Somewhat affronted, Serena Kate wrinkled her pretty nose.

"It's wet and cold. Besides… Too much water'll rust your stomach."

This little quip and the instinctive act of kindness earned her a heartfelt smile.

"Oh, well… You're the nurse," Ruthanne answered warmly and chanced another small sip from the can.

"Sure you're okay?" the redhead inquired earnestly.

"I am, thank you," Ruthanne decided with a nod. "Won't feel it until tomorrow. Right now, I'd better get back to work."

With Ches seated in the wheelchair once again, she leaned through the bars and dropped a loving kiss onto his forehead. Ches appreciated the sweetness of the moment, but it did nothing to quell his rising suspicions as she turned away.

"You're not gonna ride—"

She turned back to him for a moment and if a smile can communicate stubbornness, hers did.

"I know you'd like to protect me, Ches. That's awfully sweet, too, but if I don't ride him, your Aunt Sis will. Don't try to tell me you'd do any different if cerebral palsy hadn't robbed... Besides, m'darlin, there'd be no chance for love if I didn't have your respect."

A lump rose in Ches's throat, but he felt his heart expand with an unspeakable warmth.

"Love you, hardhead?" he whispered to her back as she turned to speak to the crowd. "Reckon I already do!"

"This colt's not mean, just unhandled and rough around the edges," she called in a voice that carried while maintaining an unforced, ladylike quality. "You've already seen his worst. So, when I climb back up there, the least y'all can do is pull your hands out of your pockets and bid."

Everything went still and quiet as Ruthanne stuck her foot into the stirrup. Serena Kate's eyes widened at the other girl's bravery, and her reluctant murmur broke unexpectedly into the silence.

"That's the thing, Ches... Being loved and petted was fun for a while, but I never really cared about your respect. Not the way she does, anyhow. I wouldn't crawl back into that saddle for love nor money!"

The sorrel stallion tiptoed around the ring, blowing and snorting at every shadow, but made no effort to unseat his rider a second time. Ches heard the unfiltered self-assessment in Serena Kate's words but never felt their impact until Ruthanne stepped safely to the ground and led her mount from the ring.

*Beyond the Parmalee Bottom* 195

Angling the wheelchair, he reached automatically to pull the redhead down into a comforting embrace but drew back at the last second. Expecting the hug from long habit, Serena Kate patted his shoulder uncertainly.

"You're a mother," he said, rising involuntarily to her defense. "Became one before you ever really grew up yourself... That's bound to impact the risks you'll take. I've always respected your commitment to the twins."

"Yeah, but—"

"I missed you an awful lot, Serena Kate. Missed you every single day for a year. Pretty much kept on that way, too, until you married and the Lord dropped Ruthanne into my path. Anyhow," he faltered, winding down, "thank you for the Tylenol."

She dismissed the uncomfortable conversation with a shrug and a whimsical little smile. Then, blinking away the tears that pooled in her eyes, she started a long, slow climb to rejoin Ethan at the top of the bleachers.

"One thing for sure, Ches... Your little lady was a real star tonight! No trick riding routine could've gone over any better. I believe that big red scamp brought more than if he'd never bucked a-tall."

Miss Sis addressed herself to Ches, but she looked squarely at Ruthanne who beamed under the praise. The three of them sat together, tired but contented, having closed the books on one more horse sale.

"You need to take care of yourself back there in that alley," Ches said to Ruthanne and then grinned mischievously at his aunt. "Miss Sis will collect the fifteen-dollar saddle and ride fee on a grizzly bear!"

Sis smiled back tolerantly but pulled a wrinkled sheet of paper from the pearl-snap pocket of her western blouse.

"Saddle and ride's stamped on this ticket, not handwritten," she replied archly in reference to the ink stamps Ches used to handle paperwork.

"St-stamped on?" he questioned but then sighed heavily. "Forgive me, Ruthanne? Nash and the McKendrick boys worked in the alley when I first came... I can hear Aunt Sis now, 'Just collect the money, Ches. That crew out back'll do the riding.'"

"And why should it be any different these days?" Ruthanne scoffed good-naturedly. "A girl don't learn to trick ride without gettin' the wind knocked out of her a time or two."

"Say what you want to," Ches told her. "Using that saddle-and-ride stamp is a whole different deal with my sweetheart back there in the alley."

"Can't say I expected first aid from Serena Kate," she quipped, changing the subject, "but I was glad enough to get it."

"Serena Kate's a sweet girl for all her faults. Always has been, and I reckon she always will be. But that's neither here nor there... You're takin' the day off tomorrow, little miss. You need the rest, and I know a young fella who enjoys every spare minute he can get with you."

"You're right as usual, Aunt Sis," Ches admitted with a smile, "but I hate to leave you with the checkout and loading. Besides, poor Ruthanne may not make it out of bed tomorrow."

"I sometimes feel old and decrepit," Ruthanne admitted with a smile, "but I've got a good deal of bounce left in me."

"No softening bones or hip replacements for you, huh?"

"Oh, Miss Sis, I never meant to—"

"Hush, now," came the lighthearted answer. "I'm just teasin' you. I handled this sale by myself until Ches came along. I don't ever want to go back to that, but surely I can manage one Saturday checkout. Y'all take it easy tomorrow and enjoy the day."

Sis headed down to the sale barn early on Saturday, and Andrew left a little later, taking Cassidy to town for a father-daughter breakfast. Alone at the big house, Ches fed the dogs, motored back inside to wash his hands, and guided the wheelchair right out again. He caught himself rolling aimlessly from one end of the back porch to the other and then smiled as he thought of Aunt Sis and her endless pacing.

"Might as well set up the laptop," he muttered, "and see about proofing one more article."

Just then, though, the cell phone buzzed in his shirt pocket.

"Morning, Ches! I'm cookin' Pap's breakfast if you want to come on over here."

"Why so early, Ruthanne? Aren't you tired and sore?"

"Well, yes... But you know I'm always up early."

"You curl up on that loveseat," he directed, "and don't budge. I'll cook Pap's breakfast and yours, too."

"Ooff," she groaned. "If I curl up anywhere this morning, I may never get uncurled. Besides, everything's just about done. Pap usually eats biscuits or an apple fritter with his ham and eggs, but I just took a batch of muffins out of the oven. It'll be on the table time you get here."

"Anything I can bring you?"

If not for muffled kitchen noises and the faint sound of her breath, Ches would have started to wonder about the connection, but Ruthanne finally spoke.

"Do you think Miss Sis might have some ointment or liniment or..."

"Sure; I'll find something."

Though not much inclined to bend over backwards for company, Pap Prescott seemed glad enough to get a little conversation with his breakfast. Ruthanne finally slipped in a word or two at the end of one of her grandfather's stories.

"Sorry I'm not dressed, Ches, but my back's awful sore for regular clothes."

"Quit apologizing, Ruthie," Pap broke in dismissively, indicating her loose-fitting pajamas and matching bed jacket as he spoke. "You already changed out of your gown into that getup, fixed your hair about three times, and... Anyhow, I doubt the boy expected a Sunday dress this early on Saturday morning."

Color tinted Ruthanne's cheeks, but she smiled at Ches and gave her head a rueful shake. They talked on for a while with the two young people dropping occasional bits and pieces into a steady but entertaining monologue.

Pap finally rose from the table with a yawn to hunt through the house for his guitar case and hat. Taking on a day of visiting with all the enthusiasm he might show for a taxing chore, he wandered off up town to check on the old folks at Pinevale.

"Go on in the den, or out to the porch, and find us a comfortable seat," Ches said when left alone with the young lady. "I'll clean up in here and be right along."

"Oh, I couldn't let you…"

"Why not? Aunt Sis lets me help out sometimes, and she's just about the perfect hostess."

"Yes, but y'all do it together."

"I won't get your kitchen all mixed up trying to put stuff away, but I can at least wash dishes and leave them in the rack to dry. Now, please, go sit down."

A few minutes later Ches left his wheelchair in the kitchen and dropped to the floor to negotiate the stepdown and join Ruthanne in the sunken den. Comfortable enough to be himself and move around in the easiest possible way, he crossed the room on his knees. When she started up off the couch to take the plastic sack he carried, he motioned her back and claimed a seat beside her.

"It's real sweet of you, cleaning up the kitchen that way, but I'm afraid Pap won't thank you for encouraging my laziness."

"Seems like we've had this conversation before, Miss Prescott," he countered teasingly. "You. Are. Not. Lazy. On second thought, what's it matter if you're just a tad lazy now and again? There's nothing in this world cuter than a sleepy little pup or a drowsy kitten."

"Aww… Did Miss Sis set you down and teach you how to melt a girl's heart, or does it just come naturally?"

They shared a smile and lapsed into an easy silence. Being a Durham and much like his aunt, Ches seldom enjoyed idleness, but Ruthanne's complete relaxation enveloped him like a warm blanket. Without wearing much perfume, the young lady gave off a light, clean fragrance that seemed to come directly from her. She smelled a little like fresh-baked muffins today. Other times, her scent mixed just as nicely with the distinctive odor of horses.

Ruthanne's eyelids soon drifted shut, but Ches gazed contentedly at her pretty face. The rhythm of her breathing captivated his attention completely, allowing time to glide by with no particular notice. She rested lightly against the arm of the sofa, not to draw away from him but to keep from pressing her bruised back into the cushions. After a while, a slight shift in her position brought a muffled groan.

"My poor baby…"

The words came out softly, but Ches hadn't intended to speak at all. Ruthanne kept her eyes closed, but her mouth curved automatically into a smile.

"I'm not asleep, Ches. We can talk if you want to…"

"Oh," he said, a little bit startled to discover she had been listening, "I never meant to embarrass you or anything."

"Don't be silly. Poor baby sounds much nicer than, 'Quit fooling around, and get back on your horse.'"

"Huh?"

"Can't you just hear Pap? 'A fall in the practice pen is one thing, but we've got a payin' show this afternoon.'"

"Poor baby, poor baby, poor baby!" he crooned, reaching up tentatively to run his fingers through her hair.

"Mmm," she murmured appreciatively as he switched from playing with her hair to a gentle massage on the back of her neck.

"I'd rub your back, too. Only… You're so sore, and I couldn't stand it if I hurt you. Say," he remembered, turning to rummage in the grocery bag, "I brought along some Absorbine liniment. Pretty stout, but Aunt Sis swears by it. Not just for the horses, either."

"Thank you, m'darlin," she replied dreamily. "I'll put some on directly, but I'm not goin' anywhere right this minute."

Encouraged by a deep and utterly peaceful sigh, he kept right on rubbing her neck. Later, as he considered her discomfort, Ches felt the need to pamper her just a bit more.

"Could I... Would you feel comfortable letting me help with the liniment?"

She sat up straight, giving the question serious thought in spite of her drowsy contentment. The move actually brought them closer together, but Ches stopped rubbing and folded his hands to wait for her answer.

"Well, I mean... I could take off my jacket, raise the blouse a little and still be more or less decent, especially layin' flat on my tummy."

"That carpet goes back to the 1960s or '70s," Ches mused as if changing the subject, "and I don't..."

"It's alright," Ruthanne answered softly, following his gaze down to the thick, gold shag. "I rented one of those rug doctor things."

"Stretch out and get comfortable if you feel like it. I'll run get us a cup towel."

Ches waited for her nod and then left the room without looking back.

"Oh, me..."

He heard her words and the involuntary moan that accompanied them, but also figured Ruthanne might want a little privacy as she eased herself off the couch and got settled.

The unbruised sliver of her back that showed just under the raised blouse lacked the sun-kissed glow of her face. Even so, it looked smooth, soft, and perfectly healthy. Ches sucked air through his teeth, grimacing as he compared that narrow strip of unblemished skin to the angry purple just below it.

"Poor baby," he repeated sympathetically and then returned to the matter at hand. "This stuff goes on cold and then kind of burns the soreness away. Not very pleasant at first, but it ought to give you some relief."

"I'm ready."

Ruthanne spoke the words earnestly but smiled into her throw pillow. Ches obviously hated the idea of adding to her discomfort. In fact, such gentleness and concern made her feel like some kind of delicate treasure. She tensed up and took in a sharp little breath as he applied the medicine but downplayed her reaction for his sake.

Excess liquid trickled off her lower back and down her sides, but Ches dabbed it away, bringing the towel into play before anything ran onto the floor. He gave the liniment some time to do its job and then eased into a light backrub. Unpracticed but gentle, his fingers carefully avoided the bruised area while working some of the soreness from the muscles around it.

Ruthanne Prescott was a kind, beautiful person and basically unaccustomed to tender love and care. Occasional noises of satisfaction from the back of her throat stirred yearnings that Ches could never put into words.

"Oh, pretty girl... Oh, yes... We'll make it all better."

"Pretty?" Ruthanne quavered, feeling a rush of embarrassment as his fingers walked through the small but unwelcome accumulation of flesh that curved outward from just over her hips. "But I've gotten so out of shape, and now I'm all bruised up."

"Believe me, sugar pie," he answered in complete and unguarded honesty, "there's nothing wrong with your shape!"

"Please, Ches... I needed to lose ten pounds before we came off the road. Now, it's more like fifteen or twenty."

"You might as well hush; I don't believe a word of it."

"Well, it's the truth," she almost sniffled.

"Listen, Aunt Sis gained a little weight back when she gave up smoking. You should've heard her fuss and carry on, but then she married Uncle Andrew and kind of quit worrying about it. Things took their natural up-and-down course, and she doesn't weigh much more today than she did when I first came to stay on the homeplace with her over sixteen years ago."

"Yes, but she's so active and full of nervous energy. I'm just too—"

"You're just too pretty for words. And while we're on the subject, that's probably enough back rubbing. I best get out of here and take a little air."

When his hands stopped massaging her and reached up to tug the blouse gingerly back into place, Ruthanne felt their slight tremor and realized the depth of feeling behind his words. She got up on her knees, turned to face him, and rested her head on his shoulder in a brief but tender embrace.

"Thank you, m'darlin," and the intimate murmur transitioned into her usual pleasant drawl. "You were so sweet to rub my back. Now that I actually feel like moving, a little stroll around the yard might be just the thing. Get your wheelchair and head out front. I won't be a minute."

Ches and Ruthanne were responsible adults who knew and loved the Lord, but it took everything he had to leave her there. Climbing back into the wheelchair, he made his way outside and slipped automatically into a heartfelt prayer. He thanked God sincerely for all of Ruthanne's lovely qualities and for her presence in his life.

"Mercy," he breathed in closing, "it don't take much to turn wonderful blessings into half-baked excuses for sin. I reckon that's a part of the human condition, but thank You, Lord, for bringing us through."

Ruthanne came out moments later with the pale rose jacket back on over her matching pajamas and a leftover muffin in one hand.

"It's a good thing you think I'm so pretty... 'Cause dieting is just about hopeless."

She added a resigned sigh for good measure, but any feelings of self-reproach melted away under his lovestruck smile.

The fall day felt almost like Indian summer, and sunshine warmed Ruthanne's back and shoulders through the delicate material of her jacket. Ches rolled down the improvised ramp, opened the door on his van, and reached inside for the Stetson. Finished with her muffin, Ruthanne brushed her hands together in a fastidious little gesture and stepped down into the yard to join him.

"Sure you're up to a walk?" he inquired solicitously.

"Yes; I really do feel better now."

"That's good, but you don't want to overdo it."

She lifted his hat in a playful but somewhat daring move, placed it atop her own head for safekeeping, and ran her hand through his close-cut hair.

"Aww… You're mighty sweet to worry, but I'm not striking out on a cross-country hike. This feels nice on my fingertips," she finished absentmindedly, making another pass through his hair.

"Ain't so bad on this end, either."

She handed over the hat with a smile, knowing full well he would want to reset it himself, and they started off together. They strolled over the front yard quietly at first, but on the second trip around, Ches ventured a gentle inquiry.

"What do you dream about, sugar pie?"

"Lots of nights I don't dream a-tall." Ches smiled, realizing she had misunderstood his question but choosing not to interrupt her. "Other times, I dream about childhood days at Fairview. And then, once in a while, there's this nightmare. It seems kinda silly in the light of day."

"Nightmare?"

"Uh, huh… The only one I can remember in my whole adult life, but it comes around pretty regular. See, I used to do this trick where I'd get going full tilt, hanging off the side of one horse and then transition to another. It always got quite a reaction from the crowd. I reckon they figured me a goner every time."

"Sounds like a nail biter alright. I'll bet it was Pap's idea."

"It made a good finale… Thimble's no trick horse, but you couldn't scare him with a charge of dynamite. The idea was to drop off Button's side, land in Thimble's saddle, and end up hanging from his opposite side. The little fella is short legged but steady. We'd have to lap him a time or two before their strides matched up right. Then I'd make the jump; easy as falling off a log."

"Yeah, I'll bet."

"Oh, I fell several times in practice but no more than I did with the other advanced tricks. The thing is, when I make my jump in the dream, Thimble's gone. Not just a stride or two behind as if I'd mistimed it in real life, but gone. Nowhere in the arena... I just keep falling and falling. 'Ruthanne Prescott,' I think in this kind of detached way, 'if you ever hit the ground, it's sure gonna hurt!'"

"Like they say, it's not the fall but the sudden stop..."

"Not really that scary, I guess, in the big scheme of things. But I wake up all tense with my heart going ninety to nothing. It's more of a nuisance than anything else."

Finally, Ruthanne paused beside a dormant muscadine arbor and eyed the decorative metal swing beneath it.

"Take the wheelchair; it's softer. I'll sit on the swing."

"Ches..." she murmured reluctantly, "I'm not an invalid."

"No, but you are my sweet little miss, and your back does hurt. Now, sit down and talk to me some more. Do all the girls in South Carolina sound as pretty as you?"

"Are all the boys in East Texas natural-born sweet talkers?" she shot back.

"I kinda hate to tell you after such a good conversation," he began, taking her hand as she settled comfortably into the wheelchair, "but I wasn't necessarily asking about nighttime dreams."

"Oh, you mean..."

"Won't you tell me about your hopes for the future?"

"Well, Ches, you might say I'm already living some of it. I always dreamt of settling down in one place with a home of my own. Some folks might not think much of a rented place way out in the country. Still, Gram always intended me to be the lady of the house, and now I am. Having you over to breakfast, for instance. Can't say I ever figured on greeting company in my pajamas, but bronc horses being what they are…"

Ches's heart glowed at the thought of Ruthanne living out her dreams, and that warmth made him uncharacteristically bold.

"Playing hostess for Pap is one thing, Miss Prescott, but I wonder… Could you ever see yourself as the lady of my house?"

"I'm not telling," she quipped, leaning forward to bounce a fingertip ever so lightly off the end of his nose, "but that just might be the rest of the dream."

"I sure do love you, little miss."

"I love you, too, Ches. Now, turnabout's fair play. Tell me some of your dreams."

"You mean, besides you? Well… I always dreamed of living here in McKendrick and working alongside Aunt Sis. I feel like this is where the Good Lord intended me. He gave me this community and a deep set of roots to draw on when the going gets rough."

"Of course," she qualified, "God Himself is our ultimate source of strength."

Ches nodded in ready agreement but continued his original train of thought.

"Daddy encouraged me to pursue some kind of non-agricultural career, but I certainly don't mind writing. It helps make a living. We can't have you acting as hostess in some tumbled-down shack. Still, I'll always be a horseman at heart."

"That fritter stand of ours made the average shotgun shack look pretty good," she remembered with a smile. "But Ches… My dream of a real home seemed pretty farfetched out there tramping from one county fair to the next. Don't you ever dream of something a little unrealistic, the sort of hope that's not quite a sure thing?"

"Now that you mention it," he began with a Texas-sized grin.

"Ah, ah, ah…" She cautioned, raising a finger to stop him. "You've practically already got me, so you needn't weight your answer down with romance."

"Well," he said, turning serious, "the future rests in God's hands. I feel so blessed that it's hard to... You know, I do catch myself daydreaming from time to time about a therapeutic riding program. Horses have added a great deal to my life, and I'd like to share that with other disabled individuals, especially children."

"Aww, I think that's a wonderful idea. And why not? You've got a readymade facility at the sale barn. Mounting ramp already in place... Short Stuff, Thimble, and Buttons... Even Pumpkin might do for more advanced riders. What's holding you back?"

"I'm not physically able, and there's never been anybody else to take on the role of instructor."

"Ches Durham, Miss Sis would walk over hot coals if you so much as implied you wanted her to, much less asked."

"Maybe so, but I never talked to her about it."

"Well, for pity's sake. Why not?"

"I don't know. Aunt Sis managed to pass some of her knowledge along to me, but I'm a whole lot like her. All she had to do was imagine her own legs hanging half-dead on either side of a horse, with most of her balance gone, and then go from there. She's so patient and kind toward me. Always has been, but you've seen her with Cassidy."

"As much as I love your cousin, Ches, teenage girls can be a trial for any mother."

"That's not the point. We can't have her threatening crippled children with a good thrashing every time they leave a gate open or don't think of their horse first. Poor Aunt Sis would end up miserable and ninety percent of the riders along with her."

"Sounds like you've put some real thought into this."

"Yeah, but I never get anywhere with it. My ideal instructor would need to be as good with horses as the boss lady but as calm and unhurried as—"

The thought hit him so suddenly that it snapped his mouth shut.

"Maybe your aunt's a bit too high strung to head up a therapeutic riding program, but I've often wished I was more like her. Calm and unhurried, that's me. Maybe it comes from too many slow circles with those Shetlands."

"Ruthanne, you're—"

"Pap's awful laidback. I wonder sometimes if it passed through the blood or just rubbed off on me. Take weight loss, for instance. I can be worried sick one minute and enjoying some sort of gooey homemade goodness the next. From what I've seen, the boss lady meets her problems head on."

"I admire every little thing about Aunt Sis, but some folks might call it foolhardy, running to meet trouble. Whatever's coming next, she's in a hurry to get there. You've got an easygoing, natural grace that I... She... We can only admire."

"I'll do it, Ches. I mean, we don't have much extra money laying 'round, and I'm not sure what kind of training it takes. But I'll put the time in, and you know I'm not scared to work."

"Oh, Ruthanne... You'd really do that?"

"Yes, silly. I'll be your therapeutic riding instructor. We'll just put all this easygoing, natural grace where the rubber meets the road."

"You'd have to take an examination through the AHCB if we go that route. I've looked into it before, and they offer the test twice a year. Don't you worry none; we can see about those little details together. And if I know my Aunt Sis, she'll be behind us all the way."

"Now, then, that's all settled..."

Ruthanne trailed off with a smile and presented her cheek for a kiss. Ches happily obliged, and a few minutes later, transferred back to his wheelchair. Gazing up at her adoringly, he patted his lap. "Hop on and let me carry you back up to the house. Oh, come on," he added when she flashed him a scandalized look. "Even Aunt Sis catches a ride now and again."

"That I'd like to see," Ruthanne quipped but then snuggled agreeably into his lap.

Ches motored slowly back toward the house, choosing the smoothest path to avoid jolting his passenger. He relished the soft warmth as Ruthanne cuddled a little closer. They exchanged silly smiles at the door as she fumbled it open from his lap. The pair sat contentedly in the kitchen for several minutes before Ches finally spoke.

"You can stay right there forever as far as I'm concerned, but you'll probably be more comfortable back on the couch."

"Feels like I've been sitting one place or another all day. This spot is definitely a favorite, but..." Trailing off, she rose to her feet with a yawn and a stretch. "I'm not nearly as sore as I was this morning. A little saddle time before church or between services tomorrow would probably jostle it right on out."

"Therapeutic riding," Ches agreed with a nod.

Ruthanne's eyes widened slightly as she read the wall clock.

"Maybe I'm not such a great Southern hostess after all. I've been so caught up in this 'poor baby' treatment of yours that I let us skip dinner altogether. Pap wouldn't put up with that for a minute."

"You've spent the day resting comfortably, and that's exactly what I wanted. I never noticed the time passing any more than you did, and I expect Pap got him another dinner out of the marketing staff at Pinevale. They're eyeing the old rascal as a prospective resident."

"He's all I've got, Ches, aside from you and Miss Sis. I'd just about die before——"

"I know that, and Pap knows that. But, being a true opportunist..."

"You've got him pegged alright," she admitted with a fond smile. "We'll just have an early supper. What sounds good?"

"Life with Pap may feel like running a short-order kitchen, but I've had too much fun spoiling you today to let you cook supper. I'll make a quick trip into town and get us something. You can meet me down at the sale barn. I've been wanting to show you the books. We'll eat down there and visit, just the two of us, so you won't need to change clothes."

"I can't leave the house without getting dressed! You're very sweet and thoughtful, but I've probably lounged around long enough. If I'm going to change and come down to the sale barn, I might as well ride into town with you."

"You look beautiful just the way you are, Ruthanne. Those pajamas are nicer than a lot of the everyday clothes I see around, so pretty and modest."

"If they weren't modest and a little on the flattering side," she observed matter-of-factly, "I never would've let you see 'em. But they're still pajamas. Wait just a minute, and let me get changed."

When she returned in boots, jeans, and a knitted top with her hair freshly braided, they headed out to the van.

"I'll sit over here in the wheelchair. You drive, if you're up to it, and use that heated seat on your back."

Before picking up supper, they swung by the nursing home.

"The grub in here won't fetch no prizes," Pap commented, after taking his noon and evening meals in the dining hall, "but it's free."

Reclining in a corner of Lonnie Ray's room, he strummed muted chords on the guitar. Having drifted in and out of consciousness all day, the patient mustered a weak grin as his eyes settled on Ches's face.

"You been horseback today?"

"Tomorrow, I expect. Started in courtin' first thing this morning and ain't got through yet."

"Well, you don't say… I told you there'd be more than one filly in the herd."

"Yes, sir. That's the way I recall it."

"You wound up with a good one, boy," and his gaze went uncharacteristically soft as it flicked to Ruthanne. "She checks in on me real regular, and I didn't even know her 'fore I took sick. Right pretty little thing, she is, too."

"Good to know your eyesight ain't played out," Ches answered dryly.

Ruthanne blushed ever so slightly but returned the compliment.

"I sat there on my horse and watched you deal with that fella who thought he'd get a little rough with Miss Sis. If anybody ever earned a good choking... Well, you'll always be a hero in my book. Besides, you rode for the Durhams just like I'm doing now. We stick together; that's just how it works."

"I'm glad Ches is a good Baptist 'cause he sure ain't no poker player!"

"Sir?"

"Let me tell you something, little lady. You can get promoted off the ridin' crew just anytime you get ready."

# Chapter Twelve

Ruthanne's blush grew noticeably deeper, but Ches squeezed her hand reassuringly. Stepping closer to the bed, she caught the old man's gaze and held it.

"On the riding crew or in the big house," she declared in a steady but love-softened voice, "we'll stick together."

"She'll do, Ches. She'll do." Then, in a more serious tone, "How 'bout praying with me?"

"Sure, Lonnie Ray, but I can get Brother Waller to come by just anytime."

"He's been by. Him and some other folks from the church. I never even gave 'em the time of day so long as I had my full strength. They've been mighty good in spite of it all, but you and Miss Sis led me to the Lord."

Ruthanne took one hand, work-roughened and withered but still surprisingly strong, and Ches moved around the bed to grasp the other. Pap laid the flat of his palm across the strings to quiet them and snatched off his hat as the prayer began.

Ches thanked the Lord for his friend's salvation and asked for comfort and guidance in his final days. When he finished and raised his head, the sight of tears on the old man's weathered cheeks almost proved too much for him.

"Plain and simple words from the heart," Pap observed from his corner. "No preacher could've said it much better."

"I wish I could do something, boy… Something for the Lord. Time I come to know Him, though, I was already good and used up."

"You're doing it, Lonnie Ray," Ches answered around the lump in his throat, "just by waiting here for things to play out His way. Shucks, you ain't hollerin' for your britches and cussin' a blue streak along with it. Anybody who ever knew you sure ought to see the Lord's hand at work."

The old cowhand's dry chuckle went a long way toward dissolving that lump, and Ches finally managed to swallow the rest of it.

"Give us some church music, Pap," Ruthanne instructed quietly. When he plucked out a familiar melody, her sweet voice took it up. The words came soft and gentle yet clear and strong.

"On a hill far away stood an old rugged cross…"

Lonnie Ray eased back into sleep before the song ended, and the young couple nodded to Pap as they slipped quietly from the room.

Supper came in two brown paper sacks from a local burger joint. Ruthanne settled on a "number one" with homestyle fries while Ches ordered just the patty with pinto beans and fried okra.

"You can hold doors and wash dishes and I don't know what all," Ruthanne teased gently, "but avoiding carbohydrates is one thing you simply cannot do for me. I hate to tell you, m'darlin, but that ain't how it works."

"Ruthanne, you don't even need to…" Dropping an argument he could never win, Ches swallowed hard and revealed his true reasoning. "I'd make a prize catch for sure, with burger fixings all down the front of my shirt. A piece of meat, I can handle."

The pair went quiet on their way back to the van, and Ruthanne drove a mile or so down the McKendrick road before she trusted herself to speak.

"You don't have a single thing to prove, Ches Durham. I love you! Truth be told, I don't think about your so-called limitations except to admire what you've overcome."

"I love you, too, Ruthanne, and I'd never want to embarrass you. Not like I'm makin' any great sacrifice," he admitted with a grin. "I don't care all that much for store-bought bread. Hamburger buns, neither. Aunt Sis fed me too good for too long."

"You know those muffins we ate this morning?" she ventured with a reluctant half smile.

"Sure; I really enjoyed them."

"Maybe so, but they were sort of a cowardly substitution."

"Do what?"

"I didn't want to fix biscuits because I know how much you like the way Miss Sis makes 'em. Gram's... My biscuits are tasty enough, I suppose, but they're little bitty things. She rolled the dough out and cut her biscuits with an old snuff glass, so that's the way I've always done it. Same glass and everything. Pap could eat five of them on the sickest mornin' he ever stumbled out of bed. They turn out pretty and dainty, but one of the boss lady's biscuits will make four of mine."

"Everybody's homemade biscuit comes out different. Besides, I would never compare you to... Nobody's perfect, Ruthanne. The Lord drove that point home right sharply while I was strugglin' to let go of Serena Kate. I learned my lesson, sugar pie, and you're as close to perfection as I'd ever want to get. You don't need to dazzle crowds as a trick rider or lose any weight or duplicate my aunt's biscuits. All I want is you, just the way you are."

Sudden tears threatened, but she blinked them away with a smile.

"Looks like we're on the same page, Ches. Being with you is a pleasure, not an embarrassment. You hang onto that, and I'll try to remember just how precious I am in your eyes. The little diet and exercise comments have become a sort of defensive reflex for me... With all your sweet compliments, though, I'm not apt to do much about it. Probably might as well hush up and be thankful for my pretty smile."

"Suits me," he quipped. "I can't take but just so much of you running down my very best girl!"

Ches rolled ahead of her into the sale barn, turning on lights. He unlocked the inner office and motioned her toward a worn library table alongside the boss lady's desk. Ruthanne, a natural-born hostess whatever her surroundings, laid their meal out neatly. They bowed their heads for a blessing, and a few minutes later, she glanced up with a tasty fry poised in one hand.

"Now," she inquired brightly, "how come you wanted me to see the books?"

"Aunt Sis and I do things pretty much in step, just comes naturally for us. It's been a blessing, but some folks probably reckon I'm just coasting along on her lifetime of work and good judgment. And, well, I couldn't stand to have you think that way."

"Ches, I never... Still, the boss lady might figure poking around in the bank statements and such is a little above my paygrade."

"Oh, I've already talked to her."

"Naturally," Ruthanne answered with a smile and a bemused shake of her head, "but I still don't quite understand why I need to look at your books."

"Remember what Lonnie Ray told you about getting promoted off the riding crew? Well, you'd better think that deal over. We ain't never bounced a check, and the riding hands always get paid."

"Hold on there, m'darlin. Just like you wouldn't want me to think you'd scooted along through life on Miss Sis's cotton sack... I don't aim to have it whispered around that I'm after what you've got instead of you."

"They'd better not say it where I can hear 'em. Nobody knows about this little business meeting, just me and you and Aunt Sis. Besides... If a girl wanted to marry money, there's way too many prospects out there to waste any time on me. Long story short, I think you ought to know just where we stand."

"You're enough, Ches. Real faith, kindness, integrity, and the way you look at me—"

"I understand, but a prospective husband ought to be able to care for his bride. I can offer you certain things in this life, sugar pie but not without your help."

"I'll do whatever's needed; surely you know that by now."

"The Lord is always enough. Still, the thought of losing Aunt Sis throws a pretty big scare into me. A sizable piece of my heart's bound to go with her. Then, too, I could hire a full regiment of U.S. cavalry and still not make this old place run without her. But, me and you together... Anyhow, just take a look at the books."

"I'm here, Ches, and I aim to stand hitched. Miss Sis is fairly young yet; I don't want to think about saying goodbye to her any more than you do. Still, if that day ever comes, we'll face it together."

"Ruthanne, you just don't know what that—"

Leaning in close, she brushed away a single tear and then trailed her finger gently down his cheek.

"Don't cry, now. I'll get to bawlin' and ruin what little bit of makeup I've got on."

They finished their meal in the warm glow of shared laughter. After spreading a series of ledgers across the table, Ches waited quietly while Ruthanne examined each one.

"With Short Stuff and Buttons and Thimble stacked up around here," he began teasingly, "I'll bet you thought I just sort of accumulated horses. I sold eight head in that last auction. There's six on the books for Aunt Sis and ten that we owned together. Two dozen total out of two hundred and five in the sale. We collect a ten percent commission on consignment horses or a fifteen-dollar PO fee on whatever don't sell."

"I never questioned the number of horses you kept. Well, excepting a little twinge of guilt knowing you held on to Buttons and Thimble to spare my feelings. Love 'em all, honey child. But don't fall in love with none of 'em, thus saith Miss Sis."

"She always warned against falling in love with a horse," he qualified. "Buttons and Thimble are here because I love you. We'd have to keep something gentle for Cassidy, anyhow, and they'll fit into the therapeutic riding program."

"Yes, only, with everything Buttons knows and Thimble matching up so good... They ought to fetch some real money, especially if we advertise them right."

"Reckon your heart's up to that?"

"If 'thus saith Miss Sis' is good enough for you, m'darlin, it's good enough for me, too."

"I'll let you make that call, Ruthanne."

"They belong to you," she reminded him hesitantly.

"Yep, but if you're sure about letting them go, this can be your first decision on the business end of things. Just think of it as a sort of graduation off the riding crew."

"You mean I'd get to choose where they go?"

"You'd handle the whole deal. Just remember what I gave for them."

"You paid me good and still bought them at a reasonable figure," she reflected, eyes sparkling with sudden enthusiasm. "There's gentle horses out there that'll serve our purpose without the advanced training or flashy looks it takes to bring in the big bucks. We're in the right spot to get 'em, too. I like that sort of charcoal line-backed dun that Miss Sis picked up last week. She acts plumb gentle, and I talked the boss lady into holding her out of the sale. Let me ride her tomorrow, and I'll find out what we've got."

"I've been trading horses and managing my own money for the better part of fifteen years now," he said, trying to sum things up for her. "Bought the Doc Parmalee place, everything but his house, from my parents. Me and Aunt Sis run cattle and horses on it, and besides, it joins the homeplace."

"You've got cows on Giles Parmalee's land over by us, too, don't you?"

"Uh, huh, I lease pasture from Giles. Those cattle are mine straight out, but I kind of let Uncle Andrew manage them like he does for Aunt Sis and for the partnership. Don't get me wrong; we watch them pretty close. But Aunt Sis gets a bigger kick out of riding hard after some old bunch quitter, whooping encouragement to her dogs, than from putting pencil to paper to assess the cow's mothering ability."

"One hundred head of cattle outright, or thereabouts, partnership on two hundred head, half of a monthly horse sale, plus the trading... And then there's your magazine articles." She ticked each asset off on her fingers and then handed him a goofy grin. "Why, Chester Joel Durham, you'll see the dollar signs rolling behind my eyes just any minute!"

"It adds up to a whole bunch of work, sugar pie, and not much else in today's world. Still... I count myself blessed even if some folks don't see it like that. This old place made a man out of me, and Daddy didn't mind that a-tall. As an accountant, though, he figures my earning power is grossly underutilized."

"Working the homeplace and the horse sale keeps you happy, m'darlin. Your articles generate more income and give you a nice creative outlet to boot. Your daddy just doesn't want you left in a bind without Miss Sis. Not that you depend on her financially, but as your partner, she plays a vital role in the business. Mr. Durham hasn't yet realized that I can fix you up a nice little insurance policy with just two words."

"Insurance... What words?"

"I do," she answered softly, but her voice gained strength under his loving smile. "Like you said, Ches, together we'll keep this old place running. What you've got here may not add up to much nowadays, but it'll buy and sell a lot of fritters. I didn't exactly grow up livin' high on the hog."

The rocking chairs out front generally accommodated sale day customers, but Ches and Ruthanne lingered on their way to the van.

"Big old moon and plenty of stars out tonight."

"Mmm," she replied softly. "Pretty as a picture."

"Something I can't quite get around," he confessed after a long silence. "How could I have been so wrong about Serena Kate? The two of us grew up together.

*Beyond the Parmalee Bottom* 219

If she couldn't overlook the wheelchair to find happiness with me, how can you? Please understand, sugar pie, I'd never doubt your sincerity. I just don't want us to run headlong into something and then have you wake up some morning to regret throwing your life away."

"We're not running headlong," she assured him, so calm it seemed almost startling. "I've finally settled down in one place long enough to enjoy being courted and fussed over by the neighbor boy. Something tells me this oughtn't be rushed."

"Oh, Ruthanne..."

Reaching for her hand, Ches gave it a gentle tug. Without further encouragement, she left her own rocker and settled onto his lap.

"You weren't wrong about Serena Kate, m-darlin'," she murmured with her head resting comfortably against his chest.

"Wh— How can you say that?" he blurted.

"Oh, I'd love to hate her. Guard my little jealousies, and feel ever so superior knowing I'd never hurt you that way... But I've watched her take care of the residents at Pinevale, seen her devotion to the twins, and even caught glimpses of the respect she feels for you and Miss Sis. You weren't wrong, Ches. You thought she was a very special person with a heart as big as Texas. She is. You may be kind of a sucker for a big-eyed female with a sad story, but that doesn't necessarily make you a poor judge of character."

"What do you mean, sucker?"

"Oh, come on, Ches," she breathed, tilting her head slightly to look up at him. "Poor little orphan girl spends childhood looking after Pap while he drags her all across the southeast from one fairground to another... I would never intentionally use my background to trap you. Still, here I am curled up safe and warm in your lap."

"You hear me complaining, don't you?"

"As for your physical handicap," she continued with only the trace of a smile, "I'd venture to guess that's not why Serena Kate left in the first place. She's toting a good deal of baggage, and the most complicated emotion she cares to discuss is a heartfelt desire for the next Mountain Dew. Serena Kate's fond of you, m-darlin. She loves her friend Ches, and she knew you could make her life easy and comfortable."

"Then why…"

"Guilt or conscience or maybe the Lord, something got to working on that great big heart of hers. Not sure how to match your kind of devotion, she took herself completely out of the picture. It might be just as simple as that."

Ches rocked them gently back and forth. Eyes closed, he drank in Ruthanne's scent and the warm comfort of her weight on his lap. He thanked God quite reverently, but a touch of humor played around the edges of his mind. Cerebral palsy hadn't been enough to keep him out of the saddle, but if he could stay right here with this lovely lady snuggled close against him…

"Living on my own never seemed very practical," he finally ventured, "and I'm not exactly geared for it anyhow. You know I spend most of my time with Aunt Sis. If not there, I'm with Mom and Daddy on the old Doc Parmalee place. Thing is… I've been saving for a long time, Ruthanne, and I reckon we could buy a nice little home for ourselves."

"I've got Pap to consider," she replied gently. "Our rent house will do nicely for the time being. But how would you feel if I moved my church membership to McKendrick Missionary Baptist?"

"Really! Oh, sugar pie, I just can't tell you… We both know a church home is a matter for prayer and consideration, but I reckon you've already taken care of that part."

"Growing up without the love and security that comes out of family roots, I prayed and cried and poured my heart out before God. And He's been mighty good to me, Ches. In His own perfect timing, He led me right here to you and the whole Durham legacy. In the morning, or just any time you get a chance, look up the first chapter of Ruth. Read verses sixteen and seventeen, m-darlin, and you'll know exactly how I feel."

"Ruthanne, what could you possibly see in me? What did I ever do to deserve… Never mind; don't answer that. Just know how very grateful I am."

*Beyond the Parmalee Bottom* 221

"You're the one giving me... Well, we could argue about that all day. I'm reasonably sure they'll send my letter from Holly Springs, but I'll have to get ahold of Aunt Lurlene and figure out whether or not they actually excluded Pap. All that business happened so long ago..."

"Pap's a character, alright, but what did the old rascal ever do to get himself excluded?"

"Oh," she admitted reluctantly, "I expect there was reason enough if anybody cared to look, but the real trouble didn't start until he let Fairview go to the bank. Aunt Lurlene is Gram's youngest sister. She'd be about sixty, now, and never did act too concerned about it all. If you want to know the truth, though, the rest of the bunch got some kinda hot."

"You mean they brought family business into the church?"

"Pap didn't exactly help matters. Told everybody the old place was just one big rock pile with half an inch of topsoil spread over it. He said later that the light in Gram's eyes was the only reason he ever wanted to hold Fairview. When she died, he just up and quit. Always was sort of fiddle-footed. Of course, the rest of 'em had their own lives and never showed much interest in the land until after it was just about gone."

He waited several minutes after her story trailed off and then returned to the subject of a future home.

"Aunt Sis has always kind of hinted that I ought to start married life in the big house, but I don't know that I could bear to see her leave it. She's never lived anywhere else, not ever."

"What about Cassidy? Later on, I mean."

"Uncle Andrew's a good provider. Aunt Sis figures he can take care of their girl. She's always claimed the Durham homeplace will come to me. They own the old McKendrick house up town, too. It's the idea of her moving off the homeplace that I can't quite get my head around."

"That McKendrick home really is large," she reflected. "The big in 'big house' is more of a notion than a size."

"You noticed, huh? It's a regular money pit, too, hot in the summertime and drafty in the winter cold. But Aunt Sis loves it up there, and so do I. Our... If we... If the Lord ever blessed you and me with children, they'd make the sixth generation."

"If you're huntin' somebody to talk you out of a sentimental notion, Ches, don't look at me. My heart's a'flutter right this minute. That hill kind of overlooks everything... Right handy to the sale barn, too. See there," she quipped triumphantly, "our dreams are as practical as anybody's."

"That's my girl," he declared, laughing joyfully even as he hugged her close.

"Your aunt practically draws her lifeblood from the homeplace and horse sale. She's a fine, Christian lady, and she's got her family now. Still, you know how it is with her."

"I know how she is about me, too. And, sugar pie, if y'all didn't love and appreciate one another, she'd be worse than any mother-in-law."

"That makes me your perfect match," she answered lightly. "The competition probably wouldn't put up with it."

"Oh, yes, all that competition," Ches shot back, matching her silliness. "We've been turnin' away two or three applicants a day for years now."

"All I can say," she drawled, eyes dancing, "is thank goodness for Miss Sis and her whip."

"I reckon we've got plenty of time yet to figure out living arrangements," he said when they finally stopped laughing.

"We could always try to buy the Giles Parmalee house," she offered speculatively." "Live there ourselves or swap it to Miss Sis. I know you don't much like the thought of her leaving the big house, but that's not accounting for all the happiness she'd get out of seeing us settled there."

"You're awful wise, my sweet girl, wise beyond your years."

"Let's don't talk about years, Ches. Sometimes I feel—"

He laid a finger against her lips, stopping her in mid-sentence.

"Hush, now," he murmured gently. "If you were any younger or prettier or... I just couldn't stand it. On that note, I'd better get you home before Pap comes looking."

"I'm afraid doing right is pretty much up to us," she answered with a sigh. "Pap loves me, bless his heart, but he's got the attention span of a child and all the motivation of a lazy yard dog. Unless, of course, there's a quick dollar involved."

The admission tugged at his heartstrings, and words poured out in a rush.

"I'll be here for you, sugar pie, from now on. You deserve all the love and consideration I can give. God comes first, but you will always be my biggest blessing!"

"Don't go making any promises you can't keep," she half teased. "Miss Sis falls in there somewhere below the Lord and just over top of me."

"She'll understand, Ruthanne. I know she will."

"I'm not so sure," she answered speculatively. "You and Uncle Andrew get along just fine, but he steps mighty careful. Cassidy even warned me. 'Don't aggravate Mother while Ches is around, and don't cross Ches in front of Mother.'"

"Her kind of loyalty runs deep, alright, but that doesn't mean—"

"Hush, now," she murmured, consciously repeating his own words back to him. "As long as we keep God first and all love one another, I don't see where the rest of it could make that much difference."

With that, she hopped off his lap, kissed him lightly, and strolled away toward the van. Moonlight and denim set off her receding wiggle so perfectly that most of a minute ticked by before he scrambled out of the rocker and into his wheelchair to follow.

"How does your back feel?" Ches inquired as she started the van and shifted into reverse.

*Beyond the Parmalee Bottom* 224

"Was there something wrong with my back?" she quipped. "You did a fine job of petting and fussing over me, Ches. I'm as good as new!"

"You needn't jump off a horse every time you want a little attention. I enjoy it as much as you do. Looks like a pretty full day tomorrow. Did you want to squeeze in a ride on that new mare or hold off?"

"First thing in the morning? It won't hurt Pap to scramble his own eggs once in a while."

"First thing in the morning," he agreed, "and bring Pap along. We can't have the old rascal out of sorts. Aunt Sis'll feed him."

"Thanks, Ches. I know you want to take me home, and walk me to the door, and all that, but…"

"You're right," he conceded. "It'd make more sense for you to drop me at the big house and bring the van back in the morning. Just give me a call once you're inside the house."

"Mercy," she teased, "I hadn't heard about the latest rural crime wave."

"You could turn an ankle or something," he defended with a shrug. "Besides, I'll sleep better knowing you're home safe."

The teasing light left her eyes rather suddenly, and she seemed to focus intently on the gravel road as it wound its way up the hill.

"Well," she finally sniffled, "when you put it like that…"

Ches knew his mom would be up watching the ten o'clock news, so he sent her a goodnight text after the phone call from Ruthanne. Slipping into bed under one of Grandmother Durham's handmade quilts, he prayed a short but grateful prayer and then drifted off to sleep amid the familiar night sounds of the big house.

"Good morning, beautiful!" he called brightly from the kitchen door.

"Mighty glad to see you, too," Pap groused but then slipped Ches a wink.

"Good morning, Ches," Ruthanne answered warmly, and then her smile took in the whole room. "Morning, y'all. We're fixin' to take a little ride, Miss Sis. Anything I can do down at the barn?"

"Nothing special. I guess you saw Buttons tied to the old oak? You might turn him out for me if you're not gonna ride him this morning."

"Did my boy do something wrong and get himself hooked onto the tree of knowledge?"

"No," Sis answered lightly. "I kept him up for a night horse."

"Thought you generally penned a night horse down at the sale barn?"

"It's quail season, sugar. Andrew's in cahoots with the doctor, making sure I walk until I'm sick of it. As long as we're chasing after those bird dogs of his on foot, I can go back to the colonel's old system and keep a horse ready to hand."

"Don't try and fool me," Andrew chided lovingly. "You enjoy it."

"Well, carrying that little .410 over my arm sure beats walking for the sake of walking. Your dogs are a pretty sight, too, when they get down to business. Mostly, though," she admitted with a reluctant smile, "I enjoy watching you have fun."

"Can't say I share the feeling," he teased. "I'm just about burnt out watching you a'horseback!"

Both couples laughed at the little joke, and Sis stepped away from the stove long enough to drape an arm across his shoulders. Seated across the kitchen table from her dad, Cassidy looked like an unwilling dress-up doll with her own personal thundercloud hovering overhead.

"How are you people so happy this early in the morning?" she grumped.

Sullen resignation contrasted sharply with hand-rolled curls and the stiff formality of a vintage Sunday dress. The young teen's obvious plight won a sympathetic scowl from Pap, but Ruthanne missed it altogether.

"Cassidy, hon," the older girl observed in passing, "that little dress is just darling on you, and Miss Sis must've spent hours on your hair!"

"I wish you had the darling little dress and the hairdo along with it," Cassidy muttered, keeping the words safely under her breath.

"How about a pretty smile to go with the pretty outfit," Ches drawled.

His voice held the mild warning tone generally used on cow dog puppies that had yet to do anything wrong but were about to make a mistake.

"Thanks, Ruthanne," Cassidy amended, and with a little effort, her expression almost matched the words. "Let Mother do your hair some early morning. I'm sure you'd both enjoy it…"

Swinging up onto her trick horse, Ruthanne jogged down to the barn. Before she could turn the paint out, Ches decided he might as well just ride Buttons. Once in the saddle and strapped down, he found the sturdy gelding responsive and eager to please. Roxy gave her pups the slip. Knowing this would be a fairly short jaunt through the pasture, Ches kept quiet and let her range out front with the other dogs.

"Cassidy's right, you know," he decided as their ride got under way. "Aunt Sis would love fooling with your hair. That kind of thing is good to occupy her hands whenever she can't busy herself outside."

"Years and years since anybody pampered me that-a-way. Well, not counting your wonderful back rub."

"I love seeing you relax. Just anything I can do to make that happen… Say, you know what puts Aunt Sis right to sleep? Having her hair washed. Ms. Lillian is a sure-enough beauty operator, not a glorified barber like that bunch up town, and one of the sweetest ladies you'll ever meet. I'll pay for it, Ruthanne, if you'd like to go."

"Why, Ches, is that your way of telling me you're tired of this plain old braid floppin' down around my shoulders?"

The accusation, lighthearted though it was, nearly stole his voice. They rode five or six more strides in silence before Ches reined to a stop.

"I wouldn't change one single solitary thing about you," he exclaimed, leaning forward in the saddle for emphasis. "I'm always amazed that you can do that braid so quickly and have it look so neat. Your hair's real pretty when you brush it out, too."

"You're awful sweet, Ches, but I was just playin' around. I'll ask Miss Sis to make the appointment if you think it's something I'd enjoy."

"You wouldn't have to go every week or change up your hairstyle or... Just go whenever you want that little bit of extra attention. As much time as we spend up at Pinevale lately, you could probably catch Ms. Lillian when she comes in to do Aunt Hattie and her other ladies, but that wouldn't be quite the same as going out to the beauty shop."

Ches started his horse off at a walk once more and Ruthanne kept pace.

"Whatever you say, m-darlin.'"

"Her husband, Bowie Tate, is my good pal and a first-class collector of assorted stuff. He's generally got an antique tractor or a hand carved walking cane or maybe something as simple as an old piece of harness, and it's always worth looking at. He'll have a grin and some kind of wisecrack for you, too."

"Is the beauty shop in their home?"

"It's there on the place, sits between the house and the road."

"Maybe I could take them a pie or a cake or somethin' when I go. This new baking hobby of mine is turnin' out more than I know what to do with."

"I don't know of a finer Christian couple. You would've met them both already, but they go to church in the county seat. Bowie was raised up there at the edge of town. Ms. Lillian grew up out here, or at least, I think that's how it goes."

"You and Miss Sis know the entire family history of everybody in a sixty-mile radius, especially if they ever fooled with livestock."

"The Tates run a few cows, but they're not much on horses. Bowie figures they've outlasted most all their usefulness."

"What a notion…"

The young couple rode through three bunches of cattle that morning. Cooler nights had knocked the grass back some, pretty much stopping growth, but the pastures seemed to be holding. Barring a killing frost, Ches reflected, the cattle ought to make it well into November before they needed much hay or feed. Calves looked good, too, and just about ready to pull.

"How does the mare handle?" he finally inquired.

"There's nothing fancy about her, but I can work on that. Her color's kinda neat, and she's gentle as a dog. Just a five-year-old, too. Be here a long time."

"You think she might suit Cassidy?"

"M-darlin… Cassidy don't know whether or not she's ridin' a good one, and she don't care. All your cousin wants is something pretty that won't hurt her. I can make this mare come around to where she'll work for you. Short Stuff's aging on up, ain't he?"

"July made sixteen years since the accident. I brought him and his mama up out of high water in the Parmalee bottom that day. Just a green kid, all by my lonesome, but too worried over Aunt Sis to even think about being scared. It don't seem like the little booger ought to be that old. Time sure gets away."

"I've heard y'all mention the accident. Read about it in one of your early articles, too, but you never have told me that story."

"Don't you ever get tired of listening to my yarns?"

"Ain't yet," she replied with a smile, "but I'll be sure and let you know."

Ruthanne dove headlong into the familiar cadence of his storytelling. She felt a little silly, knowing Miss Sis was safe at home in the kitchen, but blinked back tears just the same. Already aware of the bond between Ches and his aunt, she gained more insight through his memories of that long-gone summer day.

"The old Dolly mare died before Short Stuff ever really got old enough to wean. Giles practically gave him to me, and I spent every spare minute with my colt. Nash cut him as a yearling, and the boss lady went to riding him the next year.

*Beyond the Parmalee Bottom* 229

Little horse was born gentle and plenty smart. Aunt Sis finished him out with a Cadillac handle and then turned us loose."

"The little fella has carried you a lot of miles in safety. I love him for that. Miss Sis does, too, no matter what she might say about not getting attached to any one horse in particular."

"The Lord's given me an awful lot through my horses, especially Short Stuff. If our therapeutic riding program can share just a little bit of that, it ought to really touch some lives."

"You just said a mouthful, Ches. If we keep the Lord in the center of it... Maybe use it as a kind of an outreach. We don't have to beat folks over the head with a Bible, m-darlin. Just tell them all the Lord's done for us and make it clear that we view therapeutic riding as part of our service to Him. We could even do some Scripture memorization with the youngsters."

"Adults, too," he seconded, but the conversation brought to mind a more immediate question, one that caused a tingle of excitement and made his breath come a little short. "Are you fixin' to join the church this morning, sugar pie?"

"Not just yet... We've got the nursing home visit, and Miss Sis is a little bit edgy about that unfinished business between Serena Kate's husband and Lonnie Ray. Takes more than Ethan Fisher to worry her, but I reckon she'll want us on hand."

# Chapter Thirteen

With Ethan taking on some financial responsibility, Serena Kate no longer spent every waking minute at Pinevale. It felt a little strange, being there on a day off, but the couple walked in the front door just as Miss Sis finished her third hymn on the old and faintly tinny piano.

Observing their entrance, Ruthanne caught Ches's eye and then dropped a hand lightly onto the boss lady's shoulder.

"Y'all go on," she whispered. "I'll take care of the singalong, just send Pap out here with that guitar."

"Don't quit, now," Serena Kate objected as Sis rose from her place. "I missed hearing you play. I missed a lot of things, exiled up there to the far north country and all."

"The way I recall it, somebody exiled herself." The familiar drawl carried a bit of an edge, but her next words came out softer. "Anything particular you'd like to hear?"

"Oh, I don't know... *Come Unto Me?*"

Miss Sis turned back to the piano, letting her fingers glide over the keys to produce a familiar introduction. "Hear the Blessed Savior, calling the oppressed;

oh, ye heavy laden, come to Me and rest!'"

The song started out as a group effort. Soon, though, Ches and the nursing home residents found themselves completely enthralled. Serena Kate's bell-like soprano, Ruthanne's flawless, slightly lower tone, and Miss Sis with her rich alto formed an almost heavenly blend. Giles Parmalee's bass churned out a little more gravel than Andrew's smooth vocals, but at the moment, Andrew was home cleaning shotguns.

Even the singers took note. Ruthanne's eyes widened slightly, and the boss lady smiled in unexpected pleasure. Such beautiful harmony, from those three women in particular, hit Ches considerably harder than he would have expected. He watched until a haze of tears blurred the scene and then flipped the power switch on his wheelchair. Motoring from the room, he rounded a corner to listen in private. Miss Sis saw him go and her playing faltered ever so slightly. But Ruthanne's hand on her back and a reassuring nod carried them through the remainder of the song.

"Wow, I did not see that coming!" Serena Kate's exhilarated whisper followed a minute or two of absolute stillness. "What's the matter with Ches, though? I thought we sounded really good. Better than good…"

"He's just fine." Ruthanne spoke with absolute certainty, and out in the hallway, Ches loved her for it. "Probably gone to fetch Pap and give Lonnie Ray a little advance warn— notice."

The words sent Ches off like a shot. He pulled himself together in route, beat Pap back to the activity room, and tried to express his appreciation.

"You ladies sounded wonderful together." He smiled warmly at Aunt Sis but then caught Ruthanne's gaze, telegraphing his heartfelt admiration. "Even Mr. Giles done—"

"I'm not much on religious songs," Ethan Fisher interrupted, raising Serena Kate momentarily into the air, "but that was beyond awesome!"

Ches allowed his smile to broaden into a grin. Approval, much less envy, of Ethan felt more than a little strange, but Serena Kate's squeals of laughter and mock protest made him long to hoist Ruthanne high overhead and see her million-dollar smile.

When the burly fellow set his wife down and turned his attention to Miss Sis, all self-assurance seemed to desert him. He made an immediate bobble by offering his hand first. Rather than shake it, she smiled tolerantly and allowed him to assist her in rising.

"I don't know the first thing about religious songs," she quipped lightly. "*Come Unto Me* is good, old-fashioned church music. Your wife can sing just like a little angel. Started before she learned to talk plain. Anyhow... If you want to see Lonnie Ray, we'd best get to it."

"Ethan's promised me his best behavior," Serena Kate confided quietly. "Whatever happens, don't you let Miss Sis scare him plumb off... Please, Ches?"

"You're not coming along?"

She cast him an uncertain look, but directed a question of her own to Ruthanne.

"Does Mr. Pap play church songs?"

"Mister Pap..." the old fellow echoed indignantly, collapsing in a chair to remove his guitar from its case. "I play 'em frontwards, backwards, and sideways with a fiddle tune or two mixed in for good measure."

"It's been a long time since I got to sing like this, Ches. I'd love to stay, but I won't enjoy it much unless you're looking out for Ethan in the midst of that wolf den. He's the only husband I've got, you know."

"My Aunt Sis and good old Lonnie Ray are gonna be in that room... When it comes to folks I'm looking out for, Ethan Fisher will have to get in line. His best behavior just better be good enough."

"Third slot on the list sounds alright. I've always trusted you."

"That's wantin' to sing powerful bad, or could it be you don't place overmuch value on Ethan's hide?"

Giles spoke the words with a smile, but that hard-edged grin offered very little reassurance as he turned his mobility scooter and fell in behind Ches. Pap talked quietly with Ruthanne and Serena Kate for a minute and then struck a chord on the guitar. Making his way down the hall, Ches heard the girls venture into a close duet of *Whispering Hope.*

Miss Sis entered the sickroom ahead of them all, rapping lightly on the doorframe.

"Hey, there, cowboy..." she said softly, approaching the bed, and Lonnie Ray smiled up at her. "How do, Sonny Boy?" she added, acknowledging his presence.

"The old man said you was bringin' him a visitor..."

"And you came to watch his back?" she ventured, smiling her approval.

"No'm, I figured you had that pretty well handled. I just came to say my thanks for all you and the horse-sale crowd have done over the last month or so."

Dismissing any need for thanks, Sis gave him a quick nod and turned her attention back to Lonnie Ray.

"I reckon this kid's got good intentions, but if he tries your wind or your patience, we'll tend to it."

With that, she joined Ches and Giles by the door, making way for Ethan to step up near the bed.

"Ethan Fisher, Mr. Leggett... Remember grabbing me by the throat and telling me to find work or get out of the county?"

The old cowhand's mouth twisted upward at the corners.

"I may be dying," Lonnie Ray drawled without a trace of concern, "but there ain't nothing wrong with my mind. I see you standing there, so I reckon you hunted up a job."

"Yes, sir, I did. And I want to thank you. Serena is the absolute greatest thing to ever happen to me, but believe it or not, you choking me is right up near the top."

"Sure enough?"

"Seems like I've bumped along all my life knowing I could do better but not sure doing better was worth the effort. I know now, Mr. Leggett. It's definitely worth the effort. I'm helping to support our little family and learning a lot from my boss in the process. It's made a big difference for Serena, not feeling like she has to do everything herself. Even those redheaded daughters of hers seem happier."

"Who you working for?"

"Mr. Stanley, the painter, hired me as his helper."

"There ain't a harder working man around than Billy John Stanley. Rascal's less than ten years behind me and still painting houses."

"You're telling me! It's all I can do to keep up with him. Like I said, though, I'm learning a lot. It feels pretty good to bring home a paycheck, too."

"I'm sorry, kid."

"No, sir, you don't need to apolo—"

"I'm sorry you had to wait this late in life to figure out the benefits of hard work. Lots of ways, maybe, I shortchanged Sonny Boy. But I taught him how to work."

"Taught me, too. I think it's called a crash course!"

"Hard work's important, alright. But putting a hand to the boss lady, that's where you stepped in it. She… She's… Our Miss Sis is—"

Rising emotion worsened Lonnie Ray's labored breathing, and he trailed off unwillingly.

"Take it easy," Sonny Boy drawled. "I'll talk for you. Just about all the old-time cowboys and stockmen around here look on Miss Sis as their special pet. Good men, most of them, but kinda rough. Colonel Durham's little girl was the only softness some of 'em encountered in a day's work."

"Look," Ethan interrupted as tactfully as he knew how, "I know I messed up big time…"

"They watched their little pet grow up and came to admire every one of her ladylike graces, but guts and backbone earned their respect."

"Tell him," Lonnie Ray demanded hoarsely. "Tell him 'bout the time you come a-running to the big house with trouble dogging your heels."

"Which time?" Sonny Boy joked, but uncompromising eyes pinned him with a glare.

"You tell it, or I will."

"I reckon the old man wants you to know just how we all fit together and maybe something about the way it works around here. I was a wild, rough young fella right out of school. Had a fast car and wasn't what you'd call burdened down with good sense. Why, I'll never know, but some of us kids used to aggravate the local law just for the chance to outrun them."

"That may be," Giles rumbled low from his corner of the room, "but you're the only one had my daughter in his car."

"I hear you, Giles," Sonny Boy answered ruefully, fingering the stubble along his jaw. "I hear you. City police chief up at the county seat got kinda full of his own importance, and swore out a couple of grudge warrants, one for me and one for Rose Parmalee. Finally found a young county deputy who'd help him serve those papers without taking it through the high sheriff."

"What did the sheriff have to do with it?" Ethan wondered, interested in spite of himself.

"Marvin Wainwright? My name showed up on his desk every few months in them days. But he never saw no arrest warrants with Parmalee lettered across the top and would've likely smelled a rat. Old Marvin never much liked that city cop in the first place. Anyhow, this one Saturday in particular, Mister Police Chief got to pushin' us pretty hard and blew right on by the city limit sign just like he couldn't read."

"What did you do then?" Ethan wanted to know.

"My old man was out at McKendrick working for Miss Sis, and I'd heard plenty of talk about the way things used to be. See, if the law wanted somebody off the

Durham place, they'd send word and let the colonel bring 'em to town. Nobody wanted to just waltz out there to the sale barn and try to cart off one of his hands."

"Really?"

"My grandfather was a God-fearing man," Ches assured the newcomer. "Law-abiding citizen, too, but he never tolerated much outside interference when it came to running the homeplace."

"The old colonel drew a hard line and made it stick," Sonny Boy recalled. "Then, after his passing, Sis tried her very best to take up the slack. I figured Dad and old Nash might be inclined to help me some, but I knew Miss Sis would put up a sure-enough fight before they took her little cousin Rosie right out of the big house."

"Anybody ought to know that," Lonnie Ray commented dryly, "but it's the first thinkin' you done that day."

"Miss Sis had gone inside to fetch some more blackleg vaccine when I slid us up into the front yard. She stepped out onto the porch and never asked not one question. She caught the tear tracks on Rose's face and saw me throw a glance back over my shoulder. 'Get that cotton-pickin' race car out of sight,' she told me and then reached behind the doorjamb for a shotgun."

"Nah, man… Are you people for real?"

"She called Nash and Dad in, too. They had all kinds of signals between 'em. Sis can do a bobwhite or a whippoorwill so real it'll make you look twice."

"Sure enough," Ches seconded, "or just throw her head back and give out an old-fashioned Texas yell."

"When I got through tellin' about our troubles, she sent Rosie on down the hall to a back bedroom. Told her to stretch out and get a little rest. 'Keep an eye on things, Lonnie Ray. I believe I'll call Uncle Doc.'"

"What kind of doctor, and why did she want him?" Ethan inquired.

"Old Doc Parmalee would pull a sore tooth, set a broke arm, or deliver a baby, but what she wanted was a little help with the legal hornet's nest I'd stirred up."

Knowing Aunt Sis as he did and having heard plenty of stories about her Uncle Doc Parmalee, Ches could just about replay that phone call in his head.

"Get ahold of Racehorse Harry Haughton, Uncle Doc, and then tell Judge Potter he'd better start brushing up on his domino game."

"Domino game?"

"If the old gentleman's gone senile enough to sign a warrant on your great niece—"

"No call for a lawyer," he decided on a sharp intake of breath. "Nash'll take to the warpath just as sure as…"

"Not me," she corrected with a soft chuckle. "They may've put a warrant out for Rosie. I don't know what all's behind it, but I've got her here with me. If Racehorse Harry can't straighten it out, we will."

"Did you call Giles?"

"No, sir… I called you. Rose might not appreciate us getting her daddy involved."

"Keep her out of sight if you want to, but I'm calling him. I'll tell him there's trouble moving in on the big house, and we've got to buy Racehorse Harry some time. You may need a little help."

"Do what you think best, Uncle Doc, but I won't need Giles unless the lid blows off."

"He'll be there, darling, and I'm coming, too. But just hold that lid down, you hear?"

Recalling these words, part advice and part plea, from one who had watched Aunt Sis grow up never failed to make Ches smile. Yes sir, old Doc Parmalee knew her well. Sonny Boy, for his part, lapsed into silence as if the story were over and done. Determined not to look like an anxious kid or clueless outsider, Ethan clinched his jaw muscles. By the time impatience finally got the better of him, he almost stuttered.

"You can't stop now, man! T-tell us what happened..."

"Time she hung the receiver back in its cradle, we could hear the sirens comin' down the road. The boss lady motioned for me to stay put. She stepped out on the porch to meet them, cool as a cucumber and emptyhanded, too. Mister Police Chief might've been blind mad, but that kid deputy came in with his eyes wide open. Sunlight gives a peculiar kind of glint bouncin' off a gun barrel. He saw Lonnie Ray Leggett sidle over to get behind the woodpile and Nash Holloway already peeping 'round a corner of the old smokehouse. A rougher pair never drew breath."

"Do you remember what Aunt Sis told them?" Ches inquired. Having heard the story multiple times didn't keep him from enjoying it.

"Oh, she talked real polite and ladylike, if a tad frosty... Told them this little misunderstanding would have to be straightened out up town, but they wouldn't find me or Rosie in her house."

"No way," Ethan breathed doubtfully. "She lied?"

One long stride carried Sonny Boy Leggett to the bedside where he laid a restraining hand on his father's shoulder.

"Steady, old man," he murmured soothingly. "The kid just ain't never been taught no better."

"It'd serve him well to learn and learn fast," Lonnie Ray seethed through clenched teeth.

"Lied just ain't a healthy word 'round here... Anyhow, she never told no story. Wasn't nobody fixin' to find me and Rosie in the big house 'cause Miss Sis didn't aim to let 'em look. She wasn't but one long step from the doorway and that shotgun, just a-smiling and listening to them jaw at her when Giles came flyin' up the road, Doc Parmalee right behind him, and Sheriff Wainwright trailing the old doctor."

"So, how did it all end up?"

"You do like things spelled out, don't you, kid? I thought the high sheriff was fixin' to have him a stroke. 'Before you two idiots start some kind of a private war out here... Count her guns and then count yours! And you'd better figure me on the fence, 'cause right this minute I'm undecided.'"

"Such plain talk from old Wainwright shook that city cop right out of his quarrelsome mood," Giles remembered with a dry chuckle.

"Racehorse Harry got Rose's name plumb off the books, mostly because she never done nothing wrong in the first place, and argued my deal down to a fine. Miss Sis paid him and covered the fine, too," Sonny Boy continued. "Naturally, I put in some time workin' off my debt."

"What's it like, working for her?" Ethan inquired, and the awestruck apprehension in his voice sounded almost comical."

"Well... I split firewood, dug post holes, and done the kind of odd jobs her riding hands never much favored. Miss Sis quoted me from the Bible all about authorities and powers being established by God. When that didn't sink in too good, she promised to cut the shirt right off my back with that whip if I dragged her little cousin into another brush with the law. Me and Rosie kinda went our separate ways, and that just about wraps up the story."

"I never liked you much, Sonny Boy, but sometimes I wonder," Giles admitted almost wistfully.

"Well, sir, I doubt Rose could've put up with me all these years. Still, if she'd married me instead of that Plano dentist... It ain't likely you'd be rustin' away in this rest home, not with your health reasonable good, and I reckon there'd be Parmalee cattle grazin' your place."

"I've pondered on that, time to time, and maybe even a salty little grandson or two. Kinda gives a fella the indigestion..."

"Aw, well... Don't let it fret you. Lots of water's gone under the bridge. Miss Sis'll scoop up the old place when you're gone and think about you whenever she rides over it."

"Fisher," Lonnie Ray rasped, effectively ending the other conversation.

"Yes, sir," Ethan answered quickly, stepping back up to the bed.

"I'm right proud you come by. Old and wore out as I am, I'm still a brand-new Christian. The Lord do move in mysterious ways...Ain't nobody ever thanked me for strangling 'em before today."

"I don't know anything much about God," Ethan admitted, "but consider yourself thanked."

"My time's gettin' short, Fisher, and none too enjoyable at that. Long as I'm laying here, though, I'll pray for you."

"Means a lot," Ethan said, nearly choking on his emotions.

"Say, Ches... I'm about wore out with company for today, but I want to see little miss before y'all leave. Can't keep much of nothin' on my stomach. When I do eat a bite, it's usually something she brought up here. I'm telling you; that's a mighty fine little lady."

Ches reflected on his special connection to Ruthanne and what a blessing she was in his life. He also felt the last bit of worry over Serena Kate slip away. Shared memories gave the redhead a permanent place in his heart. He would have liked to see her married to a gentleman. But to make the first step along that road, and be any kind of a husband, you had to be a man. Despite earlier misgivings, Ethan Fisher seemed to be at least that much.

"Yes, sir. I'll send her to you."

Rolling back toward the activity room, Ches found himself praying once again for forgiveness. No matter how many times he realized his own worthlessness apart from Christ, the temptation to judge others according to a private set of standards remained strong. Old Colonel Durham's standards, passed down meticulously by Aunt Sis and all wrapped up with a Christian heritage, generally served him well. But... The notion that a man who wouldn't meet certain obligations hardly deserved the air he breathed failed to stand up in light of Biblical truth. While Lonnie Ray's swift choking had obviously turned out for the best, past envy and bitterness toward Ethan Fisher gave Ches ample cause for repentance.

As usual the knowledge of having done wrong cut deep, but God's mercy and forgiveness provided great comfort. He joined enthusiastically in the last verse of *What a Friend We Have in Jesus*. At the end of the song, he caught Ruthanne's eye.

"Where's Ethan?" Serena Kate interrupted before he could speak. "Surely he didn't go out a window?"

"He's fine; handled himself real well." Then, to his own sweetheart, "Lonnie Ray's asking for you."

"Alright," Ruthanne answered quietly.

Gliding out of the room, she slowed just enough to trail a hand across his shoulder in passing.

"*I'll Fly Away*," Pap announced, striking a chord from his guitar, but Serena Kate made her way through the singers and stopped beside Ches.

"Your little miss didn't waste any time making herself a place in the community. My girls just love her to death, and I'm coming around, too. If an old hardcase like Lonnie Ray Leggett's fond of her... I wish people would give Ethan a chance, but you know how it is."

"I misjudged your husband, Serena Kate, or rather I judged him based on the actions I'd seen. Trouble is, I didn't have any business judging him a-tall."

"Ches, I know things haven't..."

"As far as comparing him to Ruthanne... This community is part of who I am. In finding somebody who could get along with me, I naturally found a young lady who'd fit in here. You ran off and left this place behind. You wanted different, and that's what you got."

"He's not as different as you think, Ches," she whispered just under the enthusiastic voices that surrounded them. "His great-grandparents homesteaded up there in North Dakota. Took a lifetime of hard luck, but the next generation finally lost the ranch. His dad was born to the saddle and never forgot that way of life, but he ended up driving a truck over the road. And Ethan... Well, I expect he's done just about the best he could do under the circumstances."

"A ranch kid, huh, or he might have been if things had gone different... I never would've guessed it. Why don't you and Ethan come take a ride with us sometime?"

"Do all your social activities revolve around a horse?" she quipped, but a smile softened the words. "I'll holler at Ruthanne before long. I'm sure the two of us can set it up. And Ches... Thanks."

The week passed more or less uneventfully, and on Saturday, Cassidy agreed to help Ches out with a little extra typing. As they sat together at the computer, the young teen gazed out the window. She watched with mild disapproval as her parents trooped happily off behind a pair of bird dogs.

"Don't you think it's a little cruel?" Her nostrils flared slightly as she asked the question, taking in a good, deep breath in preparation for a dramatic sigh. "Raising those birds just to be released and shot at?"

"The dogs have to be worked," Ches explained patiently. "Those birds are no different than chickens raised for meat, only fried quail goes a lot better with your mother's biscuits and gravy."

"I'm no vegetarian, Ches, but you people are literally trying to clog my arteries."

"I guarantee you it's healthier than fast food. Just look at Ms. Edna, Aunt Hattie, and Giles Parmalee. They didn't get to be that old on green salads. Your dad loves to work his dogs, and it's probably good for Miss Sis. You'll never see her sweating on a treadmill. It's just not who she is."

"At least Mother and I agree on one thing. Treadmills are the absolute worst."

"Listen, tiny britches... You won't have to worry none about exercise for several more years."

"Yeah," she answered with a goofy grin that included her signature eyeroll. "I guess."

"Don't believe everything that comes across your Facebook, cuz. Sit back, watch your parents, and learn a little bit. They take good care of their animals and the land, too. A lot of these critters wouldn't have any purpose at all if me and Aunt Sis and a few others scattered around weren't bound and determined to stick to our way of life."

"Yeah, who else would want to listen to a bunch of squawking guineas?"

"Say, before we get started with this article, I need to ask you something. Me and Ruthanne talked about selling Buttons and Thimble as a performing pair. But I can hang on to Buttons if you want."

"Mother would probably buy them from you."

"I'm not about to charge my Aunt Sis just to keep an extra riding horse around, but with a steady girl to think about, I'd like to make a dollar wherever we can."

"And Ruthanne's okay with selling them?"

"Truth be told, she put the idea in my head. Don't worry. We'll keep you something good to ride. I can get along alright with Pumpkin, and your mother can ride anything with hooves and hair. So, I'd even let you ride Short Stuff until something else comes along."

"You'd do that for me? Short Stuff won't take any beauty prizes, but I have to admit he's something special."

"Beauty prizes? There ain't many quarter horses put together as good as my little fella. Time you learned to look for something besides flash and chrome… You'll be graduating high school before too long. We can't send you out into the world to judge horse stock on color. It'd disgrace the whole family!"

Cassidy harrumphed but then laughed good-naturedly.

"I'll probably move to some big city and impress everyone with my artistic flair… Until y'all come to visit, looking like the Beverly Hillbillies."

"Who says we'll visit?" Ches shot back playfully. "The family ain't moved in the last hundred and forty years. Aunt Sis figures anybody that wants us can surely find us."

"True, if she was going to visit anybody, she would've visited you in Dallas. But there's always Dad… He can usually pull her out of her comfort zone. You and the old people don't exactly help matters, catering to her every wish and whim.

Why would she want to go anywhere when she can stay right here and be queen of the realm?"

"Your mother's done things for me that nobody else could do, and she's helped people around here when nobody else cared enough to bother."

Though he kept his voice level, it vibrated with emotion, and Cassidy tried to swallow her grin.

"Oh, yes... I'm familiar with her magnificence. Sell the horses if you want to, Ches. Riding Buttons has taught me at least one thing. I'll trust you and Mother to pick another good one for me. Now, let's get on with whatever you wanted to write."

"You're sure?"

"Yes, and I'm glad you're getting serious about Ruthanne. She's great! Just enough like Mother to please you without being another pain in my neck. I like Serena Kate, too, but she's almost too laid back and kind of unpredictable."

"Not enough like Aunt Sis, huh?"

"Hey, I never said Mother was all bad. Dependability has its plus side. I'd bet more on Miss Sis being Miss Sis than on the sun coming up tomorrow. But she'd never actually let me gamble, not in a million years."

"You've got it all figured out, don't you, cuz?"

Allowing her grin to break forth, she countered his teasing with an overly sweet drawl.

"Well, I am the boss lady's daughter."

Having helped Miss Sis with the feeding and taken care of the barn chores, Ruthanne set about cleaning tack. She applied a light coat of oil to anything that needed it, washed her hands in the ladies' room, and then paused in the narrow hallway outside the office.

Ches would find her as soon as he finished writing, and the thought made her smile. He treated her like some kind of precious gift. She enjoyed it but couldn't

*Beyond the Parmalee Bottom* 245

help wondering if he would ever realize all he had done for her. It was just about dinnertime, but with Pap spending so many of his days up at Pinevale, she had started imitating Miss Sis, either skip the noon meal or grab whatever came handy. She could go home now with the best of intentions, but a nice piece of cake would be her simplest and most satisfying option.

"Home," she said aloud, and the word rolled musically off her tongue.

The sale barn was home. The entire Durham place was home. The little community of McKendrick was home, too, but the rent house was her own little nest. She might even curl up on the couch with that piece of cake. In the end, however, curiosity won out over her sweet tooth.

Off the clock for Saturday afternoon, she dropped into a rolling office chair behind the payout window, switched on the barn's only computer, and typed therapeutic horseback riding into the search engine.

With just a few clicks, she pulled up a website for the national organization and found plenty of reading material. Antiquated but durable telephones scattered throughout the building rang at top volume. This setup usually compensated for horse sale racket, but today it shattered the stillness of the nearly empty barn. Ruthanne sat bolt upright, forty minutes of research suddenly forgotten. She drew in a ragged breath, chuckled at her own reaction, and lifted the receiver.

"Durham Auction Company; this's Ruthanne."

"Didn't know if I'd catch anybody around the barn, but you're just the person I wanted to talk to…" A young woman's nervous laughter rippled through the phone line ahead of the next words. "This is Serena Kate."

"Oh, how are you this afternoon? Everything okay with the twins?"

"Sure; they're fine. I'm doing pretty good, too. Got off work at noon today."

"Me, too. Although I could be riding if I just wanted something to do. There's always plenty of work around here."

"Tell me about it! I grew up right in the middle of that three-ring circus."

"I love every minute of it," Ruthanne assured her cheerfully.

*Beyond the Parmalee Bottom* 246

"Yeah," Serena Kate replied, sounding somewhat jaded, "you probably do."

"Well," Ruthanne ventured after several moments of silence, "if the girls don't need anything… Is there something I can do for you?"

"Oh, yeah… Ches… Well, he kinda invited me and Ethan to take a ride with y'all. One of those sort of general invitations… You know how men are. I figured we girls would come nearer making it happen, especially if we put our heads together."

"That's sounds real nice. Listen, I'm not sure what Ethan said to Lonnie Ray or vice versa. When they buried the hatchet, though, it went a long way with Ches."

"And how do you feel about my husband?"

"Me? Really and truly? I love him to death," and ready humor lurked just beneath the surface of Ruthanne's words. "I like you a lot better as Mrs. Ethan Fisher than I would as my arch rival."

"Arch rival?" The unexpected words hung between them for a minute until Serena Kate dissolved into a fit of laughter. Ruthanne joined in with a chuckle and then laughed until she snorted, prodding the other girl into renewed hilarity. Finally, though, Serena Kate regained some control of her voice. "I'm suddenly very thankful to be Mrs. Ethan Fisher. You act all sweet, little miss, but I'd hate to face you at twenty paces over a dueling pistol."

"Bullwhip…" Ruthanne panted slightly, but the effort to catch her breath did nothing to hide her mischievous tone.

"W-what did you just say to me?" Serena Kate stuttered between gales of laughter.

"Well, I'm not completely out of touch. Dueling pistols went out with the hoop skirt!"

"As your friend, or at least a concerned observer, I feel like you're spending way too much time with Miss Sis."

"Thank you, Serena Kate. That's just about the nicest thing I've heard all day."

Then, after a slight pause, "We could plan this ride to death and try to outdo one another with fancied up picnic food, but that surely ain't what Ches had in mind. I'll catch us up some horses if y'all want to head this way."

"Works for me; I haven't cooked in three weeks. It's been longer than that since I rode a horse, so you pick me out a gentle one."

A quick phone call brought Ches up to speed and gained his ready approval.

"What do you want for horses?" she questioned as an afterthought.

"You better ride Buttons," he decided. "I built the ad today, a good one, too, with the writeup and pictures you gave me. Anyhow, there may not be too many more chances... Catch Pumpkin for me if Miss Sis ain't usin' her. We'll put Serena Kate on Short Stuff. She can ride, but she never was too confident about it."

"Look here, Ches, I'm not easy to make jealous but to let her ride your horse..."

"No, Ruthanne... Mercy, no. Don't you get the wrong idea. Put her on that running-bred gray if that's the way you feel about it."

"I'm only teasing, Ches. Short Stuff is probably a good idea. Being a pony and matching my horse like he does, Thimble might not do much for her pride. What'll I catch for Ethan?"

"Might be another use for the running-bred gray. Naw... Ethan's supposed to be a ranch kid, but I wouldn't do him that-a-way. The little sorrel mare ought to work."

"Sounds good. Come on down here quick as you can. I know you and Ethan are on better footing lately, but I'd rather have you a'horseback to meet him than dangling in the air when he gets here."

"Miss Ruthanne Prescott... I sure do love you!"

"I love you, too," she replied with a slight catch in her voice.

Ruthanne worked fast and Ches sat confidently atop Pumpkin, gentle but hair-triggered because Miss Sis liked her that way, by the time the other couple arrived.

"Glad y'all could come," he said by way of welcome, "and the weather's made to order."

"It is pretty," Serena Kate agreed, taking in the fall day. Then, as an afterthought, "Miss Sis and Andrew out working the bird dogs? I think she's just about forgiven me, but that doesn't mean I want to ride up unexpectedly while she's armed."

Ches returned her contagious grin but didn't find the comment particularly funny. Nevertheless, he looked on with grudging approval as she and Ethan worked together to saddle their horses. The big North Dakota native swung a cumbersome high-backed rig into place for his wife. Serena Kate, schooled by Miss Sis in her youth, doublechecked the adjustment buckles and potential weak spots on her husband's borrowed tack.

"Aunt Sis would never harm you," he finally said, trying to keep his tone appropriately light, "and you know it."

"Yeah, but the boss lady's notion of actual harm is probably different than yours or mine. I'm a little old for a spanking, Ches. She might consider a good pepperin' with birdshot a reasonable substitute."

"They hunted awhile this morning, but that little .410 is safely back in the rack. I'm not sure what all Aunt Sis might be up to this afternoon."

"Wow, Ruthanne, you must be more of a distraction than I ever was. Ches don't generally lose track of Miss Sis."

To everyone's surprise, Ruthanne smiled warmly.

"I don't know," she quipped. "It may have taken both of us to sidetrack him that much."

"Help a fella out, Ethan. They're ganging up on me."

Ethan glanced up, and a genuine smile replaced his usual blank expression. He climbed into the saddle, looking a bit awkward and out of practice, before voicing his answer.

"You're the tall-talking Texan. Use some of that keen southern wit to dig yourself out of the hole. I'm just a square head from the North Dakota Badlands, myself."

"That-a-way," Ches drawled, "just throw me right under the bus."

"Nothing personal, man… Remember, I married a super cute Texas redhead. Like to watch her in action, too, but I'm not as dumb as I look. There are lots of advantages to keeping your head down and staying quiet."

They rode across the gravel parking lot in front of the sale barn, and Ruthanne leaned expertly from her saddle to open a gate into one of the larger pastures. The other riders passed through, and Ches pulled his horse up short to wait while she closed the gate.

"I'll be sore tomorrow," Serena Kate admitted, "but even after all this time, being out here on horseback feels an awful lot like home."

"Always will," Ches assured her.

"I rode my grandfather's horses," Ethan ventured, "but I don't feel particularly at home in the saddle."

"Oh, I'm not saying I'm any kind of a topnotch rider," his wife qualified, "but Miss Sis made sure we logged plenty of hours on horseback. Not much else to do around here really."

"I know what you mean. I was in the same boat until Dad moved us to town where I discovered the arcade. Not exactly first-class entertainment, but the pinball machine never bit, kicked, or stepped on me."

"Well," she teased, "I've got the advantage there. Ches put me on his personal horse. Short Stuff is downright famous around here, but I've never seen that thing you're riding."

"Sure you have. We saw Ruthanne on this mare the day you and I rode along in the wagon. The day Mr. Leggett turned my life around and you left me on the side of the road in the middle of nowhere, remember?"

"I'm not the one who made you walk back," she reminded him good-naturedly, cutting her eyes toward Ches.

He thought privately that hours, days, or even years wasted in that arcade had set Ethan up for Lonnie Ray's choking but felt more than content to ride quietly along beside Ruthanne. As they rode, he recalled just how heartbroken he had been when Serena Kate left, and reflected on the rich blessings of God.

In all His wisdom and perfect timing, the Lord provided Ruthanne as the ideal match. Not only that, He gave Serena Kate a good life with a husband who obviously needed her support and encouragement. In an extra outpouring of love and tenderness that was just beginning to dawn on Ches, God chose to restore the sweet friendship they had always enjoyed.

Tears gathered in his eyes even as he smiled, but the reverie proved short lived. A pair of bobwhite quail launched skyward right under the nose of the sorrel mare. Her laziness evaporated, and Ethan Fisher felt the reins snatched through his fingers. Childhood reflexes took over, and he gripped instinctively with his lower body.

"Do something! Help him!" Serena Kate shrieked as the mare went by Short Stuff in one long jump.

Having seen lots of bucking episodes, Ches and Ruthanne shared a smile at what they considered a major overreaction. All amusement disappeared in the next instant when Ethan's left leg suddenly deserted him.

"Look out," Ches exclaimed. He ducked instinctively as a good-sized object whirled past his ear, glinting metallically in the sunlight. "What in tarnation was that?"

# Chapter Fourteen

The leg, a high-tech combination of titanium and various plastics, flipped end over end as it arced through the air. Ruthanne turned pale, losing her usual unwavering calm. The gorgeous hazel eyes went as big as saucers and her mouth dropped open.

"Do something!" Serena Kate repeated, adding to the general confusion.

Instead of answering, Ches steadied his fractious horse and then reached over to touch Ruthanne's arm.

"Easy, sugar pie. We'll be alright. There's no way I can get ahold of his horse, but you can."

Ruthanne's pretty mouth snapped shut, and she shook her head to clear it.

"Sure, Ches. I'll get her."

"Gotta hand it to Ethan," Ches drawled as his sweetheart sprang into action. "He's the best one-legged bronc rider I ever saw."

"This is no laughing matter, Ches," Serena Kate fumed, her fear giving way to anger as they watched Ruthanne swoop in to lend a hand. "Why didn't you put him on a more reliable horse?"

"Why didn't you tell me your husband had a leg off?" he shot back, still partially distracted by Pumpkin's nervous antics. "There ain't many horses reliable when a covey of quail breaks right under their noses. Old Pumpkin shied about ten feet! I'd be layin' over yonder somewhere, if I wasn't strapped down tight."

"Covey of quail?" she challenged. "All I saw was two birds."

"Two was more than enough, don't you reckon? Used to be wild bobwhite quail in these parts. Not anymore, but with Uncle Andrew and Aunt Sis releasing birds pretty steady throughout the fall, we see 'em in pairs or little bunches nearly every day."

"Did you ever think about warning the people who come over here to ride with you? Those little ground rockets are more dangerous than Miss Sis and her shotgun."

"You're on Short Stuff," he pointed out, suddenly tickled by the whole situation. "He's as good as any horse that ever walked, but all you done was sit there and holler. Anyhow, Ruthanne's just about put an end to the rodeo."

"So, I'm not a trick rider," Serena Kate grumbled, but an unwilling smile tugged at the corners of her mouth.

"You best go hunt up that leg," Ches told her, one old friend to another, as Ethan and Ruthanne rode back to join them. "Still had the tennis shoe on when it come by me."

"Hey, man," Ethan Fisher confided a minute later, "I've been trying to figure out a way to tell you we had more in common than you thought. Guess it's all out in the open now."

"My legs don't work too good," came the smiling answer, "but everything's more or less permanently attached. A sudden departure like that don't do much for balance. You latched down on that saddle horn real good, though. Kinda reminded me of the early days and trying to ride without this safety rigging."

"Holding on seemed like the best option," Ethan shrugged with a smile of his own. "Where does Serena think she's going? Surely she wouldn't wait this long to act all embarrassed about what I haven't got."

"Don't sell your wife short, buddy. She's gone to look for the leg. Cotton-pickin' thing just about took my head off, but we kinda lost track of it in all the excitement."

Serena Kate's gentle touch and professional experience as a caregiver allowed her to reset Ethan's prosthetic limb with ease. In fact, he never left the saddle. Ruthanne offered to switch horses, but after a moment's thought, he declined.

"I want my most capable rescuer well mounted, just in case. This little horse lost her head for a minute, but she's not mean."

The young people laughed and chatted all the way back to the barn. All four rehashed the near trainwreck. Then, Ches and Serena Kate entertained the other two with childhood stories. A few dealt with their own antics, but the really good tales centered on Miss Sis.

"Saturday night and no place to go," Ches joked in a drawling tone as Ruthanne disconnected the lift cables and watched him settle back into his wheelchair. "Denver Stubbs and his wife are supposed to be cookin' steaks on the old square in McKendrick this evening."

"You mean there's another café up and running in the old bank building?" Serena Kate asked somewhat incredulously.

"It's been a pretty regular cycle for most of our lives," he recalled, clueing in Ruthanne and Ethan. "Grand opening and then, six or eight weeks later, they'll have a going out of business sign in the window. One old boy never did take it down, but he made pretty fair chili."

"Sounds like he was a better cook than decorator," Ethan observed. "I can relate to that."

"Yeah, but he never was too much businessman either. Denver and his missus have worked up a new plan. Catfish on Friday night, burgers and steaks on Saturday… They hope to draw weekend customers from miles around. I guess they'll wash dishes and count money the rest of the week."

"I wish 'em lots of luck," Serena Kate observed, "but if we're going, we'd better go tonight. No restaurant can last long in McKendrick. People eat at home or drive on into big town."

"I don't know," Ches speculated. "Denver and his wife are semi-retired. If their expectations ain't too high... They're buying beef from us and other local producers, so I know it's good."

"If Nash was still living, he'd supply them with fresh, river-caught catfish."

The redhead smiled as she spoke, and when it spilled over into a chuckle, Ches offered an explanation.

"Nash claimed to fish with trotlines, but everybody around here knew he had nets out."

"Everybody but Miss Sis."

The lighthearted challenge in Serena Kate's words left Ethan completely stumped, but a sudden smile illuminated Ruthanne's features. She had come to McKendrick a few years after Nash's death but understood the mutual loyalty that tied him to the Durham family, a particularly strong bond where Miss Sis was concerned.

"The boss lady probably knew, or at least suspected, but as long as everybody called 'em trotlines, she needn't compromise her integrity to protect him."

Ethan nodded as a vague sort of understanding dawned, but Serena Kate spoke right up.

"Ches, your girlfriend... Beg pardon, your young lady, is a little scary. I was born into this community with its unspoken codes, but I never could put everything into words. Whenever we started out into deep water, I just had to watch Miss Sis and try to decide what I was supposed to do."

"Ruthanne's a little like me," Ches acknowledged with a smile. "We weren't born in McKendrick, but we got here as soon as we could."

All the horses tended, they piled into Ches's minivan with Ruthanne at the wheel and headed off to supper.

"The twins trooped off with Cassidy," Serena Kate said conversationally from the back seat. "They wanted to cheer her on at play practice. Surely to goodness they won't stir up too much trouble."

"Those little redheaded girls are fast becoming young ladies," Ruthanne confided over her shoulder. "They'll do fine."

"That right, Ches?"

"Sure… They've always been sweet, and now they're learning how to dial back the rowdy."

"I'm glad you think so. Otherwise, I'd wonder whose little redheaded girls Ruthanne was talkin' about."

All four enjoyed another laugh, and then somehow Ethan began to share early memories of life on his grandparents' ranch. Ches smiled to himself, listening with eyes half closed as both girls chimed in enthusiastically. They discussed the basic similarities and fascinating differences which marked rural life in South Carolina, East Texas, and North Dakota.

A long line of piney woods horse traders, the Durhams could talk with the best of them, but Ches also liked to listen. The conversation hardly slackened as they settled at a table in the crowded front room of downtown McKendrick's only brick building. The notion of Ruthanne and Serena Kate as true friends left him first astonished, then excited, and finally grateful.

Watching two of his favorite people enjoy one another's company gave the evening a warm glow that extended even to the outsider of the group. Having already laid aside his original contempt, Ches determined to be a source of encouragement in the other man's life. As the girls planned an outing for the four of them to go and see Cassidy in the school musical, he turned his attention to Ethan.

"Say," he ventured at the end of their meal, "I owe you an apology. Most of us around here took you for a lazy bum, but we didn't know about the leg."

"I was a lazy bum, Ches," Ethan answered with a wide smile. "Slick roads and one bad night on a motorcycle didn't make me that way, either. I'm missing a leg, sure, but you never let your physical problems hold you back. I needed a splash of cold water to the face, needed it for a long time. Mr. Leggett must have been all out of cold water, but he knew how to improvise."

"Don't go giving me any credit for the way I live. You'd be makin' a bad

*Beyond the Parmalee Bottom* 257

mistake. The Lord's always kept His hand on me. I'd say He put old Lonnie Ray in your path. But in my case, He used an East Texas belle. About three inches over five feet tall, sweet as sugar and tough as nails."

"Yeah?"

"My parents are great people, and I probably would've turned out alright anyhow. With Aunt Sis in the picture, it was practically guaranteed!"

"She's almost a force of nature," Ethan agreed with a nod, "but not all of us get an Aunt Sis."

"Maybe that kind of lady... That kind of person, man or woman, is pretty rare today, but Aunt Sis is just human. The Lord worked through her to put me where I am today. Your turning point came a little later in life, but you seem inclined to make the most of it."

"I'm doing my best, man. You can believe that."

"The thing is, we can't just turn over a new leaf. It won't never last. You need to get to know the One who put a hard-edged old cowboy in the middle of a deserted county road at just the right time."

Serena Kate's cellphone played the little tune that signaled an incoming call. Conversations continued all over the packed room, but her table went silent as she stuck a finger in her ear and made an effort to listen.

"Okay... Yes, I understand. Thanks for calling."

Despite his devotion to Ruthanne and the change in priorities that came with it, Ches had years of experience at reading Serena Kate. Much to his satisfaction, though, Ethan asked the question before he could.

"Are the twins okay?"

"They're fine," she answered in a disconcerted tone, biting anxiously at her fingernails from long habit. "That was Roberta. She's working the night shift up at Pinevale."

"Little Herman Holloway's wife, Roberta?" Ches clarified, delaying the bad news for just another moment or two.

"Yeah… She says Miss Sis and whoever else wants to see Lonnie Ray alive had better get up there right quick."

"Let's go; I'll call Aunt Sis on the way."

Behind the wheel once again, Ruthanne matched their speed to the urgency of the situation while remaining cautious and basically unruffled. Ches called his aunt and then lapsed into prayerful silence. Ethan chatted nervously for the first minute or two but gave it up when no one bothered to respond. Ruthanne kept her attention on the road while Serena Kate focused on larger-than-life memories of Lonnie Ray Leggett. Horseman, cattleman, and general rip roarer…

Pap Prescott glanced up at his granddaughter as the young people rushed into the room behind Ches and his wheelchair.

"I would've called you, Ruthie, but the night nurse took care of it."

As if on cue, a tall black woman in her late forties or early fifties appeared at the doorway.

"I talked to Herman just now," she informed them quietly, speaking of her husband. "He's fixing to call your brothers, Serena Kate. Unless…"

Instead of answering, the redhead nodded somewhat numbly. The death of a patient never failed to tug at her heartstrings. Losing a figure from her childhood, albeit a stern and slightly terrifying one, brought an extra measure of grief.

"We sure appreciate it, Roberta," Ches put in. "Ain't stopped long enough to call the McKendrick boys, but Aunt Sis is on her way."

Nodding quiet acceptance of his thanks, she spoke on more practical matters.

"Herman leaves the house before five o'clock every morning. Still, I expect he'll come on out here. Never wanted our kids growing up around the barn, but that won't even cross his mind tonight. All you horse-sale folks stick like glue."

Ches heard her, but his attention shifted quickly to the hospital bed. Ethan, on the other hand, soaked up her words and filed them away in the back of his mind. Giles, Hattie, and Pap already sat close around the bed, but Ches threaded his wheelchair between them.

"'Bout time you got here," Lonnie Ray rasped between ragged breaths, a grin playing weakly at the corners of his mouth.

"I'm here now." Ches's voice went rough with emotion, but his own grin never wavered. "And Miss Sis is on her way."

"Don't figure I'll last 'til she gets here," the old man admitted, "but I'll see her again. Same goes for Sonny Boy, I hope. How... How come you ain't..."

Lonnie Ray's breath failed him, but Ches read the message plainly enough in his scowl.

"Uncle Andrew's with her. She wants me here. Besides," he added, still grinning even as he blinked back tears, "it ain't quite like losing the colonel. Surely you don't think she'd cripple a horse over you."

The scowl disappeared instantly and even the spasmodic breathing seemed to ease.

"It'll take me a mighty long while to thank the Good Lord for not givin' up on me. But if I ever get around to it, boy, me and the old colonel are gonna have us a talk about you."

"Look out, now... Don't know if I like the sound of that."

Lonnie Ray chuckled a little but then fumbled for the boy's hand.

"You was a good kid, Ches, and you're a good man. This old world's a-changing fast. Miss Sis can't help bracing against it, but that don't exactly make things easy on her. You and little miss stick close beside her."

"We'll stick. McKendrick ain't fixin' to change all that much, no how. Aunt Sis won't have it."

"Stay after Sonny Boy for me, would you?" Lonnie Ray asked with his last bit of strength. "Kid's bound to come around."

Instead of moving up closer to Ches, as some might have expected, Ruthanne stepped over to Serena Kate and whispered something in her ear.

"How does it start?" the redhead inquired in a fretful whisper.

"We read of a place," Ruthanne answered calmly.

She laid a steadying hand against Serena Kate's back, and this bit of reassurance somehow anchored the other girl. Her high, clear soprano wavered at first but gained strength from Ruthanne's soothing harmony. Lonnie Ray Leggett never knew how to quit a fight, but their sweet voices and the sweeter promise, "How beautiful Heaven must be", gradually eased his final struggle.

Ches felt the iron-hard grip on his right hand loosen slightly but took it as a sign of relaxation. The girls sang through the beloved old hymn, and as they entered the chorus for the last time, Ches felt a familiar presence close beside him.

"Got here as soon as I could, honey," Aunt Sis murmured, giving his shoulder a loving squeeze. "I'm glad y'all were with him."

That said, she leaned past her nephew and gently closed the old horseman's eyes. Roberta Holloway glanced briefly at her watch and then noted the time on a clipboard at the foot of the bed. Finished with the duet, Serena Kate caught her co-worker's attention.

"Shouldn't we check?" she asked in an uncertain whisper.

"Don't you reckon she knows?" the older woman replied in what, for her, was a gentle tone.

"Thank you for sending word, Roberta." Then, to the room as a whole, "I'm sorry I didn't make it in time. Used to think the goodbyes would get easier as I got older but—"

"The old rapscallion died like a gentleman," Hattie observed, and despite the unsentimental characterization, her tone held a kind of awe. "Only by the grace of God... You can take comfort in that, Sis."

"Yes," Ruthanne agreed and her voice conveyed a quiet dignity. "You hold on a little tighter than most, but that's something we all love about our Miss Sis."

Thinking back on Nash's death and other shared losses, Ches spent several days glued to his aunt while Ruthanne transitioned seamlessly into the background. Quiet and capable, she attended to everyday tasks with all of her usual grace. Ches recognized the selfless conduct of a true lady but missed everything from her honey-sweet voice to the lovely little imperfection in her gait, remnant of an old injury to the right knee. Every reassuring smile from the corner of a room and every late-night text message full of tender concern highlighted the void her actual absence would surely leave.

Ches prayed about these feelings, careful not to place Ruthanne ahead of his love for the Lord, and then found time for a meaningful talk with his parents. His new resolve to move forward called for a visit with Miss Sis as well, but that would have to come later when his aunt wasn't bogged down in final obligations to a longtime friend.

Instead of asking pointed questions about the money, a subdued Sonny Boy Leggett only wanted to know if there was enough and what he could do to help. Ches quietly suggested Ethan Fisher as a pallbearer. Though somewhat rattled by firsthand exposure to the frailty of life, the young man saw this inclusion as a sign of gradual acceptance into his wife's tightknit community.

As his father's one-time employer and informal legal advisor, Miss Sis helped Sonny Boy tie up loose ends. This took a week or so, but Ruthanne figured life must be returning to normal when Ches asked her to take a Saturday evening ride.

"Before supper or after?" she asked with a smile.

"Let's make it a picnic. Just the two of us…"

"That new mare I picked out for you is coming along nicely. You need to try her one day soon, but we can do that just about any time."

"Give the mare a name yet?" he wondered casually.

"Cassidy's been calling her Faith," Ruthanne answered, wrinkling her nose slightly. "Doesn't sound too much like a horse, but she never asked me."

"Cassidy... When was she around the barn long enough to name a horse?"

"For pity's sake, Ches," she replied, shaking her head in gentle amusement, "the child had to spend her time somewhere over the last week and a half."

"What do you mean?"

"You and Miss Sis treat every death around here like some sort of state funeral. There's nothing wrong with it," she added hurriedly. "I find the whole rigmarole very comforting myself, but Cassidy doesn't understand that kind of thing. She barely knew Lonnie Ray Leggett. Some old hardcase dies and all of a sudden, her mother's practically off limits."

"I never really thought of it that way."

"Of course not... You and Miss Sis did what needed doing, just like you've always done. And Cassidy drifted on down to the barn. She followed me around, complained about various odors, and named your new horse."

"Faith, huh? Unlikely name, I'll grant you, but maybe it's fitting at that. I messed my life up pretty good, trying to handle things on my own. Hardheaded and tenderhearted ain't exactly the best combination, but the Lord never gave up on me. His timing is always perfect."

"Yes, it is," she agreed softly.

"There's another way faith comes into the deal, sugar pie. You picked this mare for me, and there's nobody I'd rather trust to put the miles on and give her a nice, light handle."

"Not even Miss Sis?"

"Not even Miss Sis."

Tilting her head cutely to one side, Ruthanne soaked up his simple statement of confidence before she spoke again.

"Listen, my suppers aren't real handy to tie on behind the saddle. Why don't we take the team and wagon?"

"Oh, I didn't mean for you to cook. We could always buy some chicken or something."

"Fixing our supper is no hardship, Ches. Pretending to enjoy store-bought chicken, on the other hand…"

"Alright, little miss, alright…" he said with an affectionate chuckle. "I'll get ahold of Scooter and see if he'll hitch the team for me this evening. No use in you having to do everything."

"It don't matter who puts the harness on as long as you let me drive 'em again. I really enjoyed that."

"I like driving myself, but not enough to say no to you."

"You'll like supper; I promise."

Leaving his wheelchair up at the big house, Ches borrowed Uncle Andrew's side-by-side and made his way down to the barn. Working alone proved slow, but it filled the hours that lay between him and a special evening with Ruthanne. Alone was mostly a figure of speech, seeing as how Roxy dog shadowed his every move. At this stage of the game, she could still scold her growing puppies and make them stay behind in the back yard.

Gentle, but naturally hostile to dogs, Mack and General struck out with their front feet as Roxy maneuvered them into a small pen. Such blows had crippled and even killed lesser canines, but the agile little cur gave the appearance of chuckling as she trotted happily back to her master.

Ches laid his crutches aside, perched on a rolling stool in the tack room, and grabbed an age-softened rag to wipe down the harness. That done, he picked up a halter with lead rope attached and weighed it thoughtfully in his hand. Having haltered Short Stuff more than once, he knew it could be done, but the mules weren't familiar with his crutches or the somewhat awkward movements that accompanied their use.

"You still figure to ask her this evening, honey? What all can I do to help?"

Anybody else might have startled Ches, but the boss lady's presence was too familiar to ever catch him off guard.

*Beyond the Parmalee Bottom* 264

"Yes, ma'am… Just pray for me; you've already done a plenty."

"What did Pap have to say?"

"Oh, can't you just about hear him? 'Be better to her than I have, son, and that'll make you a good start.'"

"He ain't askin' much there," Sis articulated dryly, "the way he drug that poor child from pillar to post…"

"Ruthanne latched on to the old rascal about like I did with you," Ches observed. "You just happened to be rooted in one spot. Thing is, the notion of settling down here with me would bore lots of young ladies half to death, but Ruthanne's already seen the other side of life."

"Mmm, I never thought about it just that way."

"Aunt Sis, do you sure enough want me… Want us to have Grandmother's ring and the wedding band, too?"

"It's just a simple gold ring, Ches, and one little diamond. If you think she'd like something fancier, I can still take you shopping."

"Ruthanne? She'll love anything that's come down through the family, but are you ready to part with it?"

"After you found your way back here, Ches, I used to squeeze that wedding band in the palm of my hand and pray. Mama's rings have belonged to your young lady for a long time. Exactly when and where to slip 'em onto her finger… Now, that's up to you."

Ches gave his aunt a tight squeeze and kissed her lightly on the cheek.

"Thank you," he whispered and then cleared his throat before turning to a more immediate subject. "How'd you get her ring size, anyway?"

"Cassidy… She couldn't believe it, checked and rechecked, but swears Mama's rings fit perfectly without any need for resizing."

"You don't think Ruthanne got suspicious?"

"Naw, they were just playin' around with Cassidy's old jewelry making kit. One of those phases she went through…"

"And Cassidy doesn't mind giving up the ring?"

"Lord help us, honey, that daughter of mine has no interest in anything old. Your mom's platinum ring with all those flashy stones in it is more her speed. Besides, she's happy for you and Ruthanne. Tickled that we let her in on the surprise, too."

"You raised a mighty sweet girl," he declared as if to reassure her.

"Sometimes, Ches, I think she must see me as this crazy horse lady who glides around the edges of her life. I'm a few calendar years beyond most of the other mothers and at least a generation or two older when it comes to my thinking. All I can say is Andrew's done a mighty fine job with her." Miss Sis laughed shortly and then indicated Roxy in her familiar spot by the tack room door. "I declare, that little gyp watches you like a hawk."

"Yes'm… Kinda puts me in mind of the way old Rhett hovered 'round you."

"Mmm, even looks a little like her grandpappy. Don't expect I'll ever have another dog like him. One in a lifetime is a blessing, Ches. Best enjoy Roxy while she's here."

"She's a dandy," he agreed earnestly. "But I've been watching one of her sons, only black pup in the litter."

"Think he'll make a good one, huh?"

"Maybe as good as Roxy or Rhett."

"Time'll tell, I reckon. Better let me catch those mules, honey. I can't fault your Durham hardheadedness, but I know for certain sure that it'll get you into a bind now and again."

Ches grinned a little guiltily, handed her the halter, and watched as she rose on tiptoe to grab its mate off the wall.

"Now, how would you know anything about being hardheaded?" he inquired with a chuckle.

He pictured his parents' horror at the notion of him catching mules out of the lot and compared it to the loving pride and faint amusement visible on her face. Thankful for Mom and Daddy, he knew that their protection had spared him a lot of hard knocks. But Aunt Sis was a gift, too, and the warm glow of gratitude swept through him.

"Say," he began hesitantly, taking a seat on the gasoline mule to watch while she caught the live ones. "You're not upset because I talked to Mom and Daddy first? Things got awful busy, and I just—"

"Hush, now, honey..." The words came out soft and yet unquestionably firm, as if she were soothing a startled colt. "They're your parents, after all. The two of us have a special bond, and they've been mighty good about it over the years. Still, something like this... You done just right."

"Ethan Fisher reminded me the other day that not everybody gets an Aunt Sis."

"Come again?"

"When I'm caught up in the middle of something, you can step back, look it over, and tell me exactly what I'll think later. Hearing you say I done right... That's a mighty rare kind of validation."

"I've always known we looked at life just about the same way but ain't never found the words to lay it out so plain. That's why you're the writer in the family, and I just piddle around tradin' horses."

"Piddle around? I never wanted anything more than to be just like you. I hope you know that."

"That's settin' your sights a mite low, honey," she drawled, flashing him a grin that blocked further protest. "Want me to go ahead and hitch the team?"

"Yes'm, if you'll make a round with me."

"Sure will!"

"You could've sold Mack and General half a dozen times," he commented as his aunt circled the mules for a final check of their harness."

"Mmm, but ain't no telling what it would cost us to replace them."

"Seems like mules are kinda high these days," he agreed with a nod.

"Some folks swear by mules, Ches, and others just swear at 'em. They come 'bout like horses, though. Good, bad, and indifferent…"

"You talking about mules, or people?" he quipped, clambering up into the wagon.

A smiling wink gave him answer enough. When he was squarely planted in the driver's seat with lines in hand, she untied the mules and climbed up beside him.

"Reckon I'll hang on to these boys," she declared as they started off, "leastways until somebody wants a crackerjack team worse than we do."

"On the subject of swappin' stock, Ruthanne's been riding one of your horses especially for me. I reckon we ought to settle up on that deal."

"I know the mare, honey. Bought her in a little bunch, and the rest of 'em paid out right well. Go on and take her if she suits you."

"Aunt Sis, I'm getting a little old for you to be keepin' me in riding stock free of charge. Ruthanne's got the mare coming along real good. She ought to bring you a fancy price."

"Fiddlesticks; it'll all come out in the wash. Looking back, now, I guess the colonel furnished my horses right up until he died."

"Yes'm, but you rode alongside him for a living."

"Ches, I want you to have the mare, and I'm not about to sell her to you. Why, I don't even know for sure what I gave—"

"Hold it, Miss Sis. Wait just a minute," he drawled in loving amusement. "Don't try to pull that stuff on me. If you bought that mare in a bunch, you know just exactly where you had her figured and how much she ought to bring. Let me know, and we'll clear her off the books."

She nodded reluctantly, gazed off into the distance for a long moment and finally spoke again with a note of tenderness trembling in her voice.

"Thanks, honey, for sticking close by me while we got Lonnie Ray laid to rest."

Placing his driving lines momentarily in one hand, Ches reached over and pulled her into a hug.

"No need to thank me. Sometimes it feels like I ought to thank Uncle Andrew, or maybe apologize for always being right up in the middle of everything."

"You're a part of me, Ches Durham. Andrew knows that. Besides, I would've been hard pressed to find a more patient and understanding husband. He'd a lot rather see me at ease, bless his heart. When you're not around... Gone to the Hill Country, for instance, that gets to be a pretty tall order."

"If I'd ever guessed you needed me here, Aunt Sis..."

"I know it, but your old aunt's not plumb helpless yet. Besides, you met Ruthanne on that trip."

"Know something?" he ventured after a minute or two of silence. "I believe God's timing is every bit as important as His blessings and protection."

"Right as rain," she agreed softly. "Andrew is one of my dearest treasures, but with my heart set so completely on the past... Why, I might've run the man slap off."

"Run him off?" Ches asked, genuinely bewildered. "You're a wonderful lady, an absolute beauty, and fearless on a horse! What else could anybody want?"

"Pshaw... It's just a blessing you managed to soften me up before Andrew came along."

"Maybe the Lord used me to show you that change wasn't all bad, Aunt Sis, but you were always plenty soft where I was concerned."

She smiled, shaking her head a little at his ability to hit so accurately on the truth. The rest of the ride passed in long stretches of comfortable silence interspersed with short exchanges about this horse, that deal, and the upcoming sale. Stepping down from the wagon in front of the big house, Miss Sis cleared her throat and spoke gently.

"Enjoy your evening with Ruthanne, honey. It's something you'll both look back on and hold mighty dear."

"Yes'm... Part of me wishes you could be there with us, but I guess maybe that ain't how it's done."

"I'd like to catch a horse and trail up close enough to hear the proposal," she said with a teasing kind of chuckle in her voice. "Don't seem to ride as quiet along the edge of the woods as I once did, though. Horses must be gettin' clumsier, don't you think?"

"Bound to be," he agreed huskily, fighting a sudden lump in his throat.

Miss Sis nodded at him, a decisive gesture that carried all her support and approval, and then walked through the yard gate and up toward the house.

"Aunt Sis," he called softly. Pausing at the top of the steps, she squared her delicate little shoulders and turned slowly to face him. "I love you more than I could ever say. What you said about holding on to this evening... I'll always remember the way you look right now, standing there on the porch so pretty and brave."

"I love you a bushel and a peck, honey. Ruthanne, too... The colonel raised his little lady to be tough, but if you don't speak to those mules and get out of here right quick, I might just break down and bawl."

She raised her right hand in farewell, giving him the briefest glimpse of a crumpled lace handkerchief.

"Get ahead!"

Mack and General lunged into their collars, and the abrupt start helped to settle his nerves. Ches considered pulling the team back to a walk but decided the brisk trot suited him better. After all, Ruthanne waited just beyond the Parmalee bottom.

# Chapter Fifteen

The 1960s brick home sat out in the open. Large shade trees marked it at either end, but in the absence of a yard fence, Ches brought his team to a stop right up alongside the front door. He felt next to useless watching Ruthanne make three trips just to get their picnic supper into the wagon. She glided easily back and forth, though, and fairly bubbled with pleasant conversation.

"I've worked a'horseback for my living nearly as long as I can remember, Ches. There's nothing quite like the beauty of God's creation, but I sure enjoy bustling 'round my very own kitchen for a change. Makes me feel like a little girl again, playing house or some such thing."

"Really? Aunt Sis can't stand to be cooped up very long a-tall."

Instead of workday blue jeans and dusty riding boots, shiny black Ropers peeped from under a long denim skirt. She carried a light jacket over one arm to wear in the cool of the evening, but the ruffled apricot blouse suited her sun-kissed complexion. A simple gold locket provided the finishing touch.

Had old Pap Prescott spilled the beans? Surely not, Ches decided, mainly because her gorgeous hair hung half-forgotten in the familiar practicality of a single braid. Her kind of beauty never called out for attention, but it was there, as natural and unpretentious as warmth from the sun.

Ches shifted to the lefthand seat as Ruthanne made her way up through the back of the wagon. She brushed his cheek with a kiss and then settled down to take the mules in hand.

"I've missed you, m-darlin."

"I missed you, too, pretty girl," he murmured as she set the team in motion.

"Pretty?" Ruthanne faltered briefly and then accepted the compliment with a bemused little smile. "So long as we're taking the wagon and not riding... I figured I might as well dress up a little. Hope you don't think this getup's too frilly? For a picnic supper, I mean."

"I reckon it's just about perfect. Then again, you could make a cotton sack look fancy."

"I know we talked about fried chicken, but your Uncle Andrew let me have a mess of fresh quail."

"How fresh?" he asked with a note of suspicion in his voice. "I hope you didn't have to clean and pluck birds."

"Well, no, but I can't say I'd mind all that much. You'll have to put up with my little bitty biscuits, but there's lima beans and coconut pie, too."

"Mercy," Ches breathed. "Did you leave anything in the house for Pap to eat?"

"If Pap thought he'd be going hungry," she laughed, "he'd pile right up in the back of the wagon. He's gone to Pinevale again this evening. The horse-sale crowd up there is kinda lost these days. They like to hear him pick that guitar, and it helps occupy him, too."

"Yeah, having Lonnie Ray to sit with kept 'em right busy, and now..."

"Pap claims he's getting out of my hair, but he wouldn't be spendin' time up there if it didn't suit him. Say, Ches, am I headed right?"

"You're driving, little miss. We can ease on up to McKendrick and eat our dinner in the churchyard or make us a circle back to the swimming hole or..."

"Too cool to even soak our feet, but that swimming hole makes a mighty nice spot. Let's take a good-sized loop, m-darlin. I ate a bite or two getting it cooked, and you can snack on the wagon if need be. Daylight may run short on us, but the team's feeling good, and this fall evening is too pretty to waste."

Ches looked away briefly, tamping down a powerful rush of emotion but couldn't keep his eyes off her for very long.

"What did I ever do to deserve you?" he finally asked quietly.

"Let's see here... You rescued me out of a road camp. That ought to count for something," Ruthanne answered with a musical hint of laughter in her voice. When he shook his head doubtfully, though, her lighthearted expression went all soft and tender. "Don't you remember, Ches?"

"Remember what?" he inquired almost hesitantly.

"The way you ran Tiny off that night and then convinced Pap to load up and pull out before I found myself in that kind of a tight again. That kind, or maybe worse..."

They rode along in silence for a while, listening to the measured fall of hoofbeats on the blacktop.

"I don't know just how to put this," he began reluctantly, "but I feel like it's got to be said."

"Just lay it out straight, m-darlin. Pretend you're talkin' to old Roxy or Short Stuff if it helps."

"Ruthanne... Little miss, I... You don't owe me anything. Whatever I've done, or whatever you think I've done, it's been a pleasure. The same goes for Aunt Sis and the rest of 'em. We all love you, and I... You put everybody else first, me or Pap or any of the horse-sale crowd."

"Ches, don't—"

"Look at me, now," he interrupted gently. "Hurts me to ask, but somebody's got to look out for you. Ever wonder about giving yourself a chance with an able-bodied man? Right kind of fella could take the load off your shoulders and maybe even saddle *your* horse for a change."

"Chester... Joel... Durham," she sniffled, ending up with a final choked-off sob. "If I didn't know better, I'd figure you're trying to cut me loose without hurting my feelings too awful much. I've never wanted anybody else, m-darlin. No more than Miss Sis would've replaced you with a nephew who could quick-swap from horse to horse on sale night or rope bronc mules out of the pasture."

Ruthanne shifted the driving lines to one hand, nestled into his lap, and wrapped her free arm around him in a fiercely tight embrace. Mack and General, left momentarily to their own devices, kept to the road and held a steady pace.

"I think you're both plumb crazy, but it works out pretty good for me." After this murmured statement of love and relief, his next words sounded almost abrupt. "Yonder comes a car..."

Still perched in his lap, Ruthanne spoke reassuringly to the mules and brought both hands back into play as she navigated along the righthand edge of the narrow county road. They met the car without incident, and Ches admired her handling of the team. Before he could mention it, though, she shifted around to look up at him.

"I love you, m-darlin, and I always will," she declared. Then, flashing him a whimsical little smile, "Now, let's not hear any more about another fella. And while we're on the subject... I hope you and Serena Kate can hang onto that special friendship, but I'm not exactly above settin' the dogs after some other girl if I ever caught one makin' eyes."

Ches laughed, and ducked his head to rub noses as he held her tightly against him.

"Love you, too, little miss! I'll consider myself duly warned."

"Never said I'd sic no dogs on you," she quipped without missing a beat.

They enjoyed a nice ride, and daylight was fading fast by the time Ruthanne stepped from the wagon. She tied the team to a welded pipe hitching rail that Jim Rex McKendrick had constructed when the colonel's wooden version finally rotted down. Ches climbed slowly to the ground while she spread their picnic blanket under a large, old oak tree overlooking the swimming hole.

The homecooked supper tasted delicious, and Ches found himself particularly thankful for it. Not because he might be fortunate enough to marry an excellent cook but because it provided a distraction from his nervous anticipation. After their coconut pie, he reached quite naturally for her hand.

"Finest meal I ever ate, Ruthanne, and still not half as good as the company."

"Pshaw, I just—"

"Look out, now. If you tell me how you threw all this together without half trying, I'm apt to dunk you in the creek for telling tales."

"Well, maybe I did put in a little effort. But I've enjoyed every minute, from the cooking to the wagon ride to the picnic." Then with a long, wavering sigh, "Tell you the truth, Ches, I'm not real anxious to see it end. I could sit here with you half the night, but if we drag around much longer, Miss Sis is bound to figure we've run into trouble."

"The boss lady won't be out lookin' tonight," he said, smiling even though Ruthanne couldn't quite make it out in the failing light, "and anybody else who took a notion to bother us would just about have to fight her."

"How come?"

"Don't fret, Ruthanne. I'll take you home directly. First, though, I've got something on my mind."

"Surely not, Ches. We've already cried and laughed and done most everything in between."

"Yeah, I reckon... But there's just one more question." Still holding onto her left hand, he removed a small diamond ring from the folds of his aunt's handkerchief and slid it partway onto her finger. "Marry me, Miss Prescott?"

Ruthanne never said yes, no, or I'd like to think about it. She just buried her face against his neck and sobbed for five long minutes. Feeling her nod, Ches slipped the ring securely into place and then held her while she cried.

"Of... Of course, I'll marry you. Sorry for bawling, Ches," she finally managed. "I know you wanted me to bat my eyelashes and say, 'Oh, I expect so,' but I'll never be as cool and collected as Miss Sis."

"I'm just glad you nodded. Had me scared to death there for a minute." Then, recalling the only other proposal he had ever witnessed, "Uncle Andrew was smooth as glass about it all, and Aunt Sis couldn't very well let him outdo her. Besides, she was slap out of breath. Three days gone from the hospital and fresh off a hard six-hour ride…"

"Shortness of breath or her complete lack of nerves under pressure," Ruthanne mused. "Either way, it makes for a good story."

General and Mack jogged them home through the moonlight. Ches gazed lovingly at Ruthanne as she drove but spent much of the time in silent prayer.

"Hard as it is to imagine, Dear Heavenly Father, I reckon Ruthanne is even more precious to You than to me. Thank you, Lord, for putting this amazing young lady in my life. You knew just how the deal would turn out before You ever brought me home to spend that first summer with Aunt Sis. Let Serena Kate go ramblin' off to the Dakotas and break my heart… Called me back to that dismal camp a-way out yonder in the land of mesquite thorns and prickly pear… Then, too, only You could know what Ruthanne's endured chasing all over the country after old Pap Prescott. Help me, Lord, to always be the kind of husband she needs. The kind who'll bring You honor and glory."

"You've gone awful quiet, m-darlin," Ruthanne teased lovingly, "but it's too late for second thoughts."

Ches almost laughed aloud but contented himself with a wide grin.

Interlacing fingers as they talked had become almost second nature, but the driving lines naturally interfered. By happy accident, Ruthanne's perfect posture left a convenient space between the seat and the small of her back, just right for his reassuring hand.

"Second thoughts? Not hardly," he quipped, dismissing the very notion with a soft chuckle.

Ruthanne would have parked the wagon under a side shed and unhitched the team as usual, but Ches redirected her attention with a gentle touch on the arm. Following his gaze, Ruthanne noticed the glow of a porchlight up at the big house and what looked like several extra vehicles parked out front.

"Are we late for an engagement party you neglected to mention?"

"Nothing planned," he answered, smiling at her in the darkness, "but we might as well drive on up there. Most anything that happens around here eventually circles back through the big house."

"That's the truth," she admitted with an amused little shake of her head, "and I ought to know it by now."

"I figured Aunt Sis and Pap might sit up waiting for us…"

"Naturally… But that looks like a whole welcoming committee."

Ches managed to climb down from the wagon and get his crutches under him before Cassidy bounded off the porch with most of their family crowding through the doorway behind her. Shifting temporarily to one crutch, he took Daddy's outstretched hand and then leaned into a tight embrace. Life on the homeplace would never be anything more than a hobby to Terry Durham. But the bookkeeper's pallor was long gone from his face, and his handshake felt steel-strong. Mom stepped up for a hug, and Ches wiped clumsily at the happy tears on her cheeks.

Looking around for Aunt Sis in all the confusion, he realized with a rush of love and gratitude that she had gone straight to Ruthanne. They looked almost like sisters, he thought, foreheads practically touching as they clasped each other's hands and poured out their hearts in murmured conversation. Pap Prescott, thankful for whatever feminine advice Miss Sis might offer, waited patiently a step or two behind.

"I finally snag the lead in a school play, and y'all have to come along and get engaged," Cassidy teased as they trooped inside. "Way to steal my thunder."

"Sweetheart, we never—"

"Know something, Ruthanne? Being too serious makes you gullible. I knew you'd like Grandmother's ring! Planning a big wedding might actually give us a little excitement around here."

The younger girl's enthusiasm brought a warm smile to Ruthanne's face, but at the words "big wedding", she and Ches exchanged a meaningful glance.

"Oh… We just want a simple little ceremony."

"You would," the younger girl grumped.

"None of Gram's folks would come, anyhow. Except maybe Aunt Lurlene… Pap's already here and the Durham bunch, too. Me and Ches can enjoy our engagement for a while and then gather y'all up some Sunday afternoon to watch us tie the knot. No fuss, no bother, and no money thrown away…"

"No planning, no anticipation, and I'll probably have to wear last year's Easter dress," Cassidy predicted with a dramatic sigh.

Ruthanne leaned over and gave Cassidy a quick peck on the cheek.

"Oh, cheer up. The big production will just have to wait until your wedding day."

"Yeah, maybe if Aunt Jenna and I get our way. Mother thinks like you. 'Fresh flowers cost how much? Why, I could buy a pretty decent kind of a horse for that. Go to trading on him, and cover a month's worth of expenses. We've got some real pretty blossoms right here around the house, anyhow.'"

Several lively conversations bounced back and forth across the old parlor, but when Cassidy's impersonation of Miss Sis accidentally filled a brief silence, laughter erupted from every corner.

"We ought to get ahold of Judd and Shirley," Ches confided quietly, scooting a little closer to Ruthanne on the loveseat. "She'll act mad as a hornet. Just her way of having a little fun with us because I didn't say anything beforehand."

"Oh, for pity's sake," his fiancée giggled. Miss sis and your folks… And I know you talked to Pap. Why, if you'd kept on going, the whole country might've known before I did."

"That's the way I figured it," he agreed. "Got to stop somewhere. Now, then, we can tell everybody! Your Aunt Lurlene and—"

"Oh, Ches, I heard back from her just last night. 'Course, I had no idea..."

"What did she say about your church membership?"

"Probably took some tall talking on her part way back when, but they didn't exclude Pap after all. We can both join the church at McKendrick on promise of letter."

"I love you, little miss. A bushel and a peck..."

"I love you, too. It's been a long time coming, m-darlin, but Pap figures we can talk to Brother Waller in the morning and walk the aisle tomorrow evening."

"We'll be mighty glad to have y'all. They may ask Pap to lead singing before too long."

Ruthanne plucked tentatively at his sleeve as an awkward question entered her mind. The gesture seemed faintly out of step with her usual easy calm but achingly tender nonetheless.

"You thought about Serena Kate?"

"I hadn't," he admitted. "Not in particular..."

"She's bound to be happy for us, but still... I'll talk to her, m-darlin, if that'll make it any easier."

Ches felt his heart swell until it threatened to burst with love and joy. How many times in this one evening could the Lord manage to remind him what a jewel Ruthanne truly was? He smiled in gratitude and squeezed her hand but gently shook his head.

Early Sunday morning, he caught Serena Kate in the main hallway at Pinevale and asked for her help unloading some things. They ventured out into the cool fall air and paused beside the minivan.

"It's always good to see you, Ches, but why bring goodies right now? Won't y'all be here after church?"

"Yeah, but these apple fritters are hot and fresh. Besides, I kinda needed a chance to talk to you."

"Really?" she questioned, brow furrowing in mild curiosity. "Look, whatever Ethan's done, I'm sure he didn't mean—"

"Ethan's just fine," he assured her with a passing smile. "If you're happy, I'm happy. Besides, he ain't likely to cross Aunt Sis again, not after the last time."

"I sure hope not," she declared almost cheerfully. "Now, what's on your mind?"

"It's Ruthanne… I asked her to marry me last night. She said yes, and I thought you ought to hear it from me." Turning half away from him, the redhead propped one shoulder against his van and stood there in silence for a minute. "Serena Kate?"

Blinking back unexpected tears, she mustered up a shaky smile.

"So, she gets my best friend while I'm left with a plate of the famous apple fritters and a case of Mountain Dew?"

Caught off guard, Ches relied on gentle teasing until he could gather his thoughts for a serious answer.

"Fritters oughta jumpstart your sugar rush. Pretty tasty, too. You might've come out on the long end of that swap."

"Perfect," she sniffled, "just perfect. I'll probably end up all chubby again."

"You still think of me as your best friend?" he asked quietly.

Serena Kate drummed her fingers mindlessly on the sloping hood, breaking rhythm every so often to bite at the nails.

"Well, yeah… I know it's kinda weird after every— But Miss Sis is old enough to be my mother. You and her are the ones who've always…"

"You're not losing a friend, only gaining Ruthanne. And let me tell you; little miss is a friend worth having."

"I'm very happy for you both, Ches. It just takes some getting used to is all."

"I understand," he said, quietly offering his support. "When you went away, I—"

"Ugh, don't remind me."

"I came through alright... Aunt Sis wouldn't have it any other way."

"Miss Sis," she half sobbed through a teary-eyed grin, "uncompromising belle of the horse sale."

"The Lord has plans we can't always understand, Serena Kate. I used to think Aunt Sis and the homeplace were all I'd ever need in this life. If you hadn't opened up a hole in my heart, I might've passed by Ruthanne without a second glance."

"We still going to Cassidy's play?"

"Me and Ruthanne, you and Ethan... Not exactly the way I used to picture it, but old friends like us ought to stick together."

"For sure!" Serena Kate declared with a sudden smile and then pulled him into a hug.

The day turned out busy and full of well wishes, but before it ended, Ches shed tears of his own. Arm in arm with her grandfather, Ruthanne walked the aisle and became a member of McKendrick Missionary Baptist Church. The church family had taken her as their own sometime back, accepting Pap as part of the package, but the act of joining made for a very special evening.

Over the next few days, Ches and his little miss proved almost inseparable. Without sacrificing her ladylike decorum, Ruthanne took every opportunity to hold his hand or brush a kiss on his cheek or perch for a moment on his lap, none of which he minded in the least. They felt no particular rush to discuss wedding plans, but Cassidy insisted that any couple as old-fashioned and hopelessly in love as they were needed a June wedding.

"It'll be hot as the dickens," Miss Sis objected in halfhearted practicality, but romantic notions carried the day.

Come Saturday evening, they enjoyed a couples' outing with Serena Kate and

Ethan Fisher. The musical production turned out well. Cassidy, in particular, made a pretty little dark-haired Laurey with perfect accent and delivery.

"Not bad for a high school play," Ethan decided. "Kind of brought the story to life."

"Miss Sis seen it yet?" Serena Kate wondered, arching an eyebrow. "It's almost eerie how much Cassidy…"

"None of us knew teenage Miss Sis," Ruthanne mused, "but Cassidy could've fooled me."

"The boss lady's here," Ches told them with a grin, tilting his head to indicate direction. "She's made every performance and been humming *Surrey with the Fringe on Top* in between times. Cassidy pretends to be a little put off by all that motherly approval. Truth be told, though, I think she likes it just fine."

They hung around for a few minutes, content to visit while waiting for the right moment to congratulate their starlet. Ches knew most everybody in the crowd, but his aunt's quiet voice proved unmistakable.

"Bring Ruthanne by the house 'fore you take her home tonight," she invited from just over his left shoulder.

"Right quick?" he responded, turning a searching glance on her face.

"No, honey… It'll take us a little bit to make it home and get settled. Y'all finish your evening with Serena Kate and them. Just come on by whenever it suits you."

"Yes'm… They may want to swing by the Dairy Queen, but we'll see you directly."

"Ain't she pretty, Ches?" Miss Sis observed softly as her attention shifted to the stage where Cassidy posed for various photographs.

"Can't help it," he agreed. "She's your daughter."

"She doesn't want our kind of life, honey, and that's alright. I just wish I knew what kind she did want."

"Well, Aunt Sis, I guarantee you one thing. She'll live it with plenty of gumption. Your girl may turn up her nose at the smell of horses, but she's got more than her share of the old Durham spark."

Serena Kate chided the others a little, declaring the fall night too cold for ice cream, but enjoyed her Blizzard just the same. The twins came in later with a group of friends, so Ruthanne and Ches drove the whole family back to their apartment before heading to McKendrick.

"Are you very sleepy?" he asked once they had the minivan to themselves.

"No, m-darlin. I'm okay to drive."

"Oh, I know that, but Aunt Sis asked us to stop by the big house."

"Trouble?" she wanted to know.

Ches couldn't help smiling as he watched her spine straighten and her delicate chin tilt ever so slightly upward.

"I sure do love you, little miss. No trouble, or at least, she didn't act that way. Just happy and kind of lost in thought."

"I love you, too, Ches. And we both know that means loving Miss Sis. It's more or less part of the deal."

"She sure thinks the world of you."

"Well, don't ever doubt the way I feel about her. She's a very special lady!"

The usual passel of cur dogs surged around the house and out from under it to meet them. Despite her small frame, Roxy pushed the others aside and claimed her rightful spot close to Ches. When he stopped the wheelchair for a minute, she laid her head in his lap with a long, contented sigh.

"I'm glad you talked to Pap before we got engaged, m-darlin, but it looks like I missed my talk with Roxy. Poor thing still thinks she's the only girl in your life."

"She like to've bit Serena Kate one time. Guess maybe we hugged a little too long."

"I knew that dog had good sense," Ruthanne quipped without missing a beat.

Only her genuine friendship with Serena Kate and a teasing note in her voice let Ches in on the joke. She seemed practically immune to the petty, hateful kind of jealousy. But jealousy came in cuter forms, too.

They traveled the length of the old dog run to find Miss Sis and her little family on the wide back porch. Darkness obscured their view down the hill to the sale barn, but a near-perfect starry sky made up the difference.

"Night air's a touch brisk, but I kinda like it," Miss Sis offered by way of greeting. "There's a fire if y'all had rather move inside."

Cassidy, still in costume and still over the moon, didn't seem to mind the cool of the evening. Andrew stood, offering his seat to Ruthanne, and she slipped readily into place beside Miss Sis.

"This'll do," she decided with a warm and all-encompassing smile.

Ches maneuvered into the swing on the other side of his aunt and nodded his thanks as Uncle Andrew settled into a rocker.

"Anybody want a cup of coffee?" Miss Sis asked, half rising as she spoke, but the two young people pulled her gently back down between them.

"I don't want any coffee, Miss Sis," Ruthanne told her almost playfully, "but I would like to know why you called this little meeting. The suspense is killing me. Unless you ordered these stars up special and wanted us to admire—"

"Tell me about it," Cassidy exclaimed. "She's been acting funny all day. Staring off into the distance, fiddling with Grandmother's old knickknacks, and toting that bullwhip through the house like she was at the sale barn or something. Dad is usually my interpreter, but I can't get a peep out of him this time."

The girl darted back and forth in front of them, words tumbling out in a rush. Between the old-fashioned gingham dress and near frantic pacing, only a cigarette and the curling tendril of smoke were lacking to recreate an earlier picture of her mother.

Doing his best to live by faith, Ches tried to leave the future in God's capable hands. Even so, he shied away from the possibility of a health scare for his aunt. She was Miss Sis. Colonel Durham's daughter… The embodiment of everything he knew and loved about their rural community…

Aunt Sis was the connection to yesterday and the heartbeat of today. Only the Good Lord knew for sure about tomorrow, but Ches wanted her in it. Though he could usually pick up on anything bothering the boss lady, Cassidy's nervous chatter planted the seeds of doubt. His aunt's next words- and more particularly the easy, drawling humor in her voice- brought a welcome sense of relief.

"Interpreter? Now, that's a bunch of foolishness. If you want to know something, why not just ask me?"

"Far be it from me to come before the queen without a summons," and Cassidy's mock bow swept her almost down to the worn pine boards of the porch. "Not with that bullwhip hanging loose and easy in your hand."

"For crying out loud, child… Would you be still, and try to make a little sense when you talk. We're fixing to tend to a piece of family business. I figure you're old enough to want in on it, but I can't hear myself think with you clatterin' back and forth that-a-way."

"Family business?" Ches inquired softly.

"Yes, honey, the little matter of deciding where you and Ruthanne want to start married life."

"We've talked about it some but haven't made any definite plans. I'm not going anywhere, so don't let that worry you. We'll settle in somewhere around McKendrick."

"Ches, I've been accused of being a little bossy. But not with you, I hope. Always tried to treat you like a partner. I may give advice, but—"

"Aunt Sis," he interrupted gently, "you ain't heard me complaining. Just say what's on your mind."

"Well, honey, I'd like for y'all to live right here."

"I've always felt welcome in the big house. You made it my home, too. Even so, y'all don't want us underfoot all the time."

"You could never be underfoot, honey, nor Ruthanne either. Be that as it may, the two of you will need a little space to start a life together."

"Well, now, I—"

"Me and Andrew spent some time with Giles Parmalee today. Made a deal for his house and land. Of course, he signed everything over to the daughters years ago. But the day that old rascal can't handle his girls, I'll just sell out and quit."

"I don't understand," Ruthanne put in gently. "Why would you and Uncle Andrew buy us a house?"

"No, sweetheart," Sis explained without missing a beat. "That's for us. You and Ches will take over here. Y'all can fix up Nash's little house for Pap so he'll be close by. I warn you, though, this old place gets to be just like Grand Central Station sometimes. Kinfolk in and out at all hours of the day and night... Might take a little getting used to at first, but there comes a point where you wouldn't have it any other way."

"Mother, you don't mean... We're not actually..."

Cassidy's mouth fell open, but nobody stopped to answer her unfinished question.

"I never knew Daddy to lock a door," Miss Sis continued, voice thick with nostalgia. "Friends can come in any time, and nobody huntin' trouble ever had the nerve to try."

"It may take a while, Aunt Sis, but I'll pay you for the house and whatever land you'll let go."

Ches made the declaration in all seriousness, but his aunt waved it away.

"You see, Ches," Andrew volunteered, "the Durham homeplace kind of came with your aunt. Money I would've spent housing a family went into additional investments."

"I know you've done well, Uncle Andrew, but that's got nothing to do with me. Nobody else gets a free house when they get married, and I never expected one, either. Houses have to be worked for, paid for."

"The big house is paid for, honey," Sis declared, placing a gentle hand on his. "Great-Granddaddy Durham, Granddaddy, the colonel, and me... We've all put in blood, sweat, and tears so that you and Ruthanne would have a place to live. You've done your share, too, and I won't hear any different."

"We're moving?" Cassidy squealed, joy wrestling with disbelief in her voice. "This can't be happening! After I begged and pleaded and cried for a normal house with real air conditioning... Ches decides to get married, and just like that, we're moving?"

# Chapter Sixteen

(East Texas: late March, 2016)

"By this time next year, you'll be tied down and henpecked," Scooter predicted wryly as they moved away from the sale barn into the predawn darkness. "How come Ruthanne's not riding with us?"

"You noticed Aunt Sis generally skips this one?" Ches queried. "Easter dresses ain't exactly made for the saddle. How long we been doing this anyway?"

"Good many years, but I never did know what got it started in the first place. Even the boss lady rides horseback to church now and again. Why get up in the middle of the night and trot in for sunrise service?"

Nobody spoke for a minute or so, but their horses walked jauntily into the cool, damp morning.

"Rained us out a couple of times... But you've always shown up, willing and ready, because I wanted to ride."

"First time, it seemed like a new adventure. Then, it kinda got to be our thing to do on Easter. Andrew and your daddy rode with us a time or two. And Pop, before he quit the country. Generally speaking, though, it's just me and you. I never really stopped to think about a reason until now."

"Easter is a special time, a time to celebrate the good news of Jesus Christ. Far as I'm concerned, our little ride just adds to it. We soak up the beauty of His creation, do some praying as we ride along, and still get to church in plenty of time to lay things out for the breakfast crew. Then, too, our horses are on hand for the kids to pet and pose with for some of their Easter pictures."

"You ain't foolin' me," Scooter shot back with a grin in his voice. "All that sounds good, but what you really like is to look at the people who complain about having to get up so early with a kind of a surprised expression and say, 'Me and Scooter came in a'horseback.'"

"Well, it don't hurt my feelings none."

"Suits Miss Sis pretty good, I guess. Her eyes light up every time you make that little crack. She'll toss her head, too, like a horse strainin' at the bit on a brisk kind of a morning."

"Never figured you paid all that much attention," Ches admitted, smiling at the mental picture.

"I may talk a lot," Scooter drawled, "but there ain't much gets by me. Speaking of which, how come you asked me to ride old Short Stuff?"

"You've swapped nearly every year, but he was my only ride for so long that folks kind of look for him on Easter Sunday morning. So, when I decided to bring Faith…"

"Guess I've been on the little fella… Trotted him over to you if nothing else, but I can't remember for certain."

At the church, Ches transitioned from the saddle to his friend's shoulder. Scooter set him on his knees in front of the door and moved off to tie the horses. The vapor lamp attached to a nearby highline pole afforded the only glimmer of illumination in the predawn darkness. Working within this small circle of light, Ches unlocked the fellowship hall and crawled over the threshold to his waiting wheelchair.

By the time he and Scooter got everything set up, Daddy, Uncle Andrew, and other men of the church arrived to start breakfast. They had a kitchen full of help, so Ches waited outside. These few minutes- a quiet spring morning, the promise of life all around, and the smell of hot bacon grease- had become part and parcel of the whole Easter experience.

Pap Prescott wasn't quite early enough to do any cooking, but he and Ruthanne didn't miss it by much. As the old man grew more comfortable with the church family and folks in the community, he put aside much of his brash showman's exterior. Taking a backseat for the first time in his life, he seemed content to watch as the quiet magnetism of his granddaughter's personality won her a place in their hearts.

Ruthann glided along just ahead of him, carrying a large tray of apple fritters and looking vision-like in a classic A-line dress. She wore her hair in some kind of ornate bun, with matching lavender ribbon braided in and a sprig or two of baby's breath for good measure. The updo suggested painstaking work, maybe even Miss Lillian's touch. But her pretty face bore a dreamy detachment that made her look fresh from sleep.

"Happy Easter, m-darlin," and if the joyful greeting came out sounding a little drowsy, her loving smile made all the difference.

Opening the door, Ches scooted his wheelchair aside and then brushed her arm lightly as she passed.

"Morning, pretty girl," he finally breathed.

Though she moved with a horsewoman's grace, and her youthful complexion shimmered under a light suntan, the trim athleticism of a self-taught trick rider had relaxed into softer feminine lines. Not the most welcome adjustment for Ruthanne, but to Ches, a near-perfect expression of her inner beauty.

"Fella can't hardly miss the amazement all over your face when you look at her," Pap Prescott drawled, and the tone of voice carried more sincerity than Ches had ever heard from this happy-go-lucky individual. "Something special about that girl, and she didn't get it from me. Her Gram, now... But you're steadier than I ever was and smart enough to take good care of her."

"Ruthanne is a blessing! A treasure... And I—"

Always slightly uncomfortable with matters of the heart, Pap coughed loudly and put an end to the conversation.

"Best go pick us out a few songs."

Easter Sunday at McKendrick Missionary Baptist Church called for a pretty standard list of hymns, but Ches let him go with a wry smile.

Still outside, he greeted visitors and church members alike. Aunt Sis arrived with a sleepy headed Cassidy, hugged her nephew, and then peered through the half-open door toward the kitchen.

"Looks like they've got it all under control," she decided with a nod and then came back to hover close beside him.

"I've always liked Easter best," he confided softly, "out of all the special church services."

"I know it," she agreed wholeheartedly. "Springtime in general makes my blood pump a little faster. Horses start sheddin' that old winter hair, and there ain't nothing like green grass to make 'em shine. Then, too, perfect riding weather puts folks in the mood to buy and sell. Over and above all that, Easter is a wonderful time to stop and consider the Resurrection and everything it means to us."

"Yes, ma'am! And having Ruthanne here..."

"Spring of the year brings new beginnings, honey, and it won't be long 'til you and Ruthanne set about building a life together. Seems fitting, don't you think?"

"Ruthanne kinda ties everything together," he ventured, smiling up at his beloved aunt. "This new life ought to fit into the old one like a missing puzzle piece."

"Now, Pap, he'd be that extra piece, or maybe the one with a little warp to it. But we've took in our share of rascals over the years. Leastways, this one's got a singing voice."

The sunrise part of Easter Sunday service consisted of an outdoor devotional. Content and grateful- with Aunt Sis on one side of him, Ruthanne on the other, and his parents close by- Ches listened in rapt attention. Brother Waller's voice communicated all the solemn joy of the occasion as he read aloud from Mark 16.

And when the sabbath was past, Mary Magdalene, and Mary the mother of James, and Salome, had bought sweet spices, that they might come and anoint him. And very early in the morning the first day of the week, they came unto the sepulchre at the rising of the sun. And they said among themselves, Who shall roll us away the stone from the door of the sepulchre? And when they looked, they saw that the stone was rolled away: for it was very great. And entering into the sepulchre, they saw a young man sitting on the right side, clothed in a long white garment; and they were affrighted. And he saith unto them, Be not affrighted: Ye seek Jesus of Nazareth, which was crucified: he is risen; he is not here: behold the place where they laid him. But go your way, tell his disciples and Peter that he goeth before you into Galilee: there shall ye see him, as he said unto you.

Back inside, Ruthanne fixed plate after plate. Fetching Pap's breakfast seemed only natural for her, but it didn't stop there. Ches accepted the plate she brought him with thanks and then watched her do the same for anyone else who would allow it. This went on until Serena Kate eased up next to her in the small kitchen area.

"Get you some food, and go sit down beside Ches," the redhead instructed succinctly. "Otherwise, he won't eat more than a bite or two of that plate you fixed."

"Wha—"

"You're his precious girl, thereby entitled to as much love, security, and over-all pampering as he can figure out how to give." Though she delivered the explanation bluntly, Serena Kate kept her usual sarcasm to a minimum. "I held that position myself, once upon a time, or something close to it. Ain't no room in the plan for you to be running yourself ragged."

"Oh, I never thought…"

"That's alright," Serena Kate answered, lips quirking into a brief smile. "You're just new on the job."

Ruthanne took a seat and smiled as she observed the truth of Serena Kate's statement first hand. Her very presence, settled in comfortably beside him with a plate of her own, made all the difference for Ches. She did her share of the cleanup but made it a point to join him on their pew as soon as possible.

The young couple sat on the lefthand side of the sanctuary just behind Miss Sis, Andrew, and, because of his newfound part in the song service, Pap. When she wasn't floating between these two front rows, Cassidy sat further back, joining either the McKendrick twins or her Aunt Jenna and Uncle Terry.

Despite his early morning, a big breakfast, and the comfort of Ruthanne's hand nestled into his own, rousing hymns like *Christ Arose* fueled a mounting sense of exultation. Phineas Absalom Prescott swung his hand rhythmically, keeping time, and provided the congregation with a strong voice to follow.

"Miss Sis can flat play that piano!"

Ruthanne's enthusiasm and the sweet tingle of her breath as she whispered in his ear produced a wide grin.

"Nobody plays quite like Aunt Sis," he agreed. "She and Pap make a good team."

Though unfailingly correct in his song leading, Andrew had obviously missed singing the bass line. Pap's rollicking style proved closer to the familiar sound of bygone years.

Ruthanne stepped out into the aisle when the time came for special music, pausing just long enough for Cassidy to join her. Aunt Sis stood, allowing her daughter to settle onto the piano bench, and Serena Kate made her way up from the back row. Feeling it more than he heard it, Ches picked up on a collective intake of breath throughout the room.

The trio lined up just behind their pianist, and Miss Sis slipped an arm around each of the young ladies. Ruthanne dropped a hand onto Cassidy's shoulder, instinctively linking her to the group.

"I'm grateful to have all my girls in church with me these days," Sis ventured, and the voice that steadied Ches and so many others in every kind of situation trembled slightly under the weight of her emotions. "Y'all pray for us, and we'll try to sing *Blessed Assurance*."

Cassidy's playing usually sounded timid and uncertain, but she had practiced this particular song so many times that it flowed out in a pretty fair approximation of her mother's signature style. Ches sat ramrod straight in the pew but let his tears flow as three beloved voices blended in near-perfect harmony.

"Blessed assurance, Jesus is mine! Oh, what a foretaste of glory divine!" Time played tricks on Ches, seeming to stand still, yet the song ended all too quickly. Cassidy surprised everyone, including herself, with a sweeping run on the piano that ushered in the final chorus. "This is my story, this is my song, praising my Savior all the day long!"

Serena Kate, Ethan Fisher, and the twins joined the regular crew at the big house. Hattie and Giles, liberated from Pinevale for the day, each brought along some out-of-town children and grandchildren. This loud, joyful group filled the kitchen and dining room before spilling off the wide porches and into the yard. Still young at fifty-seven, Miss Sis wore the mantle of family matriarch with the unquestioning assurance of one born to the role.

The table and sideboard practically groaned under platters of fried quail, two hams, baked beans, potato salad, deviled eggs, and last year's snap beans. Having worked alongside Miss Sis to prepare this bounty, Ruthanne turned out several dozen yeast rolls and an astounding list of desserts all by herself. Like Ms. Jenna, Serena Kate stuck to the safety of paper napkins and ice for the tea.

"Know what they've done?" Terry Durham inquired in a mischievous stage whisper. "Put y'all to washing dishes... Just as neat as you please."

Jenna responded with a soft and somewhat ironic chuckle. More sleep deprived than usual, Serena Kate found the statement wildly funny, and her reaction created a humor all its own.

"How does it feel, Miss Sis?" the redhead asked, turning unexpectedly solemn as the shared laughter died away. "Your last Easter dinner in the big house..."

"Pshaw," the boss lady answered with a smile. "Last time as hostess in the big house, maybe... But I'll be up here so regular that Ruthanne's apt to decide I'm worse than a bad penny. Ches, honey, go ahead and return thanks."

*Beyond the Parmalee Bottom* 295

"Yes'm…" Ches forced the answer around a sentimental lump in his throat, but once in prayer, the words came easily enough.

A few minutes of comparative silence followed the blessing, broken only by exclamations over the food as they all fixed a plate.

"How's everything going with the therapy program?" Uncle Andrew asked five or ten minutes into the meal.

"Fine and dandy… Ruthanne's just wonderful with our riders. Perfect for the job!"

"I don't doubt it, Ches, not one bit," Giles Parmalee intoned, gesturing with a half-eaten quail breast in one large hand to make his point. "But you might be just a little partial."

"Watch for birdshot, Mr. Parmalee," Jenna Durham interjected fretfully.

"I've been eatin' birds all my life, missy. Pick out your own shot, and don't worry none about me."

"Ruthanne lives up to my bragging and then some," Ches continued. "Just ask Ethan… Very first rider to sign up with us."

"They already got my leg bucked off," Ethan recalled, showing the influence of country wit all around him. "So, I thought… How much worse can it get? He's right, though. Ruthanne is good. Learned all about stretches and how to maximize the therapeutic value of horseback riding in that course she took. I've done without physical therapy for years."

"Ches, too," Jenna lamented. "I've tried and tried to book him a massage, but he's much too hardheaded for that."

"Serena Kate talked me into my first massage. Now, I go whenever I can afford it. Ches probably needs one, but I guess it's not exactly the cowboy thing to do."

"Sure ain't. I'm not going up town and let some stranger… Besides, a few months from now, me and Ruthanne can take it by turns, and nobody'll ever know the difference."

To Ches, this was a simple statement of fact. But laughter broke out around the table, only increasing when Andrew added his two cents.

"I have a lot more experience with that peculiar Durham logic than most of you," he asserted with a chuckle. "Guess who rubs Miss Sis down every time some half-wild bronc pounds a new kink into her back?"

Of all the desserts Ruthanne had to offer, she seemed quietly proud of the banana pudding.

"Old family recipe?" Serena Kate inquired.

"Not mine," the other girl answered cheerfully. "I learned how to make it watching Shirley Matthews from Anacoco, Louisiana."

"Aww, Ms. Shirley and Mr. Judd... 'Course they probably hate me after the way I..."

"They do not," Ruthanne objected, propelled halfway up from her chair by a sudden impulse to comfort the redhead. Glancing to her fiancé in hopes of handing the difficult conversation off, she found him otherwise occupied and forged ahead on her own. "Besides, I've never heard Ches breath a negative word about you! If he won't say such things to me, he sure wouldn't say them to anybody else."

"Guess not," Serena Kate agreed, only a little placated, "but I can't see Miss Sis holding much of anything back."

"Well," Ruthanne drawled knowingly, "it's just possible that you don't understand the boss lady as completely as you think."

Aside from tasting good, the banana pudding reminded Ches that he and Ruthanne needed to put in an Easter phone call to Louisiana. They enjoyed a brief visit and then turned their attention back to the friends and relatives who filled the big house on this special occasion.

The crowd thinned as evening settled in, and Ches guided his wheelchair out the back door. Aunt Sis, already in the porch swing, motioned him into place beside her. Their little chats covered everything from seemingly insurmountable problems to lighthearted banter. When she set the swing in motion without glancing around for Ruthanne, he figured this one for a day-to-day kind of discussion.

"Cassidy's got white-sand beaches on her mind," she began with a rather put-upon sigh. "Besides, it's about time Andrew saw his mother and the other folks back in Georgia."

"Uncle Andrew's old stomping grounds are kinda short on oceanfront views," he quipped. "That country puts me in mind of East Texas, what ain't been swallowed up by Atlanta."

"I've about let myself get talked into a family vacation. Andrew's bunch said they'd be glad to drive down and spend a few days on Tybee Island. If you think it's alright, I mean."

"You're the boss, Aunt Sis, and I wouldn't have it any other way."

"Oh, honey, I know that. They dragged me off on vacation not more than three or four years ago. I'd hate to leave you in a bind, but with Ruthanne here…"

"We'll make it just fine."

"Of course, you will. And I'll be back long before the April horse sale."

The words sounded as if she were trying to convince herself, but Ches knew this uncertainty had nothing to do with a lack of confidence in him or Ruthanne.

"Like I said, we'll make it. Unless… Do you want me to ask you not to go?"

"Well, yes. But I'll not put that off on you. Ches, honey, have you ever been to a beach? Sand everywhere! About like a watermelon field… Only, you can't grow much of anything 'round all that salt water. Years ago, I went off to Galveston with a group of girls. Ten minutes of sunbathing near cooked me. I found one little bitty patch of shade and did my dead-level best to chain smoke the boredom away."

"That bad, huh?"

"Worse," she confided with a little shudder. "If I go, though, I'm taking my saddle. Most every beach has at least one opportunist selling rides on a string of deadheaded horses. Take on the troublemakers, and it'll generally get you a free ride or two. One of those Galveston plugs and a rotten cinch taught me a memorable lesson about riding someone else's tack. I cleaned sand out of my ears for a month!"

"No?" he blurted, genuine sympathy fighting back a chuckle.

"And you want to know the pitiful part?" That was the highlight of my whole trip. After you've done absolutely nothin' for a few days, hitting the ground becomes a viable alternative."

"I reckon you got back on and rode him…"

"Bareback," she admitted with a grin, "and I figure it took that particular plug a good long while to sour out again. Couldn't blame the horse for that bad cinch, but you can just imagine the kind of mood I was in after all that 'relaxing' beach time."

"If Uncle Andrew and Cassidy are set on it, I guess you ought to go along. They're pretty good about putting up with our shenanigans. Book the trip, and I'll pray for you."

"Maybe it's pretty silly to dread this kind of little jaunt," she mused, "but I hear folks talk about needing a vacation and know for sure how blessed I am. God gave me the homeplace, put me right in the middle of this way of life, and I've never been completely happy anywhere else. Thanks, honey, for always understanding."

"Ain't much of a mystery," he confided, hand closing gently over hers. "I can spend fifteen minutes up town and come away homesick."

Departure for the beach trip was nearly three weeks out, but days passed like minutes. Aunt Sis filled the time tying up loose ends and issuing an endless stream of instructions. She never once doubted her nephew's abilities, but taking a step back from the day-to-day operation proved difficult.

"You might tell Ruthanne she can start moving some of her things into the big house while we're gone."

"You told her at least three times yesterday," he recalled with a gentle chuckle.

*Beyond the Parmalee Bottom* 299

"Guess maybe I did at that... You'll be in and out during the day, I reckon, but if Ruthanne wanted to spend a night or two..."

"You aim for her to test drive the house?"

"Not so much that," she clarified with a chuckle of her own. "But you'll be staying with your parents. That'll leave the big house empty, and an old home don't hold up well without folks in it."

"Ruthanne can stay up there as much as she wants, but I'll be around to see after the dogs."

"I know you'll feed our stock dogs running loose on the yard, honey. But you might look in on those birdbrains out back while you're at it. Andrew's got his pens fitted out with automatic waterers. Feeders, too, but it pays to keep a watch. They'd probably like to hear your voice now and then."

The frantic pace of his aunt's preparations served mainly to distract her from the upcoming trip, but there were plenty of daily chores that still needed doing. Ruthanne conducted therapeutic riding sessions every Monday, Wednesday, and Friday.

Observing her tender manner with young or fearful riders, Ches fell deeper in love as each day passed. He usually took on the role of encourager, sharing the positive impact of horses in his own life. But years of practice on horseback sometimes compensated for physical limitations, allowing him to take the lead on outside trails or guide newer riders through manmade obstacles in the arena.

"Know something, little miss?"

"Mmm?" and Ches saw his own adoration reflected back as she looked up to where he sat in the saddle.

"The youngsters probably wonder if I'm an extra instructor or just your star pupil. Don't make me much difference, teacher or student... Just so I get to watch you move around and hear that pretty voice."

She found countless opportunities to include him in the sessions, particularly when it came to new stretches or other techniques to increase the mobility-related benefits of his hours on horseback. Likewise, he did everything he could to lighten her load as instructor. They needed able-bodied help from time to time, but family and friends, including Ches's decidedly non-horsey mother, stepped up to the plate. These volunteers received their pay in smiles, hugs, and laughter from the grateful riders.

The hours Ethan Fisher put in with old man Stanley's painting crew varied according to the weather. Like Ches, he sometimes blurred the line between recipient and volunteer. Several of the kids quickly surpassed Ethan's skill on horseback, but he often managed to lend a hand from the ground.

"Before I forget..." Miss Sis paused with a hand on the passenger door of Uncle Andrew's Buick, and her slow drawl took on a hurried edge. "Jesse Lee's putting together some cheaper type horses at Reklaw. Get somebody to drive for you, and take the long trailer down there."

"Yes'm..."

"Cull the worst of 'em if need be, but I'm sure he'd like to sell the whole bunch. You know how to work that kind of a deal without me telling you, honey. Only... I'd rather study on Jesse Lee and them nags than what's ahead of me."

"I'll get the horses bought right and try to keep Jess happy at the same time," he said, comforting her with a hug.

"Sure; I know that."

"I declare, you two act like we've just come from a funeral," Andrew interjected, sympathetic despite his joking words. "Like I said, Ches, you're welcome to come along if—"

"No," they chorused, rejecting the notion outright. But Ches broke off, allowing his aunt to finish the sentence.

"Who'd run things around here, look after the homeplace?"

"Just a suggestion..." Andrew said, raising both hands in a placating gesture. "Y'all are a different breed," he added with a chuckle, "but I'm pretty fond of you both. I'll wait through the last-minute instructions and the teary-eyed kiss on the forehead, but do you reckon we could leave sometime this morning?"

"Not without saying goodbye to me," Ruthanne called as she rode into the yard on Faith, dropped lightly down beside the wheelchair, and handed Ches her bridle reins.

"You're out and about early, sweetheart," Sis greeted her with a hug, "but I'm awful glad. It'd near-about break my heart to look back and see Ches on the porch all alone."

Instead of answering, Ruthanne stepped back to stand beside Ches and dropped an arm lightly across his shoulders.

"See, they're fine," Cassidy quipped from inside the car. "Let's go before erosion claims my spot on the beach!"

Ruthanne and Ches took care of the usual round of chores, conducted several therapy sessions, and even drove down to Reklaw where they picked up a trailer load of horses.

The next day, she clipped manes, detangled tails, and administered wormer along with shots of penicillin. Some for runny noses, some for matted eyes, and some on general principle... Ches called in extra help to make the work easier and safer, but Ruthanne definitely took the lead in processing new arrivals.

"You bought a nice bunch of horses, m-darlin. A little rough around the edges, maybe, but they cleaned up pretty good.

"Aunt Sis had the deal just about wrapped up," he deferred. "Now, we've got to decide which ones to put straight into the April sale and which ones to hold for summer grazing."

"Some of them might be worth a little education. Pick out the ones you like, and I'll put a few rides on 'em."

"Thanks, sugar pie, but you're just too good in the saddle. Don't waste all that skill on fifty-dollar horses."

"There's not a fifty-dollar horse left in the country," she reminded him with a quick little snort of laughter.

"No, but inflation don't do much for their quality."

"It's awful sweet of you to place such a high value on my time, but enough wet saddle blankets will improve any horse, and folks generally pay for that improvement."

"You're right," he admitted with a chuckle. "Fifty-dollar horses built the Durham Auction Company. Old Nash ain't here to ride 'em anymore, and I may be a little overprotective when it comes to my best girl."

"Nash never rode them all," she reminded him lightheartedly, "not according to the stories I've heard. If fifty-dollar horses were good enough for Miss Sis, they're plenty good for a future in-law."

"I love you, little miss, but you don't exactly play fair when it comes to an argument."

"Discussion," she corrected lightly. "I love you, too."

"Sounds like the boss lady's holding up well," he volunteered, neatly sidetracked by the mention of his aunt, "and they'll be home Friday evening. Anyhow, I think she's spent most of the trip visiting with her mother-in-law on a third-floor balcony."

"Reigning queen of all she surveys," Ruthanne quipped, her voice warm with genuine affection.

"Well, it lets her stay out of the sand and still keep an eye on Cassidy. But I expect she'd rather be sitting in the porch swing and lookin' down on the sale barn."

"Why don't I fix us a bite of supper up there, m-darlin? Then, I reckon we ought to try out that old swing for a while before you go on down to your mom's house."

The charming notion made him smile, but Ches couldn't resist turning her own little joke back on her.

"The queen's away," he teased, "and maybe the princess wants a good look at her new domain."

"You think Miss Sis would approve?" she asked quietly, worry clouding her pretty face.

"I know she would," he declared, reaching up to her from the wheelchair.

"Ches," she protested without actually resisting the hug, "I'm all sweaty."

"Angel dew," he whispered, releasing a contented sigh against her neck.

Their pleasant evening together felt almost dreamlike, but the next day found Ruthanne doing necessary chores around the barn while Ches began a session with his typist. A longstanding arrangement with the *Ranch Horse Gazette* generated all the extra money a thrifty bachelor might need. As the wedding date drew closer, though, he reminded himself that writing freelance articles had a great deal in common with the livestock business. Both offered plenty of freedom while making good use of his natural talents, but only hard work and consistency kept his income from drying up.

As the hours slipped by, he churned out a steady stream of magazine articles, blog posts, and online advertisements. Ches didn't favor the notion of giving up his active role on the homeplace, not even for the benefits of a steady paycheck, but he knew for sure that Ruthanne mustn't ever want for anything.

Startled by his cellphone in the middle of the afternoon, he recognized Bowie Tate's voice on the other end, but the labored breathing seemed out of place.

"Say, Ches, glad I caught you…"

"Hey, everything alright?"

"Well… It is, and it ain't. I'm stuck with a bunch-quitting cow that needs to get her a new address. She's in this little pasture by the house. Her calf, too. Along with another cow and calf, a good bull yearling, and an old barren cow. We tried, but they just won't go in the lot."

"Did you call up to Willard's?"

"Yeah; Lillian told me about Miss Sis being out of town. Besides… That's where I bought the high-headed fool. I called up there, but Raymond says they're runnin' in ten different directions. She'd make a good cow, black with a bald face, but starved down some and wild as a deer.

"Well, sir…"

"She's done spoiled everything else in that little bunch, and I'm fed up with the deal. When I started to the house for my rifle, Lillian thought we'd better call you."

Ches thought of Mr. Bowie Tate as a good-natured friend with a ready laugh, but enough failed attempts to pen a snaky bunch of cattle could shorten anybody's fuse.

"Tell you what… Put that rifle back in the closet, and get you a glass of ice water. I'll make some phone calls. If nothing else works out, me and Ruthanne will come out there and gather 'em."

"That's how Lillian figured it, but I don't… Shucks, Ches, you and me been friends a long time. Reckon I'll leave it in your hands. We can always go back to the rifle if need be."

Ches and his typist wrapped things up quickly, and even as she headed for the door, he dialed Scooter McKendrick.

"What's up?" Scooter asked without preamble. After listening to the explanation, he blew out a long breath. "Hate to say it, bud, but I just can't help you. Big Ray's getting ready for his spring stocker sale. He's got everybody who can limp around on foot, or sit a horse without falling off, working today. I'm down here in Coushatta, Louisiana picking up a load of Brangus bulls."

"Thought you was an auctioneer, not a truck driver."

"Told you; we're swamped… Bowie would do better to wait 'til next week, but sounds to me like he's got his dander up. Miss Sis and them are due back soon, ain't they?"

"Day after tomorrow, but…"

"Listen, you be careful. Don't do nothin' I wouldn't do."

"That ought to give a fella some room," Ches shot back, chuckling as he ended the call.

Loading his wheelchair into the van, he set out to hunt up Ruthanne. Instead, he found Ethan Fisher.

"Hey, man. Am I early or late?"

"For what?" Ches wanted to know.

"My horseback ride… Ruthanne's not here. Kinda weird to find this place deserted. You're the first one I've seen moving around."

"Get in," Ches instructed.

"Okay, sure…"

Dismissing what seemed like a needless prickle of unease, he drove them straight to the rent house where Ruthanne still lived with her grandfather. No one came to the door or answered the cellphone they shared, but Ches continued to downplay his concern.

"The old van's gone," he observed, methodically wiping the sweatband inside his straw hat. "She must be off somewhere with Pap. Ain't much telling what that old rascal might get up to. You busy the rest of the day?"

"Not really, Serena's at work and—"

"Look here, Ethan. Can you drive a truck and trailer? How about saddling my horse?"

"You tell me what to do, Ches, and I'll do it. My dad used to say something like, 'I can take that trailer where most guys couldn't walk and carry a steering wheel.' I'm not the truck driver he was, but I think we can manage."

Ruthanne's sudden disappearance seemed odd. She never missed a therapeutic riding session without making the appropriate arrangements. Levelheaded young lady that she was, Ches felt no inclination to keep track of her every move. She would turn up by nightfall, full of apologies for missing supper and still chuckling over one of Pap's hairbrained notions.

In the meantime, an old friend needed some cattle caught. Ches never minded working in his aunt's protective shadow, but the more he thought about doing this chore on his own... Anybody calling himself a horseman, and grown enough to take a wife, ought to could pen a little set of cows between now and dark.

"Let's you and me go help a neighbor," he quipped with a conspiratorial grin.

Ches picked old Short Stuff, for safety's sake, and doublechecked the tack after Ethan finished saddling him.

"Should we take another horse for me?" the tall North Dakotan wondered.

"I'll be doing good to get the job done and take care of myself without looking out for you," Ches answered, unusually blunt in his haste. "Besides, somebody's got to open and shut the gate."

Climbing into the one-ton truck, with a gooseneck trailer still hooked behind, Ches gave a few directions and then turned his attention to the cellphone.

"I appreciate the gesture and all," Bowie began hesitantly, sounding more like himself this time, "but we can't have you hurt over a fool cow. Besides, you know how I feel about setting dogs after my cattle. I never let the colonel do it. Nor Miss Sis, either, and I don't see any reason to start now."

"Don't aim to get hurt, Mr. Bowie, and I ain't bringing a trailer full of dogs. But you might as well know that Roxy goes where I do. I'm no good on this kind of a job without her. We've got Rox and one other dog loaded."

"Ches, I just don't... Hold on; Lillian wants to talk at you."

"Miss Sis wouldn't much like you taking all this on by yourself," the beauty operator fretted in soft, lilting tones. "But I'm awful glad you're coming. Bowie didn't exactly tell you all of it. We've got both four-wheelers run out of gas, his heavy walking stick busted to splinters, and not one cow in the pen."

"Well, ma'am, I'll be more than glad to help if I can."

"I know that... Listen, son, you turn loose as many dogs as it takes. He'll just have to look the other way."

"A fella would be hard pressed to find two sweeter or more God-fearing people," he informed Ethan, gesturing to indicate an upcoming turn. "But it sounds like this old cow must've stirred up quite a ruckus, hurt feelings and all. Then again, it won't do much for the cow's feelings when Roxy's hangin' off her ear."

"You people, Southerners or East Texans or whatever you want to be called, are mildly insane. Every single one I know could look into an oncoming wildfire and find something to laugh at, but are you sure this is safe? Riding out alone, I mean."

Sharp retorts came instantly to mind, but they all felt out of place. Despite his earlier snap judgements, or maybe because of them, he had tried to cultivate some kind of friendship with Ethan. Excluding little miss and most of his blood kin, Ches held Serena Kate and the twins dearer than anybody else in the world. The least he could do was try to live out a Godly example before this husband and step-father.

"Our little community holds most everything I ever wanted in life," he admitted quietly. "Hanging 'round home, though, a fella gets tagged as the kid. Calendar years, articles written, auctioneer's license, nothing much changes it. But if I can pen a few cows for one of the old timers, somebody who knew the colonel, watched Aunt Sis grow up, and then me..."

"This Mr. Tate, he qualifies?"

"Yeah, if you want to put it that-a-way. He's a longtime friend and neighbor. Might be I'd get a little bigger kick out of doing this for Lonnie Ray, or Giles. One of the old boys who used to catch cows for everybody else... But Mr. Bowie's still around, and he needs our help."

"I get it. This is about proving yourself. Becoming a man and all like that?"

"Not hardly... I don't care what folks think, except maybe for Ruthanne and my Aunt Sis. But they already figure I hung the moon. Don't you see, Ethan? If I can do this little job of work, just me and my horse and my dog ... I'll feel like a grown man. Pullin' my own weight, same as old Colonel Durham or anybody else."

"Grown or not," Ethan yelped on an outburst of laughter, "you're a dynamite motivational speaker! I know a one-legged Yankee who'll do just about anything he can to help you pull off this daredevil scheme."

# Chapter Seventeen

Ethan operated the winch smoothly enough, but Mr. and Mrs. Tate gazed up uncertainly as Ches hung suspended in the air above his saddled horse.

"This can wait on Miss Sis or some of the Willard bunch. Cow really ain't doing much harm. Made me mad, is all."

"We've come this far," Ches quipped, smiling as he settled comfortably into place. "I'd appreciate it if you'd let me try."

"You mean I get a choice?" the old gentleman harrumphed. "If we called the colonel out, he generally decided what was fixin' to happen. Miss Sis might sugarcoat it some, but she takes more or less the same approach."

"They knew what was needed and just took care of it," Ches ventured.

"Yes," Ms. Lillian agreed, "and we were usually in a bind before we ever called them. Remember that first year they vaccinated our calves for blackleg?"

"Yeah," Bowie admitted with a chuckle. "Chester sized up my tumbledown lot and tossed a look over his shoulder at Miss Sis, Nash, and Lonnie Ray. 'Take down your ropes. This'll work smoother out in the open.' Of course, I went to jumping up and down. Chester, you're apt to kill one that way! Chasing them down a'horseback…"

"What did he say to that?"

"Looked over at me, and I've seen that same grin on Miss Sis time to time. 'How many you lost to the blackleg this year?'"

"Is that the same lot?" the young rider inquired, arching an eyebrow.

"We built that one the next fall."

The answer came from Ms. Lillian, but Bowie couldn't hold back a chuckle as he elaborated.

"Forty-odd years ago, now, and out of used lumber. You having second thoughts?"

"If you say go ahead, I think we can load 'em alright."

All of a sudden, Bowie Tate didn't give two hoots for the cow one way or the other. He cared a whole lot more about the obstacles his young friend had overcome to offer help.

"Anybody ever tell you, Ches, that you look just like a Durham sitting up there on that horse? Ride on out and get 'em."

"Yes, sir. Does everything in this little trap go to town?"

"No, just the nut, her calf, and that big barren cow."

"Alrighty… I could try to peel off what we want a'horseback, but that pen won't stand the pressure. Back our truck up to the chute, and we can straight load them all. They'll be easy enough to sort on that long trailer."

"What about my truck and trailer?"

"Park it out yonder," Ches suggested, making a diagonal motion with one arm, "so it makes a kind of wing going into the lot. Me and Roxy will carry them one time around the pasture and then pour everything right through that gap."

"All the way around the pasture…" Ethan muttered, literally scratching his head. "The cows are right there looking at us. Why not just bring them through the gate?"

"He's got a reason," Ms. Lillian answered cheerfully. Then, making a shooing motion with her hands, "Best not take all day switching those trailers."

Roxy trotted happily along beside the horse, more or less ignoring the little bunch of cattle until Ches spoke. Relying more on pitch than volume, he tossed the words out on an urgent, driving hiss.

"Go to 'em, Rox. Get around!"

His aunt's Rip dog, tied up short in the back of the truck, whined pitifully as the little red gyp sprang into action. The cattle tried to scatter at first, but they all moved away from his horse. Short Stuff pricked his ears, ready to give chase at a moment's notice. Ches's stomach churned in nervous excitement.

He sympathized with the horse's eagerness but knew a much better way to get the job done. One hand stroking the bay's neck, he held to a steady walk and let Roxy do the legwork. She seemed to be everywhere at once. Barking a challenge, biting the occasional nose, and generally redirecting things until the cattle bunched up against her constant pressure. By the time they reached a back corner of the small pasture, Ches found himself pushing a compact little knot of cattle along in front of his horse.

Roxy kept up her agitation from the front and both sides but responded to her master's voice as they turned to follow the east fence.

"Easy, Rox… Gotta let 'em go somewhere."

The little bunch of "unmanageable" cattle funneled right past Mr. Bowie's truck and through the waiting gate. Ches saw the black, white-faced cow throw up her head as she entered the pen, but her bunch-quitting impulse kicked in too late. Raising his voice for the first time, he let out a whoop and allowed Short Stuff to lunge forward.

With this extra push, the cattle never stopped to try the rickety enclosure but bounded right up onto the trailer. Ethan set out to close off the corral, but a squall from Mr. Bowie changed his direction.

"Trailer! Shut the trailer gate!"

Ches pulled his horse up short to avoid the narrow loading chute, grinning broadly as Ethan slammed the trailer gate and pinned it in place.

"Get out, Rox... Good girl; we got 'em!"

Roxy was not in the trailer amongst the plunging, stomping cattle. She had too much sense for that, but the phrase get out- delivered in a certain tone- told her their work was all done.

Ches rode out of the corral and up beside the long trailer. There, he moved Short Stuff around and used his voice a little to help Mr. Bowie and Ethan as they sorted cattle back and forth between cut gates on the trailer.

"What do we owe you, son?" Ms. Lillian inquired, looking up to him with checkbook and pen in hand.

"Aw, just fix a head of hair for me, and we'll call it even."

"Which head of hair?" she wondered lightheartedly.

Ches looked down at her, mildly perplexed.

"Whichever comes in first, I reckon."

"I'll take care of Ruthanne for you," she offered warmly, "and Miss Sis, too."

"Gotta figure in the price of that bullet he saved me..." Well satisfied with the whole outcome, Bowie flashed a sunny grin and pulled his wife into a sidelong hug. "Miss Sis couldn't have done it any better herself!"

"Don't sell her short," Ches cautioned, and loving pride mingled with amusement in his voice. "She'd climb up on the side of that trailer and sort 'em while y'all sat in the shade."

"Probably want us out of the way, alright. But what makes you think she'd be all that concerned for our comfort? Shade is for a sweated horse or a pack of tired dogs."

The three men shared a laugh, and it caused Ches to shift his attention.

"You done good, Ethan. Thanks for the help."

"Don't mention it. Trailer gate made a satisfying bang, once Mr. Bowie got me pointed in the right direction."

"My trailer's got a new floor in it. Y'all might as well take the horse and dogs on home. I'll drop the good cattle at my other pasture, take what's left up town for Raymond and Scooter to resell, and circle by your place to swap trucks."

"Ordinarily, I'd just ride along with you, but for all we know, Ethan's on the clock. Besides... I ought to get on back and see about Ruthanne."

"She sick?"

"No, sir... Just out of pocket when we left. I couldn't find her anywhere."

"Kinda hurts my feelings to know I'm not his first choice of sidekick," Ethan joked. "As far as being on the clock... This turned out to be a lot of fun, and my wife likes haircuts, too."

"Heaven help us," Ms. Lillian muttered on a sigh but then answered him more directly. "I don't fix hair to suit the younger girls, but I'll give her a nice, relaxing shampoo anytime she wants it."

"Serena and Ruthanne are about the same age. If anything, my wife is a year or two..." Ethan's words trailed off slowly as he considered the difference in their hairstyles. Finally, he dismissed the whole subject with a grin and a shrug. "Ches mentioned something about going to help a neighbor. He said get in, and I did."

"Quick thinking," Bowie drawled with a mischievous twinkle in his eye, "for a Yankee."

Still riding an unexpected rush of adrenaline, Ethan talked more on the way home than he ever had around any of the Durham bunch. Ches smiled tolerantly, accepting the well-meant congratulations, but an uneasy feeling in the pit of his stomach kept him silent. Thoughts of Ruthanne, not worry exactly but nagging concern, played back and forth across his mind. Where had she gone, what was she doing, and how could he help her?

Ches admired his little miss almost as much as he loved her. Ruthanne Prescott had proven herself quietly capable time and time again. But a clear head and quick, willing hands didn't necessarily mean she wouldn't overload herself trying to help someone else or work her fingers to the bone while Pap sat easy in the shade. Slipping the cellphone from his shirt pocket, he fiddled with it until Ethan finally noticed.

"Go ahead and call her again," he suggested. "Been three hours since we left."

"We'll be home directly," Ches answered, giving his head a little shake. "She's just fine. I'm getting as fretful as Aunt Hattie, and that's all there is to it."

From lifelong habit, Ches wanted his horse unsaddled and turned out before he took off in search of Ruthanne. Ethan performed the chore and then, for whatever reason, hopped back into the minivan. They checked all through the big house first and then circled back to her current home on the old Giles Parmalee place.

Finding the door unlocked, Ches guided his wheelchair slowly into the kitchen. If he hesitated over entering the house, Ethan followed with even greater reluctance. Ruthanne's cellphone lay on the table, placed carefully atop a sheet of old-fashioned stationery. A few lines of cursive handwriting, neat and unmistakably feminine, hit him like a mule kick to the belly.

Gone back East on urgent business... It hurts me to leave you alone, but Miss Sis will be home soon. The two of you have faced so much together, and I know you will handle this just as well. I'm asking you to trust me, my darling. All my love and prayers, Ruthanne.

Downcast on the drive back into town, Ethan Fisher took out his own cellphone and placed a call to his wife.

"Babe, I'm not sure exactly what the problem is. But you might want to get out here and check on Ches."

"Check on Ches..." she repeated in a light almost singsong voice. "If he's been run over, stepped on, or rope burned, it ain't the first time."

"Ruthanne left him this note."

"What kind of note?"

"What am I supposed to do, read over his shoulder?"

"Well, yeah."

"I just know he stared at it for what seemed like a long time, put it down like he thought it might shatter, and finally vomited into the kitchen sink."

"And what did you do?"

"What do you think? I left him there at Ruthanne's where we found the note, walked back over to the sale barn to get my car, and now I'm calling you."

"Ethan," she snapped, turning his own name into a reprimand.

"He's your frien— Well, whatever he is, this is not my problem."

"Of all times for Miss Sis to take off and go…" Her voice sounded as though she might break down and cry at any moment, but then it changed suddenly. "Oh, if I ever get ahold of Ruthanne, I'll scratch her eyes out! Ches is just like the boss lady, too loyal for his own good. They can face most anything, but for somebody they love to up and leave without…"

Ethan, more tactless than uncaring, spoke into the heavy silence.

"Isn't that just about what you did?"

"Yeah," she sniffled, and the next words came out just under her breath, bitter with hardening resolve. "But I'll still scratch her eyes out."

Serena Kate arrived to find Giles Parmalee's brick home completely deserted, and the built-in mindset of a healthcare professional addressed the practical side of things first. She splashed a little Clorox in the kitchen sink and rinsed it clean. Only then did she allow her heart, full of instincts from childhood, to lead her on up to the big house.

She knew exactly where to find Ches Durham in time of trouble. He sat alone on the wide back porch, staring down toward the sale barn with a far-off look on his face. Serena Kate trailed her fingers briefly through his dark hair and eyed a place in the swing beside him. Ultimately, though, she settled down on the top step, quartering around to face her oldest friend.

They sat that way in silence for a long time while Serena Kate wracked her brain for the right words, but it was Ches who finally spoke.

"Aunt Sis had it right all along. We take care of this old place, and it takes care of us. Land won't jump out from under you like a pitching horse or break your heart the way people do. Only thing in this world fit to hang any hopes onto, aside from God Almighty."

"Oh... Oh, no," she stuttered, fresh tears welling in her eyes while his expression remained almost blank. "Miss Sis might've felt that way once, but you showed up and... Everything changed after that. She found Andrew, and little Cassidy came along."

"Yeah, that's why I thought maybe... I'm happy for Aunt Sis and all, but I reckon the homeplace will just have to be enough for me."

"Come right down to it, Ches, there's only God to count on. I know you love this old place, but it can't love you back. Dirt is just dirt. Think about those people out yonder in the Dust Bowl who watched their land dry up and blow away. Them, and every poor sucker who's ever lost out to the bank."

"Thought you slept through history class," he shot back with a scowl.

"Most of it," she admitted breezily. "But I remember watching that Dust Bowl footage- people loading up to make a run for California- and thinking, 'No way... Miss Sis would probably hold us all here until we choked to death on the grit.'"

"Time is filled with swift transition," Ches quoted, emotion overriding any attempt to sing the old lyric. "Naught of earth unmoved can stand. Build your hopes on things eternal. Hold to God's unchanging hand."

"Remember what your Uncle Elmer used to say?" she asked with a tremulous little smile.

"'Pretty song, but it ain't scriptural.' I always knew what he meant, too. God holds on to us, and not the other way around."

"Exactly."

"Thanks for the advice, Serena Kate, but I never meant to belittle God's role in my life."

"Not so much advice... Call it a friendly reminder."

"God gave me the homeplace to help get me through. The homeplace and Aunt Sis and you're back now... Even that knot-head husband of yours ain't as bad as I had him figured. I'm gonna be just fine, sweetheart, but the thing is... I still love Ruthanne more than I could ever say. I want her to be safe and happy and well cared for, but there ain't a blessed thing I can do about it. I felt almost this helpless when you left, wondering what would become of you and them little redheaded twins."

"We made it home, didn't we? The Lord will look after Ruthanne same as He takes care of the rest of us. You could always pray for her."

"I am... Prayed for you, too, when I didn't know what else to do. Would you help me, Serena Kate?"

"Pray for that perfect little belle? Oh, Ches... I'd like to strangle her, and Miss Sis may really do it if she ever gets a chance. Still, something don't smell right about this. Ruthanne's not me. She always seemed so well adjusted. Like I said, the perfect little belle. I've been praying mostly for the strength not to hate her guts, but I suppose I could add her personal wellbeing to the list. Just for you." Serena Kate hitched herself up off the step and scooted across the smooth-worn boards of the porch until her back rested against his knees. "And, Ches, I'm so very sorry for running out the way... I didn't have to watch you go through it back then, but now..."

Ches squeezed her shoulder by way of an answer, and that head full of flaming red curls fell naturally into his lap.

"Get outta here," he prodded gently after more than an hour. "You've got a family waiting up town. Besides, we're not as young as we used to be. You'll be stiff as a board from sitting that-a-way."

"I'm not leaving you here like this without calling Terry and Jenna."

"No," and the answer came on a reflex. "Aunt Sis'll—"

"Look, I know you feel about like a coyote with his foot caught in the trap. 'Fraid you'll snap at somebody if you let 'em get too close? Not Miss Sis, maybe, but us regular folks…"

"Pretty much sums it up," he admitted with the ghost of a smile.

"Well, that's too bad. They're your parents, and they can run the risk of gettin' bit same as I can."

Sure enough, Serena Kate rallied the troops and set up a tag-team effort to keep Ches occupied. Terry and Jenna Durham arrived not long after she left with matching worried looks and a small duffel bag.

"Been a long time since I stayed all night up here at the big house," Terry mused, "but we figured this is where you'd want to be."

Daddy followed that statement with a halting attempt at conversation. Recalling how Ruthanne had fallen suddenly into their lives on the heels of Serena Kate's unexpected wedding, he suggested in no uncertain terms that it might not hurt to look around for a while the next time. Mom, usually bursting with advice, remained compassionately silent. When Scooter showed up early the next morning, Ches was back in the porch swing.

"You been to bed?"

"Yeah, but it didn't do me no whole lot of good."

"I know you ain't much of a coffee drinker, but we'll get you a couple of Serena Kate's Mountain Dews or something. Miss Sis is off kicking up her heels, and I might need some backup for that big stocker sale. It'll run all day and into the night."

"Can't say I feel much like it, but help me feed everything, and we'll go."

Figuring everybody had their own load to tote, Ches perched beside his friend up above the crowd at Willard's Livestock Exchange and hoped his misery wouldn't show. He recalled many times- after a painful injury, a sudden shock, or even a death in the family- when his eyes stung at the sight of Aunt Sis on public display way up in an auctioneer's box. He also remembered how cool and collected she looked at these times, smiling through her heartache and calling for the next horse to sell.

"Say, Ches…" Sonny Boy Leggett started to talk over the noise of the crowd but changed his mind. Trotting easily up the steep metal steps, he knelt down to speak at closer range. "Somebody told me y'all bought the old Giles Parmalee place. I knew you had pasture leased over there, but—"

"Uncle Andrew and Aunt Sis bought it. I'm still leasing the place, only from them."

"I eased over there yesterday to catch me a few of them perch."

"You know we don't care. Any more than Giles…"

"Yeah, but… Listen, Ches, does your little lady still live there with her granddaddy?" Throat tightening, Ches managed a nod. "Didn't take much note at the time, but I seen a county car roll up to the house. Ain't none of us quite as hard-edged as my old man. But I got to thinkin' how funny he was about keeping an eye out, and well… With Miss Sis gone from home, I figured you oughta know"

"Thanks, Sonny Boy. I owe you for this," and as the man rose to his feet, Ches put a hand out to stop him. "Can you manage the first couple of hours?" he asked Scooter.

"Might go 'til this evening if I don't swallow one of these blasted flies."

"I'll try to make it back before you give plumb out," and then to Sonny Boy, "help me down these steps."

Fifteen minutes later, he sat in his wheelchair across the desk from Sheriff Lance Wainwright.

"No one was arrested, Ches. I sent a man out there to serve some papers, and that's really all I can say about it."

"What kind of papers?"

"I told you; I can't say. Regulations…"

"Which deputy?"

"Can't tell you that, either."

"Did you call Aunt Sis before you sent somebody out our way?"

"Wake up, Ches. This is 2016. I'd be a running joke for every peace officer in the state if they knew I had to call and ask her, please, before serving a legal document. Y'all have been a lot of help to this department over the years. Maybe saved Uncle Marvin's hide a time or two… But I'm not Uncle Marvin. We have protocols and procedures to follow. You ought to see the stack of forms I process every day. Nowhere on the checklist does it say call Miss Sis first!"

"I'm gonna have to agree with you," Ches practically snarled. "You ain't no Marvin Wainwright. Times may change, and you may change. But we don't… Next time you better make that call."

Just then, Tom Wallace rapped on the half-open door of the inner office.

"Dinnertime, Lance. I'll be back directly." The old deputy's weather-beaten face belied the softness of his recent desk job, but kindness glinted behind a pair of bifocals. "Trail along with me, Chester?"

Ches whipped his head around, startled out of his rising anger by the quiet invitation. No one ever called him Chester, and old Tom must have done it on purpose.

"Don't you tell him anything. Violates all kinds of regulations…"

"We're going to lunch. Unless you're coming along, just stick your nose back in that computer."

They made it as far as the front sidewalk before Ches voiced his inquiry.

"Thank you kindly for the invitation, but I ain't got time for lunch. Just give it to me straight."

Tom never stopped walking but slackened his pace, allowing Ches to pull alongside.

"Lance asked me to serve them papers. I reminded him how we've always done it, but he's too big and important to make a little old phone call. Nobody else wanted the chore, either. They sent that new kid. Sent him in blind... Marvin would roll in his grave."

"You see the papers?"

"Yeah... Some kind of summons to appear for questioning in Marlboro County, South Carolina. Duplicate, one on old man Prescott and another on that sweet little granddaughter of his. Kid said they took it pretty well. Miss Ruthanne turned kinda white all of a sudden, but Prescott acted like he'd delivered an invitation to Sunday supper."

"Thanks, Tom... You'll do to ride with any day."

"I should've took it on myself to call, but Lance keeps us all so hamstrung... He's hamstrung himself, if you want to know the truth. Feels like he's got to come out of Marvin's shadow, but your aunt and the rest of them old timers only backed him for sheriff because of the last name."

"Old timers? You're older than Aunt Sis..."

"Yeah, but I ain't Colonel Durham's daughter."

Ches left the man with a handshake, and for reasons he couldn't quite explain, drove over to Pinevale. Though opinionated, Aunt Hattie had long ago excluded herself from these no-nonsense councils. Instead, Ches and Serena Kate drifted into Giles Parmalee's room.

"Miss Sis can see to Lance soon as she gets back," the old man rumbled in his unmistakable voice. "You better figure a way to get out to South Carolina. Your aunt loves you something fierce, son. Unless you want that girl drug back by the hair of the head—"

"No... No, sir. You're right, but I can't hardly drive all that way on my own."

"I'd take off and go with you, but it might cost me my job," Serena Kate put in regretfully.

"No, I'm not asking—"

"Call Mr. Judd and Ms. Shirley," she suggested, a smile breaking over her face. "Those are some traveling folks! If they're off work, they'll go."

Ches returned to the auctioneer's box, settled in his mind and ready to work. Little miss hadn't deserted him on some passing whim. Probably mortified, bless her heart. Trouble dogged Pap Prescott, but Ruthanne had no cause for embarrassment. Together, they could see it through.

Having advised Aunt Sis to finish out the family vacation, Ches didn't expect her until the middle of the next day. However, a gentle hand on his shoulder woke him long before the guinea hens ever stirred.

"You been to bed?" he murmured, echoing Scooter's question from the previous morning. Miss Sis placed a finger to her lips and then answered softly.

"I can sleep anytime. Right now, we've got things to do."

Not a hair out of place from the long car ride, she looked ready for church in a lilac blouse, white skirt with floral pattern, hose, and high heels. Ches slipped into the freshly starched blue jeans and pearl-snap shirt she laid out for him and kept silent to avoid waking anyone else. "We're not starting off after Ruthanne at this time of the morning, are we?" he questioned once inside the van.

"Trailing behind the colonel left me plenty tough," she said with a chuckle, "but I'll have to have a nap before we make South Carolina."

"Good; you don't need to... I'm headed over to Mr. Judd and Ms. Shirley's later today. The three of us will strike out from there."

She shot him a look, questioning and almost hurt.

"We can handle our own trouble, always have."

"Yes'm, but I may be gone for a week or two. We've got the April sale coming up, and well, this is something I need to do myself. You'd be one step ahead, looking out for me all the way."

"That's what I'm here for, honey. It's what Daddy did for me, and—"

"You buried the colonel on a Thursday, climbed back into the auctioneer's box Friday evening, and then turned around and did it all over again the next week. How can we cancel a monthly sale just because my sweetheart got called into court? No, ma'am... I need you here."

"Whatever you think best, honey," she whispered, blinking back tears as she guided the minivan down dark, treelined roads toward the county seat.

Ches began to suspect where they might be going, but he knew better than to ask for clarification. A man just had to stay ready and watch her for his next move. Sure enough, she drove straight to town and down into a relatively new subdivision.

"You coming?" she asked, pausing to look back as she stepped out the driver's door.

"Yes'm. What about a pistol?"

"Don't be silly," but when he opened the glovebox, she threw her head back and laughed. "No, I meant leave it here."

A quick glance at his cellphone told Ches it was ten minutes until five o'clock in the morning, and the rapid clatter of heels on the cobblestone walk told him that Sheriff Lance Wainwright was about to get a rude awakening.

"You do know town people don't get up this early?" he confided as he came up behind her in the doorway.

Aunt Sis threw him a quick wink before she began a rapid, insistent tapping on the door. When Lance finally pulled back the curtain for a peep, Ches saw blond hair standing on end every which way and a sleek semi-automatic handgun.

"Put that thing away before it goes off," Aunt Sis chided as the door swung open. She spoke in the same friendly, tolerant tone she might use with a bothersome child, brushing past the sheriff and into his house. "I'm fixing to cook your breakfast so we can get on the move."

*Beyond the Parmalee Bottom* 325

"Cook my…" He trailed off then, and his sleep-clouded gaze shifted down to the wheelchair. "Come right in; everybody else is… Look, my wife and kids are asleep. I was asleep. You're the cause of all this, Ches, so can you at least tell me what she's up to?"

Having no real idea of what his aunt's plan might be, or whether she had one, Ches flashed a grin.

"Can't do it… Regulations."

While Miss Sis worked over the stove, Lance slumped into a chair and began rubbing his temples. Ches had no clue what his aunt might be thinking, but he knew she was making more noise than necessary and dirtying every dish that came to hand. Later, as the Wainwright kids tumbled onto the scene, she set bacon and eggs on the table as well as pancakes with plenty of syrup.

"I think that's turkey bacon, Ches, but it's all I could find."

"Thanks for breakfast," the oldest daughter chirped, "but our school bus doesn't come for three more hours…"

"No school today, sweetheart, unless you want to call it a fieldtrip to the farm."

Mrs. Wainwright entered the room and started to protest, but Sis cut it off with a smile and a cup of fresh coffee.

"Look, lady," the sheriff complained, "you can't just march into my home and take over everything."

"You still got a saddle?"

"Uncle Marvin's is around here somewhere, but you know I don't ride. Maybe once a year in the parade…"

"Don't ride? Oh, well… How do you feel about a shovel and wheelbarrow?"

"I don't quite follow you…"

"We've got a horse sale coming in less than two weeks, and you ran off my top hand."

*Beyond the Parmalee Bottom* 326

"I'm not gonna shovel... I can't just... The Commissioners' Court meets today! Hold on, Miss Sis. You don't want to burn any bridges here."

"Ruthanne Prescott is more than a riding hand, Lance. She's family." Leaning across the table, Sis dropped her pleasant tone and spoke for his ears alone. "Colonel Durham would've broke your jaw when you answered the door. Mama taught me softer ways, but if that child is runnin' scared... If she comes to harm because you couldn't make a simple phone call before serving that overblown piece of out-of-state paper... I'll do more than burn bridges."

Lance took a nervous gulp of his coffee without regard for its scalding temperature.

"Oww! Okay... Okay... Yes, ma'am..."

"And the next time Ches comes into your office asking for a little information, he'd better get triplicate photocopies and a firm handshake."

"Yes, ma'am, I'll see to it. Look, I never meant... But you don't really expect me and my family to come out there and work all day?"

"Reckon we could manage without you," she said, "but I'll just leave it up to Ches."

Though laced with maple syrup, her unspoken code proved simple and direct. "Show a little respect, and you'll be treated accordingly. Invade my territory, and I'll invade yours."

Ches understood this straightforward approach, but it made few allowances for the pressures of modern law enforcement. A faint warning bell in the back of his mind said Lance Wainwright was not the enemy. Thankful for any man willing to stand and serve, he decided to get Lance off the hook without compromising his aunt's strategy.

"Unwillin' help never accomplished much," he drawled, offering a grim echo of his familiar smile. "What I've got to do now is find Ruthanne."

# Chapter Eighteen

(South Carolina Upcountry: Mid-April 2016)

"We ought to get us a place to stay before you start combing the town," Mr. Judd suggested casually. "If Ruthanne's exhausted or rattled or fresh from the county lockup, she'll need a little rest before we start that long drive back to McKendrick."

"County lockup!"

"You never know," the goodhearted jokester answered. "I've busted Shirley out more than once."

"I have never been to jail in my life!" Shirley countered, launching a ball of napkins at him from the minivan's rear seat.

Ches's smile looked a little weary around the edges, but it held a great deal of appreciation for the good-natured banter between husband and wife. Their trips usually consisted of him tagging along with Judd and Shirley, but this time they had logged more than eight hundred miles just because he asked.

"If they've got Ruthanne in jail," Judd ventured, "like as not, we'll all land in there with her. You should've seen the look on Ches's face when I said county lockup."

"If you'll hush for two seconds, Judd Matthews, I might find us a place to stay."

"Me and Ches'll spot a hotel while you're busy pelting folks with paper towel."

"Don't underestimate Google, and besides, I'm all out of napkins. Hey, Ches... Tell me the name of that farm again?"

"What farm?"

"You know... The plantation... Ruthanne's family home."

"Fairview," he recalled instantly, feeling the same rush of tenderness as if he'd spoken Ruthanne's own name, "but it's long gone to the bank. Thanks mostly to Pap and his topnotch management skills..."

"Well... Somebody's lettin' out rooms, Fairview Bed and Breakfast."

"Book it," Judd advised. Then, with his signature grin, "Might as well get the whole house, long as Ches is paying."

"Tell 'em we've just come into Bennettsville, and it might be kinda late before we get out that-a-way." Ches murmured his request, turning around to look at Shirley as the call rang in her ear. "I'd like to have Ruthanne beside me the first time we step into her old home."

"Sounds reasonable to me," Judd agreed, lowering his own voice to speak under Shirley's conversation. "I just hope it don't take us several days to find her. Being this close, do you think she might drift on over toward McColl?"

"Might," Ches answered doubtfully. "But they got called back here on a legal matter, and Bennettsville is the county seat. If Ruthanne was over around home, surely her aunt would know it. Granted, Aunt Lurlene could've been hedging just like me, but she claimed not to have heard anything since the news of our engagement."

"Hold it!" Shirley cried from the backseat.

Judd flinched, but resisted the impulse to slam on his brakes.

"I wish you wouldn't holler that-a-way. What's the matter? They don't want to hold the rooms until we get there?"

"No… I mean, yeah. The rooms are fine, but is that a Ferris wheel?"

"Not just a Ferris wheel," Ches realized instantly. "That old broke down thing is Tiny's wheel! Let's get over there."

"Didn't you and this Tiny character butt heads?" Judd asked, brow furrowing in an effort to recall the story.

"Yes, sir… May do it again, but that particular bunch of carnival folk turning up right here and now is a little too much coincidence for me."

"Fair's not overcrowded," Shirley observed under her breath as they pulled in to park.

"Ain't no fair," Judd decided. "Looks to me like they're squattin' here, maybe waiting."

"Y'all stay in the van," Ches directed flatly. "I'll be back before you know it."

"Fat chance, buddy," Shirley huffed. "I may not be as rough and ready as Miss Sis, but I'll at least get close enough to see what happens."

"Alright," Ches relented, swallowing a grin as he navigated down the wheelchair ramp. "Let's stay away from the Ferris wheel and look for the pony ride setup. Gilderoy may not be a friend, exactly, but I don't figure him for an enemy."

"That all depends on how bad Pap skinned him over them ponies," Judd muttered, and the three started their walk with a shared chuckle.

As it turned out, they bumped into Mrs. Gilderoy before locating either her husband or the ponies. The woman's dark eyes sized them up in one perceptive glance, and Ches suddenly understood how she managed to pass herself off as a fortune teller.

"You and your friends should not be here, not even with Tiny in jail. His boys… They watch, and they listen. Maybe he go free again. Who can tell?"

"Ruthanne?" he breathed, conveying several questions with the single word.

The woman's previously unreadable face lit for an instant, and a smile tugged at the corners of her mouth. Taking in this flash of goodwill, Ches paid little attention to Judd's whispered comment.

"If Pap skinned 'em, I reckon she's over it."

"Your young lady come here to visit the little horses, but I send her away. This is not a safe place for those who would stand against Tiny."

"Ma'am... I don't care about Tiny one way or the other. Where's Ruthanne?"

At Mrs. Gilderoy's gentle touch, Ches steeled himself for unwelcome news, but she simply turned his left hand over to inspect the palm.

"You and Ruthie live long and happy life togeth—"

Ches snatched his hand back like she had scalded it.

"No, ma'am. No, thank you. When the Good Lord gets ready for me, He'll take me. I wouldn't have it any other way. Where is Ruthanne now, today?"

"There is a public campground, near this same highway, and just beyond the far edge of town."

"Thank you... Thank you kindly."

As they turned to go, a soft chuckle drifted through the sunlit spring afternoon.

"You and Ruthie make good match. She, too, is very Baptist."

Always the designated navigator, Shirley searched the internet for nearby campgrounds, but they spotted the actual RV park just about the time its name popped up on her screen. Judd threaded them between rows of travel trailers until Ches leaned suddenly from his window and gave a long, shrill whoop. The full-size maroon van with "Hot Apple Fritters and the Prescott Ponies" emblazoned on the side hunkered between two fifth-wheel campers.

Judd slammed the minivan into park and jabbed buttons until the wheelchair

*Beyond the Parmalee Bottom* 332

ramp deployed.

"You testing every door?" Shirley wanted to know.

"Just look at Ches," he exclaimed, blinking back happy tears to which he would never admit. "I didn't want him to go head first out the window!"

Ruthanne knew a Durham holler when she heard it, even from the far side of the campground. Depositing her small purchase unceremoniously on the porch, she sprinted away from the on-site convenience store and toward the familiar sound.

Pap Prescott's head poked out of the old van like a turtle from its shell. Ches started to speak, but the sight of Ruthanne jumping over somebody's waterline and ducking low-hanging wind chimes as she cut across neighboring lots refocused his attention. A little more careful for fear of high centering the wheelchair or smacking into something, he nevertheless rushed to meet her.

Somewhat breathless from the mad dash, she fell unselfconsciously across his lap, gazed up adoringly for a long moment, and then shifted her gaze to look all around them.

"I... Wasn't... Sure..." she panted, "Whether I was coming to a h-happy reunion or s-some kind of fight."

"Fight?" he repeated through laughter and tears. "I could never—"

"No, it sounded like you were puttin' the cow dogs onto something."

"And you came running to a good scrap?"

"I came running to see you, m-darlin... But whenever I find you in a scrap, I'll fall right in there."

"You mean that?"

"Of course, I do. Say, what are you doing all the way..."

Her tears came then, hot and quick. Ches gathered her a little tighter into his arms and commenced a slight rocking motion that moved them gently back and forth.

*Beyond the Parmalee Bottom* 333

"Shh… Shh, everything's gonna be alright. Whatever the trouble is, we'll face it together."

"Ches," she finally managed, "I'm not crying over the little fix that brought us here."

"Then, what?"

"I'm crying because I just realized you didn't figure on me coming back. How could you think… Oh, m-darlin, I'd never run off and leave you behind. And without a goodbye or even a backward glance?"

"I'm awful sorry I misread the signs, but things looked kinda bad."

"Don't you apologize to me, Ches Durham! I wish now I'd told you everything, but it all happened so fast. Then, too, I was ashamed to drag you and Miss Sis into—"

"Whenever I find you in a scrap," he echoed softly, lips hovering next to her ear, "I'll fall right in there."

"Oh, Ches…"

"Save your breath, little miss, right along with all that embarrassment," he murmured, turning to face the onlookers with her still in his lap. "I'd like to hear this story right from the horse's mouth. Talk fast, Pap."

"No trouble, no trouble at all," the old showman drawled, patting the air in front of him as he began his oration. "Ruthie girl, I had no notion you'd got yourself so worked up and embarrassed over this deal. No call for shame, you'll see. I'll tell you right now, Ches, it's my fault we left in haste, but I sure didn't know you all figured to trail right after us. In future, son, just give me a little time. We'll circle back."

"In future," Ches retorted dryly, "you can circle back whenever the notion strikes you, but Ruthanne stays with me."

"Be that as it may," Pap continued, acknowledging the interruption with a curt nod, "Ruthanne's not in any trouble. For once in my life, I'm not either. Why, I set the whole deal up, and it's clickin' right along."

*Beyond the Parmalee Bottom* 334

"Set it up?" little miss gasped, rising to stand beside Ches as he stiffened into that alert, motionless pose reminiscent of his Aunt Sis or maybe a snake just before it strikes.

A hot rush of anger nearly overpowered the respect due Ruthanne's grandfather. However, the undeniable urge to laugh brought a gradual relaxation of his posture.

"Why, you conniving old rascal," he drawled, but Pap spoke over the outburst of laughter that followed.

"You was there, Ches, the night this whole mess started. Remember telling me all about how Tiny backed Ruthanne up against the horse trailer? Maybe you thought I kinda shrugged it off," and the old man smiled as he tapped his forehead. "But these wheels is always turning."

"Beg pardon, Pap. I've drug Mr. Judd and Ms. Shirley half way across the country. Are you coming to some kind of a point?"

"Surely am, son. I surely am. You see... My cousin, Dude Prescott, is the circuit solicitor of Marlboro County."

"Circuit... Say what?"

"You know, like a district attorney. I called him from the next town. Ruthie operates our mobile phone more than I do. Anyhow, I kinda put the black mark on that overgrowed scoundrel. When Tiny and the bunch finally ventured up this way, Dude couldn't say for sure where I was. He's a Prescott, though, and a smart boy. Just got the court to issue them papers on me and Ruthie and let somebody else do the legwork, huntin' us down."

"What kind of folks name a rollin' stone like you Phineas Absalom Prescott and call the future district attorney Dude? Anyhow, I wish you'd told somebody 'bout this scheme of yours. You've upset Ruthanne, led us on this wild goose chase, and... Aunt Sis barged into Sheriff Wainwright's house at five o'clock in the morning and started cookin' breakfast!"

"She did what?"

"Hard to complain when a lady cooks breakfast for you."

*Beyond the Parmalee Bottom* 335

Pap's belly laugh died suddenly as Judd's lighthearted comment captured his attention. Ches almost smiled as worry and then faint horror chased one another across the normally untroubled face.

"She wouldn't... She didn't... Was there anything in it?"

"Poison is a coward's vengence," Ches snapped. "She ain't geared that way. Worst I've ever known her to do is leave a few bullwhip tracks on somebody. Not for revenge, mind you. Just getting her point across in the here and now or teachin' valuable lessons for the future."

"Never meant to cause no trouble, Ches. I set this little deal in motion and then put it on the back burner. How was I to know if Tiny and them would ever ramble way up here into my little old home county."

This justification was as much apology as Pap was likely to offer, so Ches moved on to practicalities.

"What are the charges? We ran him off before anything could happen to Ruthanne. Besides, I don't want her put on the spot. Gettin' up in open court to tell how some big galoot made her feel like a snared rabbit..."

"Charges? You name it, and old Tiny's done it. He's guilty as homemade sin. Dude won't have to drag up nothing involving Ruthanne, not directly. He'll send Tiny down the river for that little gambling ring that runs along with the carnival."

"Gambling ring?"

"Sure. Why do you think he was so mad at me that night? It takes a good deal of luck to cheat an honest game. But once I get the feel of a rigged layout, son, I can play it like an organ." Ruthanne's face lost all color, flamed red, and then went pale again. Pap, for his part, looked a little sheepish. "I know I oughtn't to have done it, but the money was just too easy."

"Oh, Pap..." Ruthanne murmured from the back of her throat.

"Whenever we'd run short on cash, I'd ease by there of an evening and pick up what I needed. Then, if I spotted a friendly kind of local yokel in the game who'd just about lost his shirt, I'd throw money his way for the fun of it. Tiny's boys couldn't hardly stand it, but when you're runnin' a crooked game, you don't jump up and holler cheat."

This little speech sent Judd and Shirley into waves of laughter. Ches bit his tongue to keep from joining in, but he watched Ruthanne carefully as the signs of mild nausea began to fade. Finally, one corner of her mouth twitched, and he allowed himself a little chuckle.

"Have you told Ruthanne where we're staying?" Shirley asked gently as the laughter died down.

"Nice place," he said casually. "We thought you'd like it. But first, give me the rundown. What comes next?"

"Pap and I appear in court for the first time tomorrow afternoon, Ches. Who knows how long things might drag out from there?"

"I'll be in that courtroom with you. In the meantime, though, you can show me around our quaint little bed and breakfast."

"Quaint little... People don't generally need rooms in their hometown, m-darlin. If there was a bed and breakfast runnin' in the county when we lived here, I never knew it."

"We thought you'd like this one in particular," he repeated. "They call it Fairview Bed and Breakfast."

"You don't mean? We can really stay at... Oh, that'll make this whole awful mess worthwhile. I'll show you every little... The orchard, Ches! I bet it's just chockfull of apple blossoms!"

"Easy, now, Ruthie," Pap crooned in a grave but gentle tone. "We don't know if there's so much as an apple tree left standing. Not unless Ches has already..."

"No, sir."

"I suppose you're right, Pap," Ruthanne admitted. "We don't know, but I intend to find out."

"Y'all go ahead on," he replied dismissively. "I feel more at home in a campground these days than I would under that roof."

Ches's throat tightened as he watched Ruthanne's joy deflate.

"Well, I can't just leave you here."

"I'll stay with him myself if that's what it takes," Ches declared. "You're goin' to a hot bath and a soft bed."

"Sounds lovely... But the best part of seeing Fairview again will be sharing it with you, m-darlin. I can't do that if you're camped out here with Pap."

"I aged past the babysitter stage many moons ago," the old man grumbled. "Meet me on the courthouse steps a little before two o'clock tomorrow afternoon, and we'll nail Tiny's hide to the wall."

Leaving Ches's side for the first time since his arrival, Ruthanne rose on tiptoe and kissed her grandfather's cheek.

"Just give me a minute, Ches," she tossed over her shoulder. "I'll be ready before y'all can turn the van around."

"Easy does it, little miss. You're worth waitin' on..."

Later that evening, the young couple sat together on the shaded veranda of Ruthanne's former home.

"Mr. Judd and Ms. Shirley will think I'm some kind of emotional wreck after this trip," she sighed. "I've laughed and cried and..."

"They understand. You went from a bad shock, thanks to Pap and his shenanigans, to the unexpected joy of coming home again." Then, as the thought hit him, "You gonna show me the orchard before dark?"

Excited, she half rose from the wicker loveseat only to nestle in beside him once more.

"I walked off down there when we first came, and it's breathtaking. Apple trees in full blossom... But somehow, m-darlin, I don't want you to see it from the wheelchair."

*Beyond the Parmalee Bottom* 338

"I'll get the crutches and walk," he volunteered eagerly. "You'll have to stop and rest me like a played-out horse, but we'll make it."

"A couple of played-out horses may be just what we need! Did you bring your saddle?"

"Mom and Daddy gave us funny looks, but Aunt Sis packed it right along with the rest of my stuff. Now, what are you up to?"

"Please don't misunderstand me, Ches... Nothing slows you down. I don't mind the wheelchair in the least. For whatever reason, though, I feel a certain closeness when we're together a'horseback. On equal terms, you know?"

"Equal terms my foot," he quipped with a grin. "You can ride circles around me."

"That's not the point," she answered softly. "You'd say Miss Sis can ride circles around you, too, but the sight of her up on a horse won't ever give me that funny little flutter a-way down in my stomach."

"Stomach?"

"Laugh if you want to, but sometimes I think my heart's down there. Anyhow, m-darlin, you cut quite a dashing figure in the saddle."

"Me, strapped down like a sack of potatoes?"

"That safety belt compensates for your balance, and that's all. You sit a horse with your head high and your shoulders back."

"Kinda like Aunt Sis... Only on me, it's flutter worthy?"

"Now you're just teasing me."

He was teasing, too, right up until the playful accusation and a soft giggle from his serious-minded young lady changed the moment completely.

"You give me the flutters all on your own. No horse or nothin'..."

"You're doing alright," she admitted on a shuddering sigh as he trailed a finger

*Beyond the Parmalee Bottom* 339

ever so gently along her jawline.

All at once, Ches straightened up in his seat, giving her hand a little pat to keep from breaking contact so abruptly.

"Fella could get carried away real easy," he apologized. "The other day when I thought I'd lost you for good... Wherever you are, that's where I want to be. If we're going to take over the big house and start us a life together, I'm ready."

"Cassidy wants a June wedding," she reminded him, but her voice carried the faintest tinge of regret.

Feeling the warmth of her hand in his, Ches offered a silent prayer of gratitude, and twilight gave way to darkness before he spoke again.

"You're tired, sugar pie," he ventured, kissing her lightly on the forehead.

"My body's tired and a little sore..."

"All that driving and the stress, too."

"Still, my mind's running ninety to nothing. No matter how long this legal rigmarole drags on, I don't want you paying for more than a few days here at Fairview. We need to make the most of them."

"Tell me what you're thinking."

"Those Shetlands wouldn't do us much good, but I know Gilderoy would lease me the little palomino pony we bought in Louisiana. One of the neighbors has an old paint mule running in the pasture."

"Saw it as we came in..."

"We took that mule in to break when I was nine or ten years old."

"You did the training and Pap got paid?"

"I suppose," she admitted, with a playful sort of smile, "but we had the mule all summer. Pap did work her in the garden just a little. First thing in the morning, I'll go over and see if I can't rent Gilderoy's little horse and a trailer, too. The mule probably won't cost us anything as long as I'm willing to clean her up some and knock the rough edges off. If I run at it like Miss Sis would and make things happen, we oughta have time for a nice little ride before I'm due in court. Mercy," she quipped, affecting a little shudder. "Just what every girl wants to say to her fiancé! Before I'm due in court…"

Ches hated to see Ruthanne push herself, obviously overdoing it on the heels of a long road trip. But he couldn't turn down the chance to ride over Fairview with her, not when she wanted this little jaunt even more than he did.

Naturally, he insisted on going with her back to the encampment. Gilderoy's wife repeated her ominous words of caution, but the man himself simply counted Ches's money and wished him a pleasant ride. The neighbor lady greeted Ruthanne warmly, imparted the sad news of her husband's passing, and decided they could do whatever they wanted with the mule.

Ches could only shake his head as Ruthanne climbed into the loft of the plantation's last remaining barn, dug around in a forgotten corner, and came up with a fairly ancient set of horseshoeing tools.

"At least let me hold her foot up while you work on it," he chided. "You're not exactly built for wrestling livestock."

"Ches…" she gasped in real distress. "A mule can kick frontwards, backwards, and sideways! You know that as well as I do."

"What are you, kick-proof?"

"Maybe not, but you'd have to get down on your knees to hold that foot up for me. At least I can keep my head outta the line of fire."

He laughed suddenly, but Ruthanne's jaw took on a stubborn set.

"It ain't funny, Ches Durham. I won't have you crawling around under that mule."

"No, look…"

She turned then and followed his gaze to where the little mule stood half asleep with Judd busily trimming off excess hoof. Ever nurturing, Ruthanne crossed the wide hallway in the barn to lay a hand on Judd's shoulder.

"Don't you have back trouble?" she inquired gently.

"You've heard 'em talk about a strong back and a weak mind?"

"Yes, sir, but what does that have to do with—"

"Ain't much point in havin' all that," he joked, looking up from his task with a grin, "if I'm not gonna use it."

Whenever Ruthanne really got tickled, her laugh contained a precious little snort that melted Ches's heart every single time.

"If you insist on taking care of that," she told Judd, eyes still alight with laughter, "I'll just step up on this little yella horse and make sure he's got his mind in the right place."

A few minutes later, Shirley held the mule's head for Ruthanne to mount while Judd settled Ches into place atop the palomino.

"Riding stock's kinda mismatched," Judd commented to his wife as they stood together in the barn door, "but I reckon those two kids paired off just about right."

"Ruthanne is a blessing," Shirley agreed. "Not just for Ches, but to all of us who love him."

"Any girl brave enough to get past his Aunt Sis..." Judd trailed off with a chuckle.

"Ches wouldn't be who he is today without Miss Sis, and Ruthanne's mature enough to appreciate their special bond. In fact, she's developed her own deep ties to the boss lady."

"Never said it was a bad thing... Miss Sis wanted the very best for Ches, the very best or nothing at all."

The mule snuck in a couple of playful jumps as they left, but Ruthanne corrected the problem with two or three stinging licks across the shoulders. Ches couldn't help smiling as he watched her in action.

"Where'd you come up with the quirt?"

"Found it in the loft," she answered with a smile in her voice. "Just a dried-up piece of leatherwork, now, but it's one Gram used quite a bit. I never meant to leave it behind."

"Yeah, a little grownup twelve-year-old with Pap on your hands... Hard to believe you'd forget anything."

"Do you think it would be dishonest, Ches, to take it home with us?"

"Little miss," and he gave her a smiling shake of his head. "You're just about too good for this old world. I'll buy the thing if that's what it takes to make you feel right, but we ain't leavin' it here for the rats to eat."

Ruthanne purposely guided them away from the apple orchard, saving it as a little grand finale. Though she shared an occasional memory of her brief but happy childhood, they rode mostly in silence, lost in the pleasure of each other's company. When they finally wandered down to the orchard, she heard his intake of breath and reined to a stop among the fragrant blossoms.

"Well," she ventured softly. "I learned to trick ride up yonder 'round the barn, and I guess you could say the apple fritters started right here. Lordy, we traveled up and down the road. Those years weren't altogether unhappy, m-darlin, but when you came into my life, you brought back so much of what I thought was gone forever. Loving you and being loved... It's sweeter than I could've ever imagined."

The yellow Choctaw pony shifted slightly under Ches as he reached across for his lady's hand, and she asked the mule for a step or two, moving with him.

"Marry me, Ruthanne?"

"Oh," and the word came on a breathy whisper. "Surely you don't think I'd up and change my mind."

"No, but will you marry me right here in the apple orchard?"

The instantaneous joy of her smile gave way to momentary hesitation.

"Fairview holds wonderful memories for me," she finally managed, "but my heart's back in East Texas. Right alongside yours, Chester Joel Durham."

"You just don't know what that means to me, Ruthanne, but Lord willing, there's a lifetime ahead of us on the Durham place. Here at Fairview, we've got right now. Why not make one more special memory?"

"All this courtroom business may be a tempest in a teapot," she answered on a soft laugh. "Still, I don't much like the thought of it hangin' over our wedding day." Ches started a silent countdown of the long weeks until June, but her tender, drawling question changed everything. "How about tomorrow, m-darlin?"

# Acknowledgments

Sharing my characters and their stories with others is a delightful experience for which I must extend my personal thanks to every reader. Ms. Delorese Quackenbush typed the bulk of this manuscript and then worked tirelessly on cover design. Without her consistent effort, practical advice, and generous encouragement, the story may never have come to completion. I am truly and deeply grateful. Special thanks to Hallie Gage and Nell Ann Untiedt at the Mount Enterprise branch of the Rusk County Library for their time, talents, and support. Much love and appreciation to Michelle Simmons for her creative efforts as a "personal audio-book narrator" and for reading the manuscript. Daddy and Momma, Kenneth and Rhonda Keeling, deserve more gratitude than I could ever express. I am continually thankful for every member of Friendship Missionary Baptist Church in the Jumbo Community and, most of all, for Jesus Christ as my Lord and Savior.

**Author's Note**: This novel is, of course, a work of fiction. Any resemblance to actual persons or events is purely coincidental. My aunts (Donna Howeth, Linda Sledge, and Lorene Pless) read the manuscript and offered valuable suggestions, but all errors are my own. Mandy Davis Thompson, twin sister to the famous Jenny, began reading this manuscript. Life got in the way, but she provided very timely encouragement as did my favorite saddle pal, Madi Grace, and her father Ryan Tandy.

## About the Author

Blessed with a fulfilling life despite (and in some ways because of) the physical limitations of cerebral palsy, Jake Keeling teaches U.S. and Texas history as an adjunct instructor at East Texas Baptist University in Marshall. His father and several trusted riding buddies go to great lengths in supporting his love of horses and mules. Involvement with the family cattle operation continues a six-generation connection to the land. Deeply humbled by the opportunity, Keeling counts it a privilege to serve his church family as a deacon in Friendship Missionary Baptist Church.

**Jumbo Exchange and Communications**
8515 State Hwy. 315
Long Branch, TX 75669
903.658.0128
jumboexchangeandcommunications@gmail.com
or
visit our Facebook page

CPSIA information can be obtained
at www.ICGtesting.com
Printed in the USA
LVHW080549080922
727813LV00014B/483